Dark & Dangerous

Brooding Heroes Romance Collection

Alison Reid

Dark & Dangerous - Brooding Heroes Romance Collection

by Alison Reid

ISBN: 978-1-7644837-2-8

Independently published

Introduction to...

Dark & Dangerous

Brooding Heroes Romance Collection

Welcome to **Dark & Dangerous**—a collection of intense romances featuring brooding heroes, irresistible alpha males, and women strong enough to challenge them.

Each novel in this box set is a complete standalone romance, written in the spirit of classic Mills & Boon with a modern edge. You'll experience slow-burning tension, enemies-to-lovers dynamics, high-stakes romance, and emotional journeys that prove even the most dangerous men are vulnerable to love.

Inside these pages are stories of heartbreak and betrayal, second chances, revenge and redemption, and love that refuses to be tamed. There is no cheating, and every story delivers a guaranteed happily-ever-after.

Whether you're reading these heroes for the first time or returning to familiar faces, **Dark & Dangerous** invites you to get lost in a binge-worthy collection where passion runs deep, danger lurks around every corner, and love is always worth the risk.

Enjoy the journey.

Table of Contents

The Billionaire's Regret

Alison Reid

A complete standalone romance

Previously published individually

Prologue

Melissa stepped into the living room, leaving behind the hum of laughter and celebration on the terrace. It was her twenty-first birthday—a night that was supposed to be perfect. Yet, as she scanned the room, a flicker of unease crept up her spine.

She had been looking for Michael, her boyfriend of nearly three years. The love of her life. The man she was certain she would spend forever with.

But he wasn't there.

She was sure he asked her to meet him here at this time.

Instead, Brian—his cousin—was standing near the bar, a glass of whiskey in his hand. The dim lighting cast shadows across his face, making his expression unreadable.

"Oh, hello, Brian," she said, offering a polite smile. "What are you doing in here all alone?"

Brian turned toward her, swirling the amber liquid in his glass. "Needed a break."

"Oh, okay," she said, glancing around. "Have you seen Michael?"

He took a slow sip, watching her over the rim of his glass. Then, he took a step closer.

"No, I haven't." He tilted his head slightly, studying her. "You and Michael are close, huh?"

Melissa frowned. "Yes, of course. We've been together for nearly three years now."

Brian nodded, his gaze darkening. "You know... I think you're too good for him."

She let out a soft laugh, shaking her head. "Don't be silly."

But Brian didn't laugh.

Instead, he stepped closer. Too close.

"You know, I've always liked you, Melissa." His voice was low, almost teasing, but there was something unsettling beneath it.

Melissa forced a polite smile. "Thank you, Brian, but I'm very fond of Michael." More than fond—she loved him with all her heart.

The sharp scent of whiskey and expensive cologne filled her nose as he set his glass down on the coffee table.

Then, before she could react, he lunged.

"Brian, stop!" she gasped, stumbling back, but he was faster.

His hands gripped her arms, strong and unyielding. "You and I should get together," he murmured, his voice thick with alcohol and something far more dangerous.

Panic shot through her. "Let me go, Brian."

He didn't.

Instead, he shoved her backward, the breath knocking from her lungs as she landed hard on the sofa. His weight followed, pressing her down, trapping her. Her arms were crushed between their bodies, pinned uselessly.

"Brian, please—"

Her words were cut off as his mouth crashed onto hers, rough and punishing. The sharp tang of whiskey invaded her senses, making her stomach turn. She twisted, trying to pull away, but he was relentless.

She tasted blood.

Her own.

Terror paralysed her. She couldn't move. Couldn't scream.

Brian's weight pressed her deeper into the couch, his breath hot and reeking of whiskey as he muttered something against her lips. His hands roamed, gripping her wrists, pinned between their bodies as he ground himself against her.

Melissa froze in horror.

She could feel him.

The hard, unmistakable proof of what he wanted, pressing against her thigh. A violent shudder tore through her, disgust and fear crashing over her in suffocating waves.

"No," she whimpered, her voice barely a breath.

Brian only chuckled darkly, his fingers bruising as he forced her wrists above her head, trapping them there with one hand. His free hand slid lower, past the hem of her dress, his fingers skimming her thigh.

Melissa bucked against him, twisting, fighting, but he was too strong. His body caged hers completely, pinning her down like prey beneath a predator.

Tears burned her eyes.

No, no, no—

Desperation clawed at her chest. Her fingers curled into fists, nails digging into her own palms. He was too strong, but she had to do something—

And then, she felt it.

One hand.

His grip had loosened, just slightly, shifting as he reached for her leg.

It was all she needed.

With every ounce of strength she had, Melissa yanked her hand free and lashed out. Her fingernails raked across Brian's face, catching his cheek, dragging down hard.

His roar of pain was deafening.

He jerked back, clutching his face, blood welling beneath the deep, angry scratches.

Melissa didn't wait.

She shoved him with everything she had, scrambling out from under him. Her heart pounded as she staggered to her feet, gasping for breath.

Brian's glare was murderous, his chest heaving, his lips twisted in rage.

But she didn't care. She had to get away—now.

Melissa shoved off the sofa, her legs trembling beneath her as she bolted toward the stairs. Her breath came in short, panicked gasps, her pulse roaring in her ears. Just a few more steps—

Then a hand grabbed her arm.

She twisted, ready to scream—

"Melissa!"

The familiar voice cut through her panic just in time. It wasn't Brian. It wasn't another threat. It was—

Sarah.

Her sister's eyes were wide with concern, her grip firm but gentle. "What's wrong?" she asked, searching Melissa's face.

That was all it took.

Melissa crumpled. A sob tore from her throat, her body shaking violently as the terror finally consumed her.

Sarah didn't hesitate. Wrapping an arm around Melissa, she guided her quickly upstairs, away from prying eyes, away from him. Once inside her bedroom, she shut the door firmly, locking it before turning back to her sister.

Melissa collapsed onto the edge of the bed, her breaths ragged, her hands shaking uncontrollably. Sarah knelt in front of her, gripping her hands.

"Melissa, talk to me," she pleaded, her voice gentle but urgent. "What happened?"

Melissa tried to speak, but the words got stuck. Her throat felt raw, like she had been screaming even though no sound had come out. She shook her head, tears spilling down her cheeks.

Sarah's brows furrowed, her worry deepening. "I saw Brian come out of the living room after you, was it him?" she asked, her voice low, tense.

Melissa squeezed her eyes shut, more tears escaping as she gave a small, broken nod.

For a moment, Sarah was completely still.

Then, her grip on Melissa's hands tightened. "That bastard." The fury in her voice was sharp, deadly.

Melissa flinched, still trembling.

Sarah exhaled sharply; her fists still clenched as she knelt in front of Melissa. With a shaking breath, she gently brushed the damp hair from her sister's face, her touch at odds with the storm raging in her eyes.

"Did he—did he hurt you?" Her voice wavered slightly, as if she were afraid of the answer.

Melissa hesitated before whispering, "He tried."

A sharp breath left Sarah's lips.

A storm of rage darkened her eyes. She stood abruptly; fists clenched at her sides. "I'm going to kill him."

Melissa's head shot up, panic flashing through her. "No! Please, Sarah, don't—"

But Sarah was already pacing, her entire body vibrating with fury. "He forced himself on you," she spat, her voice shaking. "In our house. On your birthday." She whirled around, eyes blazing. "He needs to pay for this. I swear to God, Melissa, I'll—"

Melissa grabbed her wrist, her grip desperate. "Please don't. I just—I just want to forget."

Sarah stared at her, her expression torn between heartbreak and rage.

Then, slowly, she sat back down beside Melissa and pulled her into a tight embrace.

"I won't let him get away with this," she whispered, her voice unbreakable. "I promise you."

Melissa buried her face in her sister's shoulder, sobbing quietly. Her entire body trembled, the shock still rattling through her bones.

"Please, no," she choked out between shaky breaths. "Just—just find Michael. Bring him here. I need him."

Sarah hesitated for only a second before nodding. "Of course. I'll be back soon."

She pulled away and hurried out of the room, leaving Melissa alone, wrapped in a suffocating silence. She curled in on herself, hugging her arms tightly around her body, as if that could hold her together.

Minutes passed. Then longer. Sarah was gone for what felt like forever.

When the door finally opened, Melissa sat up quickly, her heart pounding. But one look at Sarah's face sent a fresh wave of panic through her.

Her sister looked… uneasy. Troubled.

Melissa's stomach clenched. "Where's Michael?" she whispered, her voice raw.

Sarah hesitated.

Then, carefully, she said, "He left."

Melissa blinked. "What?" She shook her head, gripping the blanket around her shoulders. "No, he—he wouldn't just leave. Why would he—"

Sarah bit her lip, looking like she was struggling to find the right words. "I don't know, Mel." She sighed. "I looked everywhere. He's gone."

Melissa felt like the air had been sucked from her lungs.

Gone?

He left?

Without saying goodbye.

She shook her head again, refusing to believe it. "No," she whispered. "He wouldn't do that. He wouldn't leave me."

But Sarah's expression didn't change.

Melissa's chest caved in, the weight of those two words—He left—suffocating her.

She thought she had been broken before.

But this? This was a different kind of pain.

Chapter One

"Melissa, you have to."

Graham, her best friend in the world, stared at her like this was the most obvious thing in the world.

"I'm no model, Graham," Melissa protested, crossing her arms.

"You could be," he shot back. "You're better looking than half these models here. You're tall, slender, graceful, gorgeous—what more do you need?"

Melissa felt like she was going to be sick.

Her top model—the one who was supposed to wear the dress, her dress—had been in a car accident on the way here. Thankfully, she was okay, but her ankle was sprained, and there was no way she could walk the runway.

Which meant disaster.

Melissa's entire show had been leading up to this moment—the unveiling of her pièce de résistance, a wedding gown that had already been whispered about in the industry. And now, the only person in the room who could fit into it... was her.

She exhaled sharply, running a hand through her hair.

This wasn't how tonight was supposed to go.

She was a designer from Sydney, Australia, who had finally made it to Europe. Her career was soaring, her designs were flying off the shelves, and everything was falling into place.

Except this.

"Ahhh," she groaned, pressing her fingers to her temples. "I can't believe this is happening."

Graham smiled then because he knew—she was going to do it.

Graham Ellis was Melissa's most trusted friend and business partner at M&G Designs. Most people assumed they were a couple—but that was exactly what she wanted them to think.

Melissa encouraged the misconception, knowing it kept unwanted attention at bay. She had no patience for men who saw her as a challenge, and Graham, ever loyal, played along without complaint.

Not that it mattered—Graham was gay, though he didn't advertise it. He was a private person, content to let the world make its own assumptions. And Melissa—twenty-five, almost twenty-six, and still a virgin—had long since lost any interest in romantic entanglements.

Not after Michael Anderson shattered her heart.

Not after Brian Anderson tried to take what she never wanted to give.

This was why Graham and Melissa were perfect for each other.

If either of them needed a date for an event, they were there. If one needed a plus-one to avoid awkward questions, the other stepped in. Their love was real, just not romantic. And they would do anything for each other.

Melissa sighed. "Okay, Graham. But if I make a fool out of myself, I will kill you."

Graham grinned. "I love you too, sweetheart."

He snapped his fingers at his assistant. "Bring the gown."

Melissa stripped down to her underwear without hesitation. She felt comfortable with Graham—there was no awkwardness, no self-consciousness.

Graham gave her an exaggerated once-over, then smirked. "If only I wasn't—" He lowered his voice to a playful whisper. "—gay, I'd be on you like a moth to a flame."

Melissa giggled. "No wonder everyone thinks we're together."

"Let them think what they want." He kissed her cheek just as Julia, his assistant, walked in, carrying the dress.

"Thanks, Julia," Melissa said, running her fingers over the fabric. "Help me get it on."

The wedding gown was her masterpiece. It was a vision of timeless elegance—crafted from layers of the softest silk and delicate Chantilly lace, the bodice sculpted to perfection with intricate embroidery that shimmered under the lights. Tiny pearls were hand-stitched along the neckline, leading to sheer illusion sleeves adorned with delicate floral appliqués. The skirt flowed in cascading layers, airy yet dramatic, designed to float effortlessly with every step. And the back—her favourite part—featured a row of tiny, fabric-covered buttons running down to a sweeping train, the very definition of romance.

Melissa had designed it to be unforgettable.

And now, she would be the one wearing it.

As they dressed her, Melissa's mind drifted to the man she once thought she would wear a dress like this for.

Michael Anderson.

The love of her life—at least, he had been once.

But he had shattered her heart when he disappeared without a word on her twenty-first birthday. That night had been a nightmare. First, Brian assaulted her—thankfully, she had fought him off—but then, before she could even process what had happened, Michael was gone. Not just from her party, but from her life. From the country.

Her heart had never recovered.

"There," Graham said, stepping back to admire her with awe in his eyes. "This gown is truly a masterpiece, Mel. You look absolutely stunning."

Julia nodded enthusiastically. "You look amazing, Melissa."

Melissa let out a slow breath, worry flickering across her face. "Do I look like a bride?"

Graham clapped his hands. "You look magnificent. And it's nearly time."

They walked out of the dressing area and into the backstage chaos, where models and staff hurried around, finalising the show. Standing near the runway entrance was Luke, the male model assigned to escort her down.

Luke was devastatingly handsome—tall, dark-haired, with sharp cheekbones and a confident, easy-going smile. And he was *very* interested in Melissa.

Too interested.

He had asked her out more times than she could count, sent flowers to her office, even left flirtatious little notes. He was charming, no doubt. But Melissa wasn't interested in charm. Not anymore.

Luke's eyes widened the second he saw her. He let out a low whistle, shaking his head. "You look… stunning. No, gorgeous. No—there are no words."

Melissa groaned, feeling the warmth rise in her cheeks. "Stop, Luke. I can't walk down there looking like a beetroot."

She *hated* how easily she blushed.

Luke grinned, clearly enjoying her reaction. "Fine, fine. But if I trip on that runway, just know it's because I was too busy staring at you."

Melissa rolled her eyes, but she couldn't help but laugh.

She had no idea that, in the audience, the one man she had spent years trying to forget was about to see her.

As Melissa and Luke got ready, Graham was giving last-minute instructions.

"Okay, Mel, follow Luke's lead. He knows where to stop and kiss."

"What?!"

Luke grinned. "The bride and groom have to kiss, Melissa. Surely, you're not scared."

Melissa stiffened, masking her discomfort with a forced smile. "No, no, of course not."

Graham patted her shoulder reassuringly and handed her the bridal bouquet. "You'll be fine." Then he turned a sharp look on Luke. "But don't you get too loose with my girl, Luke."

Luke grimaced playfully. "She's yours for now, but not for much longer."

Melissa rolled her eyes. "I'm right here, guys."

Then the music started. Their cue.

Luke extended his arm, and Melissa placed her hand lightly on it as he guided her out. She was *shaking*. She knew she had the height, the figure, even the looks, but she had never wanted to be a model.

As they reached the entrance of the runway, Luke bent down and whispered in her ear, "I've got you, honey."

To the audience, it probably looked like a tender, romantic moment. To Melissa, it felt *too* familiar. Too intimate.

But there was no time to dwell on it.

They stepped onto the runway, walking in perfect sync. Melissa kept her chin lifted, her shoulders straight, her expression serene—or as close to serene as she could manage.

The moment was surreal. The bright lights, the sea of faces watching her, the way her gown flowed with each step. The glare from the overhead spotlights was blinding, turning the audience into a shadowy blur. Melissa knew they were there—hundreds of people watching her every move—but she couldn't make out individual faces beyond the first row. She wasn't looking at them anyway, she was to busy concentrating on what she needed to do.

Then—gasps.

Melissa's breath caught. *Did they like the gown?*

At the end of the runway, Luke turned to her, cupping her face. The kiss was supposed to be brief—a light touch, a theatrical moment. But Luke took full advantage, pressing his lips to hers with far too much enthusiasm, his grip lingering just a little too long.

Melissa froze, shock rippling through her. The heat of the stage lights, the hum of the audience—it all blurred into the background as discomfort curled in her stomach. Before she could react, Luke pulled back, his lips grazing her ear.

"You taste so good, honey," he murmured.

Melissa's stomach twisted in protest.

What she didn't know—what she couldn't know—was that someone in the audience had gone rigid.

Michael Anderson.

Michael's entire body locked up. His fist tightened until his knuckles went white, his jaw clenched so hard it ached. A slow, burning heat coiled in his chest, spreading through his limbs like wildfire. He had imagined this moment a hundred times—seeing her again. But not like this. *Never this.*

Oblivious, Luke took her hand once more, guiding her back up the runway. Just before they reached the exit, he stopped again—turning to her with a smirk. Then, to Melissa's utter disbelief, he leaned in and kissed her again.

This time, the crowd erupted in cheers.

But Michael… Michael saw red.

They walked off the runway, and the moment they were out of sight of the audience, Melissa swung around to face Luke, her eyes flashing.

"Was that really necessary?" she demanded, crossing her arms.

Luke held up his hands in mock surrender, a smirk still playing on his lips. "What? I was just doing what I was told. You heard the crowd, they loved it."

Graham, sensing Melissa's growing frustration, stepped in smoothly. "Luke, stop harassing my woman," he said, draping an arm over Melissa's shoulder protectively.

Melissa exhaled sharply, shoving past Luke. "Seriously, Luke?" she muttered, her voice laced with frustration as she stormed off toward the dressing room, the heavy train of the gown trailing behind her.

Melissa needed to get out of this dress and put some distance between herself and Luke. They still had the after-party to attend, but right now, all she wanted was a moment to breathe.

Graham watched her go, then turned to Luke, his smile vanishing. "Keep pushing her, and you'll get nowhere."

Luke smirked, unfazed. "She'll come around. She's just not ready yet—but she will be. Sooner or later, she'll be mine."

Graham's expression darkened, his voice turning cold. "She doesn't belong to anyone, Luke. But one thing's for damn sure—she doesn't want you."

Chapter Two

Michael Anderson commanded attention the moment he entered a room.

Tall—easily over six foot three—with a powerful, athletic build honed by years of discipline in the gym. Broad shoulders tapered to a trim waist, every movement exuding strength and control. His sharp jawline, high cheekbones, and thick, dark brown hair made him strikingly masculine, but it was his eyes that held people captive—an intense, piercing blue, like the depths of the ocean before a storm.

Cold. Unreadable. Calculating in business. But when provoked? Fiery. Dangerous.

He had built an empire through sheer will and ruthless ambition, and every custom-tailored suit only emphasised the raw power he exuded. He was a man who knew what he wanted—and always got it.

Tonight, what he wanted was a designer. Someone capable of creating five exclusive gowns to complement his latest high end jewellery collection.

He settled into his seat near the runway, absently nodding as Sherry—his date for the evening—gushed about their excellent placement.

Michael barely glanced at her. *Why was he even with this woman?*

Vapid. Shallow. No depth. No substance. Sure, she had a great body, but that was all.

And wasn't that exactly what he wanted?

Something quick. Something meaningless.

Something that wouldn't hurt.

The show began. Gowns flowed down the runway, elegant, intricate, some impressive enough to hold his attention. But only one dress mattered—the wedding gown. The centrepiece of the collection. If it was as exquisite as he'd heard, he might have found his designer.

The lights dimmed. A hush fell over the crowd. The first few notes of the bridal chorus swelled through the speakers, rich and haunting.

Then she walked out.

Michael went still.

His breath stalled in his throat, his entire body locking up as if someone had sucker-punched him.

Melissa Shaw.

The woman who shattered his heart. The only woman who ever could.

And he'd be damned if he let it happen again.

But God help him—he wasn't prepared for this.

She was stunning. More breathtaking than he remembered. The soft, golden glow of the runway lights bathed her in an almost ethereal light, illuminating every perfect curve, every graceful step. The silk of her wedding gown clung to her like a lover's touch, cascading around her in a way that made her look untouchable. Unreal.

His chest tightened.

A wedding dress.

Michael's fingers curled into fists at his sides. The sight of her in white—his Melissa, walking with another man—sent a sharp, visceral ache through him.

For a fleeting moment, something raw stirred inside him. Something dark. Something he thought he had buried long ago.

Then his jaw clenched. His face hardened.

And that's when it happened.

The male model beside her—tall, chiselled, effortless—cupped her face.

And kissed her.

What. The. Hell.

Michael's stomach plummeted. A flicker of disbelief surged through him, colliding with something far more dangerous.

The moment passed; the models moved on.

She had moved on.

While he had spent years drowning in heartbreak, she was here—thriving. Untouched by the devastation she had left behind. Untouched by him.

Then it happened again.

The male model kissed her a second time.

A slow, seething burn ignited in Michael's gut.

Mine.

The possessive thought slammed into him before he could stop it. Before he could remind himself that he had no right.

And then she was gone.

The music swelled. The lights shifted. The show continued.

But Michael.

He was frozen.

Because the past—the one he had spent years trying to outrun—had just come rushing back, swift, and brutal.

Her twenty-first birthday. Almost five years ago.

The night he had planned to propose.

Michael had rehearsed the moment in his head a thousand times. How he would take her hand, drop to one knee, and tell her that she was it for him. That he wanted forever with her.

The velvet box had been burning a hole in his pocket all evening, the diamond inside waiting to slip onto her finger, where it belonged.

But then—

He had walked in on them.

Brian. His own cousin.

Melissa. Beneath him on the couch.

Their bodies tangled together, Brian's mouth covering hers—too intimate, too familiar.

Michael's world tilted.

For a few agonising seconds, he couldn't move. Couldn't breathe.

His brain refused to process what his eyes were seeing. No. It wasn't real. It couldn't be.

His chest tightened, breath locking in his throat, his pulse thundering so violently it felt like his heart might shatter beneath the pressure.

This wasn't possible.

This wasn't her.

Melissa loved him. She loved him. She wouldn't do this.

And yet—

She was right there. Beneath another man.

Beneath Brian.

A sickness crawled up Michael's throat, thick and suffocating.

He had asked her to meet him here—at this exact time. Had she planned this? Had she wanted him to see them together?

His fingers curled around the small box in his pocket, the weight of it suddenly unbearable. His grip tightened until his knuckles turned white, his entire body bracing against the sharp, gut-wrenching betrayal.

There had to be an explanation.

Some kind of mistake.

Some reason why the love of his life was in another man's arms, her body pressed so closely to his it was as if she belonged there.

But they hadn't even noticed him standing there.

Hadn't noticed the way his world had just caved in.

A sickening realisation crept in, cold and slow, wrapping around his ribs like a vice.

Melissa had never let him touch her like that. Never let him take things further than soft kisses and lingering caresses.

She had told him she wasn't ready.

Told him she was a virgin.

Had it all been a lie?

His stomach twisted violently.

Maybe this was why she had always pulled away. Maybe she hadn't been waiting for the right time.

Maybe she had been waiting for someone else.

Rage coiled in his gut, hot and blinding.

Melissa. With Brian.

A jagged, raw sound built in his chest, but he swallowed it down. Choking on it. Drowning in it.

His fingers loosened. The velvet box slipped from his grasp, landing with a dull, lifeless thud against the carpet.

He didn't pick it up.

Didn't say a word.

Didn't make a sound.

He just turned around and walked out.

Walked away from the only woman he had ever loved.

And never looked back.

Sherry's voice yanked him from the memory, dragging him back to the present like a harsh snap of reality.

She slipped her arm through his, her perfectly manicured fingers resting lightly against the fabric of his suit. "That wedding dress was exquisite, wasn't it, darling?"

Michael barely registered her words. His mind was still caught somewhere between the past and the devastating present, tangled in the image of Melissa—*his Melissa*—walking down that runway in white.

"Mm, yes, it was," he replied absently, his voice distant.

Sherry pouted, tilting her head to study him. "What's wrong?"

"Nothing."

He forced his lips into a half-smile, slipping from her grasp as he rose from his seat. Around them, the audience was beginning to move, heading toward the reception area where champagne and small talk awaited. He fell into step with them, walking through the grand hall like a man moving on autopilot.

But his mind was elsewhere.

Melissa.

My God, she looked good.

Better than he remembered.

Years had passed, but time had only made her more breathtaking. More poised. More effortlessly stunning. She had always carried herself with grace, but tonight… tonight she looked untouchable. Like something crafted from silk and moonlight, something that didn't belong to this world.

And that gown—*Jesus.*

It had been exquisite on her. Sculpting her in all the right places, flowing around her like it had been made just for her. Every step she took had been mesmerising, commanding the room without effort.

Michael exhaled slowly, willing his pulse to settle.

Then his gaze dropped to the program in his hand.

Designed by M&G Designs.

His brows pulled together slightly.

Whoever this designer was, they were good. *Damn good.* There was an elegance to the work, a precision in the craftsmanship that set them apart from the usual luxury brands he dealt with.

Michael had been searching for fresh talent. Someone who could bring something new—something exceptional—to his next project.

This M&G Designs might be exactly what he was looking for.

His grip tightened on the paper.

And if the models were attending the after-party?

Even better.

Because God help him—he needed to see Melissa again.

"There you are, Michael. Glad you could make it," Margaret Moore said as she approached, pressing a light kiss to his cheek.

"Hello, Margaret," he greeted with a smile.

"Did you enjoy the show?"

"Yes," he said, then added, "You were right about that wedding dress."

Margaret chuckled, swirling the champagne in her glass with an air of satisfaction. "I told you—M&G Designs are all the rage right now. Their pieces have been making waves in the industry." She leaned in slightly, lowering her voice as if sharing a secret. "Graham, one of the owners, mentioned they had a bit of a crisis backstage, but it all worked out in the end."

Michael kept his expression neutral, but his mind latched onto that detail. *A crisis?*

"Could you introduce me to them?" he asked smoothly.

Margaret's eyes lit up. "Of course." She scanned the room before spotting someone across the crowd. "Oh, there's Graham." She gestured for Michael to follow. "Come, come."

Michael moved through the sea of well-dressed elites, nodding politely when necessary but barely paying attention. His focus was locked on the man Margaret was leading him toward—a tall, blonde-haired figure with striking green eyes.

Handsome. Confident. The kind of man who had presence.

As they reached him, Margaret placed a manicured hand on Graham's arm to get his attention. "Graham Ellis, this is the gentleman I was telling you about—Michael Anderson."

Graham turned, his easy smile radiating warmth and professionalism. He extended his hand. "Nice to meet you, Mr. Anderson."

"Call me Michael," he replied, shaking his hand firmly. He didn't miss the strength in Graham's grip—measured, deliberate.

"I have to say, your designs are excellent," Michael continued. "Especially that wedding dress."

A flicker of pride crossed Graham's face before he shook his head. "Thank you, but I can't take the credit for that one," he admitted. "That was my business partner's creation."

Michael raised an eyebrow. "I heard you had a disaster backstage?"

"Oh yes," Graham said, chuckling wryly. "The model scheduled to wear the wedding gown had an accident on the way here and couldn't make it."

Michael frowned slightly. "I hope she's alright?"

"Yes, just a sprained ankle, thank goodness."

Michael nodded, feigning casual interest. "So, you found another model last-minute?" He paused, choosing his words carefully. "She did an excellent job."

Graham shook his head. "No, no. She wasn't a model."

Margaret, who had been watching the exchange with an almost knowing glint in her eyes, chimed in with a sly smile.

"She's the designer, Michael."

Everything inside him went still.

The noise of the crowded reception faded to a distant hum.

His chest tightened, his entire body locking into place.

No.

He hadn't dared to believe it. Hadn't even considered the possibility.

But the moment Margaret said it, he knew.

Before he could react—before he could even breathe—Graham turned slightly, calling over his shoulder.

"Melissa, sweetheart, come meet Michael Anderson."

Chapter Three

Melissa froze.

Her heart stopped.

She never thought she'd see him again.

Michael Anderson.

The man who had loved her. The man who had left her.

She hated him.

Or at least, she told herself she did.

Because the alternative—the storm of emotions surging through her, the memories clawing their way to the surface—was too much.

It had been years.

Years of telling herself she had moved on. That she didn't care. That he no longer had power over her.

And yet, all it took was one name. One look. One second of eye contact for the past to come roaring back.

He had vanished.

No warning. No explanation. Just gone.

On her twenty-first birthday.

The night that should have been filled with laughter, love, and the promise of forever had turned into devastation.

And yet, before that night… he had been everything.

She could still remember the way he used to hold her, his strong arms wrapped around her like he never wanted to let go. The way his lips would brush against her ear as he whispered sweet promises that once made her believe in forever. The way his fingers traced lazy patterns on her skin, as if he couldn't bear not to touch her.

She had loved him with everything she had.

And then, he had disappeared.

Now, here he was.

Michael turned.

Their eyes met.

The air between them crackled with tension—so many words left unspoken, so many wounds left unhealed.

For a split second, she could almost feel his touch again. Could almost hear his voice whispering her name like it was sacred. Could almost believe that the years between them hadn't been filled with silence and heartbreak.

But then, reality came crashing down.

Because Michael Anderson wasn't hers anymore.

Maybe he never had been.

For a brief moment, time stilled.

The world around them blurred into a distant haze—the chatter of the after-party, the clinking of champagne glasses, the low hum of music—none of it existed.

All that mattered was the space between them.

Thick with history.

Heavy with the weight of everything left unsaid.

Up close, she was even more stunning than he remembered.

Her sun-kissed skin glowed under the soft lighting, flawless and smooth. The red velvet gown she wore clung to her curves like a second skin, the daring slit running up her leg reminiscent of Pretty Woman. Her golden honey-brown hair cascaded in waves down her shoulders, reaching her waist in soft, effortless beauty.

But it was her eyes that held him captive.

Doe-brown. Almond-shaped. Deep enough to drown in, mysterious enough to make a man lose himself.

They made her look almost exotic.

Like a forbidden temptation.

And then there were her lips.

Pink. Pouty.

Kissable.

She had looked beautiful on the runway.

Up close, she was breathtaking.

Michael's jaw clenched.

She was tall—almost six feet in heels—and yet somehow, she still made him feel like the one at a disadvantage.

She was poised. Untouchable.

Like she had never been shattered. Like she had never spent a single sleepless night thinking of him.

And God, that burned.

Melissa was the first to break the silence.

She held out her hand, her expression cool, unreadable.

"It's been a while, Michael. How are you?"

Michael took her hand, but instead of shaking it, he brought it to his lips. His gaze never wavered from hers as he brushed a slow, deliberate kiss across her knuckles.

"Melissa, you look ravishing as always."

A sharp, electric charge sliced up her arm, straight to her heart.

Her breath hitched.

She tried to pull away, but he held on just a moment longer, his grip firm, possessive. When he finally released her, her fingers tingled where his lips had touched.

Before Melissa could recover, Graham stepped beside her, slipping an arm around her waist.

Possessive. Familiar.

Michael's jaw tightened as he watched Graham's hand settle on her hip. A casual gesture—one that shouldn't have meant anything.

But it did.

Because it wasn't his hand.

Every instinct in him screamed to rip it away.

"You know Michael, sweetheart?" Graham asked, his tone light, oblivious to the tension suffocating the space between them.

Melissa didn't flinch. Didn't stiffen.

She barely even blinked.

"Yes," she said smoothly, as if his touch hadn't just unravelled something inside her. As if Michael wasn't standing right in front of her, looking at her like she was the past he hadn't been able to bury. "Michael and I used to live next door to each other in Sydney."

The lie slid off her tongue effortlessly.

A half-truth.

Because neighbours didn't kiss until they were breathless. Neighbours didn't whisper dreams into the dark, making promises meant to last a lifetime.

Neighbours didn't break each other's hearts.

"What a small world," Margaret commented with a warm smile, completely unaware of the storm raging beneath the surface.

Michael barely heard her.

His gaze remained locked on Melissa, searching, dissecting.

"How long has it been?" he asked, voice deceptively casual, as if he truly didn't remember.

Liar.

A flash of something crossed Melissa's face. Something raw.

Hurt.

For the smallest fraction of a second, her mask slipped.

Then she pulled it back into place, her expression unreadable once more.

"Five years, Michael," she said, her voice laced with quiet bitterness. "You left on my twenty-first birthday... remember?"

The words cut deeper than she wanted them to.

She hated how they still tasted of betrayal. Of sleepless nights and unanswered questions.

Michael didn't answer.

Didn't acknowledge the accusation woven between the syllables.

Instead, he tilted his head slightly, studying her.

Her shoulders were squared, her posture flawless, every inch of her screaming confidence and control.

But her fingers trembled slightly where they rested against her gown.

And Michael saw it.

He saw everything.

His voice dropped lower, softer.

"Your designs are outstanding," he murmured, the words brushing against her like a touch. Almost admiring. Almost… something else.

Melissa's lips pressed together.

Because she knew that tone.

And she knew better than to trust it.

"Thank you," she said simply.

But her voice wasn't soft.

It was steel.

Before the tension could thicken, Graham turned to Michael with an easy, polite smile. "It was nice meeting you, Mr. Anderson, but I need to catch up with a few people."

Michael barely acknowledged him. His focus remained locked on Melissa.

Graham, however, wasn't done.

He leaned in to kiss Melissa's cheek, his lips brushing close to her ear as he whispered, "Don't be too hard on him, Mel."

Michael's jaw tensed.

Melissa felt the shift in energy—like a thundercloud rolling in, thick with impending storm.

Instead of reacting, she simply gave Graham a sweet, amused look, her fingers ghosting over his arm before she pressed a light kiss to his cheek.

Graham smirked knowingly before walking away, disappearing into the crowd.

Michael watched the exchange with sharp eyes, irritation curling inside him like a slow burn.

Too familiar.

Too intimate.

He exhaled sharply, his gaze narrowing slightly as realisation dawned. Were Melissa and Graham sleeping together?

Melissa realised, Graham had figured it out.

Melissa didn't know when exactly it had clicked, but it was clear as day—Graham knew Michael was the man who had shattered her heart.

Just as Michael was about to say something else, movement at Melissa's side caught his attention.

The male model from the runway approached, slipping in beside her with the kind of ease that spoke of familiarity. He handed her a glass of champagne, his fingers brushing against hers a little longer than necessary.

"I thought you might need this, honey," the newcomer said warmly.

Then, in a low whisper—one meant to be discreet but loud enough for anyone nearby to hear—he added, "When are you going to get rid of Graham and realise, I'm the one for you?"

Michael's jaw clenched.

Melissa rolled her eyes but played along, tilting her head up at him with a teasing smile. "Stop it, Luke. You know I would never get rid of Graham."

She said it sweetly, with just the right amount of affection, her tone light and playful.

But Michael didn't miss the way Luke's hand lingered at the small of her back, fingers skimming her waist like he had every right to touch her.

His fingers curled into fists at his sides.

Who the hell was this guy?

Melissa accepted the glass and turned back to Michael. "Luke Helm, meet Michael Anderson. Michael, this is Luke."

Luke's eyes flicked toward him, widening slightly in recognition. "The Michael Anderson? From Anderson Gems?"

Michael inclined his head. "That's me."

Luke extended his hand, his expression unreadable. "Pleasure to meet you."

Michael shook it, his grip firm, deliberate. "Likewise."

The moment stretched between them—assessing, measuring.

Luke didn't look away first.

Sherry, still clinging to Michael's arm, let out a dramatic sigh before giving him a little tug. "Aren't you going to introduce me, darling?"

Melissa arched a perfectly shaped brow, amusement flickering across her face. Michael caught the quick flash of satisfaction in her eyes before she masked it, her lips curving ever so slightly.

Damn her.

She was enjoying this.

Michael forced himself to turn slightly, making the introductions with as little enthusiasm as possible.

"This is Sherry Monroe," he said flatly. Then, with even less warmth, he gestured toward Melissa. "Sherry, this is Melissa Shaw."

Sherry's lips parted into a saccharine smile, her gaze flicking over Melissa with the kind of appraisal that women did so well—sharp, quick, and vaguely territorial.

"Lovely to finally meet you," Sherry said, her tone just a little too sweet.

Melissa smiled back, her expression polite. "Likewise."

But Michael wasn't fooled.

This was a battle.

And Melissa Shaw had just fired the first shot.

Not that it was a fair fight.

Melissa would outgun Sherry in beauty, poise, and intellect without even trying. There was no need for cattiness or theatrics—Melissa's mere existence was enough to render the competition irrelevant.

Margaret excused herself, offering a polite smile before disappearing into the crowd, leaving only the four of them—Melissa, Luke, Michael, and Sherry—standing in the charged space.

Michael turned to Luke; his expression composed but unreadable. "Luke, would you mind dancing with Sherry while I talk to Melissa about some business?"

Luke hesitated for the briefest moment, his sharp gaze flicking between them. Then, with a carefully measured smile, he extended his hand toward Sherry. "Of course."

Sherry, clearly reluctant to leave Michael's side, let out a dramatic little sigh before accepting Luke's hand. "Well, if you insist."

Michael barely spared them a glance as Luke led her onto the dance floor, his focus entirely on the woman before him.

Melissa.

He turned back to her, taking her in fully. Now that they were alone, the space between them felt heavier—charged with everything left unsaid.

"You look good, Angel." His voice was low, rough around the edges.

"So do you." Her response was polite, distant. Her posture remained composed as she took another sip of champagne, her expression unreadable. "But please don't call me that. My name is Melissa."

She didn't flinch, didn't waver. Just a simple, direct rejection.

He had no right to call her Angel anymore. Not after he left her without a word.

"As you wish," he murmured.

"I do."

A beat of silence stretched between them before he asked, "How long have you been in Paris?"

"Three years." She met his gaze head-on, unwavering. "What did you want to discuss?"

Straight to business. No warmth. No invitation for small talk.

Michael exhaled slowly. He had expected frostiness, but this was ice-cold.

Michael noted the crispness in her tone, the subtle way she was keeping him at arm's length, as if she had already decided he had nothing to offer her.

"I have a business proposition," he said.

Melissa exhaled lightly, setting her champagne flute down on a nearby tray. "You should talk to Graham. He handles most of the business decisions. I just design."

"You prefer it that way?"

She gave a small, elegant nod. "I do."

Then, holding out her hand, she said simply, "Can I have your phone?"

Michael hesitated for a beat before pulling it from his pocket, unlocking it, and placing it in her palm.

Melissa took it without a word, her fingers moving deftly across the screen. A moment later, she handed it back.

"Graham's number," she said smoothly.

Michael glanced down at the screen, his eyes flicking over the contact information she had entered. Then, without looking up, he asked, "What about your number?"

Melissa's lips curled into a slow, knowing smile. "I'm very careful about who I give my number to, Michael."

His grip tightened around his phone. His pulse kicked up a notch.

"You didn't have that problem five years ago."

The playful light in Melissa's eyes flickered out. Her expression darkened, her brows knitting together.

"What is that supposed to mean?"

He opened his mouth to answer, to say something sharp, something he wasn't sure he even meant—

But before he could, Luke and Sherry returned.

Melissa exhaled, schooling her expression back into polite indifference as she reached for her champagne flute.

Whatever Michael had been about to say would have to wait.

Sherry wasted no time slipping her arm through his, pressing close—*too close*—as if to stake her claim. Her long, manicured nails skimmed his sleeve, her perfume cloying in the small space between them.

Melissa barely suppressed a smirk. He's all yours, darling.

If Sherry thought she was going to provoke a reaction, she was sorely mistaken. Melissa had spent years perfecting the art of detachment, of keeping her emotions locked away behind an impenetrable wall. She wasn't about to let Michael Anderson—or his desperate companion—break through now.

Instead, she turned to Luke with a light, effortless smile. "Would you like to dance?"

Luke's face lit up with excitement. "Honey, I'd go to the moon and back for you."

With exaggerated charm, he lifted her hand to his lips, pressing a playful kiss to her knuckles before sweeping her toward the dance floor.

Melissa laughed, letting him lead, her fingers resting lightly on his shoulder. He pulled her in close, his palm warm against the small of her back, guiding her effortlessly into the rhythm of the music.

But she felt it—the weight of a gaze burning into her from across the room.

Michael.

His entire body had gone rigid, his jaw set, his broad shoulders tight with restrained tension.

Melissa didn't have to look to know that his hands had curled into fists, his expression darkening as he watched her move in Luke's arms.

Anger burned through him like a lit fuse.

And Melissa?

She let him burn.

Chapter Four

By the time Melissa made it back to her apartment, it was late. The evening had drained her, leaving her exhausted in a way that had nothing to do with the time.

It had taken longer than she expected to shake off Luke—not that he wasn't charming. He was sweet, persistent, always good for a laugh. But tonight, she hadn't been in the mood for company. She never should have asked him to dance.

But standing there, trapped in Michael's gaze, had been unbearable.

It ripped open wounds she had spent years pretending had faded into scars. But they hadn't—not really. One look at him, and the past came surging back, sharp, and relentless.

The heartbreak. The betrayal. The unanswered questions that still haunted her in the quiet moments.

With a weary sigh, she kicked off her heels, the cool floor soothing against her aching feet, and padded into the kitchen. She reached for a bottle of wine, pouring herself a generous glass.

She took a slow sip, savouring the rich taste as she stared out the window at the glittering Paris skyline. The city stretched before her—beautiful, endless, full of possibilities.

She had built a new life here. A good life.

And she would be damned if she let Michael Anderson ruin it.

A knock sounded at her door.

Melissa closed her eyes for a brief moment, inhaling deeply. She didn't need to guess who it was.

Setting down her glass, she moved to the door and pulled it open.

Sure enough, Graham stood on the other side, arms crossed, an unmistakable gleam of mischief in his green eyes.

"So," he drawled, stepping inside without waiting for an invitation. "He's the Michael, huh?"

Melissa sighed, shutting the door behind him. "Yes."

She watched as he made a beeline for her wine rack, inspecting the selection before casually pouring himself a glass—like he owned the place, like he always did.

She arched a brow. "Make yourself at home, why don't you?"

Graham smirked, lifting his glass in a toast. "Don't mind if I do."

Melissa rolled her eyes, but a small, reluctant smile tugged at her lips.

Because if there was one thing about Graham, it was this—he always knew when she needed him.

He sprawled onto her couch, one leg draped over the armrest, as if he had no plans to leave anytime soon. "So, what did you two talk about?"

"A business proposition."

Graham raised an eyebrow. "Oh?"

"I gave him your number," she said, crossing her arms. "If you think it's worth considering, let me know. Otherwise, I don't want to hear it."

Graham took a slow sip of wine, studying her over the rim of his glass. "You know it will be," he said finally. "He's Michael Anderson. Anderson Gems."

Melissa sighed, rubbing her temple. "Yes, Graham, I know who he is." Her voice softened, almost to herself. "But to me, he's just the Michael who broke my heart."

Graham let out a low whistle, swirling the wine in his glass. "Damn, Mel. No wonder you never wanted to talk about him."

Melissa leaned against the counter; arms crossed. "Because it doesn't matter anymore."

Graham raised an eyebrow. "Doesn't it?"

Melissa's voice was steady, but her fingers tightened around the wine glass. She wanted to believe the words—needed to. But why had her heart clenched the moment she saw him? Why had the air in that reception hall suddenly felt too thin?

"I moved on, Graham," she said, forcing her grip to relax. "I built a life here, and I don't need him waltzing back in like nothing happened."

He studied her for a moment, then shook his head with a smirk. "You should've seen your face when you saw him."

Melissa stiffened. "What's that supposed to mean?"

"That you haven't moved on as much as you think." He took another sip of wine, completely unfazed by her glare. "You still care, Mel. And I think he does too."

She scoffed. "I care that he left me without a word. I care that he made me feel worthless. I care that after five years; he suddenly thinks he can walk back into my life and pretend nothing happened."

Graham studied her for a long moment before speaking. "So… he doesn't know what Brian did to you?"

Her jaw tightened. "No. How would he? I never saw Michael after I fought Brian off."

Graham's grip on his glass tightened, his knuckles whitening. "I hate that you went through that, Mel. No woman deserves that."

Melissa grimaced. "I was lucky. Some women… some women aren't as lucky as I was."

But even as she said the words, the memory surfaced—sharp, raw, and suffocating.

Brian pinning her down, his weight crushing her against the couch. His breath, hot and reeking of whiskey, ghosting over her skin as he forced his lips onto hers. The sheer panic that had seized her, the terror of knowing she couldn't move, couldn't break free.

Until she did.

She had managed to free her hand, her nails slashing across his face. She remembered the shock in his eyes, then the fury. The blood dripping from his cheek. For a split second, she had thought he would kill her.

She shivered.

Graham's gaze darkened as he watched her, the muscles in his jaw working. Slowly, he swirled the wine in his glass. "Do you want me to back off? Let him know we're not together?"

His voice was gentle, but the question carried weight.

Melissa inhaled deeply, forcing the memories away. When she met Graham's eyes again, hers were steady, unreadable.

"No," she said finally, her voice quiet but firm. "Let him think what he wants."

Graham gave her a teasing smirk.

Melissa ran a hand through her hair, letting out a tired sigh. "Graham, I am not interested in Michael Anderson. He told me he loved me, then left without a word and never came back." Her voice tightened. "Why would I ever open myself up to that kind of hurt again?"

Graham wrapped her in a warm hug. "You know I'm here for you, Mel."

She leaned into him, letting the warmth of his presence ground her. For a moment, the weight of everything—the past, Michael, Brian—felt a little lighter.

"I know," she murmured. "I love you, Graham."

"I love you too." He gave her shoulder a reassuring squeeze before pulling back, his expression thoughtful. "And you know what else?"

"What?"

His lips curved into a slow, mischievous grin. "You should make him regret it."

Melissa frowned. "What?"

Graham's grin widened. "You're Melissa Shaw. You built your own fashion empire. You don't need to let some guy from your past throw you off balance." He crossed his arms. "Make him see exactly what he lost."

Melissa stared at him for a moment before reaching for the bottle of wine. She poured herself a generous glass, lifted it to her lips, and took a slow, measured sip, letting the bitterness settle on her tongue. She had spent five years rebuilding herself, brick by brick, turning heartbreak into ambition, pain into power. She refused to let Michael Anderson tear it all down with a single glance.

Then, with a small, dangerous smile, she murmured, "Oh, don't worry. He will."

Chapter Five

After dropping off a very upset Sherry, Michael stepped into his hotel suite and shut the door behind him with a weary sigh. The evening had drained him—more than he cared to admit.

He loosened his tie, rolling his shoulders, but the tension didn't ease. His mind was still caught in the aftermath of his breakup with Sherry.

She hadn't taken it well.

Her voice still rang in his ears, raw with emotion, sharp with accusation.

"It's because of that model, isn't it?" she had demanded, her green eyes shimmering with unshed tears. "I saw the way you looked at her."

Michael had kept his expression unreadable. "No, Sherry." His tone had been even, steady, unyielding. "Our time has just come to an end. You knew this was temporary."

But she hadn't accepted it.

She had clung to him, her manicured nails digging into his sleeves, her breath ragged as she begged him to reconsider. Her mascara had stained his crisp white shirt, her sobs muffled against his chest.

It had taken everything in him to gently pry her off, to peel her arms from around his waist, to walk away without looking back.

Now, standing alone in the dim silence of his suite, he exhaled slowly, dragging a hand through his hair. He turned toward the massive floor-to-ceiling windows, where his own reflection stared back at him—tired, distant, troubled.

Sherry had been wrong about many things.

But she had been right about one.

It was because of that model.

Melissa.

Seeing her again had been a punch to the gut, a cruel twist of fate he hadn't been prepared for.

One look at her, and every carefully buried emotion came roaring back to the surface. The years apart hadn't dulled his hunger for her—if anything, they had only sharpened it.

The way she had looked at him tonight—poised, unreadable, a woman who had moved on—had only made him want her more.

It had taken every ounce of his self-control not to close the distance between them, not to seize her the way he had wanted to for five damn years.

Not to grab her, sling her over his shoulder, and find the nearest bed to ravish her until she was breathless and trembling beneath him.

Until she was his again.

But he couldn't.

Not yet.

Melissa wasn't the same girl he had walked away from. There was steel in her now, a fire in her gaze that dared him to try. A quiet challenge in the way she looked at him, as if she expected him to fail.

And God help him, he wanted her anyway.

Michael ripped off his jacket and tie, tossing them onto a nearby chair before striding toward the minibar. He grabbed the first bottle of whiskey he saw, pouring himself a generous glass. The amber liquid swirled as he gripped the tumbler tightly, his fingers pressing against the cool crystal.

He walked back to the window, staring out at the glittering expanse of Paris. The Eiffel Tower loomed in the distance, its golden lights flickering against the night sky.

City of love, huh? He smirked bitterly, lifting the glass to his lips. We'll see.

Melissa had looked so damn good tonight. Too good.

The red velvet dress still burned in his memory—the way it had hugged her curves, the way it had shimmered under the soft lights, the way it had made every man in the room stop and stare. But it wasn't just the dress. It was her.

The way she carried herself. The effortless grace. The quiet confidence.

Melissa had always been beautiful. But tonight, she had been breathtaking.

And he hadn't been the only one who noticed.

Michael exhaled sharply, his grip tightening around the glass as he thought about the other men who had circled her like vultures.

Graham.

Luke.

His jaw clenched at the memory. Graham had hovered around her all evening, a protective shadow at her side. And Luke—Michael's stomach twisted at the thought—had held her far too close. He had watched, his blood simmering, as Luke's hands had lingered on her waist, his mouth far too close to her ear.

The only solace had been the way Melissa had seemed to brush Luke off after their dance. She had laughed, teased him, but there had been a distance there. An unwillingness.

But did that mean she hadn't wanted his attention?

Or was she just playing hard to get?

Michael wasn't so sure. And that uncertainty only fuelled the fire burning inside him.

He wasn't blind—he had seen the way Graham looked at her. The casual touches. The easy intimacy. The way he had kissed her cheek, whispered something only for her to hear.

Were they just business partners?

Or was there something more?

Michael swore under his breath, downing the rest of his whiskey in one slow swallow.

One thing was certain.

Melissa Shaw wasn't just a ghost from his past.

She was very much alive.

And he wasn't going to let her slip away again.

Michael could tell Graham was important to her—but how important?

The thought made his grip tighten around his glass, his knuckles whitening. There was an easiness between them, a familiarity that Michael didn't like. But was it friendship? Or something more?

If Graham had any kind of claim on Melissa, Michael needed to know. Because no matter what had happened between them in the past, one thing was certain—he wasn't about to walk away from her again.

Not without having her in his bed.

No matter who she was close to.

A dark thought crept into his mind, unbidden and unwelcome. It hadn't bothered her five years ago to share her affections, so why would it now?

The bitterness of it burned just as fiercely as the whiskey sliding down his throat. He set the glass down with more force than necessary, his jaw tightening. He hated that thought. Hated himself for even thinking it. But the past still had its claws in him, refusing to let go.

Damn her.

Damn the way she had looked at him tonight—shocked, wary… but undeniably affected.

She wasn't as indifferent as she wanted to be.

And that was enough.

Michael had spent years trying to erase the memory of her, convincing himself he had made the right choice in leaving. He had told himself that it was for the best, that they had been too young, that what they had would have burned out eventually.

But seeing her again had shattered all of that in an instant.

His body had responded to hers like no time had passed, as if she still belonged to him.

And she would.

Melissa could fight him. She could pretend she had moved on, that Paris had given her a new life, a new purpose, new men to fill the space he had left behind. But he knew better.

He had seen the way her breath hitched when she met his gaze. The way her fingers trembled slightly around her wine glass when she spoke his name. The way her body had tensed when he stood too close, as if she was afraid of what would happen if she let herself give in.

She wasn't over him any more than he was over her.

And if she thought she could keep him at a distance, she was wrong.

Michael Anderson of today didn't walk away from what he wanted.

And he wanted Melissa Shaw.

Michael finished his drink and set the glass down with a quiet clink. Rolling his shoulders, he made his way toward the bedroom, stripping off his shirt as he went. A hot shower was exactly what he needed—to clear his head, to rid himself of the lingering tension coiled tight in his muscles.

Just as he reached for the bathroom door, his phone buzzed on the nightstand. He almost ignored it, but when he glanced at the screen and saw Jason flashing across the display, he sighed and picked up.

"Hey, Jason, what's up?"

His younger brother's voice came through the line, brimming with excitement. "Mike, sorry to call so late, but I have some news."

Michael checked the time and smirked. "It's only one in the morning. I just got in myself. What's the news?"

Jason let out a breathless laugh. "Sarah and I are getting married."

Michael's brows lifted. "That's great, Jas! Congratulations."

"Thanks, mate," Jason said, his voice warm with happiness. "We're getting married soon, though, and I want you to be my best man."

"How soon?" Michael asked, already unbuttoning his pants, ready to jump in the shower.

"In two weeks."

Michael froze. "What? Why so soon?"

Jason hesitated for only a second before admitting, "Sarah's pregnant, and she wants to be married before she starts to show."

Michael exhaled, rubbing a hand down his face. "Damn, Jas. That's big news."

"Tell me about it," Jason chuckled. "We weren't exactly planning it, but… I'm over the moon, Mike. I love her."

Despite everything weighing on his mind, Michael couldn't help but smile. His brother deserved this kind of happiness. "I'm happy for you, Jason. Really."

"Thanks, man. So, best man?"

Michael shook his head with a small laugh. "Of course. I wouldn't miss it."

"Good," Jason said, relief in his voice. "Because Sarah's already making plans, and I think she might kill me if I didn't lock you in now."

Michael chuckled. "Wouldn't want that. Just send me the details."

"Will do. Oh, and I need you to know—Melissa is going to be Sarah's bridesmaid. I know you two have history."

Michael's grip tightened around the phone for a brief second, but he kept his voice even. "It'll be fine, Jason. We'll cope. I actually saw her tonight."

"Oh? Where?"

"At a fashion show."

Jason laughed. "What the hell were you doing at a fashion show?"

"I need a designer for my new jewellery launch in a couple of months."

"Well, I know Melissa is an amazing designer."

Michael's jaw tensed slightly. "You knew she was in Paris?"

"Yeah, of course I did. Sarah and Melissa talk at least once a week. And I have visited her there with Sarah."

Michael's brows furrowed. "You never mentioned it."

Jason sighed. "Why would I, Mike? You didn't exactly part on good terms."

Michael's stomach twisted. "What do you mean?"

Jason hesitated for a moment before saying,

"You disappeared without a word to her. Melissa was broken when you left."

Michael froze. His grip on the phone turned vice-like, knuckles white. He exhaled slowly, running a hand over his face as tension coiled in his chest.

Jason's voice softened, but there was no hesitation. "It's not my business, but she was in a bad way. And just so you know—Sarah was pretty pissed at you."

Michael swallowed, his throat suddenly dry. His fingers tapped against the phone, a restless movement betraying the unease curling in his gut. He forced his voice to stay even. "She seemed fine tonight."

Jason let out a humourless laugh. "Yeah, well, I suppose it was a long time ago."

Michael didn't respond right away. Because for the first time in five years, he had to ask himself—had he been wrong about how she felt about him? Had Melissa truly been heartbroken when he left?

No.

He clenched his jaw, pushing the thought away. It doesn't matter. I saw her with Brian.

Their breakup was her fault, not his.

She made her choice.

He had left without confronting her because he hadn't wanted her to see how shattered he was. Because if she had looked at him with anything less than guilt—if she had dared to act like she hadn't just ripped his heart out—he wasn't sure he could have survived it.

So, he had walked away.

And now? Now she was back in his life, whether either of them liked it or not.

"It will be fine. Melissa and I are adults. I'm sure we can behave for you and Sarah," he assured him.

"Thanks, mate. Can't wait to see you. It's been too long. Night, Mike."

"Night, Jas."

Hanging up, Michael tossed his phone onto the bed and ran a hand through his hair. His brother was settling down, starting a family. Meanwhile, Michael was standing here, fresh from breaking things off with a woman he barely tolerated and obsessing over the one woman who had never truly left his mind.

Melissa.

No matter how much he told himself she wasn't worth the thought, his mind refused to let her go. Seeing her tonight had only made it worse. The moment their eyes met; it was like five years had vanished—like she still belonged to him. But she didn't, did she?

She had danced with another man. She had laughed with Graham. She had moved on.

Hadn't she?

Michael exhaled sharply, shaking his head. He wasn't doing this. He wasn't letting her get under his skin again.

Striding into the bathroom, he turned on the shower, hesitating for only a second before twisting the knob to cold. Maybe that would clear his head. Maybe then he'd stop picturing the way she had looked tonight—like temptation itself wrapped in red velvet.

Or maybe, just maybe, he never stood a chance.

Chapter Six

Melissa walked into M&G Designs in Paris early, running on little sleep. Michael had haunted her dreams far too often, leaving her restless and frustrated. In the end, she had given up on sleep and come to work instead. At least here, she could be productive.

She inhaled deeply, letting the familiar scent of fabric and fresh sketches calm her. Designing had always been her escape, her sanctuary. And after last night's show, there was plenty to do. Her wedding gown had been a massive success.

Her phone rang, pulling her from her thoughts. Seeing Sarah's name flash on the screen, she smiled and answered the FaceTime call.

"Hi, Sarah," she greeted cheerfully.

"Hey, sis! How did the show go?"

Melissa leaned against her desk, tucking a strand of hair behind her ear. "It was great! The wedding gown was a hit, but I had to model it."

Sarah's eyes widened before she burst into laughter. "You? What happened to the model?"

"She sprained her ankle," Melissa explained with a sigh.

"Oh no!" Sarah laughed again. "You must have hated that!"

Melissa huffed. "There was one thing I hated more last night."

Sarah's amusement faded as she studied her sister's expression. "What's wrong, Mel?"

"Michael was there," Melissa informed her sister, her voice unsteady as tears stung the back of her eyes.

Sarah's expression shifted instantly. "Michael? What was he doing there?"

Melissa swallowed hard. "He's looking for a designer for one of his galas."

Sarah looked astounded. "And he wants you?"

"I think so… but I don't know what his angle is."

Sarah frowned, concern clear in her voice. "Mel, are you okay?"

Melissa forced a smile, pushing down the emotions threatening to rise. "I'll be fine." Wanting to shift the conversation, she asked, "What's up? Why are you calling so early?"

Sarah's face lit up with excitement as she held up her left hand, revealing a sparkling ring. "I'm getting married!"

Melissa gasped, her emotions momentarily forgotten. "Sarah! That's wonderful—congratulations!"

Sarah beamed. "Thank you! Jason's just come in."

A moment later, Jason leaned into the frame with a grin. "Hey, Mel."

"Congrats, Jas. I'm really happy for you both," Melissa said sincerely.

"Thanks, Mel," Jason replied with a warm smile.

Sarah hesitated for a moment before adding, "There's more, Mel."

Melissa frowned slightly. "More?"

Sarah's smile widened. "I'm pregnant."

Melissa's breath hitched, and before she could stop them, tears welled in her eyes and spilled over. "Oh, Sarah… that's wonderful!"

Sarah laughed softly. "I know, right? I wanted you to be one of the first to know."

Melissa wiped at her tears, her heart swelling with happiness for her sister. "I can't believe it. You're going to be a mum."

Jason wrapped an arm around Sarah, his expression filled with pride. "And she's going to be an amazing one."

Melissa smiled through her tears. "I'm so, so happy for you both."

"We're getting married in two weeks," Sarah announced excitedly.

"Two weeks!" Melissa's eyes widened in shock. "That's so soon!"

"I know, but we didn't want to wait," Sarah said, practically glowing. "And I need you here, Mel. Can you come?"

Melissa didn't hesitate. "Of course I can. I wouldn't miss it for the world."

Sarah beamed. "That means everything to me."

Melissa smiled, pushing aside the emotions swirling inside her. No matter what was going on in her own life, this was Sarah's moment, and she wouldn't let anything ruin it.

"I love you, sis," Melissa said warmly before shifting her gaze to Jason. "I take it Michael will be there?"

Jason hesitated before nodding. "Yes, Mel." His expression tightened. "Sorry."

Melissa exhaled slowly, then forced a small smile. "Don't be sorry, Jas. He's your brother. And this is about you two—your wedding, your happiness. That's all that matters."

Jason studied her for a moment, as if trying to gauge how she really felt, but Melissa kept her expression neutral. She refused to let Michael ruin this for her—or for Sarah and Jason.

Melissa forced herself to keep her voice steady. "Will Brian be there?"

Sarah's expression immediately shifted, tightening with worry. "Yes, he will be."

A tense silence stretched between them.

Jason, who had been sipping his drink casually, frowned at the sudden shift in mood. His sharp eyes flicked between them. "Wait—why don't you like Brian?"

Melissa stayed quiet, pressing her lips together. She had spent years avoiding this conversation, but now, the truth was on the verge of coming out.

Sarah hesitated, looking at Melissa for permission. "Can I tell him?"

"Tell me what?" Jason asked quickly, turning to Sarah.

Melissa inhaled deeply, then nodded. She had no choice now.

Sarah turned to Jason, her voice steady but firm. "Brian attacked Melissa on her twenty-first birthday."

Jason surged to his feet so fast that his chair scraped against the floor. His entire body went rigid, his expression darkening with barely contained fury. "What?" His voice was sharp, lethal.

He turned to Melissa, eyes flashing. "Is *that* what happened to his face that night?"

"Calm down, Jason," Sarah said quickly, reaching for his arm and pulling him back down beside her.

Jason's hands curled into tight fists, his jaw clenching so hard Melissa thought it might crack. "What the hell happened? I knew he liked you, but..." He trailed off, his throat working as he fought to keep his anger in check. Then, he turned to her, his voice lower but no less intense. "Why didn't you tell me, Mel?"

Melissa swallowed, looking down at her hands. She had spent so many years trying to bury this, trying to move past it. The last thing she had ever wanted was to bring it back to life.

But Sarah wasn't going to let her keep it buried any longer.

She sighed and took over. "Brian pinned her down and tried to force himself on her in the living room. The only way Mel got away was by scratching his face." Sarah's eyes darkened at the memory. "I found her right after she escaped. Mel was terrified."

Jason inhaled sharply, his entire body stiffening. His knuckles turned white against the table.

Melissa forced herself to look up, meeting his gaze. "It's in the past, Jason."

His expression was thunderous. "That bastard—"

"Jason." Sarah squeezed his arm in warning.

But he wasn't done. His anger burned hot, and now that he knew, there was no way in hell he was letting it go. "God, Mel, I'm so sorry," he said, his voice rough with regret.

Melissa shook her head. "No, Jason, it's not on you. He just needs to stay away from me."

"I'll make sure he stays away," Jason promised, his voice laced with deadly intent. "And I'll get Michael to help—"

"No!" Melissa cut in sharply, her heart leaping to her throat. "I don't want him to know, Jas."

Jason looked at her in disbelief. "Why the hell not?"

"Because I don't need him charging in like some avenging knight, he lost that right a long time ago," she snapped, breathing hard. "I don't need his help. I've handled this on my own, and I will keep handling it." Her voice softened just slightly. "I really didn't want you to know either, but… you're family now."

Jason exhaled, running a hand through his hair. His anger was still there, simmering beneath the surface, but Melissa could see the understanding in his eyes. He got it.

"Okay," he murmured. "I get it, Mel. But if he so much as looks at you wrong, I swear—"

Sarah reached for his hand, her voice gentle but firm. "We'll handle it, Jason."

Jason let out a heavy breath, rubbing the back of his neck. "Yeah," he muttered, though his expression made it very clear—Brian was living on borrowed time.

Graham walked into Melissa's office and immediately noticed Sarah on the screen. He grinned. "Hey, gorgeous."

Sarah laughed and waved. "Hey, Graham. You looking after my sis?"

"Of course," he said with a smirk before glancing at the screen again. "Hi, Jason."

"Hi, Graham," Jason replied. "I hope you can make it to our wedding."

Graham's brows shot up. "What!" Then his expression softened into a grin. "Congrats, you two!"

They talked for a little while longer, sharing laughter and excitement before finally saying their goodbyes. Melissa and Graham reassured Sarah and Jason that they wouldn't miss the wedding for the world.

As the call ended, Graham turned to Melissa. "Just a heads-up—I have a meeting with Michael at ten."

Melissa's body stiffened for a brief second, but then she lifted her chin. "So?"

Graham shrugged. "So, if you want to make yourself scarce…"

Melissa folded her arms. "No way. I'm not going anywhere."

A proud grin spread across Graham's face. "Good on you, girl." He leaned in and kissed her on the cheek before heading toward the door. "I'm proud of you."

Chapter Seven

At exactly ten o'clock, Michael walked into M&G Designs.

Kim, Melissa's assistant, nearly dropped the tablet she was holding, her eyes bulging as she took in the tall, striking man who had just entered. Michael Anderson was impossible to ignore—his presence seemed to command the entire room without him saying a word.

Melissa, however, remained with her back to him, her posture stiff as she feigned focus on the task at hand. She didn't need to turn around to know it was him. She felt it— the shift in the air, the quiet murmur of hushed voices as the staff noticed him.

They were standing around the large desk in the middle of the main office, reviewing notes from last night's show. If Michael expected a reaction from her, he'd be sorely disappointed.

"Kim," Melissa said, her voice smooth and composed, "I need you to organise for all the garments to be returned by this afternoon."

Kim forced herself to look away from Michael, swallowing hard. "Y-Yes, no problem, Mel. Is there anything else?"

Melissa nodded, flipping a page in her notebook as if completely unaware of the tension growing in the room. "I need you to get the pink gown we finished yesterday to Mrs. Kramer. She's expecting it before two this afternoon."

Kim hesitated for a fraction of a second before responding. "Got it."

Only then did Melissa take a steady breath, bracing herself. She could still feel Michael's eyes on her, waiting for Graham. But she wouldn't give him the satisfaction of acknowledging him. Instead, she picked up a few papers from the desk and made her way to her office without turning around, her steps measured and deliberate.

If he wanted something from her, he'd have to work for it.

As she reached her office, she heard the deep timbre of Graham's voice. "Michael, good to see you. Come on in."

Michael responded, his voice as smooth and confident as ever. "Graham."

She didn't wait to hear more. Closing her office door behind her, she exhaled slowly and moved to her desk.

The man who had shattered her heart was just a few feet away. But she refused to let him rattle her.

Melissa tried her best to concentrate on her work, but knowing Michael was in the building made it nearly impossible. Still, she forced herself to focus.

Around thirty minutes later, she was at her high drawing desk, sketching a new design, when a knock sounded at her door.

"Come in," she said without looking up, her pencil gliding across the page.

"Mel, sweetheart, Michael has a very interesting proposition for us," Graham informed her.

Still not looking up, she finished the line she was working on. "Oh? If you're sure, Graham. Just give me a sec."

Graham chuckled. "Sorry, Michael, she gets consumed in her work."

Michael stayed silent, just watching her work. His intense gaze was almost tangible, but Melissa refused to acknowledge it. She felt the weight of his gaze, but she refused to look up, keeping her pencil moving.

When she finished the final stroke of her design, she took a moment to fortify herself before putting her pencil down. Then, finally, she turned to face Graham and Michael. "Sorry," she said smoothly, as if she hadn't just ignored Michael's presence in her office for the last two minutes.

She gestured toward the chairs around a small table. "Please, sit."

They all took their seats, and Graham subtly shifted his chair closer to Melissa. Michael's jaw tensed.

"So," Melissa said, keeping her voice professional, "what can we do for you?"

She knew Graham had already vetted whatever proposal Michael was about to present, which meant it had to be worthwhile. But that didn't mean she had to make this easy for him.

Michael proceeded to explain, his tone all business. "I need five unique gowns designed to complement these." He reached into an envelope and pulled out five photographs, spreading them across the table.

Melissa's eyes flicked to them as he continued, "Each gown should be designed to enhance the beauty of these necklaces—one sapphire, one ruby, one emerald, one opal, and one diamond."

Curiosity piqued, Melissa picked up the photographs, studying them closely. The craftsmanship was breathtaking, each necklace a masterpiece in its own right.

"These are exquisite," she murmured, unable to hide her awe. For a moment, she forgot who had brought them, momentarily lost in their beauty.

Michael watched as Melissa studied the photographs, her fingers gently stroking the images, completely engrossed. A hint of satisfaction flickered in his eyes—he had known she wouldn't be able to resist the challenge.

"Thank you," he said, his voice calm yet firm.

Melissa finally looked up at him, her professional demeanour firmly in place. "What sort of designs did you have in mind? Any particular fabric, colour, or silhouette?"

Michael leaned forward slightly, holding her gaze. "I want each gown to embody the essence of the gemstone it represents. The sapphire should be regal, the ruby bold, the emerald timeless, the opal ethereal, and the diamond—" his lips quirked slightly— "flawless."

Melissa arched a brow, considering his words. "That's a nice concept, but I need specifics. Are we talking silk, chiffon, velvet?"

Michael smirked. "That's why I came to you, Melissa. You're the expert."

"When do you need them by?" Melissa asked, already calculating the workload in her mind.

"It's a tight timeline—eight weeks," Michael informed her.

Her eyes widened in shock. "That's quite ambitious."

"Yes, it is." His tone was steady, unwavering.

"Especially when I need to be in Sydney in two weeks," she added, knowing full well that Jason had likely told him the news.

Michael didn't flinch. "Yes, Jason and Sarah's wedding."

His gaze held hers, and for a brief moment, something unspoken passed between them. He knew she'd be there. She knew he'd be there. There was no avoiding each other now.

"Do you think it's possible?" Michael asked, watching her closely.

Melissa looked from him to the photographs, considering the challenge. Finally, she nodded. "Yes, I could do it."

Michael leaned forward slightly. "On the night, your gowns will receive full exposure—front and centre."

Melissa arched a brow. "That's quite the incentive."

He smirked. "I know the value of good publicity."

Melissa looked at Graham. "I'll need to push all other projects aside for this one. Is that possible?"

"Yes," Graham confirmed. "The other designers and I can handle them. You can focus on this solely."

Satisfied, Melissa turned her attention to Michael. She exhaled, her fingers tapping lightly against the table. After a brief pause, she nodded.

"Alright. I'll do it."

Michael smiled. "Great. What do you need from me?"

Melissa glanced at the photographs again. "I can start working on the designs with these, but before I make the final decision on fabric and colour, I'd need to see the necklaces in person. Is that possible?"

"Yes, I just need a couple of days' notice," Michael explained. "As you can imagine, security is extremely tight when it comes to accessing the necklaces."

Melissa considered this for a moment. "I'll need to see them in person about four weeks before the event."

Michael nodded. "I'll make that happen." He pulled out his phone, typing a quick note before glancing up. "I'll also need your number."

Melissa hesitated for the briefest moment before reaching for a notepad on her desk. She quickly scribbled down her number and tore off the page, handing it to Michael.

"No calls after ten at night," she said firmly.

Michael smirked as he took the paper from her fingers. "I'll try to restrain myself."

Melissa's eyes flickered with a sharp edge, a fleeting moment of tension passing between them. Her lips pressed into a tight line as she met his gaze. "Let's hope so," she replied coolly, her voice steady but tinged with something more.

Michael's smirk lingered, but he said nothing more, clearly enjoying the effect he had on her.

Graham chuckled, breaking the tension. "Alright, now that's settled, I think we have a deal."

Melissa nodded, ignoring the way Michael's gaze lingered on her. "Yes, we do."

They all stood, signalling the end of their meeting. Graham extended his hand, shaking Michael's firmly before stepping aside.

Then, before Melissa could react, Michael reached for her hand. His grip was warm, confident, yet gentle as he brought it to his lips. He brushed a soft kiss over her knuckles, his eyes locking onto hers.

"Thank you, Mel," he murmured, his voice low and rich. "I look forward to working with you."

Melissa's breath hitched at the unexpected gesture, a sudden warmth spreading through her. But she quickly masked her reaction, refusing to let him see the effect he still had on her.

Michael smiled, clearly noticing her reaction, but said nothing. His sharp eyes lingered on Melissa for a second longer than necessary before he turned away.

As Graham escorted him toward the door, the rhythmic click of heels echoed down the hallway. Kim, Melissa's ever-efficient assistant, approached with a towering vase of fresh flowers, their vibrant petals spilling over the rim.

Graham glanced at them, lifting an eyebrow. "Who are they from this time?" he asked casually, though a smirk tugged at his lips.

Kim laughed as she adjusted her grip on the heavy arrangement. "Who else? Luke, of course."

Michael stiffened almost imperceptibly, but Graham caught it. His usual relaxed posture turned rigid, his jaw tightening ever so slightly. He didn't like the idea of Melissa receiving flowers from another man.

As Kim entered Melissa's office, Melissa stepped closer to the doorway, her gaze falling on the extravagant bouquet. Normally, she would have dismissed them with a polite, "Put them in the reception area." But today, with Michael standing there, watching, she hesitated. Then, with a small, deliberate smile, she said, "Put them on my desk."

Kim's eyebrows flickered up in surprise, but she recovered quickly. "Finally coming around to Luke's charm, Mel?" she teased.

Melissa let out a light laugh, shaking her head as if the notion was absurd. But Michael wasn't amused. His expression darkened ever so slightly, his gaze unreadable.

Graham, ever observant, noted the shift with amusement. As he guided Michael out the door, he held back a chuckle.

When he returned moments later, leaning casually against Melissa's desk, he wore a knowing grin.

"Well, well, well. Isn't he charming," he teased, his voice laced with humour. "Did you see his reaction to the flowers?"

Melissa rolled her eyes, but a faint blush betrayed her. "Don't start, Graham."

"Oh, I wouldn't dream of it," he said, clearly enjoying himself. "But let's just say, someone isn't too thrilled about dear old Luke."

Melissa shook her head, but she didn't argue.

And Graham? He was already taking mental bets on how long it would take before Michael did something about it.

Keeping her focus on the business at hand. "It's a great offer," she said instead, flipping through the photos once more.

Graham's expression turned serious. "Yes, it is. But are you going to be okay with this?"

Melissa exhaled, keeping her tone even. "I'll be fine. I should only have to see him once a week."

Graham stepped closer, placing his hands on her shoulders, gently but firmly making her meet his gaze. "Are you sure, sweetheart? Really?"

Melissa forced a small smile. "I will be fine, Graham."

When Graham left her office, Melissa sank into her chair, her gaze drifting to the oversized bouquet dominating her desk. She exhaled slowly, the weight of the moment pressing down on her. The scent of fresh roses filled the air, but it was the lingering presence of Michael that unsettled her more—the ghost of him still clinging to the room, to her thoughts, to the fragile walls she had built around her heart.

She couldn't let herself fall again. Not this time.

Not for him.

She had told herself she'd be fine. That she had moved on. That she had no choice but to. But as she sat there, staring at the flowers she suddenly wished weren't there, a quiet fear curled around her resolve.

Because deep down, she wasn't sure if she would be.

Chapter Eight

Michael was itching to call Melissa. It was Friday, four days since their meeting in her office, and she had been on his mind far more than he cared to admit. He told himself it was just business, but he knew better.

There was something about her—something that had always pulled him in, no matter how much he resisted. And that infuriatingly composed act she'd put on last time? He wasn't buying it. His fingers hovered over his phone, her number displayed on the screen, but he hesitated.

His jaw clenched as he recalled the flowers she'd received just before he left. Damn Luke again. Graham hadn't seemed the least bit bothered—too used to her getting gifts from other men.

If Melissa were his, that wouldn't sit well with him. But she's not yours, is she?

Then he thought of the way she'd dismissed him—cool, composed, utterly detached. Professional to a fault. But she hadn't been unaffected. He'd caught it—that flicker of something in her eyes when he kissed her hand.

A slow smirk tugged at his lips.

She still felt something.

And that was all the encouragement he needed.

Without another moment's hesitation, he pressed Call.

Melissa stood at her sketching desk; pencil poised over the half-finished design. When her phone rang, the screen flashed Unknown Caller.

She hesitated, pulse skipping, before answering. "Hello, Melissa Shaw speaking."

A pause. Then—

"Melissa."

Her breath caught. She knew that voice instantly.

"Michael," she said carefully, her grip tightening around the pencil. "What can I do for you?"

"I was hoping you would have dinner with me tonight."

Silence.

Melissa's fingers curled around the edge of the desk, her pulse unsteady. She should say no. She needed to say no. But the moment she heard his voice, memories she had no business clinging to resurfaced—late nights, whispered laughter, the way he used to look at her like she was the only thing that mattered. She swallowed hard. That was a long time ago. This was different. It had to be.

"Melissa, you there?" Michael's voice was smooth, but there was a hint of something else—anticipation, maybe.

"Yes, sorry," she said quickly, forcing herself to focus. "Yes, okay. I need to show you the designs I'm working on."

"Great," he said without missing a beat. "What's your address so I can pick you up?"

Melissa straightened, already shaking her head. "That's fine, Michael. I'll meet you there. Just let me know where."

Michael considered pushing, but he knew when to pick his battles. He let out a small, knowing chuckle. "Okay." He then proceeded to tell her the time and location.

"No problem," Melissa said, keeping her tone light. "I'll be there."

Melissa was ready, dressed in a simple black knee-length silk dress that flared elegantly when she moved. She paired it with matching high heels, her hair styled effortlessly, and her makeup subtle yet polished.

A knock sounded at her door, and when she opened it, Graham stood there, his eyes sweeping over her with approval.

"Don't you look stunning, sweetheart," he said with a warm smile.

She gave him a small smile in return, but before she could respond, he asked, "Are you sure you don't want me to come with you?"

Melissa shook her head. "No, I have to get used to him being around if I'm going to get through this project." She picked up her portfolio folder and purse. "Thank you for driving me."

"That's fine," Graham said, stepping aside as she locked the door behind her. "I have a date too."

Melissa perked up at that. "Oh great! Who is he?"

Graham chuckled, shaking his head. "Not telling yet—let's see how it goes first."

Melissa laughed softly. "Well, good luck." She leaned up and kissed him on the cheek. "You deserve it."

When Graham dropped her off at the restaurant, Melissa took a steadying breath before stepping out of the car. Through the large windows, she spotted Michael immediately—waiting at the bar, effortlessly composed, a glass of whiskey in his hand.

As she approached, he turned, his piercing gaze locking onto her. A slow smile curved his lips as he leaned in, pressing a kiss to her cheek.

Melissa stiffened at the brief contact, willing herself to remain unaffected. If he noticed, he didn't comment. Instead, he gestured toward the hostess, who led them to a private table near the window.

Once they were seated, drinks ordered, and the initial tension settled, Melissa got straight to business. She reached for her portfolio, flipping it open.

"I've started drafting the designs," she said, sliding the first sketch toward him.

Michael leaned in, his eyes darkening with intrigue as he studied the drawing.

The dress for the sapphire necklace was regal, just as he had suggested. It was a floor-length gown crafted in the deepest midnight blue, with a fitted bodice that accentuated the waist before flaring into an elegant, flowing skirt. The neckline was designed to frame the necklace perfectly—off-the-shoulder with delicate, shimmering embroidery that mirrored the facets of a sapphire under light. The fabric was rich, likely velvet or heavy silk, exuding sophistication, and power.

Michael exhaled slowly, his appreciation evident. "This… is incredible," he murmured, his fingers trailing along the edge of the sketch. "It captures exactly what I envisioned."

Melissa nodded, pleased with his reaction but keeping her expression neutral. She turned the page, revealing the second design.

"This is the concept for the ruby necklace," she said.

The gown was bold—fiery red, unapologetically striking. It was a sleek, body-hugging silhouette with a daring high slit and a deep V-neckline, sensual yet refined. The fabric shimmered, hinting at a blend of silk and satin that would catch the light with every movement. The dramatic open-back detail added an extra touch of allure, making it a gown designed to turn heads.

Michael's lips quirked as he studied the sketch. "Now this," he said, his voice dropping slightly, "is passion. It's fearless."

His gaze flickered to hers, something unreadable in his expression.

Melissa held his stare, refusing to let the moment unnerve her. "That was the point," she said simply.

Melissa turned another page, revealing the next design. "And this," she said, "is for the opal necklace."

Michael's gaze swept over the sketch, his expression unreadable, but she caught the way his fingers tapped lightly against the table—an unconscious sign of intrigue.

The gown was ethereal, just as he had requested. A soft, flowing creation in the palest shade of iridescent ivory, almost translucent in its delicacy. Layers of fine tulle cascaded over a fitted bodice, giving the dress a weightless, dreamlike quality. The skirt moved in airy, fluid waves, as if it floated with every step. Tiny, hand-sewn embellishments— subtle hints of opalescent shimmer—were scattered across the sheer overlay, mirroring the play of colours within the gemstone itself.

The neckline was elegant yet understated, a gentle illusion design that blended seamlessly with the skin, making it appear as though the fabric simply melted into the wearer. Soft, draped sleeves rested just off the shoulders, adding to its delicate, almost otherworldly appeal.

Michael finally exhaled, shaking his head slightly. "It's… mesmerising." His voice was lower now, more thoughtful. "Like something out of a dream."

Melissa nodded, satisfied. "That was the intention."

His gaze lifted to hers, something unreadable flickering in his eyes. "You've outdone yourself."

She held his stare for a moment before glancing back down at her sketches. Keeping things professional. Keeping her distance.

"I'll have the final two concepts for you by Wednesday. I'm flying to Sydney on Wednesday night, so if I don't get to show you here, I'll be taking my work with me," Melissa said, closing the folio and placing it next to her chair.

"You should fly with me. I'm taking the jet," Michael suggested.

Melissa hesitated. "Graham is traveling with me. I can't—"

He cut in smoothly, "He's welcome too. It'll be much more comfortable than a commercial flight."

Before she could respond, the waiter arrived to take their order.

Once the waiter left, Melissa met Michael's gaze. "Are you sure?"

"Yes. If you need to, you can work on the flight as well," he replied, effortlessly casual.

Melissa studied him through her lashes. "Thank you. That would be appreciated."

They fell into easy conversation, chatting about the weather and other trivial things. When their meals arrived, they ate in a comfortable silence.

After a few moments, Michael asked, "How did you end up in Paris?"

Melissa smiled. "I entered a design competition in Sydney and won a trip to Paris. That's where I met Graham—we hit it off right away, and he loved my designs. We decided to start a business together. My dad helped me in the beginning, but I've since paid him back, which I'm really proud of." She shrugged slightly. "And the rest is history."

"How often do you go home?" he asked.

"Not often, but Mum, Dad, Sarah, and Jason visit me at least every six months."

"Jason comes?" Surprise flickered across his face.

Melissa nodded. "Yes, Jason and I are close." She hesitated for a beat before adding, "Despite everything, he was always there for me." A small, genuine smile softened her features. "I'm so happy for them both."

Michael took a slow sip of his wine, watching her carefully. He hadn't expected that. Jason had always been protective, but knowing he had remained in her life left a strange taste in his mouth.

"Where are you based? Do you go home often?"

Michael set his knife and fork down. "I'm based in London, but I travel a lot. And no, I don't. This will be the first time in two years."

"Oh? Why so long?" she asked, tilting her head slightly.

He was going to say, *Because I didn't want to run into you.* But the words lodged in his throat. Instead, he leaned back, exhaling slowly. "Just been busy."

Chapter Nine

Just as their desserts were being served, a smooth, accented voice cut through the low hum of conversation.

"Melissa."

Both she and Michael turned toward the sound.

A tall, lean man with sharp features and an air of effortless wealth approached their table. His designer suit was immaculate, his confidence undeniable.

Melissa rose gracefully, offering a warm, practiced smile. "Gabriel, how lovely to see you."

Much to Michael's growing irritation, Gabriel stepped in close, his hand settling lightly—but possessively—on Melissa's waist as he kissed both her cheeks. He held her a little too long, his touch lingering just enough to make a point.

"And where is your other half?" Gabriel teased, his tone smooth. "Have you finally moved on from Graham? Why didn't you call me? You know how I feel about you."

Melissa laughed lightly, dismissing his flirtation with practiced ease. "No, I haven't moved on. And this is Michael Anderson." She gestured toward the table. "Michael, this is Gabriel Dubois. It's a business meeting."

Michael shook Gabriel's hand, his grip firm, his expression unreadable.

Melissa and Gabriel exchanged pleasantries for a few minutes, their conversation easy, familiar. Too familiar for Michael's liking. Then, as Gabriel leaned in to kiss her cheeks once more, his lips hovered dangerously close to hers.

"Call me when you come to your senses," he murmured.

Melissa laughed it off, her tone light. "Nice to see you, Gabriel."

Michael, on the other hand, wasn't amused. He watched Gabriel walk away, jaw tight, fingers tapping once against the table before he forced himself to relax.

Melissa slid back into her seat with a small sigh. "Sorry about that."

"He was a bit familiar," Michael said evenly, though the irritation simmering beneath his tone was impossible to miss.

Melissa shrugged, unbothered. "It comes with the territory. You get used to it."

Michael pressed his lips into a firm line. He had no right to say anything.

But by God, he wanted to.

When their coffee arrived, they lingered over it for a few minutes before Melissa set her cup down. "I should get going."

She pulled out her phone to order an Uber, but before she could confirm the ride, Michael reached across the table, his hand covering hers.

"I'll take you home," he said firmly.

"Oh, there's no need," she replied, glancing up at him.

"Yes, there is," he countered, his gaze steady, unwavering.

Michael gestured for the check and paid without hesitation.

Outside, the night air was crisp, a stark contrast to the lingering warmth of the restaurant. He placed a hand on the small of Melissa's back, guiding her toward his car. The brief contact sent a jolt through her, and she held her breath without meaning to.

He opened the door for her, and as she slid in, her dress rode up slightly, revealing more of her thigh than she would have liked. She quickly smoothed it down, hoping he hadn't noticed.

She gave him her address, and the drive was quiet, filled with a tension neither of them acknowledged.

When they arrived, Melissa reached for the door handle, ready to make a quick exit, but Michael's voice stopped her.

"I'll walk you to the door."

"There's no need," she said, glancing at him.

"Yes, there is," he said, already stepping out.

He rounded the car, opened her door, and took her hand, helping her out. His grip was steady, sure.

They walked up the short path in silence. Once at her door, she unlocked it and turned to him.

"Goodnight," she said softly.

Michael tilted his head, amusement flickering in his eyes. "Aren't you going to invite me in?"

Melissa's heart pounded. "I don't think that's a good idea," she murmured, her voice barely above a whisper.

"Why not? Because of Graham?" he asked stiffly, jealousy flashing in his eyes and tightening his tone.

Ignoring his question, she said firmly, "We need to keep our relationship on a professional level." She kept her gaze fixed on his chest, unwilling to meet his eyes.

Michael let out a quiet chuckle, low and knowing. "I think we're past that," he murmured.

With a gentle but insistent touch, he lifted her chin, forcing her to look at him. His fingers, warm and slightly rough, skimmed along her jaw, tilting her face upward until their eyes met. The heat in his gaze sent a ripple of anticipation down her spine, her breath catching in her throat.

Melissa barely had time to process the intensity between them before his lips claimed hers. The first brush was soft, almost hesitant, as if he were testing the moment, waiting for her to pull away. But she didn't. *She couldn't.*

A shiver coursed through her as his mouth moved against hers, coaxing, deepening, until restraint became an afterthought.

A bolt of pleasure shot through Michael the moment their lips met. *God,* he'd missed this. *Missed her.* She tasted like something warm and familiar, yet entirely new—a mixture of longing and unspoken promises. She felt so damn good, just like he remembered, yet somehow even better.

With a groan, he wrapped an arm around her waist, pulling her flush against him. The feel of her body against his was dizzying, intoxicating. His other hand slid into her hair, angling her head to deepen the kiss.

Melissa responded without hesitation, her free hand fisting in his shirt, as if afraid he might disappear. Her nails dug into the fabric, her grip desperate, needy. She felt the hunger in the way he kissed her, in the way his tongue teased the seam of her lips before slipping inside, tasting her, claiming her.

Heat pooled low in her stomach, a slow, smouldering ache that built with every passing second. She pressed closer, moulding herself to him, her pulse thrumming wildly as their tongues tangled in a sensual, unhurried battle.

Michael groaned against her mouth, his grip tightening. Every soft sound she made, every tiny shudder, sent another surge of desire through him, unravelling what little control he had left. He wanted more. *Needed more.*

Melissa gasped into the kiss, her chest rising and falling in quick succession. The world around them blurred, faded, ceased to exist. Nothing mattered but the heat between them, the frantic press of lips and hands, the sheer, undeniable gravity that always seemed to pull them back together.

Then, suddenly—

"Good evening, you two."

The voice cut through the charged silence like a blade.

Melissa jolted back, breathless, her heart hammering as reality crashed over her. Michael cursed under his breath, his chest rising and falling with laboured breaths.

They turned toward Graham, who stood a few feet away, arms crossed, amusement flickering in his eyes.

"Graham… we didn't hear you," she said, trying to steady her breath.

"Obviously," he replied dryly.

Michael cleared his throat, clearly irritated, knowing he had to leave. He lingered a moment before stepping back. "Goodnight, Melissa." Then, turning to Graham with a slow, triumphant smile, he added, "Graham."

With that, he walked to his car, leaving Graham watching him go.

Melissa exhaled, steadying herself before turning back to Graham—only to find him watching her with a knowing grin, one brow slightly raised.

Melissa frowned. 'What?'

Graham smirked, arms crossing. 'Oh, nothing.' His tone was pure amusement. 'Just enjoying the show.'

Heat crept up her neck. 'There was no show.'

He chuckled. 'Right. So, I didn't just witness my business partner making out with her very handsome ex on her doorstep?'

Melissa stiffened, arms crossing. 'It… it was nothing.'

Graham gave her a look. The kind that said, keep telling yourself that. "If that was nothing, I'd love to see what *something* looks like."

Melissa opened her mouth, then closed it, realising there was no winning this argument. With a sigh, she turned to open her door. "How was your date?" she asked, trying to change the subject.

"Not as eventful as yours," Graham said with a smirk.

Melissa groaned as she stepped inside, Graham following her in and shutting the door behind him. She barely made it to the couch before sinking onto it, putting her head in her hands. "It was a mistake," she muttered.

Graham sat beside her, his expression softening as he placed a reassuring hand on her shoulder. "Are you sure? He seems keen."

Melissa let out a bitter laugh, shaking her head. "That's the problem. He was keen before, too. And then he just…left." Her voice wavered, betraying the pain she had worked so hard to bury. "What happens when he does it again?" She exhaled shakily, her fingers gripping her temples. "I can't go through that again, Graham."

Graham's expression softened, and he gave her shoulder another reassuring squeeze. "Melissa… do you really believe he would do that?"

She let out a shaky breath, her fingers twisting together in her lap. "I don't know," she admitted, her voice barely above a whisper. "I mean, he left without a word. He chose to disappear from my life. What else am I supposed to think?"

Graham sighed, leaning back against the couch. "Look, I don't know the guy well, but from what I saw tonight. He didn't kiss you like someone who didn't care."

Melissa swallowed hard, wiping at the tears gathering in her eyes. "But what if that's all it was? Just a moment of attraction? What if I let myself believe it's something more, and then he walks away again?"

Graham hesitated before saying carefully, "Then maybe you need to ask him. Get your answers. Otherwise, you'll never really move on—whether that means letting him go or giving him another chance."

Melissa shook her head, frustration flickering in her eyes. "And what if I don't want to hear his answer? What if knowing hurts more than not knowing?"

Graham tilted his head, studying her. "Then you're letting fear make the choice for you."

She looked away, staring blankly at the floor. "Maybe fear is the only thing keeping me from making the same mistake twice."

Graham exhaled, rubbing a hand over his jaw. "Or maybe it's keeping you from something real."

Melissa didn't respond. She wasn't sure she had an answer.

Michael let the icy water cascade over his body, but it did nothing to cool the fire still raging in his veins. His mind replayed the kiss—the way Melissa had melted against him, the soft moan that had escaped her lips, the desperate clutch of her fingers against him.

She still felt something for him. That much was undeniable.

But then there was Graham.

He had walked in on them, yet he hadn't reacted like a jealous boyfriend. No anger. No possessiveness. Just amusement.

That meant something.

Melissa and Graham weren't together.

Then why did everyone assume they were?

Was it a front? Some kind of arrangement? Did they have an open relationship?

Michael exhaled sharply, leaning his head against the cold tile. So, she hasn't moved on. Not really.

Then why the hell had she stayed silent all these years?

A voice in the back of his mind sneered the answer before he could stop it.

You didn't give her a chance to.

His jaw tightened, a bitter realisation creeping in.

I didn't ask. I just left.

Five years ago, he'd walked in, seen Brian, and left.

No confrontation. No questions. No chance for her to explain.

Why?

Because he hadn't wanted to hear the truth? Or because he'd been too much of a coward to face it?

His stomach twisted.

Back then, his anger had been absolute. His pain, raw. Leaving had felt like survival.

Now?

Now, he wasn't so sure.

Had he really been trying to escape her?

Or had he been running from the fear that she could confirm his worst nightmare—that she had betrayed him?

Michael shut off the water abruptly, gripping the edge of the shower wall. He wasn't that naive kid anymore. He wouldn't make the same mistake twice.

He needed answers.

Why Brian? How long? Had she ever loved him? Or had Michael been a fool all along?

The questions wouldn't stop.

Five years ago, anger had made the decision for him. He'd walked away. No demands. No explanations. No truth.

Now, that buried doubt was clawing its way back.

What if he'd been wrong?

The thought hit like a gut punch.

Michael ran a hand through his wet hair, exhaling slowly. He had spent five years convincing himself that she had betrayed him. That leaving had been the right choice. That if he ever saw her again, he wouldn't feel a thing.

And yet, one kiss had shattered all of that. If he was honest, one look had shattered it.

His fingers curled into a fist.

He needed to know the truth.

And this time, he wouldn't leave without it.

Chapter Ten

On Wednesday afternoon, Melissa and Graham stepped into the private terminal at Charles de Gaulle Airport. Their luggage had already been handled. The polished floors gleamed under soft lighting, a stark contrast to the chaos of the main airport.

Michael was already waiting near the lounge, dressed in a crisp navy suit with an open-collared shirt. He greeted them with a smooth, "Melissa, Graham," nodding at each in turn.

"Michael," Melissa said politely, while Graham gave him a casual nod.

Without wasting time, Michael led them toward the tarmac, where his private jet was waiting.

The aircraft was a Gulfstream G700, sleek and powerful, its body painted a deep midnight blue with silver accents that gleamed in the daylight. The jet exuded understated luxury, with its elongated frame and tinted windows. As they approached, Graham's eyes flicked to the name elegantly scripted near the nose of the jet—Lissa.

He nudged Melissa with a knowing smirk. "He doesn't care, hey?" he muttered under his breath.

Melissa's breath hitched. Her gaze landed on the name—*Lissa*—before she quickly looked away. Her lips parted, but no words came.

At the top of the air-stairs, an impeccably dressed air steward stood waiting. He had short, neatly styled blond hair and a professional but friendly demeanour.

"Welcome back, Mr. Anderson," the steward greeted with a nod.

Michael gave a small smile. "Simon, this is Melissa Shaw and Graham Ellis. They'll be flying with us."

Simon turned to them and smiled warmly. "A pleasure to have you both onboard. Please, make yourselves comfortable."

They stepped inside, and Melissa's first thought was that it wasn't just a jet—it was a flying penthouse.

The interior was bathed in soft, warm lighting, with cream-coloured leather seats arranged in a spacious configuration. Polished walnut panelling gave the space a refined elegance, and a fully stocked bar gleamed against the far wall. A long, plush sofa lined one side, opposite a set of recliners with individual tables.

"This way," Michael said, leading them toward the rear of the jet.

He gestured toward a conference area, where a sleek glass table sat surrounded by ergonomic leather chairs. "If you need to work, there's Wi-Fi and everything you might need here."

They moved further in, passing a private lounge, where a large, curved TV was set against the wall, complete with surround sound.

"And back here," Michael said, pushing open a door, "is the master suite."

Melissa blinked. A king-sized bed, dressed in soft grey and white linens, dominated the space. There was even a marble-lined en-suite bathroom, complete with a rainfall shower.

Graham let out a low whistle. "You travel well."

Michael smirked. "I like to be comfortable."

Melissa ran her fingers lightly over the back of a leather seat, trying to ignore the weight of Michael's gaze. The name on the jet still lingered in her mind.

If he didn't care, why would he name it 'Lissa'?

Once they settled inside the luxurious cabin, Simon, the air steward, approached with a polite smile. "Mr. Anderson, we'll be taxiing shortly. I'll need everyone to take their seats and fasten their seat belts."

Michael gestured toward the plush cream leather seats. "You heard the man," he said smoothly, taking the seat beside Melissa while Graham sat across from them.

Melissa clipped her seat belt into place, her fingers brushing against the soft material of the armrest. She was still slightly distracted by the jet's name—Lissa. The realisation that Michael had named it after her sent an unsettling warmth through her chest. But then she mentally shook herself. It's just a coincidence. It has to be.

Once they were all secured, the cockpit door opened, and the pilot, a middle-aged man with a confident but approachable demeanour, stepped out. "Good afternoon, Mr. Anderson." he greeted before giving a polite nod to Melissa and Graham. "Welcome aboard Lissa. I'm Captain Harry Reynolds, and I'll be flying you to Sydney today."

He glanced at his tablet before continuing. "Our flight time will be approximately twenty hours with a short refuelling stop in Singapore. We'll be cruising at 41,000 feet, and the weather along the route looks favourable. You can expect some mild turbulence over the Indian Ocean, but nothing significant. Once we reach altitude, feel free to move about the cabin and enjoy the amenities."

Michael nodded. "Thank you, Harry."

The pilot gave a reassuring smile before returning to the cockpit. A moment later, the jet's engines rumbled to life, a smooth, powerful sound that vibrated through the cabin as they prepared for take-off.

Melissa settled into her seat, her fingers gripping the armrests lightly as the aircraft accelerated down the runway. Within moments, they lifted off, the ground falling away beneath them. As they climbed to cruising altitude, the tension in her shoulders eased.

Once they levelled out, Simon appeared, offering drinks.

Melissa declined, but Michael and Graham each requested a whiskey.

After the drinks were served, Melissa turned to Michael. "Would you mind if I went to get some work done?"

Michael nodded. "Go ahead."

With that, she disappeared into the private office at the back of the jet, leaving Graham and Michael alone.

A charged silence settled between them, broken only by the quiet hum of the aircraft. Michael exhaled slowly, running a hand along the back of his neck before finally speaking.

"Why do you two act like a couple?" His voice was calm, measured—but there was an edge to it, something he wasn't entirely sure he wanted to name.

Graham smirked, his eyes gleaming with amusement. "Took you long enough to ask."

Michael's jaw tightened. "I didn't realise it wasn't real until the other night."

Graham shrugged, swirling the amber liquid in his glass. "It's Melissa's idea."

Michael frowned. "Why?"

"She doesn't like the attention she attracts from men—especially the rich and famous."

Michael leaned forward, his grip tightening around his drink. "What do you mean?"

Graham stretched his legs out, settling in as if for a conversation he'd long expected but never rushed to have. He took a slow sip of his drink before gesturing vaguely.

"Michael, look at her. She's gorgeous, graceful, intelligent, and wealthy. You saw Luke—the male model at the show. He's just one of many who won't take no for an answer."

Michael's grip on his glass tightened, his knuckles whitening at the memory. Luke had been relentless, his hands lingering too long, his smile too self-assured. Melissa had handled him with practiced ease, brushing him off with a smirk and a flick of her wrist.

But now, Michael saw it differently.

How often did she have to do that?

How many men like Luke refused to hear no?

His mind flashed to Gabriel Dubois the other night—the way he had spoken to Melissa, the casual insinuation that he was waiting for her, the too-familiar way he touched her.

A lead weight settled in Michael's chest.

His voice came out rougher than he intended. "Why doesn't she want the attention? Why hasn't she got a boyfriend or a husband?"

The idea of her belonging to someone else made his stomach twist.

He tried to ignore it.

Graham's smirk faded, replaced by something far more serious. He studied Michael for a long moment, as if weighing his words carefully.

"She's had plenty of offers," he said at last. "If she wanted, she could have notched a list of the wealthiest, most eligible bachelors without even trying. But something happened to her in Sydney before she came to Paris…" He exhaled, swirling the liquid in his glass. "Since then, she's been wary of men. That's why she doesn't go home much."

Michael straightened, tension coiling in his shoulders. "What happened?"

His voice was sharper than he intended, edged with something he refused to name— *concern.*

Graham hesitated. A flicker of something unreadable crossed his face before he shook his head. "It's not my place to say. Just know that it frightened the hell out of her."

Michael's jaw locked. His mind raced through possibilities, each one worse than the last. Frightened wasn't a word Graham would throw around lightly. If whatever had happened had driven Melissa away from home—away from the familiarity of her old life—it had to be bad.

He exhaled slowly, forcing himself to stay composed, but frustration coiled in his chest, tangled with something sharper.

Something possessive.

Graham watched him closely, his lips curving in something between curiosity and challenge. "Why do you care so much?"

Michael didn't answer immediately. Instead, he took a slow sip of whiskey, his gaze fixed on the endless stretch of sky outside the window. He wasn't sure he wanted to say the words out loud—to admit what he was only now beginning to accept.

"You know our history?"

Graham's lips pressed into a thin line. "Yes, I know." He paused, then added, "I love Melissa. She's like my family."

His expression darkened, his voice losing its usual teasing lilt. "And I don't let anyone hurt my family."

The warning was clear.

Michael met his gaze, his expression unreadable. But deep down, one thing was certain.

He needed to know what had happened to Melissa in Sydney.

Michael leaned back in his seat, his fingers drumming against his glass as he processed Graham's words. The revelation that she had been through something frightening sent a slow burn of unease through him.

He had already been carrying the weight of his own mistakes where she was concerned. But now—now there was something else.

Something dark, lurking beneath the surface of her carefully controlled exterior.

And he *hated* not knowing.

Graham watched him with quiet amusement, but there was an edge to it—something protective. The man might have been relaxed in posture, but Michael knew better. There was steel beneath that charm, and it was clear as day in the warning he had just delivered.

Michael let out a slow breath, swirling the whiskey in his glass before taking another sip. "So, you've been playing the role of the doting boyfriend to keep men away," he mused, his voice deceptively casual.

Graham smirked. "It's a tough job, but someone's got to do it."

Michael wasn't smiling. "And she needs that? A fake relationship to keep men at a distance?"

Graham's smirk faded. His expression turned contemplative. "You saw how she handled Luke. She can hold her own, but that doesn't mean she should have to. Some men don't take no for an answer." He exhaled, his gaze darkening. "And after what happened in Sydney, she is very cautious."

Michael's fingers clenched around his drink. "You keep mentioning Sydney," he said, his voice low. "What happened?"

Graham studied him for a long moment before shaking his head. "That's for Melissa to tell you. *If* she ever wants to. But what happened in Sydney changed her life—and not for the better." He sighed, his gaze turning distant. "She deserves to be happy. She's one of the most loving, sincere, and selfless women I've ever met. I just hope one day she lets someone in."

The answer did nothing to ease the frustration coiling in Michael's chest.

He *hated* being kept in the dark—especially when it came to her.

His grip tightened around the glass as his mind raced through possibilities, each one worse than the last.

Whatever had happened to Melissa in Sydney, it had left a mark.

And now, more than ever, Michael needed to know what—*or who*—had put that fear in her eyes.

Chapter Eleven

Melissa had spent the last few hours perfecting the final two dress designs for Michael's gala. Now, with a satisfied smile, she gathered her sketches and made her way back to the main cabin.

Michael and Graham were seated, engaged in quiet conversation, but they both looked up as she approached. "I've finished the last two designs," she announced. "I'd like your opinion."

Curiosity flickered across Michael's face as he stood and walked to the sleek mahogany desk, Graham following behind. Melissa spread out the first sketch—a gown designed to embody pure flawlessness, created specifically to complement an exquisite emerald necklace.

The dress was a masterpiece of understated elegance. A figure-hugging silhouette sculpted from liquid silk in the deepest shade of midnight green, its fabric draped effortlessly, pooling into a soft, flowing train. A daring but refined off-the-shoulder neckline revealed just enough collarbone to allow the emerald necklace to take centre stage, its vibrant stones glowing against the rich fabric. Delicate, barely-there embroidery in silver thread shimmered subtly as it caught the light, resembling the faintest traces of stardust across the gown.

Michael exhaled slowly, his gaze tracing every detail of the design. "It's timeless," he murmured, almost to himself.

Melissa felt a flush of pride warm her cheeks. "That's the goal," she said softly, glancing at Michael. He hadn't taken his eyes off the sketch, his expression unreadable.

Encouraged by their reaction, she carefully pulled out the next design—a gown meant to complement the diamond necklace.

The dress was the very definition of flawless—an ethereal creation in shimmering white satin, cut to drape like liquid silver over the body. The bodice was intricately adorned with hand-sewn crystals, catching the light with every movement, mirroring the brilliance of the diamonds it was meant to enhance. A deep, elegant neckline plunged just enough to be daring but remained sophisticated, while the long, fitted sleeves added an air of classic refinement. The skirt flowed into a sweeping train, weightless yet commanding, designed to move like a whisper with each step.

Graham let out a low whistle. "It's going to be breathtaking. Whoever wears this will own the night."

Melissa smiled, but before she could respond, Graham tilted his head. "So… who's wearing this?"

She hesitated. "I haven't decided yet. I have models lined up, but I need to see which gown suits each of them best before making a final decision."

Michael's gaze lifted to hers, something flickering in his dark eyes. His voice was quiet, but firm.

"You should."

Melissa blinked, startled. "I'm not a model."

Graham chuckled; arms crossed as he leaned against the desk. "You proved that you could be."

Michael didn't smile. He simply held her gaze, unwavering. "You designed these gowns, Melissa. No one will wear them better than you."

Melissa opened her mouth to argue but faltered. She wasn't used to the spotlight. For years, her work had spoken for itself, while she remained behind the scenes. Walking the runway at her last show had been an emergency solution, not a decision she had ever considered for herself.

Her mind flickered back to that night—the flash of cameras, the murmurs of the audience, the way her heart had pounded so violently she thought she might collapse right there under the lights. She had pulled it off, but the vulnerability of standing before so many eyes, the scrutiny, had left her shaken long after the show ended.

"I don't know…" she said carefully, biting her lip.

Michael stepped closer, his voice low but insistent. "These gowns were created to embody perfection." He held her gaze. "And so were you."

Her breath caught. Something about the way he said it, the way his eyes darkened as he looked at her, made her pulse stutter.

Graham smirked. "He's right, you know. And if Michael Anderson—one of the most powerful men in Europe—says you should wear it, who are we to argue?"

Melissa rolled her eyes at Graham, but she couldn't shake the warmth that had settled in her chest.

She looked back at the sketch, trying to picture herself in the gown. The thought made her nervous. But also… excited.

Could she do it?

She glanced up at Michael again, searching his face. His features were composed, but something softer lingered in his gaze now.

Melissa exhaled, running a hand through her hair. "I'll think about it."

Michael's lips curled at the edges, just the faintest hint of satisfaction in his expression.

"You do that," he murmured, his gaze never leaving hers.

Dinner was served soon after—an exquisite meal paired with fine wine; the kind expected on a private jet. The atmosphere was surprisingly relaxed, despite the unspoken tension simmering between Michael and Melissa.

Graham, who had been enjoying himself thoroughly, chuckled as he set his fork down. "This airline food is a bit better than I'm used to."

Melissa smirked. "I don't think this qualifies as airline food."

Michael merely raised a brow, sipping his whiskey.

After dinner, Graham stretched with a satisfied sigh. "I think I'll get some sleep before we land." He turned to Melissa. "You okay?"

She nodded. "I'm fine. Get some rest."

Graham gave Michael a knowing look before heading toward the rear of the jet. Within minutes, he was reclined in one of the plush seats, dozing off almost instantly, leaving Michael and Melissa alone.

They settled into the private lounge at the front, the curved TV casting a soft glow as the movie played. The tension between them, once thick with unspoken words and unresolved emotions, had melted into something quieter. Something almost comfortable.

At some point, Melissa's eyelids grew heavy. She fought it, blinking rapidly, shifting in her seat as if sheer willpower could keep her awake. But exhaustion won. Her head dipped to the side, resting against the back of the lounge for a fleeting moment before Michael—without thinking—reached out.

With careful precision, he guided her head into his lap, his touch gentle, ensuring she was comfortable.

She murmured something in her sleep, a soft sigh escaping as her body unconsciously relaxed against him.

Michael stilled.

His gaze traced the delicate curve of her face, the way sleep had erased the guarded sharpness she carried when awake. Here, in this quiet moment, she looked so different—so vulnerable. A version of her he hadn't seen in years.

Before he could stop himself, his fingers moved, threading lightly through her silky hair. The sensation sent a strange ache through him—something both familiar and foreign. He told himself to stop, to pull back. But he didn't.

Instead, his hand kept moving, slow and absentminded, as if drawn to her by instinct alone. His other hand rested lightly on her shoulder, his thumb brushing over the soft fabric of her dress.

She was still the most beautiful woman he had ever seen.

It frustrated him—how easily she could undo him. Even now. Even after all these years.

Melissa woke with a start, her breath catching as her heart pounded against her ribs. Disoriented, she blinked rapidly, her mind struggling to piece together where she was— until she felt the warmth beneath her cheek, the steady rise and fall of his breathing.

Michael.

Her head was resting in Michael's lap.

Embarrassment crashed over her like a tidal wave.

Carefully, she tilted her head, glancing up at him. He was reclined against the lounge, eyes closed, his breathing deep and even. Asleep. Completely unaware of the intimate position they had fallen into.

Melissa swallowed hard; her pulse still erratic as she forced herself to move. Slowly— carefully—she lifted herself, doing her best not to disturb him. Every shift of her body felt amplified, the brush of fabric against fabric, the slight change in pressure where her weight had rested against him.

Once free, she adjusted her posture, smoothing down her dress with trembling fingers.

She needed to get out of here.

Slipping off the lounge as quietly as possible, she made her way toward the bathroom, her steps light against the plush carpet. The moment the door closed behind her, she braced her hands on the sink, her reflection staring back at her in the mirror.

Her cheeks were flushed, her lips slightly parted as if she'd been caught in a dream she hadn't fully escaped.

Melissa exhaled sharply, twisting the faucet on and splashing cool water onto her face. The shock of it sent a shiver through her, snapping her fully back to reality.

What the hell had just happened?

She hadn't meant to fall asleep on him. And yet, she had—so easily, so naturally, as if some part of her still trusted him, still found comfort in his presence.

Her stomach twisted at the thought.

No. It didn't mean anything.

It couldn't mean anything.

Straightening, she inhaled deeply, pressing a hand over her chest as she willed her heart to slow. After a long moment, she squared her shoulders, smoothing her dress once more before stepping back out.

As she returned to her original seat, she stole a glance at Michael. He hadn't moved, still lost in sleep, his features relaxed in a way she hadn't seen in years.

Melissa sat down, folding her hands in her lap.

She told herself to forget about it.

To pretend it never happened.

But the warmth of his touch still lingered on her skin, making it impossible to ignore the one thing she didn't want to admit.

For the first time in a long time, she had felt safe.

Approximately twelve hours after take-off, a voice came over the speakers, informing them to fasten their seatbelts for landing at Changi Airport in Singapore for refuelling. It would take thirty to sixty minutes before their flight continued to Sydney.

As the jet taxied to its designated spot, Melissa unbuckled her seatbelt and stretched slightly. Turning to Michael, she asked, "What time do you think we'll be in Sydney?"

Michael glanced at his watch before meeting her gaze. "Around 9 p.m. local time," he said. "I have a limousine waiting for us to take us home."

He smiled slightly before adding, "Mum and Dad can't wait to see you."

Melissa's brows lifted. "Oh? Did you let them know we were coming with you?"

Michael's smile deepened. "Of course."

Just before 9 p.m. Sydney time, the jet touched down smoothly on the runway. After clearing customs swiftly through the private terminal, Michael, Melissa, and Graham stepped into the waiting limousine.

As they pulled away from the airport, the city lights of Sydney blurred past the windows. The journey to Michael's family estate was a short one, made even more familiar by the fact that Melissa's own family estate sat right next door.

When they arrived, the grand entrance of the Anderson estate was warmly lit and waiting at the top of the steps were Maria and Henry Anderson.

As soon as Melissa stepped out of the car, Maria let out a delighted gasp and wrapped her in a big hug.

"Oh, dear, we have missed you!" Maria said, pulling back slightly to get a better look at her. "You look stunning as always."

Melissa smiled. "Thank you, Mrs. Anderson. It's so good to see you again." She returned the hug and pressed a light kiss to the older woman's cheek.

"Enough with the formalities," a deep voice interjected. Henry, ever the charmer, grinned as he pulled Melissa into a brief but firm hug. "You know you're practically family."

Melissa chuckled. "I suppose I'm out of practice."

Standing a few steps away, Graham smirked and nudged Michael. "Melissa seems more popular than you."

Michael chuckled, watching the warm reunion. "She always has been."

After a quick but warm reunion, Michael turned to his parents.

"I'm going to take Melissa and Graham over to her place," he informed them.

Maria nodded with a smile. "Of course, dear. We will see you in the morning."

Henry clapped Michael on the shoulder. "Good to see you, son."

With that, Michael guided Melissa and Graham back to the limousine. As they drove toward the Shaw estate, a quiet sense of nostalgia settled over Melissa. It had been years since she'd last seen home, and as the familiar wrought-iron gates came into view, a soft smile touched her lips.

Michael glanced at her. "Feels good to be home?"

She turned to him, her smile deepening. "Yeah, it really does."

As soon as the limousine rolled to a stop in the driveway, the front door burst open, and Sarah came running out, her excitement palpable.

"Melissa!" she squealed, practically launching herself at her older sister.

Melissa let out a laugh as she caught Sarah in a tight embrace, squeezing her affectionately. "Sarah! I missed you!"

"You're finally home!" Sarah pulled back just enough to beam up at her. "It's been way too long."

Jason followed at a more composed pace, a smirk playing at his lips. "Look who finally decided to grace us with her presence. What, Paris wasn't glamorous enough for you anymore?"

Then, with a softer look, he stepped forward. "It's good to see you, Mel. Even if I half expected you to come back wearing a tiara and demanding we address you as 'Madame Designer Extraordinaire.'"

Melissa laughed, stepping forward to hug him as well. "It's good to see you, Jason."

Sarah's eyes sparkled with excitement as she clasped her hands together. "Can you believe it? You're finally here for the wedding! I've been counting down the days."

Melissa's lips curved into a soft smile, warmth spreading through her chest. Sarah had always been the heart of their family—the one who made every gathering feel like home. Without thinking, Melissa reached out and squeezed her sister's hand, a silent acknowledgment of how much she had missed this, missed her.

"I wouldn't have missed it for the world," Melissa said. her voice thick with emotion.

Sarah's grin widened. "Good."

Behind them, Mr. and Mrs. Shaw stepped forward, their faces filled with quiet joy.

"Graham," Mr. Shaw greeted, shaking his hand. "It's good to see you again."

Mrs. Shaw turned to Michael with a smile. "Michael, it's been too long." She gave him a quick, motherly hug. "Thank you for bringing our daughter home."

Michael returned the embrace politely. "You're welcome. It's good to see you both again."

Sarah looped her arm through Melissa's, practically buzzing with excitement. "Come inside! We need to catch up."

Melissa laughed but didn't resist as Sarah eagerly tugged her toward the house, her heart warming at the familiar, loving chaos of home.

Once inside, they made their way to the back of the house, stepping onto the terrace, where a beautifully arranged spread of snacks and drinks awaited them. The evening air was warm and carried the faint scent of jasmine from the garden.

Kevin, Melissa's father, quickly struck up a conversation with Michael, Jason and Graham, their voices carrying in easy camaraderie, while Maria and Sarah guided Melissa to a cozy seating area.

As they settled in, Sarah leaned closer and whispered excitedly, "Did you bring the wedding dress?"

Melissa smiled. "Of course."

Sarah's eyes lit up. She had jumped at the chance to wear one of Melissa's original designs, especially knowing how much love and craftsmanship her sister put into every piece.

"I can't wait to try it on," Sarah said, practically bouncing in her seat.

"You'll look stunning in it," Melissa assured her. Sarah was nearly the same build, just a little shorter, but with a few adjustments, the dress would fit her perfectly.

Fiona, Melissa's mother, watching their exchange, smiled fondly. "It's so special that you're wearing your sister's design. It makes the wedding even more meaningful."

Sarah nodded enthusiastically. "It really does." She turned to Melissa with a teasing grin. "Now, tell me everything about Paris and Michael's Jewellery Gala."

Chapter Twelve

Melissa woke early Friday morning, the familiar sounds of birds chirping outside her childhood bedroom window bringing a sense of nostalgia. She stretched and took a deep breath, inhaling the comforting scent of freshly brewed coffee wafting from the kitchen. It felt surreal to be home again, surrounded by the warmth of her family after so many years away.

After getting dressed, she made her way downstairs, where her mother, Fiona, was already bustling around the kitchen, preparing a hearty breakfast. Sarah was seated at the dining table, sipping on a cup of tea, her eyes lighting up when she saw Melissa.

"Morning, sleepyhead," Sarah teased. "I thought Paris had turned you into one of those late risers."

Melissa chuckled as she poured herself a cup of coffee. "Not a chance. I was just savouring the feeling of being home."

They sat together, enjoying a leisurely breakfast filled with laughter and stories about the wedding plans. Fiona, ever the doting mother, fussed over Melissa, making sure she had everything she needed for the alterations.

Once breakfast was finished, Melissa turned to Sarah. "I'll get you to try the dress on this morning so I can get started on the alterations."

Sarah beamed with excitement. "I'm so excited to put it on!"

The three women moved to the spacious living room, where Melissa had already set up her sewing kit and dress. Sarah carefully stepped into the elegant white gown; her movements filled with anticipation. When she finally stood in front of the mirror, Fiona gasped.

"Oh, sweetheart, you look absolutely stunning," she said, misty-eyed.

Melissa grinned as she stepped back, hands on her hips. "Well, I have to say, it does look good on you. But let's see where we need to make adjustments."

The morning was filled with giggles and playful banter as Melissa pinned and adjusted the fabric while Sarah twirled around dramatically. Fiona reminisced about her own wedding day, sharing funny anecdotes that had both her daughters in stitches. At one point, Sarah nearly tripped over the hem, causing all three of them to dissolve into laughter.

"Careful," Melissa warned, still laughing. "I'd rather not have to stitch the whole thing back together before the wedding."

After a couple of hours of measurements, pinning, and minor alterations, they finally took a break for lunch. Fiona had prepared a beautiful spread of sandwiches, fresh fruit, and homemade lemonade, and they sat outside on the terrace, enjoying the warm afternoon sun.

Just as Melissa was about to take another bite of her sandwich, the sound of a car pulling into the driveway caught her attention.

Sarah smirked knowingly. "Sounds like the men have arrived."

Moments later, Michael and Jason stepped out onto the terrace. Michael was dressed in a crisp button-down shirt with the sleeves rolled up, his confident stride making it impossible for Melissa to look away. Jason, ever the charmer, flashed a grin as he followed.

"Hope we're not interrupting anything," Michael said, his eyes locking onto Melissa's.

Melissa swallowed hard, forcing down the sudden rush of emotions. "Not at all," she said smoothly. "Just a morning filled with wedding chaos."

Jason laughed. "Sounds about right. And how's our bride holding up?" Bending down and giving Sarah a quick kiss on the lips.

Sarah grinned. "Excited, but Melissa has been poking me with pins all morning."

Michael arched a brow. "Torturing the bride? That doesn't seem very professional."

Melissa rolled her eyes, trying to ignore the way his deep voice sent shivers down her spine. "It's part of the process. You wouldn't understand."

Michael smirked. "Oh, I understand plenty."

Melissa shot Michael a pointed look, but he only responded with a knowing smile. Fiona, ever the gracious hostess, gestured to the table. "Boys, sit down and have something to eat."

Jason settled beside Sarah, while Michael took the seat next to Melissa. Both men thanked Fiona and helped themselves to the light lunch.

As they ate, Fiona turned to Melissa. "How long will the adjustments take you to finish?"

Melissa smiled, wiping her hands on a napkin. "I'll have them done by tomorrow morning, just in time for the final fitting."

Jason perked up. "Can I see it?"

Three voices answered in unison. "No."

Michael chuckled, shaking his head. "Even I know that, Jason. You're not supposed to see the dress until she walks down the aisle on Sunday."

Jason held up his hands in surrender. "Okay, okay, sorry."

Sarah leaned into him with a teasing grin. "At least you're learning."

Jason pressed a quick kiss to her cheek. "Of course. And in case you're wondering, we got our suits sorted this morning."

Sarah beamed. "Good."

Jason smirked. "And we look awesome."

Fiona glanced up from her plate. "Who's picking up the bomboniere?"

Sarah's eyes widened. "Oh no, I completely forgot about them!"

Michael, ever the problem solver, shrugged. "I'll get them if you like."

Sarah turned to Melissa, a hopeful gleam in her eyes. "Mel, could you go with him?"

Melissa shot her sister a look that screamed, Are you serious? But Sarah only responded with an overly sweet smile, feigning innocence.

Melissa sighed, setting her fork down. "Do I have a choice?"

Sarah's eyes twinkled with mischief. "Not really."

Michael smirked, clearly enjoying the exchange. "Come on, Melissa. It's just a quick trip."

Melissa rolled her eyes. "Fine. Let's go."

Fiona smiled, pleased that the task was sorted. "The bomboniere is at the boutique in town. I already paid, so you just need to collect them."

Michael nodded. "Got it." Then he turned to Melissa with a teasing glint in his eyes. "Try to keep up."

Melissa scoffed. "Trust me, I won't be the problem."

Jason chuckled as he reached for another sandwich. "Try not to kill each other before the wedding."

Michael grinned. "No promises."

Sarah smothered a giggle as Melissa shot her another glare before following Michael outside.

The drive into town was filled with a tense silence at first, the only sound being the hum of the car engine. Melissa kept her gaze firmly on the road ahead, determined not to acknowledge the man beside her. But, of course, Michael wasn't one to let things stay quiet for long.

"You're acting like I'm dragging you to a dentist appointment," he commented, glancing at her with amusement.

Melissa exhaled sharply, crossing her arms. "I just don't see why I had to come. You're perfectly capable of picking up some wedding favours on your own."

Michael smirked. "True. But then we wouldn't get to spend all this quality time together."

She turned her head to glare at him. "Oh, how lucky for me."

Michael chuckled but didn't push further. Instead, he turned on the radio, letting the soft music fill the car. Melissa was grateful for the distraction, even if it didn't completely drown out the awareness simmering between them.

Fifteen minutes later, they arrived at the boutique. It was a charming little shop with delicate lace curtains framing the windows and a rustic wooden sign hanging above the entrance. Melissa stepped out of the car, smoothing down her dress as she walked ahead of Michael, determined to make this as quick as possible.

Inside, the shop smelled of vanilla and fresh flowers. An older woman at the counter greeted them with a warm smile. "Ah, you must be here for the Anderson/Shaw wedding order."

Michael stepped up, flashing his charming smile. "That's right."

The woman beamed as she retrieved a beautifully wrapped box. "They're all packed and ready for you."

Melissa took the box carefully, a sense of relief washing over her now that the errand was nearly done. But just as she turned to leave, the shopkeeper gave them a knowing smile.

"You two make such a lovely couple."

Melissa froze. Michael, on the other hand, chuckled, clearly amused. "Oh, thank you. She's the light of my life."

The shopkeeper beamed. "That's wonderful." She turned to Melissa, eyes twinkling. "You're a lucky girl."

Melissa forced a polite smile. "Thank you." Before Michael could add anything else, she grabbed his arm and practically dragged him toward the door.

The moment they stepped outside, Michael burst into laughter. "Did you hear that? We make a lovely couple."

Melissa groaned, marching toward the car, her voice sharp with frustration. "She's a complete stranger. She has no idea how not lovely we are. And she certainly doesn't know how cruel you can be."

Michael stiffened. His playful smirk disappeared in an instant. *Cruel?* The word struck him like a blow to the chest. *Is that what she thought of him? That he had deliberately set out to hurt her.* The worst part was, maybe she wasn't wrong. He had wanted her to suffer—at least, at first. But now… now, hearing her say it out loud made his stomach twist in a way he hadn't expected.

"What's that supposed to mean?" he asked, his voice quieter now, edged with something unreadable. He took the box from her hands and placed it carefully in the backseat, but his focus remained on her.

Melissa swallowed hard, blinking against the sting in her eyes. Her voice wavered, but she refused to look away. "You left, Michael. Without saying a word. Not goodbye. Not anything. Like I meant nothing to you." She sucked in a shaky breath, but the pain still slipped through. "Do you have any idea what that felt like?"

Michael stared at her, his expression shifting—guilt, regret, something else she couldn't quite place. "Melissa…" His voice was low, almost hesitant, as if he wasn't sure what to say.

She let out a hollow laugh, shaking her head. "No." Her hands clenched into fists at her sides. "I don't care. Let's just get back. I have work to do on the dress."

Without waiting for a response, Melissa yanked open the car door and slid inside, her jaw tight, her heart pounding.

Michael lingered for a moment, his fingers flexing at his sides as if he wanted to reach for her—but didn't dare. With a heavy sigh, he got into the driver's seat, his movements slower, more hesitant than usual.

The tension in the car was suffocating. The air between them felt thick with unspoken words, with things neither of them wanted to touch.

Melissa crossed her arms and stared out the window, her reflection glaring back at her. "Are you going to say something, or are we just going to sit in this awkward silence?"

Michael gripped the steering wheel, his knuckles whitening. He exhaled sharply through his nose. "Not here," he muttered.

Melissa turned toward him, her eyes blazing. "Not here? What, you don't want to talk about it in public?" She let out a sharp, bitter laugh. "Wouldn't want people overhearing, right? Wouldn't want them to know that you had no right to do what you did. That you treated me abominably. That there was no reason for you to hurt me like you did. None."

Michael's jaw tightened, his grip on the wheel so tight it looked like he might snap it in half. The words burned on his tongue—I saw you, Melissa. *With him.* But he swallowed them back. This wasn't the time.

"Melissa—" he started, but the moment his voice softened, her expression hardened.

"No." She shook her head, her breath shaky as she blinked rapidly, willing back the sting of tears. "Just drive, Michael."

He didn't move at first. Instead, he turned to her, searching her face, and what he saw made his stomach twist. She wasn't just angry—she was certain. Certain that he was in the wrong. That she was the one who'd been betrayed, not the other way around.

His throat worked as he looked away. Jaw set, he turned the key, and the engine roared to life. But the silence between them? That remained, heavier than ever.

Melissa clenched her jaw, staring out the window, her fingers tightening around the edge of her dress. She could feel the heat of unshed tears burning behind her eyes, but she refused to let them fall. Not now. Not in front of him. Instead, she exhaled slowly and gripped the seatbelt, as if holding onto something—anything—to keep herself from breaking apart.

Chapter Thirteen

As soon as Michael pulled into the driveway, Melissa threw open the car door and rushed out.

"Melissa," he called as he got out, but she didn't stop.

Over her shoulder, she said curtly, "You can give the box to my mother. Thanks." Then, without another glance, she disappeared into the house.

She made a beeline for the living room, dropping into an armchair and picking up the wedding dress she had been working on. Her fingers moved quickly, stitching with fierce determination, as if focusing on the delicate fabric could erase Michael from her mind.

Ten minutes later, footsteps echoed behind her. She didn't have to look up to know who it was.

"Melissa," Michael said softly.

She kept her eyes on the dress. "Go away, Michael."

Michael didn't move. Instead, he took a slow step closer, his voice steady but laced with something she couldn't quite name. "Melissa, we need to talk."

She kept her eyes on the delicate fabric in her hands, carefully adjusting the lace trim as if he weren't standing there. "No, we don't," she said flatly. "I have work to do."

Michael exhaled sharply, running a hand through his hair. "Pretend all you want, Melissa. It won't change anything."

Melissa's hands stilled mid-stitch. Her jaw tightened, but she kept her eyes on the delicate fabric. Then, with forced calm, she finally looked up, her brown eyes sharp. "Funny," she said, her voice deceptively even, "considering you walked away without a second thought."

His jaw tensed, but he didn't argue. He just stood there, watching her, as if trying to figure out what to say—what would make her listen.

Melissa turned back to her stitching, her fingers trembling slightly. "Just leave, Michael."

But he didn't. Instead, he pulled up a chair and sat down across from her. "Not this time."

Melissa smoothed the fabric of the wedding dress with steady hands, her gaze fixed on the delicate lace as if it were the only thing that mattered. She told herself she wasn't shaken, that his presence didn't send her heart into a frantic rhythm. But no matter how hard she tried to anchor herself in the task, the weight of his stare pressed against her skin, unravelling the careful detachment she had spent years perfecting.

Michael sat across from her, arms folded, his expression unreadable. "You're not going to ignore me forever, Melissa."

Her fingers stilled. She inhaled sharply and forced her shoulders to stay straight, her expression smooth. "I'm not ignoring you. I'm working."

His gaze darkened, as if he saw straight through the lie. "You're hiding."

Her pulse kicked up. She clenched her jaw and reached for another pin. "Believe what you want."

Michael leaned forward, elbows resting on his knees. He wasn't touching her, wasn't even that close, but his presence alone was enough to unsettle her. She hated how easily he slipped under her skin, how effortlessly he shattered the walls she had spent years building.

"You're trembling." His voice was softer now, more dangerous for the way it cut through her defences.

Melissa stilled. Her fingers had curled slightly, betraying the tension she refused to acknowledge. Slowly, she released the fabric, smoothing it out again with deliberate care. "I have work to do, Michael."

"I'm not leaving."

The words sent a shiver down her spine. She hated how much they affected her; how much he still affected her. He had already hurt her once—shattered her beyond repair. She couldn't let him do it again.

Forcing herself to meet his gaze, she lifted her chin. "Then sit there all night. It doesn't change anything."

Melissa set the dress aside and stood up, her fingers twitching as she curled them into fists. Her breath hitched. She blinked rapidly, but the tears came anyway—silent, unrelenting. She swiped at them, frustration flashing in her eyes. But it was useless. The pain she had buried for years was surfacing, raw and unstoppable.

"You need to go," she whispered, her voice fragile, barely holding together.

Michael stood slowly; his gaze locked on her as he took a step forward. "Melissa."

There was something in his voice—regret, longing, maybe both. She didn't want to acknowledge it, didn't want to let it seep into the cracks of her already wounded heart.

She shook her head, stepping back. "Don't," she pleaded.

But he reached for her anyway.

She flinched, instinctively trying to move away, but Michael didn't let her. His arms came around her, strong and unwavering, pulling her close.

"Let me go," Melissa choked out, her fists pressing against his chest. "Sarah and Mum are here."

But Michael didn't loosen his hold. If anything, he held her tighter, his warmth seeping into her, his steady heartbeat against her ear.

"They went out with Graham," he murmured. "There's a note on the kitchen bench."

Melissa stilled for a moment before trying to pull away, but he only softened his grip, refusing to let her go completely. She lifted her tear-streaked face to him, eyes filled with anguish. "I can't do this again," she whispered, her voice breaking. "You broke me. I can't go through that again."

Michael stilled, his breath catching in his throat. Jason's words—*She was broken*—hit him with the force of a wrecking ball. He had dismissed them, convinced she had moved on, convinced she had chosen someone else. But now, looking into her tear-filled eyes, hearing the tremble in her voice, doubt twisted inside him like a knife. Had he been wrong all this time? The thought unsettled him, made his chest tighten with something dangerously close to regret.

Had he really done that to her? But he had seen her with Brian. Hadn't he? Yet, looking into her eyes now, seeing the raw pain reflected back at him, something inside him cracked.

He didn't think. He didn't second-guess. He just acted—his lips claiming hers in a kiss that burned with everything unspoken, everything lost and found all at once.

The moment their mouths met, Melissa gasped, her hands fisting in his shirt as if she wanted to push him away but couldn't make herself do it. Michael deepened the kiss, one hand threading through her hair, the other gripping her waist, pulling her closer.

She shuddered, a soft whimper escaping her lips as his mouth moved over hers with desperate intensity. It wasn't just a kiss—it was a plea, an apology, a confession of everything he hadn't said.

Melissa wanted to fight it, but the fire he ignited in her was impossible to ignore. Her body melted against his as he backed her toward the couch, his hands roaming over her, his touch both possessive and reverent.

His lips trailed down her jaw, pressing hot kisses along her throat. "Melissa," he whispered, his breath ragged. "Tell me to stop, and I will."

But she couldn't. Despite all her pain, for the way he had hurt her—she still wanted him.

Melissa's resolve crumbled as Michael's lips moved hungrily over hers. A soft moan escaped her, and before she could stop herself, her arms wrapped around his neck, pulling him closer. His hands gripped her waist, fingers pressing into her as if afraid she would disappear.

The kiss deepened, growing more urgent. Michael's tongue traced the seam of her lips, coaxing her open, and she surrendered, letting him in. Their breaths mingled, the taste of longing and regret intertwining as his hands slid up her back, pressing her flush against him.

Melissa's breath hitched as his lips claimed hers, igniting something deep, something terrifying. She should push him away—should want to push him away. Instead, she found herself drowning in the kiss, in the heat of his hands as they anchored her against him. A war waged inside her, every logical thought telling her to stop before she fell too far, but then Michael's fingers traced along her jaw, tilting her face up to his. His kiss softened, turning reverent, coaxing rather than demanding. Stay with me. That's what it felt like he was saying. And God help her—she did.

He groaned against her mouth, his grip tightening before he suddenly broke away, his breath ragged.

In one swift motion, he bent down and scooped her into his arms.

"Michael—" she gasped, startled, but he silenced her with another kiss, his lips devouring hers as he carried her down the hallway and up the stairs.

She could feel the steady rise and fall of his chest, the way his heart pounded as he held her. Every step he took sent a shiver through her, anticipation curling low in her stomach.

By the time they reached her bedroom, her hands were gripping his shoulders, her lips trailing along his jaw. Michael kicked the door shut behind them and lowered her to stand in the middle of her bedroom.

Michael's lips claimed hers with a hunger that stole her breath. His hands slid into her hair, tilting her head as he deepened the kiss, his tongue sweeping into her mouth, tasting, possessing. Melissa moaned against him, her arms winding around his neck, pulling him closer as heat flared between them.

"Michael..." she whispered, her fingers slipping beneath his shirt, desperate to feel his skin.

He groaned at her touch, his muscles tensing under her fingertips. In one swift movement, he pulled his shirt over his head, then reached for the hem of her dress, dragging it up and over her body, leaving her bare except for panties.

His gaze darkened as he took her in, his hands roaming over her soft curves.

"God you're so beautiful." He murmured as he took her mouth in another searing kiss.

He shed his remaining clothes, his eyes darkening as they roamed over her bare skin. Melissa shivered under his gaze, anticipation curling in her stomach as he closed the space between them. When his lips followed—trailing slow, reverent kisses down her body—she gasped, her fingers threading through his hair, clinging to him as if he were the only thing keeping her grounded.

He walked her backward, his hands tracing the curve of her waist, his touch igniting a fire under her skin. When the backs of her knees hit the bed, he lifted her effortlessly, cradling her against his chest. She clung to him, her fingers tangling in his hair as he lowered her onto her bed. Her breath hitched as he lent over her. Every touch, every kiss sent shivers racing through her. Her body arched toward him as he worshiped her with his lips and hands, unravelling her until all that remained was sensation.

He couldn't wait; he needed to take her. Now. When he finally moved over her, ready to claim her, she tensed. Just for a moment. It was subtle, but he felt it. It confused him, but all thought had left him, the only thing he could think about was possessing her.

He moved with aching slowness, savouring the feel of her—until the moment resistance met him. Michael's entire body went rigid, realisation slamming into him like a freight train. His breathing turned unsteady. No... His gaze snapped to hers, searching, disbelieving. "Melissa..." His voice was husky, thick with something he couldn't name. She turned her face away, but he wouldn't let her. Gently, he cupped her jaw, tilting her back toward him. Tell me I'm wrong. But the truth was already there, written in her eyes.

"You're a virgin—" He stopped, realisation crashing over him like a tidal wave.

Melissa's breath shuddered out of her. She turned her face away, heat rising to her cheeks. 'Yes.' The word was barely a whisper, but it hit Michael like a physical blow.

Michael swallowed hard, his body tense with the effort to stay still. A curse slipped from his lips as his mind reeled. *How was this possible?*

Running a hand through his hair, he rasped, "But how—"

Melissa turned her face away, her fingers gripping the sheets. He could see the rapid rise and fall of her chest, the way her breath hitched as if she were trying to steady herself. Her lips parted, but no words came.

"Melissa," he pressed, his voice gentler now. He reached out, tilting her chin so she had no choice but to look at him. "Tell me."

Her eyes shimmered with something raw, something vulnerable. She swallowed hard, her fingers tightening around the fabric beneath her. Then, barely above a whisper, she said, "I—" Her voice faltered, uncertainty flickering across her face.

Michael's thumb brushed over her cheek, his gaze steady. "Please."

A shaky breath left her. She hesitated one more second—one second that felt like an eternity—before finally, *finally,* she whispered, "I never wanted anyone else. Only you."

The words landed like a punch to his chest. Michael sucked in a sharp breath, his entire world tilting beneath him.

"Damn it, Melissa," he rasped, leaning down to press a fierce, almost reverent kiss against her lips. "You should have told me."

She let out a breath that sounded almost like a laugh—broken, weary. "Would it have changed anything?"

Yes!

Michael closed his eyes for a brief moment, regret crashing over him. He had left her, hurt her, and now he had taken something he could never give back.

Five years.

Five years he had spent believing she had belonged to another man, that she had betrayed him without a second thought. Yet, she had been his all along—waiting, wanting only him. A mix of emotions surged through him—regret and guilt so sharp it felt like a wound, shame that clawed at his insides, and something else, something fierce and possessive that made his throat tighten.

But as he looked at her—truly looked at her—he knew one thing for certain. He would spend the rest of his life making it up to her.

Melissa met his gaze, her eyes brimming with something deeper than just passion. "I want you."

His restraint snapped. He kissed her again, slower this time, his hands moving over her body with new reverence. He worshiped her with every touch, making sure she felt nothing but pleasure, nothing but him.

When he finally started to move within her, he was gentle, murmuring her name as he coaxed her through the unfamiliar stretch of pain and pleasure. She clung to him, her nails digging into his shoulders, her body trembling beneath his.

"Look at me," he whispered.

She did, and in that moment, everything changed. This wasn't just about passion or need. It was something deeper, something that bound them together in a way neither of them could deny.

He held her gaze, his thumb tracing her cheek as he moved within her, each thrust sending waves of pleasure crashing over her. She clung to him, lost in the rhythm they created together, in the fire that consumed them both.

Michael moved slowly, reverently, until the tension in her body gave way to pleasure. Her gasp of surprise, the way her body arched against him, nearly undid him. He guided her through every wave of sensation, until she shattered beneath him, her cry lost in his mouth as he kissed her through it.

Moments later, he followed, groaning her name as he buried himself deep inside her, his body shaking with the force of his release.

He collapsed against her, his breathing ragged, his heart pounding in sync with hers. As the aftershocks faded, he pressed a lingering kiss to her temple, then to her cheek, tracing a path down to the curve of her shoulder. His arms tightened around her as if he could hold onto the moment, as if letting go meant losing something vital.

Chapter Fourteen

Melissa lay still beneath him, her own breath unsteady, her body still thrumming from his touch. But reality crept in, unravelling the fragile haze of warmth and desire. She gently eased out from under him and slipped off the bed, needing a moment to collect herself.

In the ensuite, she splashed cool water on her face and tied her robe securely around her, as if the soft fabric could shield her from whatever this was turning into. When she stepped back into the room, Michael was already dressed.

He stood by the window, his back to her, hands braced against the sill. But when he turned, the regret in his eyes was unmistakable.

Melissa's stomach tightened. "What?"

Michael hesitated. "Melissa… you wanted to know why I left."

A cold weight settled in her chest. "Yes."

He exhaled sharply, running a hand through his hair. He looked like he didn't want to say the words—like whatever he was about to reveal would change everything.

Melissa stared at him, waiting, the air between them thick with something unspoken. But when the words finally left his lips, they knocked the breath from her.

"I thought you were cheating on me," Michael said. His voice was hoarse, almost reluctant, as if he hated admitting it.

She felt the sting of it before she fully processed what he'd said. "That's ridiculous." Her laugh was sharp, humourless. "With who?"

Michael hesitated, then exhaled, as if bracing for impact. "Brian."

The name sent a violent chill down her spine. She felt the blood drain from her face, her pulse slowing into something cold and sluggish. Brian.

The memory slammed into her. His hands pinning her down. The way she had struggled, the sickening weight of his body pressing against hers. And now, Michael— *Michael*—had believed she had willingly been with him?

Her stomach twisted. "You thought I was cheating with Brian?" Her voice cracked on his name.

Michael dragged a hand down his face, his voice rough with frustration. "I saw you," he ground out. "I walked in, and he was on top of you—"

"And you just left?" The betrayal in Melissa's voice cut through the air like a blade, sharper than any wound he had ever inflicted on her. Her breath came fast and uneven, fury warring with heartbreak. "You didn't ask. You didn't wait. You didn't give me a chance to explain. You just—left?"

"I thought—"

"No." She shook her head violently, stepping back as if his words had physically struck her. "You assumed." Her voice trembled, thick with emotion, her body shaking with the force of it. "You saw what you wanted to see, and instead of talking to me, instead of trusting me, you abandoned me." Her breath hitched, her chest rising and falling too fast. "You left me to pick up the pieces, to wonder what I did wrong. Why you walked away without a word—" She sucked in a shuddering breath, her vision blurring. "You never even gave me a chance."

"Melissa—"

"You have no idea what Brian—" She stopped herself, her throat tightening. No. He had no right to know.

Michael's entire body went rigid. "What Brian..., what?"

Melissa lifted her chin, her jaw clenched so tight it ached. "No." Her voice was sharp, final. *Unforgiving.* "Get out."

His eyes darkened. "Melissa—"

"No!" Her voice cracked, but she didn't care. She stood her ground, her hands balled into trembling fists at her sides. "If you didn't trust me then, you won't trust me now." Her throat ached, the weight of everything she'd carried for years pressing down on her. "And if there's no trust, we have nothing."

He didn't move.

"Get out!"

The silence stretched between them, heavy, suffocating. Michael looked like he wanted to argue—his jaw tight, his fists clenched, his entire body radiating frustration. But something in her face—maybe the hurt, the sheer devastation, or the cold finality in her eyes—must have stopped him.

Because after a long, tense moment, his expression hardened.

And then, without another word, he turned and walked out.

Melissa stood frozen, chest rising and falling in uneven breaths, waiting—hoping—dreading—the sound of it closing behind him.

When it did, the sharp click echoed through the room like a gunshot. And just like that, she shattered all over again.

Michael left her room feeling hollow, his footsteps heavy with the weight of his own mistakes. He had believed the worst of the woman he loved. And despite everything, he still loved her—*desperately.*

He stepped out into the chilly air, but it did nothing to cool the firestorm raging inside him. His hands curled into fists at his sides as he replayed the last ten minutes over and over, each word a fresh wound, each look in her eyes another reminder of how badly he had failed her.

He had always prided himself on being a man of conviction, someone who stood by his choices. But now, for the first time, he wished he could take them all back.

Five years.

Five years of silence.

Five years of thinking he had been the one betrayed, when all along, he had been the betrayer.

Melissa's voice still echoed in his ears, raw and unforgiving.

'You didn't ask. You didn't give me a chance. You just—left.'

The words cut deeper than he wanted to admit.

What was the truth? What had Brian done?

Michael had an idea, a sickening suspicion curling in his gut, but he hoped—*God, he hoped*—he was wrong. Because if he wasn't… if his instincts were right… then he had done the unforgivable. He had walked away when she needed him most. Left her when she had been at her most vulnerable.

His chest tightened, the weight of it all pressing down on him like a vice.

He leaned against the hood of his car, dragging a shaky hand through his hair. His pulse hammered in his ears, his thoughts a tangled mess of regret and self-recrimination.

How had he not seen it? How had he let his own insecurities, his own fears, cloud everything?

The guilt was suffocating.

Five years. *Five damn years.*

And now he had to face the possibility that he hadn't just lost her.

He had failed her.

He had been so sure of what he'd seen that night. So convinced that he had been the one wronged. But in reality, he had been a coward. A coward who hadn't fought for the truth.

And Melissa—*God, Melissa*—had suffered because of it.

His stomach churned at the thought of her alone, hurting, wondering why he had abandoned her. He had thought he was protecting himself from heartbreak, but in doing so, he had destroyed the one thing that had ever truly mattered to him.

Now, standing in the wreckage of his own making, he knew one thing for certain.

He couldn't lose her again.

Michael drove home, his mind spinning, the weight of the evening pressing down on him. His hands gripped the wheel tighter than necessary, his jaw clenched so hard it ached.

When he pulled into the driveway, he saw the cars and sighed. The extended family had started to arrive for the wedding. He wasn't in the mood for company, but he knew his parents would expect him to play his part.

Forcing himself to push aside his turmoil, he greeted his uncle and aunt with as much warmth as he could fake—which wasn't much. His father then mentioned that his cousin, Brian, and Jason were in the games room playing pool.

Michael stiffened. *Brian.*

The last person he wanted to see.

Still, something made him head in that direction. Maybe it was a need to confront him, or maybe just a self-destructive urge to hear the man speak and confirm, once and for all, that Michael had made the biggest mistake of his life.

Michael wasn't sure what he had expected when he entered the games room, but it sure as hell wasn't this.

The moment he stepped inside, the scene before him froze him in place.

Jason had Brian slammed against the wall, his forearm pressed hard against the bastard's throat, pinning him there with unyielding strength. Brian struggled, his hands scrabbling uselessly at Jason's arm, his face reddening from the pressure. But Jason didn't budge.

His voice was low, furious, vibrating with barely restrained violence. "How far were you going to go?" Jason snarled. "Were you going to rape her? If she hadn't gotten her hand loose and scratched your face—how far, you bastard?"

Michael's breath hitched.

No!

Brian let out a strangled wheeze, his voice cracking from the force against his throat. "It was only a little fun," he choked out. "Melissa knew that."

Michael's blood went cold.

Everything inside him stilled for a fraction of a second.

Then rage.

Blinding. Consuming. A fury so hot it burned through his veins like fire.

Brian didn't even see Michael move. One second, he was gasping under Jason's grip—the next, he was yanked away, only for Michael's fist to slam into his face with brutal force.

The sickening crunch of bone echoed through the room.

Brian stumbled, groaning in pain, but Michael wasn't done.

He grabbed the bastard by the collar and threw him against the pool table. The edge caught Brian's ribs, knocking the air from his lungs as he crumpled onto the ground.

Michael advanced on him; his vision edged with red. His fists clenched, his breath ragged. He had never wanted to kill a man before. But right now, he was damn close.

Jason hadn't moved. He stood there, chest heaving, letting Michael take over—because he knew. He knew this wasn't just about revenge. It was about something deeper.

Michael's mind clicked all the pieces into place with sickening clarity.

Melissa hadn't been with Brian.

She had fought him.

Brian had forced her onto the couch.

Graham had told him something had happened that really frightened her.

Melissa had been attacked.

And he had left her there.

His stomach twisted. A sharp, gut-wrenching pain shot through him.

He left her.

While she must have been terrified, shaking, struggling to make sense of what was happening—he had walked away.

His jaw clenched so tightly it ached.

Michael's hands curled around Brian's shirt, dragging him upright until they were nose to nose.

"Did you touch her?" Michael's voice was quiet, deadly.

Brian's lip was bleeding, his face pale. He swallowed hard. "I—"

Michael slammed him back against the table.

"Did. You. Touch. Her?"

Brian let out a weak, pained chuckle. "Why do you care?" he sneered, though it came out as more of a wheeze. "She's not even your girlfriend anymore."

The words hit Michael like a hammer to the chest.

Five years ago, he had walked away. He had told himself he was doing the right thing.

But he hadn't been there to protect her.

His grip tightened.

Jason's voice cut through the tension. "If you don't kill him, Michael, I will." His voice was dark, edged with fury. "Because the only reason that bastard is still standing is because Melissa asked me not to do anything."

Michael's head snapped toward him.

Melissa knew Brian would be here.

And she still hadn't wanted him to know.

His throat tightened.

He had no right to her pain. No right to her wounds.

But that didn't mean he wouldn't burn the world down for her.

Michael turned back to Brian, his voice dropping into something cold. Merciless. "Listen to me very carefully." He leaned in, his lips curling in barely restrained disgust. "If you ever so much as breathe in Melissa's direction again, I swear—"

He didn't finish the sentence.

Because the look in his eyes said it all.

Brian flinched.

Michael finally let Brian go, shoving him backward with one last, disdainful glance.

Brian staggered before collapsing onto the floor, clutching his ribs. For a moment, he just sat there, breathing heavily, his eyes flickering between Michael and Jason as if debating whether to run or plead. But he wasn't stupid—he knew he had just made an enemy out of the wrong damn man.

And without another word, he scrambled to his feet and bolted for the door, leaving Michael and Jason alone in the suffocating silence.

Neither of them moved to stop him as he stumbled out of the room like a coward with his tail between his legs. He wasn't worth it.

Jason exhaled heavily, rubbing a hand over his face before turning to Michael. "When did you find out?"

Michael's hands were still curled into fists at his sides, his breath uneven. His voice came out hoarse. "Why didn't you tell me?"

Jason met his gaze—steady, but grim. "I only found out two weeks ago. And Melissa asked me not to say anything."

Michael's expression twisted, something raw and broken flashing in his eyes. "You should have told me," he said, his voice quiet but laced with an emotion Jason couldn't quite place—anger, guilt, desperation. Maybe all of them at once.

Jason sighed, rubbing the back of his neck. "I know I should have," he admitted, regret flickering across his face. "I'm sorry, man."

Michael let out a shaky breath and flopped onto the couch, his body feeling impossibly heavy under the weight of his mistake.

She had been hurt. And he hadn't been there.

Jason watched him for a long moment before sitting down beside him.

Michael dropped his head into his hands, his fingers tangling in his hair.

"I left her there, Jason," he whispered, his voice thick with despair.

Jason frowned, his stomach knotting. "What?" He shook his head, his voice filled with disbelief. "No. You wouldn't do that."

But Michael just laughed—bitter and hollow.

"I did," he said, lifting his head. His gaze was dark, haunted. "That night. I walked away. And she—she needed me."

Jason inhaled sharply, realisation dawning in his eyes.

Michael wasn't talking about tonight.

He was talking about five years ago.

Michael lifted his gaze, his eyes shimmering with guilt. "I thought she was with him willingly." His throat tightened as the words caught. "I left her. With that animal."

The admission hung heavy in the air.

Jason's breath stilled. "You left her?" His voice was quieter now, but it carried a dangerous edge.

Michael swallowed hard, his mind racing back to that night. The way Melissa had been underneath him. Her arms hadn't been around him—he had her pinned there. And he had just… walked away.

"What if—" His breath hitched. No. He couldn't think about that. He wouldn't.

But the what ifs clawed at him anyway, merciless, and unrelenting.

Jason's voice sliced through his thoughts, sharp with disbelief. "What the hell, Michael? How could you? I thought you loved her!"

"I did." Michael's voice was hoarse. "I do."

"Then why didn't you talk to her? Why didn't you ask her to explain? Why didn't you rip that bastard off her?" Jason shook his head, disgusted. "If I saw Sarah with someone, I wouldn't hesitate to haul him off her—even if she was there willingly."

Michael squeezed his eyes shut. "I was hurt."

Jason let out a bitter laugh. "You were hurt? What about Mel?" His eyes burned with fury. "She was attacked, Michael. And you left her there."

Michael flinched as the words struck like a gut punch. "I thought—"

"You thought wrong," Jason snapped. His fists clenched at his sides as he glared at his brother. "So that's why you left her? You thought she was cheating?"

"Yes." Michael's voice was barely audible, but he didn't try to defend himself.

Jason let out a harsh breath, pacing away before turning back, his anger only growing. "And now? Now does she know the truth? Because she didn't then. She was heartbroken, Michael. Lost. I saw what you did to her, and it broke my damn heart." His voice was thick with disgust. "But I trusted that you must've had a good reason. Because you're my brother."

Michael dropped his head into his hands again. "She knows now." His voice was hollow. "She threw me out of the house."

Jason scoffed. "Do you blame her?"

"No."

"Now she knows you never even gave her a chance."

"I know." The guilt was suffocating, clawing at Michael's insides like a living thing. His voice was barely above a whisper.

Jason shook his head, his disappointment cutting deeper than his anger. "She deserves better." His jaw clenched. "You're my brother, and I can't believe you did that."

Without another word, Jason stormed out, the door slamming behind him.

Michael didn't move. He sat there, staring at the door through which Jason had just stormed out, the words still echoing in his mind. *She deserves better.* The thought stung, sharper than any punch. Jason's anger was justified. *What could he say?* There were no excuses for what he had done.

The room was silent, heavy with the weight of regret and failure. *He had left her.* He had failed her when she needed him most.

His fingers tightened into fists at his sides. He had to fix this. *But how?* The trust between them was shattered, and he had no idea how to rebuild it.

The sound of footsteps pulled Michael from his thoughts, followed by the quiet creak of the door opening. He looked up, startled, as his father stepped into the room, concern etched across his face.

"Michael, I heard you and Jason arguing," Henry said, his voice calm but laced with curiosity. "What happened? You two never fight."

Michael's heart sank. His father's gaze wasn't accusing, just filled with quiet confusion—and disappointment. He opened his mouth to speak, but the words stuck in his throat.

Finally, he forced them out. "I messed up," he admitted, his voice hoarse. "I... I left Mel when she needed me. And I thought the worst of her. I hurt her, Dad. Badly. I don't know how to make it right."

His father sighed and sat beside him. "Son, I never understood why you left home—and Melissa—five years ago. I know she was shattered. She was never the same after you left. It broke your mother's heart. And mine." He paused, shaking his head. "But we didn't interfere. It was your life, your choices. Now, if you're telling me, you made the wrong one..."

"I did." The words were bitter on Michael's tongue, but they were the truth.

Henry placed a firm, steadying hand on his shoulder. "Sometimes, we make mistakes—big ones. But that doesn't mean we can't try to fix them. It won't be easy. It'll take time. But you owe it to her—and to yourself—to try."

Michael nodded, the weight of his father's words settling deep in his chest. "I know. I have to."

Henry studied him for a long moment before standing and clapping him on the back. "Then start by showing her you're sorry. No more running."

Michael pushed to his feet; his legs unsteady but his resolve stronger than it had been in years. He had already lost so much time. He couldn't lose anymore.

As he reached the door, his father's voice stopped him.

"And Michael... don't give up on her."

He turned slightly, his jaw tight. "I won't." His voice was quiet but certain. "I can't."

With that, he stepped into the hallway, heading toward his room. He had no idea how he was going to fix this mess. But one thing was clear—he had to.

Because he knew, he couldn't lose her again.

Chapter Fifteen

Melissa stood under the stream of hot water, her forehead resting against the cool tiles as silent sobs wracked her body. The sound of the water masked her tears, but it did nothing to wash away the ache spreading through her chest.

How could he think I was cheating on him?

The betrayal cut deeper than she expected, reopening wounds she had spent years convincing herself had scarred over. And with Brian of all people.

Her stomach twisted at the memory. *He left me there.*

Michael had seen her with Brian. And instead of asking, instead of believing her, he had turned his back and walked away.

A violent shudder ran through her, her arms wrapping around herself as she fought against the dark, suffocating thoughts clawing at her mind.

It could have been worse—so much worse.

If she hadn't gotten her hand free. If she hadn't scratched Brian's face. If Sarah hadn't found her.

Melissa squeezed her eyes shut. *Stop.* Just stop crying.

She forced a deep breath, willing herself to focus on something—anything—else. Your sister is counting on you.

Gritting her teeth, she reached for the soap, determined to push the emotions down, to lock them away where they couldn't touch her. She lathered the soap between her hands and ran them over her arms, her shoulders, her stomach—

And then she saw them.

The faint marks on her skin.

Her breath hitched, fingers stilling over the evidence of Michael's touch.

A faint bruise on her arm where he had gripped her too tightly in the heat of passion. The ghost of his lips lingering on her skin—her breasts, the inside of her thighs.

A fresh wave of emotion crashed over her, tightening her throat, burning behind her eyes.

Michael's lovemaking had been everything she had imagined—intense, consuming. But how could he have believed she had betrayed him? How could he have left her to fight Brian off on her own?

She didn't know how to move forward when her body ached for his touch, yet her heart was fractured beyond repair.

She swallowed hard.

Not now. Not today.

Melissa straightened, turning the water off with a sharp twist of her wrist. She had already let the past haunt her long enough today.

And she refused to let it ruin her night.

Squaring her shoulders, stepped out, wrapping herself in a towel. Sarah is more important. I need to get the wedding dress finished, then get through the wedding. She could deal with everything else—the heartbreak, the anger, the painful memories— later.

But as she caught her reflection in the mirror, her red-rimmed eyes and trembling lips betraying the turmoil within, she wasn't sure she'd ever be ready to face Michael again.

Melissa slipped back into the same dress, ensuring no one would notice anything amiss. She couldn't afford questions—not now. There was work to do. The wedding dress needed to be finished for Sarah, and that had to come first.

She returned to the living room, settling onto the couch, and forced herself to focus. Needle in hand, she worked relentlessly, stitching, adjusting, refining—anything to keep her mind from spiralling. The fabric blurred slightly as she pushed through the ache in her fingers, refusing to let exhaustion slow her down.

A couple of hours later, the sound of the front door opening made her look up. Sarah, Graham, and Fiona walked in, their voices filling the quiet space.

"Hello, sweetheart," Fiona said warmly as she approached, pressing a gentle kiss to Melissa's forehead.

Graham and Sarah smiled as they greeted her, and she returned the gesture, her voice steady despite the turmoil still simmering beneath the surface.

For now, she would pretend everything was fine.

Graham headed upstairs to rest, while Fiona disappeared into the other room to check the bomboniere she and Michael had picked up that morning.

Sarah, however, stayed behind, settling onto the couch beside Melissa. She didn't speak right away, just watched her with a small, knowing smile, though concern lingered in her eyes.

"Are you okay, Melissa?" she finally asked, her voice gentle.

Melissa forced a light tone. "Yes, I'm fine. Why?" She kept her focus on the dress, hoping Sarah wouldn't press further.

But Sarah reached out, placing a firm but comforting hand on her arm, stopping her movements.

"Mel," she said softly, "Jason called me. He told me Michael knows about Brian… and that he saw you. Jason is really angry and, he is worried about you."

Melissa's fingers curled around the fabric. A sharp sting pricked her eyes, but she forced herself to blink it away.

"Please, Sarah," she whispered, her voice raw. "I can't talk about it." She turned to her sister, pleading for understanding, but also terrified that if she started talking, she might not be able to stop. That all the pain, all the anger, all the love she still felt for Michael would come pouring out, leaving her exposed.

Sarah's expression softened. She gave Melissa's arm a reassuring squeeze. "I'm here when you need me, okay?"

Melissa nodded, swallowing past the lump in her throat. But will I ever be ready to need someone again?

Sarah studied her carefully before speaking again. "Are you going to be okay tonight? I'll understand if you don't feel up to it." Her voice was careful, filled with concern.

Melissa forced a small smile. "No, I'm fine. Your hen's night is one of my gifts to you." She exhaled, trying to shake off the weight of everything. "I need it too."

Sarah hesitated for a moment, then nodded. "Okay." She reached over and wrapped her arms around Melissa. "I love you, sis."

Melissa hugged her back tightly, drawing strength from the embrace. "I love you too."

They had an early dinner shortly after their father arrived home from the office, then the girls and Graham began getting ready for a night of fun. Melissa forced herself not to think about Michael. Tonight was about Sarah—nothing else mattered.

After their parents wished them a wonderful time, the girls stepped onto the front porch to wait for their limousine. The car would pick up Sarah's other three friends before picking her and Sarah up, then the real celebration could begin.

Melissa had chosen a short, form-fitting dress that hugged her curves, exuding confidence, and allure. The deep emerald fabric skimmed her thighs, clinging in all the right places, a striking contrast against her sun-kissed skin. It was a bold choice—one that declared she was done playing it safe, done pretending she wasn't affected by everything that had happened.

As she stepped outside, Graham raised an eyebrow, his lips twitching into a smirk as he let out a low whistle.

"Mankiller, sweetheart," he teased, shaking his head in amused disbelief. "That dress should come with a warning label."

Melissa smirked, flipping her hair over one shoulder. "It's just a dress, Graham."

He exhaled dramatically, adjusting his cuffs as he leaned against the car parked in the driveway. "Yeah, and I'm just a lawyer. That dress is dangerous, sweetheart."

Sarah laughed, linking her arm through Melissa's with a playful squeeze. "Ignore him. You look incredible."

Melissa smiled, soaking in her sister's warmth. Tonight was about Sarah, about celebrating her upcoming wedding, and she refused to let anything—not even the lingering ghosts of her past—ruin it.

Just as the thought crossed her mind, a sleek black limousine rolled up the driveway. But it wasn't theirs.

It was Michael and Jason's.

The sight of Michael stepping out of the car sent an unwelcome jolt through her, her pulse betraying her practiced indifference. He was dressed sharply, dark suit tailored to perfection, the top buttons of his shirt undone just enough to hint at the hard lines of his chest. It was infuriating how effortless he made it look—how he still managed to steal the air from her lungs with nothing more than his presence.

Melissa forced her spine to straighten, smoothing out her features into an expression of cool composure.

Jason was the first to approach, his concern evident as he wrapped her in a warm hug. "You okay?" he asked quietly, his voice just for her.

Melissa forced a bright smile, nodding. "I'm fine," she said lightly, though they both knew better.

Jason didn't push, but his eyes held a quiet understanding. He squeezed her hand before stepping back.

And then Michael moved closer.

His gaze swept over her in open admiration, lingering in a way that sent a ripple of awareness through her. Her skin prickled under his scrutiny, heat crawling up her neck despite her best efforts to ignore it. For a brief moment, it looked as if he was going to pull her into an embrace, like old habits were threatening to take over.

Her breath caught.

Would she let him?

Did she even trust herself not to?

But instead of reaching for her, Michael's voice dropped to a softer tone, laced with something unreadable.

"You look gorgeous, Mel."

The words sent a sharp pang through her chest.

He used to say things like that when he loved her—*when she thought he loved her.* Back when those words would have made her heart race for all the right reasons. Now, they were just another reminder of everything they had lost, of the wreckage they had left behind.

She forced herself to nod, keeping her expression carefully neutral. "Thanks," she murmured.

Michael hesitated, then, his gaze searching hers. "Can we talk?"

Melissa looked at him, the urge to refuse rising like a shield. But they had to do this sooner or later.

"Okay."

Silence stretched between them.

Then, finally, he spoke. "I know what Brian did to you."

Her spine went rigid. But she schooled her expression into something unreadable, giving nothing away.

Michael exhaled, his voice thick with regret. "And I know what I did to you was unforgivable."

Melissa met his gaze head-on, her own steady, unwavering. "At least I know now." Her voice didn't waver, didn't crack. "I can finally move on."

"Melissa—"

Before he could say anything more—before she could betray herself by holding his gaze too long—Melissa turned away.

Right on cue, the girls' limousine pulled up, the sleek white vehicle gleaming under the soft glow of the driveway lights.

Sarah, ever watchful, had been keeping an eye on Melissa. The moment the limousine arrived, she seized the opportunity, looping her arm through Melissa's and steering her toward the car. "We should get going," she said, her tone light but firm, leaving no room for argument.

Michael's jaw tightened almost imperceptibly, his expression unreadable. He didn't stop her, didn't call her back—but he didn't look away either. His gaze stayed on her, a lingering, searching look that sent something sharp and unwelcome twisting in her stomach.

Melissa forced herself to keep walking. To not turn around. To not let him see the effect he still had on her.

Sarah and Melissa slid into the limousine; the plush leather seats cool against their bare skin. The excited chatter of the other women inside finally began to sink in, a reminder that tonight wasn't about heartbreak or lingering feelings—it was about fun, about celebration.

Before the door could close, Jason leaned in, pressing a quick kiss to Sarah's lips. "You behave," he teased, his grin boyish and full of affection.

Sarah smirked. "No promises."

Jason chuckled before glancing at Melissa. "Bye, Mel. You too—keep it tame."

Melissa arched a brow, her lips curling into a mischievous smirk. "No way, Jas. Tonight, I'm letting loose."

Jason let out a booming laugh, shaking his head. "God help us all."

The door shut with a soft click, sealing them inside, and as the limousine pulled away, Melissa allowed herself to exhale, to let go—if only for one night.

Outside, Michael remained where he stood, watching as the car disappeared into the night, his hands shoved deep into his pockets.

Jason clapped a hand on his shoulder. "You okay, man?"

Michael didn't answer right away. His gaze lingered on the empty driveway, on the ghost of Melissa's smile.

Finally, he let out a breath, low and resigned.

"No," he admitted. "I don't think I am."

The girls' night out was everything Melissa had hoped it would be—filled with laughter, music, and endless toasts to Sarah's upcoming wedding. After leaving the Shaw estate, the celebration kicked into full gear, their limousine buzzing with energy as they sipped champagne and belted out lyrics to their favourite songs.

Sarah, glowing with happiness, giggled as one of her friends handed her a sash that read Bride-to-Be in elegant gold script, along with a tiara that she placed on her head with dramatic flair. "You all know I look ridiculous, right?" she teased, adjusting it in the mirror.

"Absolutely," Melissa agreed with a smirk, "but that's half the fun."

Their first stop was an upscale lounge with a rooftop terrace, where they raised their glasses—Sarah sticking to non-alcoholic ones due to her delicate condition—the others making a series of heartfelt, and increasingly tipsy, toasts in her honour.

"To the bride!" one of the girls cheered.

"To finding someone who puts up with your terrible taste in movies!" Melissa added playfully, earning a mock glare from Sarah and laughter from the group.

The night carried on in a blur of flashing lights and infectious energy. Their next stop was an exclusive club downtown, where the music pulsed through the air, the bass vibrating beneath their heels. The dance floor was packed, the energy intoxicating.

Melissa, determined to give her sister the perfect night, kept a watchful eye on her, ensuring she was having fun but also well taken care of. But somewhere between the second round of cocktails and the DJ switching to their favourite dance tracks, she let herself go—laughing, spinning, surrendering to the rhythm of the music.

For a while, she forgot.

She forgot the ache in her chest, the way Michael's presence had unsettled her earlier, the weight of memories she had been trying to shake loose.

For a few blissful hours, she was just Melissa—not the woman carrying heartbreak, not the woman with scars from the past. Just a woman dancing, free and uninhibited.

As she twirled on the dance floor, the lights flashing in bursts of colour around her, a tall, devastatingly handsome man caught her eye. He stood near the bar, watching her with a lazy confidence that sent a thrill through her. He was dark-haired, broad-shouldered, with smouldering eyes that held just the right amount of mischief.

A slow, knowing smile curved his lips as he moved toward her, his steps deliberate.

When he finally reached her, he leaned in just enough for his voice to be heard over the pounding bass. "You're gorgeous," he murmured, his tone smooth, effortless.

It was just a compliment. Simple. Harmless.

But the way he looked at her—with open appreciation, no hesitation, no pain, or history between them—made something shift inside her.

Melissa, feeling bold for the first time in ages, let her lips curl into a slow, teasing smile. "Thank you."

And for tonight, that was enough.

For tonight, she wasn't the woman Michael had broken. She was just Melissa, a woman in a stunning dress, being noticed.

The bass thrummed through her veins, the rhythm dictating the movement of her hips as they swayed in perfect harmony. His grip on her waist tightened just enough to make her pulse stutter, his body aligning with hers in a way that felt both effortless and intentional.

She let her head fall back slightly, revelling in the delicious friction of their bodies moving together. His hand slid lower, fingers pressing against the small of her back, guiding her, pulling her closer. Their bodies brushed, chest to chest, heat bleeding through the thin layers of their clothing.

Her breath hitched when his thigh nudged between hers, just enough to make her skin prickle with awareness. He smelled like spice and whiskey, the kind of scent that lingered, that stayed with you long after the night was over.

She shouldn't be doing this.

But God, it felt good.

For the first time in what felt like forever, she wasn't drowning in memories of Michael. She wasn't trapped in the past, in regret, in the ache of everything she had lost.

She was here. Now.

And she wasn't alone.

The stranger's lips ghosted over the curve of her jaw, not quite touching but close enough to send a shiver down her spine. Her fingers curled into the fabric of his shirt, steadying herself, or maybe keeping him right where he was.

The song slowed, the pounding rhythm giving way to something sultry, something that invited them to press just a little closer. She felt the hard planes of his body against hers, the heat of his skin seeping through her dress.

When the final note rang out, he lingered, his breath warm against her ear.

"Come out with me," he murmured, his voice deep, low, inviting.

Melissa hesitated.

A part of her wanted to say yes. To disappear into the night, into the arms of a man who saw her as nothing but beautiful. To let go, fully, without restraint.

But another part of her—one still healing, still raw—held her back.

He must have sensed her hesitation because he didn't push. Instead, he smiled—slow and knowing—as if he already understood the war waging inside her.

Without a word, he reached into his pocket and slipped a folded napkin into her palm. His fingers brushed hers, warm and deliberate, sending a quiet thrill up her spine.

"Call me," he murmured, his voice smooth, unhurried. There was no pressure, no demand. Just an offer. A possibility.

And then he kissed her.

Soft. Lingering. A whisper of warmth against her lips, enough to leave her breathless.

By the time she opened her eyes, he was already gone, swallowed by the crowd—leaving nothing behind but the ghost of his touch and the slip of paper burning in her hand.

Melissa tucked the napkin into her clutch with a grin, a flicker of amusement dancing in her eyes. She had no intention of calling.

But for tonight, it felt good to be wanted.

As Melissa made her way back to the table, her skin still tingling from the dance—and from the memory of his lips—Sarah arched a perfectly shaped brow, a knowing smirk playing on her lips.

"He was gorgeous. Don't tell me he didn't give you his number."

Melissa plopped down into her seat, reaching for her drink. The chilled glass was a welcome contrast to the warmth still lingering on her skin. She took a slow sip, letting the crisp taste of her cocktail settle before answering. "He did."

Sarah's smile widened knowingly. "And?"

Melissa twirled the stem of her glass between her fingers, her mind flickering to the folded napkin tucked inside her clutch. For a brief moment, she considered it—what it would be like to let go, to take a risk, to see where the stranger's number might lead.

But then reality set in.

She shook her head, her voice light but certain. "No. I'm going back to Paris soon. No point."

Sarah let out a dramatic sigh, leaning back in her chair. "Never say never, Mel." She picked up her own drink and gave her a pointed look over the rim. "You never know when love will happen."

Melissa let out a soft laugh, but deep down, something about Sarah's words stuck with her.

Love.

The very thing she had once believed in so fiercely. The thing she had dreamed about, fought for, built her future around—only to have it shatter in her hands.

She glanced back toward the dance floor, where the stranger had disappeared into the sea of moving bodies, and exhaled slowly.

Maybe Sarah was right. Maybe love could happen when she least expected it. Maybe, one day, she would be open to it again.

But tonight wasn't about love.

Tonight was about something else entirely.

It was about reclaiming the pieces of herself she thought she had lost.

It was about remembering who she was before heartbreak had stolen her fire.

Chapter Sixteen

Michael, Jason, Graham, and two of Jason's closest mates kicked off the bucks' night at an exclusive rooftop bar, the city lights stretching beneath them like a sea of gold. The atmosphere was lively—glasses clinking, laughter echoing, and plenty of teasing about Jason's last night of freedom.

When Brian backed out, claiming a headache, Michael felt an immediate sense of relief. He hadn't realised how much he'd been dreading the possibility of facing him until the excuse was given. The thought of being in the same room as that bastard—pretending everything was fine—was unbearable.

Instead, the night was spent in good company, with Michael making sure Jason was properly celebrated—ordering rounds of expensive whiskey, arranging a private poker game, and even pushing the groom-to-be into a few harmless dares.

But despite the easy camaraderie, Michael's mind wasn't in it. His thoughts kept drifting to Melissa. He knew she was out with Sarah, celebrating, dancing, drinking. Maybe even dancing with someone else.

The thought made his jaw clench, especially remembering how she looked tonight. That dress. Damn, she'd looked sexy—too sexy. He could still see it in his mind, the way the fabric hugged her curves, the way her bare legs seemed to go on forever, the way her lips had curved into a teasing little smirk when Jason had told her to behave.

Had she smirked like that at someone else tonight?

Jason, noticing Michael's brooding silence, nudged him with his elbow. "You're thinking about her, aren't you?"

Michael exhaled sharply, staring into his glass as he swirled the amber liquid, watching the way it clung to the sides before settling again. His grip tightened slightly. "I screwed up, Jas."

Jason smirked, taking a slow sip of his own drink. "Yeah, you did. Big time."

Michael let out a low chuckle, but there was no humour in it. "Thanks for the support."

Jason shrugged, unbothered. "Hey, you don't need support. You need a miracle."

Michael dragged a hand down his face, exhaustion weighing heavy on his shoulders. "I know. And I don't know how to fix it." His voice was quieter now, tinged with something Jason rarely heard from him—uncertainty.

Jason leaned back in his chair, watching him carefully. "Don't worry, mate—Melissa's not the type to hold a grudge."

Michael let out a hollow laugh, shaking his head. "You sure about that?" His jaw clenched as images of Melissa flashed through his mind—her guarded expression, the way she avoided his gaze, the way she had turned away from him tonight without hesitation. "She has every right to."

Jason sighed, setting his drink down. "Look, Mel's been through a lot. More than either of us realised. But deep down? She still feels something for you."

Michael scoffed, but the doubt in his eyes betrayed him. "Yeah? Then why does it feel like every time I get close, she builds another wall?"

Jason tilted his head, considering. "Because she's scared, you idiot. You left her once. She's not about to make it easy for you to walk back in and do it again."

Michael swallowed hard. *I left her.* The guilt gnawed at him, relentless. And now, knowing what had really happened with Brian—knowing he had abandoned her when she needed him the most—he wasn't sure he deserved another chance.

But deserve didn't matter.

He couldn't lose her. *Not again.*

Michael sighed, rubbing his fingers over the rim of his glass. "God, I hope you're right, Jas."

Because if Melissa was the type to hold a grudge.

He might have already lost the only woman he had ever truly loved.

The next morning, everyone was feeling a little worse for wear, but thankfully, no one had gone too overboard with the celebrations.

Melissa had finished the final adjustments on Sarah's wedding dress the day before, so now it was time for the moment of truth. In the bridal suite, Sarah stood in front of the full-length mirror as Fiona, Graham, and Melissa watched with anticipation.

As soon as Sarah stepped into the dress and Melissa fastened the last button, a hush fell over the room. The gown fit like a glove, hugging her figure perfectly, the intricate lacework catching the morning light.

Graham, never one for sentimental moments, let out a low whistle. "Damn, Sarah, you look incredible."

Fiona's eyes shimmered with tears as she clasped her hands together. "Oh, sweetheart, you look absolutely breathtaking."

Melissa, exhausted but satisfied, gave her sister a warm smile. "Told you it was perfect."

Sarah turned to her with a glowing smile. "It's more than perfect, Mel. It's everything I dreamed of."

"You deserve it." Melissa hugged her tightly, feeling a surge of love for her sister.

That evening, the celebration continued at Jason and Michael's parents' home. Melissa was happy to reconnect with Jason's family, but an undercurrent of tension ran beneath her excitement—Michael would be there. With him being Jason's brother and the best man, there was no escaping him.

Maria and Henry greeted them warmly at the door, their excitement for the upcoming wedding evident. As they stepped inside, Henry's brother and his wife were reintroduced, and then—unfortunately—Brian.

The moment Melissa spotted Brian across the room; a cold weight settled in her stomach. Instinctively, she shifted away, putting as much distance between them as possible. Her pulse kicked up, memories threatening to surface, but she forced them down. Not here. Not now.

Then she saw it—a dark bruise blooming along Brian's jawline.

Her stomach tightened. The realisation hit an instant later, her mind working faster than she could control. Michael.

Slowly, almost hesitantly, she turned her head.

Michael was already watching her.

Their eyes met across the room, an unspoken current passing between them. Melissa gave him a pointed look, silent but sharp. Michael, ever composed, merely took a slow sip of his drink, his expression unreadable. But she saw it—the flicker of satisfaction in his gaze.

He wasn't sorry.

She knew exactly who had left that bruise.

Before she could dwell on it further, Jason's voice rang out over the hum of conversation, effortlessly drawing attention.

"Well, Mel, did my fiancée behave herself last night?"

Melissa shook off the moment and turned back to the group, letting out a laugh as she swirled the amber liquid in her glass. "I made sure she was a good girl."

Sarah smirked beside her, eyes dancing with mischief. "Unlike you."

Melissa shot her a warning glance, but it was too late. Jason's interest was piqued.

"Oh, do tell," he teased, leaning forward with a grin.

Sarah, clearly relishing the moment, turned toward the rest of the group. "Melissa caught the eye of the best-looking guy in the club. And let me tell you, he was very keen on my gorgeous sister. You should have seen the way they were dancing. He couldn't keep his hands off her."

Melissa groaned, shaking her head. "Stop, sis," she protested, but she was laughing.

"I saw him slip you his number," Sarah continued, winking. "Are you going to call him?"

Melissa opened her mouth to respond, but the sudden shift in energy at the table made her pause.

Michael.

He sat stiffly in his chair, his grip tightening around his glass. His jaw was locked, his entire posture coiled like a man barely restraining himself. But it was his eyes that sent a thrill down her spine—dark, intense, burning into her like a silent warning.

Possession. Jealousy.

It was a look she knew well, one she'd once revelled in, knowing it meant she was his. But now? Now it was infuriating.

If looks could kill, she'd be in serious trouble.

Melissa's amusement faded as a spark of defiance flared inside her. *What right does he have to be angry?* He has no claim over me. He threw that away.

Lifting her chin, she met his stare head-on. "I think I will," she said coolly, deliberately.

A low whistle came from Graham, who sat back with a grin. "I told you that dress was lethal, sweetheart." His gaze flicked to Michael, clearly enjoying the tension.

Laughter rippled around the room, light-hearted and teasing.

Everyone was enjoying the moment—except Michael.

He didn't laugh. Didn't smirk. Didn't even look away.

Instead, he took another slow sip of his drink, his eyes never leaving hers. The air between them grew thick, charged with something unspoken, something raw.

A challenge.

Melissa felt the heat of it deep in her bones, her pulse quickening despite herself.

This wasn't over. Not even close.

Dinner was a lively affair, with laughter and conversation flowing freely. Despite everything, Melissa found herself enjoying the evening, momentarily pushing aside her complicated feelings.

After dinner, as the guests began to mingle with drinks and conversation, Michael finally found his moment. He approached Melissa with slow, measured steps, his expression unreadable.

"Can we talk?"

Melissa hesitated. Part of her wanted to walk away, to avoid reopening wounds that were barely beginning to scab over. But she wasn't a coward, and she wasn't childish. If nothing else, she owed herself closure.

"Alright."

She followed him outside, the cool night air wrapping around them as they stepped into the garden. The scent of jasmine lingered in the breeze, mingling with the distant sound of laughter filtering from the house.

For a few moments, silence stretched between them, heavy with unspoken words, with the weight of everything left unsaid.

Michael was the first to break it. "Melissa, I'm so sorry."

His voice was rough, stripped bare of the usual arrogance and confidence he carried so effortlessly.

She kept her gaze straight ahead, focusing on the distant glow of the garden lights. "Okay. Thanks. At least I know now."

He exhaled sharply, as if bracing himself for the next blow. "Will you ever forgive me?"

Melissa stopped walking. She turned to him, her expression honest, if not a little weary. "I don't know, Michael. I honestly don't."

Michael looked into her eyes, searching for something—hope, maybe. Redemption. Anything that told him he hadn't lost her completely. His voice was raw with emotion when he finally spoke again.

"I love you, Mel. I always have."

Melissa held his gaze, her own expression unreadable. Then, quietly, she said the words that had been echoing in her mind since the night he walked away.

"But not enough to trust me." Her voice was calm, steady. "Not enough to give me the benefit of the doubt."

Michael swallowed hard, regret flashing across his face. "I—"

He reached for her hands, but she instinctively pulled back. He didn't let go—he didn't grip her tightly, just firmly enough to keep her from slipping away.

"I was hurt," he admitted, his voice low, rough. "I know it doesn't compare to what you went through, but it's the truth."

Melissa's eyes flashed with anger. The emotions she had tried so hard to suppress surged forward.

"Brian could have ra—" Her voice caught, but she forced herself to say it. "He could have *hurt* me, Michael. And you left me there."

"I know," he cut in, his voice thick with regret. His grip on her hands tightened for a fraction of a second before he released her, as if realising he had no right to hold her anymore. "And I hate myself for it."

Her jaw clenched. "If I saw you with someone else, I would have asked you to explain yourself. I wouldn't have just walked away." Her voice wavered, but her anger held strong. "I wouldn't have left—like you did. Like I meant nothing."

Michael flinched, as if she'd struck him. "You meant—mean—everything to me," he said, his voice breaking at the edges, reaching for her hands again.

Melissa exhaled slowly, a quiet sadness settling in her eyes. She gently pulled her hands free, the warmth of his touch slipping away like a memory. When she spoke, her voice was barely above a whisper.

"No, Michael," she said, the finality in her tone like a dagger to his chest. "I didn't."

Michael took a deep breath, his voice thick with emotion. "That night, when I was looking for you, I was going to propose."

Melissa's eyes widened in shock. "What?"

"I was on a high," he continued, his expression filled with regret. "I was so in love with you. I wanted to be with you forever. But then…" He shook his head, struggling to find the words. "I just couldn't comprehend what was happening. I was devastated." He looked away, ashamed. "Then I left."

Melissa's breath hitched as tears blurred her vision. "You never came back, Michael." Her voice was barely above a whisper, but it carried years of pain. "I waited. I waited for a phone call, a message—some sign that I wasn't just… nothing to you. But there was nothing. For an entire year, I kept hoping. And when I finally stopped, it wasn't because I moved on." She swallowed hard, her voice breaking. "It was because I finally believed you had abandoned me—like I was disposable."

"No!" His voice was raw, desperate.

"Yes!" she shot back, her pain spilling over. "You left me to think I meant nothing to you. That I wasn't even worth a single explanation. That I wasn't worth fighting for."

Michael ran a hand through his hair, his frustration evident. "I thought you had moved on. And then the hurt turned to anger. I was too proud to come back. I just… I just concentrated on work."

Melissa let out a short, bitter laugh. "Well, that worked out for you. You're one of the richest men in Europe."

"That means nothing now that I know I threw away the one thing that really mattered to me," he said, his voice raw.

She looked at him, her heart aching despite everything. "Michael, I'm not a vengeful person and I don't want to be. But I can't forget what you did."

He reached for her hands again, but she took a step back. "I don't expect you to forget, Mel," he admitted. "But tell me—can you ever give me another chance?"

Melissa swallowed hard, looking at the man she had once loved with all her heart. "I don't know," she whispered. "I honestly don't."

"Please, Mel," Michael pleaded. "Give me a chance. I love you, and I swear, I will never doubt you again."

Melissa shook her head, emotion tightening her throat. "Michael, you hurt me. I was broken. My work and Graham saved me."

Michael exhaled heavily; his expression filled with regret. "And I will be forever grateful to him. But, Melissa, I want to be the one beside you now. I want to make things right."

She looked away, blinking back tears. "I don't know if you can."

Michael reached for her hands again, his grip firm, yet there was desperation in the way his fingers trembled against hers. "Yesterday, when I held you... when you clung to me like you didn't want to let go—that's where we belong, Mel." His voice was rough with emotion, his eyes pleading. "Tell me you didn't feel it, too. Tell me you don't still feel it."

He pulled her into his arms before she could resist. Her body stiffened, but the warmth of him—the scent she had once memorised—unravelled her defences.

And then, the dam broke.

A choked sob tore from her lips, followed by another, until she was clutching him as if he were the only thing keeping her from shattering completely.

Years of heartbreak, anger, and longing pouring out of her all at once. Michael held her tighter, his hand smoothing over her hair, his voice a gentle murmur in her ear.

"I'm here," he whispered. "I've got you, Mel. I'm never letting you go again."

And for the first time in a long time, she let herself believe he might mean it.

Her sobs subsided, her breathing slowly evening out. She pulled away from his arms, and though he let her go, she felt his reluctance in the way his fingers lingered against her skin.

Melissa looked up at him, her eyes red-rimmed, her face tear-streaked, but there was a quiet strength in her expression.

Michael lifted a hand, his touch unbearably tender as he brushed his thumb over her damp cheek.

"I can't, Michael," she whispered.

It felt like a knife slicing through him.

"Sarah and Jason's wedding is all I can think about right now," Melissa said, her voice steady despite the emotions swirling inside her.

Michael exhaled sharply, nodding, but the determination in his eyes didn't waver. "Okay," he said. "But I'm not letting you go, Melissa. I love you. I can't lose you again." His voice was thick with emotion. "I haven't been able to move on because you're the only woman I have ever loved or will ever love."

Melissa swallowed hard, but before she could respond, he gently cupped her face. "I know you don't believe me right now, and I don't blame you," he continued, his tone raw with sincerity. "But I'm not giving up on you. On us."

He lowered his head and kissed her, a kiss filled with love, desperation, and the weight of all the years they had lost. It wasn't just a plea—it was a promise.

Melissa kissed him back because she couldn't not. For a fleeting, reckless moment, she let herself drown in him—the familiar warmth, the way his lips moved against hers like they were meant to, like they had never stopped belonging together.

But reality came crashing down just as fast.

She tore herself away, her breath ragged, her heart pounding for all the wrong reasons. When she looked into his eyes, she saw everything she had tried to forget—love, regret, desperation.

His voice was hoarse when he asked, "Are you going to call that guy from last night?"

Melissa could have lied. It would have been easy, a small act of defiance. But lying had never been in her nature.

She held his gaze and whispered, "No."

She turned and walked away, each step heavier than the last. The night air pressed against her skin, but she barely felt it.

What was she going to do?

Could she forgive him?

Could she ever forget?

Chapter Seventeen

The wedding went off without a hitch. The grounds of Melissa's parents' estate had been transformed into a breathtaking wonderland, with twinkling fairy lights draped over ancient trees and fresh blooms lining every path. The bride was radiant in white, the groom handsome in his tailored suit, their love shining brighter than the chandelier-lit reception.

But Melissa would never forget the way Michael looked at her as she walked down the aisle in a flowing, crimson gown. His gaze was unreadable—intense, lingering, filled with something that made her pulse stutter.

Later, as they danced beneath the stars, he was attentive, his touch light but steady. He didn't mention the past few days; he didn't bring up the tension or the truth that still hovered between them. And for that, she was grateful. Just for tonight, she let herself exist in the moment, wrapped in the warmth of his presence, pretending—if only for a little while—that nothing had changed.

Jason claimed Melissa for a dance after a while, leading her onto the floor with an easy confidence. As they swayed to the music, his voice dropped low.

"Don't be too hard on him," he said, his tone gentle but firm.

Melissa let out a quiet breath, her gaze drifting to where Michael stood across the room, laughing at something one of the guests had said. He looked… happy. Like a man who had no idea how deeply he'd shattered her.

"I don't know if I can get past it," she admitted, her voice barely above a whisper. "I don't know how to, the pain is still there, Jason."

Jason gave her a knowing look. "I know, and he was in the wrong, one hundred percent. But maybe you just need time now that you know the truth." He squeezed her hand. "Or maybe you already know what you should do—you're just too scared to admit it."

Before she could respond, Graham claimed her for a dance. She had filled him in on all the gory details late last night, pouring out everything she'd been holding in.

"How are you holding up, sweetheart?" he asked, his voice full of warmth and concern.

Melissa smiled at him with love. "I don't know what I would do without you, you know that."

"Of course," he said, giving her a teasing smirk to lighten the mood.

She let out a small breath, resting her cheek briefly against his shoulder. "I don't know how I am. I'm just trying not to let it consume me."

Graham nodded, his grip on her steady and reassuring. "You know he still loves you. I saw it the first day I met him."

Melissa swallowed, her throat tight. "But is that enough? Trust is important, Graham."

"I know, honey." His voice softened. "Only you can answer that. But I'm here for you, no matter what you decide."

Michael claimed her for another dance, his grip firm yet gentle as he pulled her close. The warmth of his body, the familiar scent of him, made her chest tighten.

He leaned in, his breath warm against her ear as he whispered, "I love you."

Melissa stiffened, her heart lurching at the words. She tried not to let it distract her, tried to focus on the music, on the movement of their dance—but it was impossible to ignore the way he held her, the raw emotion in his voice.

"You mean everything to me, Mel," he murmured, his hand tightening slightly around hers, as if afraid she'd slip away.

"I need time, Michael." Melissa pulled back just enough to look him in the eye, her gaze searching his. "I don't know what's going to happen, but I can't decide until I've processed everything. Then I have to work out what's important to me."

Michael's jaw tensed, but his hands remained steady on her waist. "I'll give you all the time in the world, Angel," he said softly, his voice laced with both patience and determination. "You're worth it. But I can't let you go again."

Melissa sighed, her voice soft but firm, free of malice or anger. "You may have to, Michael."

The words hit him like a punch to the gut. Michael felt the pain to his core, but he refused to loosen his hold on her. His eyes searched hers, desperate for something—*anything*—but she had already looked away.

Even Henry claimed her for a dance, his grip gentle yet firm. "I don't know what went down with you and my son," he said, his voice low and steady. "All I know is that he is very sorry for hurting you. And he loves you."

Melissa sighed, her gaze distant. "I know he's sorry, I can see that. But sometimes, love isn't enough."

Henry studied her for a long moment before shaking his head. "I hope you're wrong," he said quietly. "Because I've always thought you two belonged together."

When Brian approached Melissa for a dance, she stiffened. She hadn't been this close to him in five years.

"Mel, could I please have this dance?" he asked hesitantly, a pained look in his eyes.

Melissa hesitated. Maybe it was time to move on. Maybe talking to him was a good idea. Taking a deep breath, she placed her hand in his outstretched one, allowing him to lead her to the dance floor.

The moment he pulled her into his arms, she tensed. Sensing it, he kept a respectful distance, and that small gesture made her relax—just a little.

"I have no excuse for what I did to you that night," he began, his voice low and strained.

Melissa looked up at him, but before she could respond, she noticed Jason, Michael, Graham, and Sarah watching them closely. They were making sure she was okay. Michael, in particular, did not look happy.

Brian continued, his voice filled with regret. "I really liked you, but I was drunk. I know that's no excuse, but I need you to know how sorry I am."

Melissa's throat tightened. "You terrified me, Brian. It took me a long time to get over that."

"I know." His gaze dropped for a moment before meeting hers again. "You didn't deserve what I did. And I am truly, truly sorry." He exhaled sharply. "I don't expect you to forgive me. I just needed you to know."

Silence stretched between them as they swayed to the soft rhythm of the music. Then, after a long pause, Melissa gave him a small, tentative smile.

"Apology accepted, Brian."

Relief flickered across his face. "Thank you, Mel. I truly wish you all the best."

As the dance came to an end, he lifted her hand and pressed a gentle kiss to her knuckles before offering her a faint, uncertain smile.

Before Melissa could step off the dance floor, she caught sight of Graham and Michael approaching. Graham got to her first, smoothly pulling her into a dance. Michael looked annoyed but, after a brief hesitation, turned away and left them to it.

Graham studied her, concern etched into his features. "Are you okay, sweetheart?"

She met his gaze and smiled, pressing a light kiss to his cheek. "I think I am Graham. He apologised… and I need to move on."

Graham exhaled, his shoulders relaxing slightly. "I'm proud of you," he murmured, holding her just a little closer.

Melissa let herself relax in Graham's arms, the weight of the past finally beginning to lift. Maybe she wasn't sure what the future held—whether Michael had a place in it or not—but she knew one thing for certain. It was time to start living again. And maybe, just maybe, one day, she'd find the kind of happiness Sarah had found with Jason.

As the night wore on, the wedding began winding down. Laughter and music filled the air as guests exchanged goodbyes. Melissa followed Sarah upstairs to help her change, knowing this would be their last quiet moment together before Sarah and Jason left for their honeymoon.

"You looked absolutely beautiful today," Melissa said softly, carefully unfastening the delicate buttons on Sarah's wedding gown. "You're so lucky Jason loves you."

Sarah turned, her eyes shining with happiness. "Thank you, Mel. I love you so much, and I couldn't have done this without you." She pulled Melissa into a tight embrace, holding her close for a lingering moment.

Downstairs, the sound of cheering erupted as Sarah and Jason made their grand exit. Melissa stood at the doorway, watching them disappear into the night, feeling a strange mix of joy and longing.

As she turned to head inside, a warm hand closed around hers.

"Walk with me?"

Melissa looked up, meeting Michael's gaze. There was something unreadable in his expression, but she nodded, allowing him to lead her through the garden. They strolled in silence, the crisp night air cooling her flushed skin, the distant hum of conversation fading into the background.

"You looked beautiful today," Michael finally said, his voice quiet but firm.

Melissa glanced at him, her lips curving into a small, hesitant smile. "Thank you."

Michael squeezed her hand gently, his thumb brushing over her knuckles. "I mean it, Melissa. You took my breath away."

She looked away, focusing on the soft glow of the garden lights. "It was a beautiful wedding," she said instead.

He exhaled, as if bracing himself. "It was." A pause. "But all I could think about was you."

Melissa's steps slowed. She wasn't sure how to respond to that. The last few days had been overwhelming, and she still wasn't sure what she was going to do.

Sensing her hesitation, Michael stopped walking and turned to face her. "I know you need time," he said, his voice steady but laced with emotion. "And I'll give it to you. But I need you to know how I feel about you."

Melissa met his gaze, waiting.

"I love you, Melissa, with all my heart, body, and soul. And I'll spend the rest of my life proving that to you."

Her breath hitched. For the briefest moment, something flickered in her eyes—pain, longing, maybe even hope—but she quickly masked it, turning her gaze toward the distant glow of the reception.

A beat of silence passed before she whispered, "We should head back."

Michael hesitated, searching her face as if hoping for more, but he only nodded. As they turned, his fingers brushed against hers one last time, a lingering touch before he finally let go.

The next day, Melissa, Michael, and Graham had to leave. Their parents weren't too thrilled about their early departure, but Michael had arranged for both families to be in London for his jewellery launch, which they were all eagerly anticipating.

As Maria hugged Melissa tightly, she smiled. "I can't wait to see the gowns you design to match the necklaces." Then, with a playful gleam in her eyes, she added, "I heard you might be wearing one."

Melissa hesitated, shifting slightly. "Oh, I don't know…" she said cautiously.

"Of course she is," Graham cut in, smirking as he draped an arm over her shoulder.

As they were boarding Michael's jet, Graham couldn't resist stirring up trouble. With a mischievous grin, he turned to Michael and asked, "So, did you name your jet after Melissa, or is that just a coincidence?"

Melissa felt her cheeks heat up and quickly looked away, pretending to adjust the strap of her bag.

Michael, however, didn't hesitate. His gaze locked onto hers as he said, "I did name it after Melissa."

Melissa's breath hitched, her heart skipping a beat. She wasn't sure how to respond, so she simply looked out the window, trying to ignore the way her pulse raced.

The flight was pleasant, but Melissa made sure to sit away from Michael this time, keeping a careful distance. She focused on conversation with Graham, flipping through a magazine, or simply gazing out the window, anything to keep from dwelling on Michael's presence just a few feet away.

As they neared Paris, Michael turned to her. "In two days, we'll be heading to London to see the necklaces," he informed her.

Melissa glanced at him, surprised. "Why London?"

"It's easier for us to go to them rather than bringing them here and then returning them," he explained. "The gala is in London after all."

She nodded slowly, taking in the information. It made sense, but something about it made her uneasy. Maybe it was the thought of being in London with him alone.

Michael gave Melissa the space she had asked for, and she kept herself busy gathering fabric samples for the gowns. The designs were finalised, but she needed to ensure the materials complemented each other perfectly. She immersed herself in work, letting the creative process distract her from everything else.

That evening, Michael called to let her know he would be picking her up at nine the next morning.

Graham was with her when she got the call. He smirked as she ended the conversation. "You're really going to make him work for it, aren't you?"

Melissa frowned. "I don't know what you mean."

Graham chuckled, crossing his arms. "You're acting like an ice queen."

"Am I?" She blinked, genuinely surprised.

"But I don't blame you," he added, pulling her into a warm hug. "He needs to work for it."

She sighed, her voice quieter. "I don't know how to act with him, Graham. I'm really confused and torn."

Graham brushed a soothing hand over her back. "You'll know when it's time, sweetheart. Just do what makes you happy."

Chapter Eighteen

Michael arrived at exactly nine as promised.

"Morning, Angel," he murmured, bending to kiss her lips.

Melissa froze but didn't pull away. He noticed—and took it as progress. A small smile played at his lips as he pulled back.

By 9:30 a.m., they were airborne, heading for London. The flight lasted just over an hour, and with the time difference, they touched down in London at 9:40 a.m. local time.

By mid-morning, they arrived at Michael's office building in the heart of London. It was an impressive glass-and-steel high-rise, towering above the bustling streets below. Inside, polished marble floors gleamed under soft lighting, and floor-to-ceiling windows offered breathtaking views of the city skyline. The quiet hum of productivity filled the air as impeccably dressed employees moved with effortless efficiency.

They went straight to the vault, where Michael's head designer, Ryan, was waiting.

Ryan's eyes lit up the moment he saw Melissa. Stepping forward, he took both her hands in his and pressed a lingering kiss on each.

"Hello, Melissa. It's a real pleasure to meet you," he said with a slow, appreciative smile. Then, turning to Michael with a teasing glint in his eye, he added, "Where have you been hiding this beauty?"

Melissa giggled. "You're a charmer."

Ryan wiggled his brows. "Is it working?"

Michael's jaw tightened. "No, it's not." His tone was deceptively smooth, but the warning in his gaze was unmistakable. Without another word, he placed a hand at the small of Melissa's back and guided her past Ryan, his touch possessive.

Inside, the air was cool and still. Michael and Ryan retrieved their keys, turning them simultaneously to unlock a door in the wall. A soft click echoed as it swung open, revealing a chamber lined with velvet trays, each holding a breathtaking piece of jewellery.

A tall table stood in the centre, where Melissa had meticulously arranged her iPad and fabric samples for the task ahead.

Michael carefully removed the necklaces one by one, presenting each to Melissa as she studied them under the light. Holding up silks, satins, and chiffons, she examined how the fabrics interacted with the gemstones.

Ryan, flipping through her designs, let out a low whistle. "Melissa, these are outstanding." His tone was laced with genuine admiration.

She smiled. "Thank you."

Michael, watching them, simply said, "She's the best."

Ryan looked at Melissa with appreciation. "I can see that."

Michael's jaw tensed at Ryan's tone, but Melissa found herself pleased by the compliment.

Turning back to her work, she made her final selections with careful consideration. Velvet for the sapphire necklace, satin for the ruby, a mix of silk and tulle for the opal, heavy silk for the emerald, and white satin for the diamond.

Michael nodded in approval. Then, with casual finality, he said, "Melissa will be wearing the diamond necklace on the night."

Her head snapped up. "Oh, I haven't decided that yet." She gave him a pointed look.

Ryan took her hand gently, his gaze warm. "You must," he insisted. "It would look exquisite on you. Your skin tone, your hair, your eyes—they would only enhance its brilliance."

Melissa felt her cheeks heat slightly at his words.

Michael, however, was less amused. He rolled the necklace between his fingers, his grip just a fraction too tight. "She'll wear it." His voice was smooth, but Melissa didn't miss the tension simmering beneath.

She arched a brow at him, amused by his possessiveness but not ready to let him dictate her choices. "We'll see."

Ryan chuckled. "Oh, Michael, I think you've met your match."

Michael smirked, locking eyes with Melissa. "I've always known that."

Michael took Melissa to an exclusive restaurant, where the food, atmosphere, and conversation were outstanding. She actually enjoyed herself immensely, feeling lighter than she had in days.

For a little while, it was easy to forget the past and simply enjoy the present.

After lunch, they took the jet back to Paris. The flight was smooth, and though Melissa remained cautious, she found herself relaxing more around Michael.

When they landed, Michael drove her home, pulling up in front of her building. He turned to her, his gaze warm. "I had a great time today."

Melissa nodded. "Me too."

For a moment, silence stretched between them, thick with unspoken words and lingering tension. Michael hesitated, as if debating whether to prolong the moment, to ask for more—an invitation inside, a reason to stay. But instead of speaking, he reached out, tucking a stray strand of hair behind her ear.

Just as she was about to say goodnight, Michael suddenly closed the distance, his lips crashing onto hers in a kiss that stole her breath. It wasn't gentle—it was deep, searing, filled with everything unsaid. Melissa gasped against his mouth, her fingers gripping the front of his shirt as she let herself drown in him.

When they finally broke apart, both breathless, he rested his forehead against hers. "Sleep well, Angel," he murmured, his voice husky.

Dazed, Melissa managed a small smile before stepping out of the car. As she walked inside, she could still feel the heat of his kiss, the press of his lips against hers. And for the first time in a long while, his gaze on her didn't feel heavy—it felt right.

The next four weeks were a blur of activity. The gowns were being made, the models had been finalised, and after some persuasion from Graham, Melissa decided to wear the white gown with the diamond necklace.

"It'll be great for your image and profile," Graham had said. "And, let's be honest, you'll look stunning."

She had to agree.

During this time, Michael respected her space. He had returned to London but made a point to call every day—sometimes just to check in, other times to share details about their days.

Their conversations became easier, more familiar, and Melissa found herself reminiscing about how things had been before everything went awry. Late-night talks that stretched for hours, the way his laughter used to make her chest tighten with warmth.

"Did you eat today?" he asked one evening, his voice warm with concern.

Melissa smiled, tucking her legs beneath her on the couch. "Yes, Michael. I'm not starving myself."

"I'm just making sure," he teased. "You get so lost in your work sometimes."

Melissa smirked, deciding to tease him. "Well, I did have a visitor today. Luke dropped by."

There was a beat of silence. "Luke?" Michael's voice had lost its warmth.

"Yes, the male model from the fashion show," she said with a smile. "He asked me out for dinner, again."

Michael let out a slow breath. "And what did you say?"

Melissa bit back a laugh at the clipped tone. "I told him no, of course."

"Good." His response was immediate, firm. Then, after a moment, he added, "I never liked that guy."

"You barely spoke to him," she pointed out, grinning.

"I didn't have to," Michael grumbled. "He was looking at you like he wanted to devour you that night."

Melissa chuckled, a warmth spreading through her chest at his possessiveness. She didn't want to admit how much she liked it. "Jealous, Michael?"

He huffed. "I don't get jealous."

"Hmm," she hummed in amusement.

Michael sighed. "Well… yes, how could I not? You're beautiful," then he added, "You tell Luke to stay in his lane."

Melissa laughed. "I have tried, but he never seems to get the message."

Michael sighed dramatically. "Maybe I should fly back and make sure he gets the message personally."

Her stomach fluttered at the thought. "Oh? And what exactly would you say to him?"

"That depends," he mused. "Would a simple 'she's taken, back off' do the trick, or do I need to be more… persuasive?"

Melissa shook her head, still smiling. His voice was laced with playful menace, but underneath it, she could hear something else—something real.

"I think you just want an excuse to come back."

A pause. Then, softly— "You're right."

Her breath hitched.

"I don't like being away from you. It's getting harder to stay away."

The quiet sincerity in his voice made her chest tighten. Her fingers curled around the fabric of the couch as she tried to steady herself.

He was dangerous, this man. Not because he was possessive, not because he was teasing, but because he had the power to undo her with just a few words. And the worst part? She wanted to be undone.

Another night, after discussing an upcoming meeting, he sighed. "I miss seeing you, Mel."

She hesitated, her heart stumbling over the quiet confession. "I…I miss you too."

Two weeks before the gala, Michael finally asked her out on a date.

"So, what do you say?" His voice was light, but there was something raw beneath it, something hopeful.

To her own surprise, she agreed straight away. "Okay," she said, a soft smile tugging at her lips. "I'll go on a date with you."

The pause on the other end was brief, but she could hear the grin in his voice when he responded. "Good. Because I wasn't planning on taking no for an answer."

Michael picked Melissa up on the next Friday evening, a week before the gala, arriving in a sleek black car that gleamed under the glow of Parisian streetlights. As he stepped out, the crisp lines of his perfectly tailored tuxedo only added to his effortless charm. He moved with purpose, his gaze locking onto hers as she opened the door.

Melissa stepped out gracefully, the soft fabric of her black dress clinging in all the right places. The cool night air kissed her bare shoulders, but it wasn't the chill that sent a shiver down her spine—it was the way Michael was looking at her.

"You look stunning," he murmured, lifting her hand to his lips for a slow, deliberate kiss.

She smiled, tilting her head slightly as she took him in. "And you," she said, her voice light, "look very handsome."

His lips curled into a smirk. "Just handsome?"

Melissa arched a brow, playing along. "Would you like another adjective?"

"I was hoping for devastatingly handsome."

She laughed softly. "Let's not get ahead of ourselves."

Michael chuckled, his hand lingering at the small of her back as he led her toward the car. "By the end of the night, I'll earn it," he promised, helping her inside.

Michael took her to the Eiffel Tower, where they rode the private elevator up to Le Jules Verne, the Michelin-starred restaurant on the second floor. The moment they stepped inside, they were enveloped in an atmosphere of refined luxury. Floor-to-ceiling windows framed breathtaking views of Paris, bathed in the golden glow of sunset. The intimate lighting, crisp white tablecloths, and soft murmur of French conversation created an ambiance that felt both grand and private.

Michael had reserved a table by the window, and as they settled in, a sommelier arrived with a bottle of vintage champagne. Their meal was an exquisite journey through French haute cuisine—delicate amuse-bouchées, a perfectly seared filet of beef for him, a decadent lobster dish for her. Each bite was a symphony of flavours, and with every sip of wine, Melissa found herself more at ease. Their conversation flowed effortlessly, laughter coming easily between them.

After dinner, instead of leaving right away, Michael took her hand and led her to The Champagne Bar at the very top of the Eiffel Tower. Below them, the city stretched out like a sea of twinkling lights, a breathtaking contrast to the dark velvet sky. The air was crisp but not cold, and the moment felt suspended in time. He handed her a flute of champagne, their fingers brushing as she took it.

Michael took a slow sip of his champagne, his gaze never leaving hers. "You know, this is the first time in a long while that I've seen you truly relax with me."

Melissa exhaled a quiet laugh. "Maybe it's the champagne."

"Or maybe it's me," he teased, a playful glint in his eye.

She arched a brow. "Oh, so now you take credit for my good mood?"

"Absolutely." He leaned in slightly, his voice softer. "I've missed this. Just talking, laughing… being with you."

Melissa looked away, her fingers tracing the delicate stem of her glass. "Michael…"

"I'm not asking for anything, Melissa," he said gently. "I know I messed up. And I know I can't change the past. But… I love seeing you smile."

She met his gaze again, searching his face. There was no arrogance there, no expectation—just sincerity.

Melissa nodded slowly, a small smile touching her lips. "I love smiling."

Michael lifted his glass again, his slow smile mirroring hers. "Then keep on smiling."

Melissa couldn't fight the warmth that spread through her at his words. There was something so disarming about the way he looked at her—like he truly saw her, not just the woman he had once loved, but the woman she had become.

She took a sip of her champagne, the crisp bubbles dancing on her tongue. "You say that like it's easy."

Michael tilted his head slightly. "Maybe it can be."

She let out a soft laugh. "You think so?"

"I think," he said, his voice steady, "that sometimes we let the past hold too much power over the present."

Melissa studied him for a moment, the golden city lights reflecting in his dark eyes. "And what if the past left scars?"

His expression turned serious. "Then you wear them, learn from them. But you don't let them keep you from happiness."

She looked down at her glass, running a finger along the rim. He made it sound so simple, yet she knew how complicated it really was. But tonight, in this moment, she wanted to believe him.

She lifted her gaze back to his and gave him a small, genuine smile. "Then I guess I'll have to keep smiling."

Michael's lips twitched upward as he lifted his glass once more. "Now that," he murmured, "is something worth drinking to."

Their glasses clinked softly in the night air, and for the first time in a long time, Melissa felt the weight on her heart grow just a little bit lighter.

When they finished their drinks, Michael stood and helped her to her feet, his hand lingering at the small of her back as he led her out to his car. The drive home was quiet but charged, tension thrumming in the space between them.

Every glance, every accidental brush of his fingers sent a quiet thrill skittering through her. The air between them was thick with something unspoken, something that had the power to change everything... if she let it.

When they arrived at her building, Michael stepped out first, coming around to open her door. Melissa looked up at him, her breath catching as their eyes met. There was something raw in his gaze—something unspoken but undeniable, a quiet intensity that sent a shiver down her spine.

At her door, he reached up, tucking a loose strand of hair behind her ear just as he had many times before. But this time, his fingers lingered, trailing down along the curve of her jaw, his touch featherlight yet searing.

"Tonight was perfect," he murmured.

Melissa swallowed hard. "Yes, it was."

Michael leaned in, hesitating just enough to let her stop him if she wanted to. But she didn't. Their breaths mingled, and then his lips met hers—slow and searching, as if he was memorising her, as if he never wanted to forget the way she felt in his arms.

Melissa melted into him, her fingers gripping his jacket, pulling him closer. The kiss deepened, a quiet sigh escaping her as she pressed against him, her entire body coming alive under his touch. Michael groaned softly, one hand sliding to the small of her back, the other threading into her hair, anchoring her to him.

When they finally broke apart, Melissa was breathless, her pulse unsteady. Michael started to pull back, as if giving her the space to reconsider, but she wasn't ready to let go. Instead, she grabbed his hand, fumbling with her keys before finally pushing the door open and pulling him inside.

"Melissa—"

She silenced him with another kiss, this one hotter, more urgent. She backed him against the closed door, her hands splaying across his chest as his grip tightened around her waist. He was holding back—she could feel it in the way his fingers flexed against her, in the restraint in his touch.

Her eyes burned with something fierce and unshakable as she whispered, "Stay."

Michael exhaled sharply, his control fraying at the edges. "Are you sure?"

Instead of answering, she reached for him, sliding his jacket off his shoulders, her fingers working deftly at the buttons of his shirt. Michael let out a low groan, his resolve snapping. He lifted her effortlessly, and she wrapped her legs around his waist as he carried her to the bedroom.

Their mouths met again in a feverish kiss; all hesitation burned away by the sheer need coursing between them. Hands roamed, bodies pressed together, each touch more desperate than the last. Clothes disappeared piece by piece, discarded without thought, until there was nothing left between them—no past, no pain, only heat, only this.

When they tumbled onto the bed, Michael covered her body with his, his lips tracing a slow, reverent path over her skin. He worshiped her, mapping every inch of her with his hands, his mouth, his whispered devotion. And Melissa let him. For the first time in years, she let herself feel—*truly feel*—the love, the longing, the years of unspoken words and unresolved emotions unravelling between them.

When he finally entered her, she gasped his name, her nails digging into his back as he filled her completely. He stilled, savouring the moment, savouring her, his forehead resting against hers. Then he began to move, slowly at first, watching her, memorising the way she looked beneath him, the way she trembled when he touched her just right.

He kissed her deeply, his thrusts growing more urgent, more demanding, until she was clinging to him, her body tightening, her breaths turning into soft, desperate cries.

"Michael—"

He silenced her with his mouth, swallowing her pleasure as she shattered around him. The feeling of her gripping him, pulling him deeper, sent him spiralling after her, a guttural groan tearing from his lips as he found his own release.

For a long moment, neither of them moved. Their bodies remained entwined, their breathing slowly returning to normal as the world settled around them.

Melissa rested her head against his chest, her fingers tracing lazy patterns over his skin. Michael held her close, pressing a lingering kiss to her hair, his grip on her firm, like he never wanted to let go.

"I love you," he murmured, his voice rough with emotion.

Melissa closed her eyes, her heart pounding for a different reason now. She wasn't ready to say it back—not yet. But for the first time, she knew that one day, she would.

Chapter Nineteen

The next morning, they spent the day together. Melissa didn't reciprocate Michael's declaration of love, but there was a quiet understanding between them—neither pushing for more nor pulling away.

They spent most of the day in bed, tangled in each other's arms, speaking in soft murmurs between lazy kisses. The outside world faded away, replaced by warmth, whispered touches, and the unspoken ache of something deeper.

Sunday passed in much the same way—a quiet, fragile truce. They didn't talk about the past or the future, only existed in the present, where words weren't needed, and their bodies spoke for them.

On Monday morning, as Michael prepared to leave, he pulled her into his arms. "I don't want to, but I have to go. The jet had to land at Lille Airport in northern France on Friday because of the crosswinds, and they haven't got much better, so I need to take a helicopter there to make my meeting in London on time."

Melissa nodded, her hands resting lightly on his chest.

"I'll see you in London on Friday for the gala on Saturday," he continued. "I'll send the jet for you and Graham. I love you."

Before she could respond, he kissed her—hard and possessive, as if imprinting himself on her before they parted.

When they finally pulled away, their goodbye was reluctant, lingering in the quiet space between them. Then, with one last look, Michael turned and left.

Michael stepped onto the tarmac, the early morning air crisp against his skin. The sleek black helicopter sat ready, its blades slicing through the dawn sky. He adjusted the cuffs of his suit jacket before climbing in, nodding at the pilot.

"Straight to Lille," Michael instructed as he buckled in. "I can't be late."

The pilot gave a curt nod. "Weather's a bit rough this morning. Some strong crosswinds."

Michael barely listened, already pulling out his phone to check his schedule. If all went as planned, he'd be in London by midday. He tapped out a quick message to his assistant, confirming his itinerary. Then, almost unconsciously, his fingers hovered over Melissa's name.

He hesitated.

She had looked so damn beautiful that morning, wrapped in the sheets, her hair tousled, sleep still in her eyes. I love you; he had told her.

She hadn't said it back.

He sighed, slipping the phone into his jacket. She feels it. I know she does. He'd see her in a few days. Maybe then—

A sharp jolt rocked the aircraft.

Michael's head snapped up. "What the hell was that?"

"Crosswinds," the pilot said, his voice suddenly tense. "Stronger than expected."

Another violent gust sent the helicopter lurching sideways. Michael gripped the armrest as alarms blared in the cockpit.

"Losing altitude!" the pilot shouted, his hands flying over the controls.

The aircraft veered sharply, dipping toward a dense expanse of forest below—Forêt de Compiegne. Trees stretched endlessly in every direction, their thick canopies an unforgiving net beneath them.

Then—a sickening snap.

One of the rotor blades clipped a treetop. The impact sent the helicopter into a deadly spin.

"Brace! Brace!" the pilot yelled.

Michael barely had time to react before the ground surged up to meet them. The world became a blur of green and metal, branches snapping like gunfire as the helicopter crashed through the treetops.

The last thing that flashed through Michael's mind before impact was Melissa.

Then, with a final, jarring impact, the aircraft hit the forest floor—hard.

And silence swallowed them whole.

Melissa stood in her office on Monday afternoon, flipping through sketches, but her mind wasn't on work. The weekend with Michael lingered in her thoughts, wrapping around her like a warm embrace. She had felt loved.

She exhaled sharply, pushing the thought aside and refocusing on her designs. The gala was days away, and everything was on track. The gowns were nearly perfect—she had arranged a few final tweaks that morning.

A soft smile tugged at her lips as she absently traced the edge of a sketch with her fingertip. Her thoughts drifted back to Sunday morning—Michael's sleepy voice murmuring against her skin, the warmth of his arms wrapped around her, the way he kissed her as if he never wanted to let go.

Her phone buzzed, snapping her out of the memory. Expecting a message from Michael, she reached for it, her pulse skipping. But it was just an email. She let out a quiet laugh at herself, shaking her head. *You're ridiculous, Melissa.*

Then the office door burst open.

Melissa turned, startled, as Graham strode in. One look at his face sent a chill down her spine. He was pale, his usual easy-going demeanour replaced by something raw and unsteady.

"Graham?" Her voice wavered. "What is it?"

He stopped in front of her, gripping her shoulders as if bracing her for impact. His hands were trembling.

"Sweetheart… it's Michael."

The world tilted.

She clutched his forearms. "What about Michael?"

Graham swallowed hard. "Henry just called. Michael's helicopter—" He hesitated, his throat working as if forcing the words out. "It crashed, Melissa. Somewhere in the Forêt de Compiegne."

Melissa's breath caught. *'No.'* The word was barely a whisper. Her vision blurred, the room tilting around her.

"They lost contact mid-flight. Search teams are looking, but… the area's remote. No signals. No wreckage found yet." His voice was hoarse, heavy with uncertainty. "Michael's missing."

The words slammed into her like a physical blow. She stumbled back, shaking her head.

Missing.

No.

Not Michael.

Her chest tightened, pain searing through her like a blade.

Graham held her steady. "Melissa, they don't know for sure. Not yet."

But she barely heard him.

All she could hear was Michael's voice from that morning. *I love you.*

She never told him how she felt.

And now he was gone.

Her knees buckled.

Darkness swallowed her whole.

"Melissa, sweetheart." The voice was distant, muffled, like it was coming from the other end of a tunnel.

She felt hands on her, steadying her, but everything was slipping—her breath, her strength, the world itself. The edges of her vision blurred, fading to black.

"Stay with me." The voice again, urgent now. Familiar. Graham.

But Melissa's world fractured. The weight of those three unbearable words pulled her under.

Michael was missing.

By Wednesday, there was still no news.

Michael's parents, Maria and Henry, along with Jason, Sarah, Melissa's parents, Fiona and Kevin, and Graham, had all gathered at Melissa's home. They clung to one another, offering what little comfort they could, but the waiting was unbearable.

Melissa was devastated. She barely spoke, barely moved. All she did was cry and sleep, unable to function under the crushing weight of uncertainty.

Graham had taken it upon himself to keep everything on track for the gala, refusing to let the event fall apart.

"When he is found, he'll want it to go ahead," he told Melissa again and again, his voice firm yet gentle. "You know he would."

But Melissa barely acknowledged him.

Melissa's parents were beside themselves with worry, but their greatest concern was Melissa. She was falling apart before their eyes. When she was awake, Sarah held her, whispering reassurances that Melissa barely registered.

She hadn't eaten properly in two days. Every time she tried, nausea overtook her, and she was sick.

The authorities had little comfort to offer. The search was slow, they said. The area was remote, difficult to navigate.

And still, there was no sign of Michael.

Every night, after making sure Melissa was settled in bed, the others would return to the nearby hotel where they were staying. But Sarah refused to leave. No matter how much they tried to persuade her, she insisted on staying to keep an eye on Melissa.

That night, as Sarah helped her to bed, Melissa whispered the same words she had every night since he had been missing.

"I should have told him."

Sarah tucked the blanket around her and smoothed her hair gently.

"He knows, Mel."

Melissa's eyes fluttered closed, exhaustion pulling her under. But sleep brought no peace—only restless dreams, haunted by Michael's voice, his touch, the warmth of his embrace.

Then, she felt it. A hand brushing against her cheek, light as a whisper. A voice—low, familiar.

"Melissa."

She stirred, frowning in her sleep. The touch came again, fingers threading gently through her hair.

"Mel, wake up."

Her breath hitched. That voice. It was impossible.

She forced her eyes open, her heart pounding. And there he was.

Michael.

Kneeling beside the bed, his blue eyes locked onto hers, filled with something raw and aching. His face was shadowed with exhaustion, his jaw rough with days of stubble, but he was here. Alive.

Melissa sucked in a sharp breath and reached for him—but her fingers met nothing but air.

She jerked back, shaking her head. No. No, this isn't real.

"Shh," Michael murmured, his voice coaxing, steady. "I'm here, angel."

Tears welled in her eyes. She squeezed them shut, willing the dream away. This was just her mind playing tricks on her. It had to be.

"You're not real," she whispered brokenly.

Michael's expression tightened with something like pain. He lifted a hand as if to cup her cheek but hesitated.

"I'm coming back to you, Mel," he said softly. "Hold on a little longer."

Melissa sobbed, curling in on herself. "You're not here," she choked out. "You're gone."

Michael exhaled sharply, his fingers ghosting over hers.

"I love you," he whispered. "I've always loved you."

A sob wracked her body as she buried her face in the pillow.

When she looked up again, he was gone.

Only silence remained.

Melissa drifted in and out of sleep, exhaustion weighing her down like a lead blanket. Her body ached, but it was nothing compared to the hollow ache in her chest.

The dream had felt so real—Michael's voice, the warmth of his embrace, the way he used to hold her as if she was his entire world. But it had to be just that. A dream. A cruel trick of her mind, born from grief, regret, and longing so deep it felt like it would swallow her whole.

She had never told him.

Not when he came back into her life. Not when he kissed her, held her, made her feel like she belonged to him again. She had been too afraid—too guarded—to say the words that had been clawing at her throat for years.

And now, maybe it was too late.

Tears pricked at her eyes. *What if I never get the chance? What if he never knows?*

A warm hand brushed against her cheek.

Her breath hitched.

Was she still dreaming? Or was she about to wake up to a reality where he was truly gone?

"Melissa."

Her eyes fluttered open, her heart hammering. The room was dim, bathed in the soft glow of the bedside lamp. And there, sitting on the edge of the bed, was him.

Michael.

Dishevelled, bruised, his shirt torn and stained with dirt, but unmistakably real.

She gasped, scrambling upright, her pulse roaring in her ears.

"No," she whispered, shaking her head. "No, this isn't real."

"It's me, angel." His voice was hoarse, rough with exhaustion. "I'm here."

Melissa's breath caught. Her fingers trembled as she reached for him, afraid that if she touched him, he'd disappear like before. But when her hand met solid warmth—his skin, his heat, his presence—her breath came out in a broken sob.

Michael caught her wrist, bringing her palm to his cheek. His stubble scratched against her skin, grounding her in the reality of him. "I made it back to you," he whispered.

A choked sound tore from Melissa's throat, raw and desperate. And then she was moving—no hesitation, no thought—just pure, overwhelming need.

She threw herself at him, her body colliding with his as a sob wrenched free from her chest. Michael caught her instantly, pulling her onto his lap, his arms locking around her like he'd never let go.

That was when the dam broke.

She sobbed against him, the weight of fear, grief, and unbearable relief crashing over her in violent, shuddering waves. Her fingers clutched at his shirt, fisting the fabric as if she could anchor herself to him, as if holding on tight enough could erase the agonising hours she'd spent thinking he was gone forever.

He smelled of earth and rain, of survival, of something deeply, intrinsically him.

"You're alive," she gasped between sobs, her voice shaking. "I thought—I thought I lost you again."

Michael's grip tightened. "Never," he swore. "I would never leave you."

"I couldn't bare to lose you," she sobbed against his skin.

Michael's arms tightened around her, his lips pressing into her hair. "I'm here, Melissa. I'm right here."

But she couldn't stop crying, couldn't stop the way her entire body trembled against his. Because for a moment—one terrifying, gut-wrenching moment—she had known what it felt like to live in a world without him. And now that he was back, she wasn't sure how to let go of the fear that still had its claws in her.

Her hands roamed over him, desperate to feel every inch of him, to convince herself he was real. His chest, his arms, the rough fabric of his torn shirt. "You were missing for days," she whispered brokenly. "We thought—"

"I know," he murmured, pressing a kiss to the top of her head. "I know, Angel."

Melissa pulled back just enough to look at him, tears streaming down her face. "I love you," she blurted, the words rushing out like they'd been locked inside her for too long.

Michael stilled, his breath catching. Then his lips parted, his gaze searching hers, as if he was memorising this moment, engraving it into his soul.

"Say it again," he rasped.

Melissa cupped his face, her thumbs brushing away the streaks of dirt. "I love you, Michael."

A shaky breath escaped him, and then he was kissing her, raw and desperate, as if he was pouring all his pain, relief, and love into her.

Melissa kissed him back just as fiercely, her fingers tangling in his hair, her body moulding to his.

When they finally broke apart, Michael rested his forehead against hers, his breath unsteady.

"I should've said it sooner," she admitted, her voice barely above a whisper.

His fingers traced the curve of her jaw. "You said it when it mattered," he murmured.

Melissa let out a small, shaky laugh, her heart full to bursting.

Michael was home.

He pressed a lingering kiss to her forehead before pulling her into a tight embrace, as if he never wanted to let go again.

"I sent Sarah with my car to the hotel," he murmured against her hair. "She's letting everyone know I'm okay."

Melissa nodded, her fingers clutching the fabric of his shirt. "Good." Her voice was barely above a whisper, thick with lingering emotions.

Michael pulled back just enough to look into her eyes. "Come with me."

She followed him into the bathroom, her heart still hammering, unwilling to let him out of her sight.

Warm steam soon filled the space, curling around them like a cocoon. But before they stepped under the water, Melissa reached for him, her hands roaming over his chest, his arms, his shoulders—everywhere. Her fingers trembled as she inspected him, searching for cuts, bruises, any sign that he wasn't as unscathed as he claimed to be.

"Melissa," Michael murmured, catching her hands in his.

"I need to be sure," she whispered, voice thick with emotion. Her palm pressed flat against his heartbeat, feeling the steady, reassuring thud beneath her fingertips. "You were on that helicopter. I need to know you're really okay."

His expression softened. He let her look, let her touch, let her reassure herself. Only when she finally exhaled, a shaky breath of relief, did he gently guide her under the spray of the shower.

There, in the warmth of the water, they took their time—washing away the remnants of fear and sorrow. Michael's touch was reverent, his hands tracing the curves of her body as if memorising every inch of her.

Melissa shivered—not from the water, but from the overwhelming love in his gaze.

And then, neither of them could hold back.

Their hands found each other with desperate urgency, their mouths colliding in a kiss that was all heat, raw need, and unspoken emotion. There was nothing hesitant about it—nothing careful. It was wild, consuming, a collision of past and present, of love and longing. A silent declaration that this was real. That after everything, they had found their way back to each other, and they weren't letting go.

Water streamed down their heated skin as they clung to one another, fingers tracing familiar yet electrifying paths. Every touch was feverish, every gasp lost in the thick steam curling around them.

With her legs wrapped around him, pressed hard against the cold tiles, he entered her in one smooth thrust. A sharp cry escaped her lips, swallowed immediately by his mouth as he kissed her deeply, possessively. It wasn't just about physical need—it was an unspoken plea, a silent vow sealed in the way their bodies moved together, in the way their hands grasped, in the way his name left her lips like a prayer.

They moved in a desperate rhythm, chasing something more than pleasure—chasing lost time, chasing the years of pain, chasing the love that had never faded, only buried beneath the weight of mistakes.

Every kiss, every thrust, every whispered name was a promise. This time, no more regrets. No more wasted time. No more running.

Melissa shattered first, her body arching, trembling as waves of pleasure crashed over her. Michael followed seconds later, his release tearing through him as he held her tight, as if he could somehow fuse them together, make this moment last forever.

Later, wrapped in fresh sheets, Melissa nestled against him, her head resting over his heart. The steady rhythm beneath her ear was a soothing reminder—he was alive, he was here, and this time, he was hers.

She tightened her arms around him, pressing a soft kiss to his chest, as if to ground herself in his warmth.

Michael brushed his fingers through her hair, his voice a low murmur against her temple. "I'm never leaving you again."

And this time, she believed him.

Michael tightened his arms around her, pressing a kiss to the top of her head. "I love you, Melissa."

She smiled, her eyes drifting shut as exhaustion and contentment washed over her. "I love you too, Michael."

And with their hearts finally at peace, they fell asleep in each other's arms.

Chapter Twenty

The day of the gala had finally arrived.

Melissa stood before the full-length mirror in Michael's London apartment, her gaze fixed on her reflection as she took in the transformation. The soft hum of anticipation lingered in the air, mingling with the weight of everything that had led her here.

Michael had insisted she come back to England with him. He hadn't just *asked*—he had *demanded*. He refused to be away from her any longer, refused to risk losing her again. And despite all her hesitations, all her fears, she hadn't been able to say no. Not when every part of her ached to be by his side.

Now, standing in the glow of the elegant space he had made sure felt like hers too, she exhaled slowly, trying to steady the nervous flutter in her stomach.

Her hair, styled by the expert hands of a renowned stylist, was swept into a delicate up-do, soft tendrils framing her face, lending her a look of both elegance and effortless grace. Her makeup, subtle yet masterfully done, enhanced her features perfectly—natural, yet undeniably radiant.

It was the kind of beauty that seemed to glow from within, as if something deep inside her had finally settled, as if she had finally stopped searching.

But it was the gown that truly took her breath away.

The white satin dress she wore was the very definition of flawless. It shimmered under the soft lighting, a liquid silver creation that clung to her figure in all the right ways, draping her body with the kind of elegance only true luxury could bestow. The fabric, smooth and luminous, caught the light with every subtle movement, as though alive with its own quiet brilliance.

The bodice of the dress was an intricate masterpiece, adorned with hand-sewn crystals that sparkled like stars caught in a soft, night sky. Each crystal seemed to have its own story, reflecting the light in a perfect dance as she shifted, creating a shimmering effect that mirrored the brilliance of the diamonds that she will wear. The neckline was a daring plunge—deep yet tasteful—striking the perfect balance between boldness and sophistication, leaving just enough to the imagination.

The long, fitted sleeves of the gown hugged her arms with a refined delicacy, adding an air of timeless grace. The skirt, though fitted through the hips, flowed outward in a sweeping train that seemed to move with a mind of its own, weightless yet commanding. It swirled around her with each movement, like a whisper of silk on a breeze. The train trailed behind her, but with a delicate motion, she could effortlessly hook it up in her hand, transforming it into a soft cloud of satin that seemed to follow her every step. It moved with a quiet grace, dignified yet effortless, as though it were an extension of her own elegance.

Melissa, looking at herself in the mirror, almost didn't recognise the woman staring back. She looked every bit the vision of elegance she had dreamed for the design, but more than that—the gown looked exquisite.

Behind her, Michael stood in the doorway, his eyes tracing every inch of her as if trying to commit the moment to memory. His breath caught in his throat. He had seen her countless times—laughing, crying, vulnerable, strong—but nothing compared to this.

She was *his*.

And he still couldn't quite believe how lucky he was.

His lips parted, but no words came. The love and admiration in his gaze spoke volumes, a silent declaration of everything he felt but struggled to put into words.

"You're…" he whispered, his voice hoarse, "perfect."

Melissa smiled softly, her heart skipping a beat at the raw sincerity in his voice.

"I'm ready," she said, turning to face him fully, her eyes sparkling with a mix of nerves and excitement.

Michael stepped forward, taking her hand gently in his. He couldn't stop looking at her, couldn't stop marvelling at the fact that she was here—with him, beside him, *his*.

"Your design is breathtaking," he said, his voice full of awe. "Everyone will be blown away."

But as far as Michael was concerned, no dress, no event, no moment in the night could ever compare to the woman standing before him.

They made their way to the limousine through the grand foyer of his apartment building, and as Melissa walked, heads turned to admire her. Each step she took seemed to draw attention, the soft rustle of her gown creating a quiet symphony of elegance. Michael walked closely beside her, his eyes never leaving her as he helped her into the car.

Once inside, the ride to the gala passed in silence, save for the steady rhythm of their breathing. Michael kept a gentle but firm grip on Melissa's hand, his thumb softly brushing over her knuckles as if anchoring her to the moment, to him.

When they arrived, they were swiftly ushered through the back entrance of the venue, where the atmosphere buzzed with anticipation. The other models were already there—poised, stunning, their gowns flowing like molten liquid under the soft lights.

Security staff delicately placed glittering necklaces around their necks, each one an extravagant masterpiece that transformed the women into living works of art.

Tonight was about the fashion and the jewels. Each model would have a male escort for the evening—someone to complement the elegance, to ensure they were attended to at all times. And Michael's role for the night? *Hers.*

Melissa barely had time to process the thought before Michael stepped forward, holding the piece meant for her.

The necklace was breathtaking—a cascade of radiant diamonds, each one catching the light in a dazzling display. It was regal, exquisite, almost too much.

As he fastened it around her throat, his fingers brushed against her skin, sending a shiver down her spine. The cool weight of the jewels pressed against her collarbone, grounding her, anchoring her to the moment.

Michael didn't move away. Instead, he gently turned her to face him, his touch lingering, his eyes roaming over her as if he had never seen anything more captivating.

"It looks like it was made for you," he murmured, his voice thick with something deep, something reverent.

Melissa met his gaze, her breath catching.

It wasn't just the necklace. She belonged here. *With him.*

"I will meet you out front," Michael murmured, pressing a gentle kiss to her cheek. His lips were soft, a moment of quiet affection before the chaos of the night began. Melissa nodded, watching him leave with a quick but reassuring glance.

The models were quickly given their instructions, each one assigned their time to walk onto the stage. They would be escorted down to the main area afterward, where they would have the chance to mingle and allow the guests to admire the new collection from Anderson Gems. The music began to swell, a subtle, elegant melody that signalled the start of the show.

But nothing could have prepared her for what happened next. When the collection was officially announced, the MC's voice rang out, "And now, presenting…the Melissa Collection."

Melissa froze, her heart pounding in her chest. Her name. Michael had named the collection after her.

One by one, the other models walked out with their escorts. The sound of gasps and applause filled the room, a symphony of admiration as each woman displayed the exquisite gowns and the jewels that accompanied them. It was an overwhelming, surreal experience for Melissa. She couldn't help but feel both awe-struck and nervous as she waited for her turn.

She was the final model; she was the only model to go solo on the runway. The last to walk the long, gleaming stage, each step feeling like a dream she wasn't sure she could fully grasp.

The crowd's murmurs of admiration filled the space as she stepped into the spotlight. The room was a sea of beautiful people, women dressed in sleek black gowns, and men in classic tuxedos, all eyes fixed on her. Melissa's gowns were the only colour in the room, their vibrancy standing out against the sea of monochrome attire. The gowns shimmered in the spotlight, each one more breathtaking than the last, while other gleaming jewels in glass cases added a touch of sparkle to the atmosphere.

At the end of the stage, Michael stood waiting, his eyes locked on her with pride, admiration, and something deeper that made her heart race. He was the one who had made this moment possible. She stepped forward, the soft rustle of her gown filling the silence, each movement showcasing not only the elegance of her designs but the brilliance of the jewellery that adorned her.

The night unfolded like a fairy tale, filled with laughter, admiration, and celebration. It was a complete success. The room buzzed with excitement, the air thick with the shimmering beauty of the jewels and the breathtaking gowns. Every moment seemed to glow with magic as guests mingled, lavishing praise on the collection. The models basked in the attention, their confidence soaring under the admiring gazes.

But for Melissa, none of it compared to the warmth of knowing the people she loved were there.

Michael's parents, Maria, Henry, and brother, Jason, had flown in, their expressions a mixture of pride and approval as they watched him stand beside her, unwavering in his devotion. Next to them, her own parents, Fiona and Kevin, and sister, Sarah—looked on with beaming smiles, their presence a steady source of comfort and encouragement for them both.

And through it all, Michael never left her side. He was her constant anchor, his hand resting on her back or intertwined with hers, a silent promise of support, pride, and something even deeper. When he looked at her, it wasn't just admiration in his eyes— it was love. And for the first time, in a long time, Melissa let herself believe she truly had everything she had ever wanted.

As the night wore on, the spotlight shifted to Michael. The guests quieted as he made his way to the stage, the room falling into an expectant hush. He cleared his throat, he spoke in the microphone the sound carrying across the space, and with a confident but warm smile, he addressed the crowd.

"Ladies and gentlemen," he began, his voice smooth, a mixture of pride and gratitude in his tone, "thank you for being here tonight, for celebrating the beauty and craftsmanship of Anderson Gems. But most importantly, thank you for celebrating the incredible talent of the woman who made tonight possible—Melissa Shaw, of M&G Designs."

A ripple of applause spread across the room as Melissa's heart fluttered in her chest. She glanced up at him, her eyes soft with emotion. Michael's smile never wavered as he continued.

"The Melissa collection," he said, holding his gaze steady on her, "is not just a reflection of my company, my vision, or my success. It's a reflection of someone who is not only a genius in her craft but also a force of nature in my life. Someone who makes every moment better just by being in it."

A warm laugh rippled through the crowd, but Melissa's gaze remained locked with his, her heart racing. His words felt like a dream.

"But tonight," Michael went on, his tone turning softer, more intimate, "there's one final thing I must do."

People looked around, some whispering in confusion, and Melissa felt her stomach tighten. *What was he talking about?*

He to her, his expression softening as he stepped off the stage and walked to Melissa, his hand extending toward her, she took it in hers.

"Melissa," he said, his voice low, almost a whisper, "you are the love of my life. I lost you for a while and I never want that to happen ever again. I can't imagine a life without you, and I don't want to."

Melissa's breath caught in her throat. *Was he...?*

Michael handed the microphone to the MC. Then slowly, dropped to one knee in front of her, a wave of gasps echoing through the room. He reached into his pocket, pulling out a small velvet box, the spotlight glinting off the stunning diamond ring inside. The crowd held its collective breath.

"Melissa," he said, his voice steady but filled with emotion, "will you marry me?"

Tears welled up in Melissa's eyes as she stared at the ring—brilliant, radiant, a symbol of everything they had been through, everything they had built. Her heart raced, her pulse quickening. *This was real. This was happening.*

Her voice was a mere whisper as she fought to steady her emotions. "Yes," she managed, her words breaking through the silence, "Yes, I will."

The room erupted into applause, cheers echoing around them, but all Melissa could focus on was Michael—his eyes filled with love, the promise of forever in his gaze.

He slid the ring onto her finger, standing to pull her into his arms as the crowd erupted into cheers. The sound faded into the background, drowned out by the wild pounding of her heart.

"You've made me the happiest man in the world," Michael whispered against her ear, his lips brushing the side of her face.

Melissa buried her face in his neck, her entire being overwhelmed with love, relief, and sheer joy. "You've made me the happiest woman." she murmured, her voice thick with emotion.

Michael pulled back just enough to look into her eyes, his thumb brushing a stray tear from her cheek. Then, with the world watching, he cupped her face and kissed her— deeply, reverently, sealing his promise with a touch that left no room for doubt.

The cheers swelled around them, but all Melissa could feel was him—his warmth, his love, his unwavering devotion. And as she kissed him back, she knew with absolute certainty that she was exactly where she was meant to be.

And in that moment, everything felt perfect. The night, the proposal, the future they were about to build together. Magic had filled the air all evening, but now, as they stood together, surrounded by the people they loved, it was clear: this was just the beginning of their forever.

Epilogue

6 months later…

Michael and Melissa walked into the living area of Sarah and Jason's new home in Sydney, their hands clasped tightly together, a reflection of the bond they shared. The soft morning light filtered through the windows, casting a warm glow over the room, and the quiet hum of family chatter filled the air.

Sarah and Jason's home had become a symbol of new beginnings, and now, it was the perfect place for them to celebrate another milestone.

As they entered, Henry and Maria, rose from their seats with smiles that matched the warmth of the room. They moved toward Michael and Melissa, their arms outstretched for hugs.

"Look at you two, so happy," Maria said, her voice filled with love as she pulled Melissa into a tight embrace.

Henry followed with a firm, proud hug for Michael, giving his son a hearty pat on the back. "We're so glad you could make it," he said, his eyes twinkling with affection. "It feels like just yesterday we were at your wedding."

Michael smiled, his eyes softening as he glanced at his wife. "It feels like we've been married forever," he said, his voice full of contentment.

Next, Fiona and Kevin, came forward with the same eager smiles. Fiona enveloped her daughter in a tight hug, her voice full of emotion. "You look so happy, darling," she said, her eyes glistening with tears of joy. "We're so proud of both of you."

Kevin pulled Michael into a warm embrace as well, his strong hands patting his son-in-law's back in approval. "It's good to see you both so in love," he said with a grin. "Everything about you two is just right."

The love between Michael and Melissa was undeniable. Everyone could see it in the way they moved together, always so in sync. Michael's hand was often resting gently on her lower back, or his fingers would graze her hand whenever they spoke. Melissa would sometimes sit on his lap, leaning into whisper something to him, a look of pure adoration in her eyes.

They hadn't been married for long—only three months—but their connection was already a beautiful testament to the love they shared. It was in every touch, every glance, every moment they spent together. They were completely at ease in each other's presence, as if the world outside had no power to disrupt the bubble of happiness they had created together.

"How's my gorgeous niece?" Melissa asked, her voice soft with curiosity as she glanced around the room.

Sarah, who had been sitting on the couch with her newborn daughter, smiled warmly at the couple. "She's asleep in the nursery," she said, her eyes full of the same warmth and joy that had defined her since Lily's arrival. "You can see her in just a moment."

"Congratulations, again," Michael said, his voice genuine as he looked at his brother and his wife. "She's perfect."

Jason, who had been standing nearby, smiled back at them, his eyes full of pride. "She's a dream come true," he replied, his tone thick with affection. "We're so glad you're here."

The air in the room was filled with a deep sense of happiness and celebration. It wasn't just about the arrival of a new life, though that was certainly part of it. It was about the way families grew, the way love multiplied, and the way bonds deepened over time.

"Let's sit down and catch up," Sarah suggested with a wide smile, her voice bubbling with excitement. "I want to hear everything—how's life been treating you both?"

Melissa exchanged a glance with Michael, her hand resting gently on his arm as they made their way to the couch.

As they sat down, the conversation quickly turned to updates on their lives. Michael and Melissa were eager to share their journey since their wedding.

"I've finally finished moving into Michael's apartment in London," Melissa began, her voice warm with pride. "It's starting to feel like home."

"And M&G Designs has been expanding," she continued, excitement creeping into her tone. "Graham's handling the Paris office while I manage things in London. The 'Melissa Collection' of necklaces has taken on a life of its own. The gowns were a massive hit, and the orders have been overwhelming—I honestly don't know how we're managing it all!"

Michael smiled at his wife's enthusiasm, his heart swelling with pride. "It's incredible to watch Melissa's success. She's worked so hard, and I couldn't be prouder."

"And our honeymoon," Melissa added, her eyes sparkling at the memory. "The Maldives were pure paradise. Just the two of us, no interruptions. It felt like we could finally breathe again after everything."

Michael laced his fingers through hers, squeezing gently as they shared a quiet, intimate look.

Then, with a slow inhale, he turned to their families, his grip on Melissa's hand tightening slightly. "Actually," he said, his voice steady but carrying an undercurrent of emotion, "there's something else we want to share."

All eyes turned to them, expectant.

Melissa bit her lip, her heartbeat picking up as she watched Michael's expression soften.

"We're having a baby," he announced, his voice rich with love and excitement.

A stunned silence filled the room for a heartbeat before it erupted into cheers and joyful exclamations. Melissa was immediately enveloped in warm embraces, her mother's teary eyes shining with happiness, Michael's parents beaming with pride.

Michael pulled her close, pressing a kiss to her temple. "I can't wait to meet our little one," he whispered, and as Melissa looked into his eyes, she knew with absolute certainty—this was everything she had ever dreamed of.

Life had certainly taken them on an unexpected journey, but looking around at the people they cherished, they couldn't help but marvel at how everything had fallen into place. Old wounds had healed, new joys had arrived, and they were exactly where they needed to be.

Surrounded by the people they loved; Michael and Melissa felt an overwhelming sense of peace. It was a reminder that everything—every twist, every turn—had led them here, to this perfect moment in time.

The End

The Blood Debt

Alison Reid

A complete standalone romance

Previously published individually

Chapter One

Catherine Grant hated fluorescent lighting.

It buzzed faintly above the boardroom table, flickering against the polished glass like a nervous tic—an unwelcome echo of the tension simmering beneath the afternoon's meeting. At twenty-nine, she was far too young to feel this bone-deep weariness, yet responsibility carved lines into a person long before age ever could. She straightened her notes, lifted her chin, and fixed her calm CEO smile into place.

The expression was practiced—warm enough to reassure, firm enough to command—but beneath it lived a woman almost no one in this room truly understood.

Tall, poised, and strikingly beautiful, Catherine carried her mother's delicate bone structure, her father's sharp jawline, and a cool elegance that made people assume she'd been born to lead. Beauty had never been a gift in her world—not in the charity sector, where sincerity was often mistaken for weakness, and certainly not under a father who prized appearances over people.

Her caramel-brown hair was pulled into a neat twist at the base of her neck, though rebellious wisps always escaped to frame her face. Her eyes—green flecked with gold—missed nothing. They rarely softened. They rarely let anyone in.

Guarded. Always guarded.

Two years ago, when her mother died and the charity nearly collapsed under grief, mismanagement, and board infighting, Catherine had rebuilt it from ruins. She had taken Evelyn Grant's dream—the charity that housed thousands of vulnerable children—and breathed life back into it with sheer will, sleepless nights, and ruthless determination no one expected from the "grieving daughter."

She did not have the luxury of breaking. She barely had the luxury of breathing.

And now, with the orphanage project finally nearing completion, she could feel everything she'd fought for balancing on a knife's edge.

Pressing her palms lightly against the table, she centred herself, letting the familiar sense of purpose rise. Smart. Principled. Stubbornly independent. These weren't qualities people praised—they were qualities she had been forced to become.

"Thank you all for being here," she said, projecting calm authority even as the flickering light above continued its irritating hum.

This was her world. Her mother's legacy. And Catherine Grant would fight for it—no matter how many shadows gathered around her.

"As you know, today we review the final proposal for the new orphanage site."

A ripple of murmurs moved around the long table. Chairs shifted. Pens clicked. Excitement. Curiosity.

She slid the presentation forward on the screen. "The land purchase will go through next month, pending the final audit of our capital expenditure accounts."

As she spoke, Catherine's eyes swept across the boardroom, noting the familiar faces and subtle nuances that always escaped casual observation. She glanced first at Lisa Grant, seated near the far end of the table. Half-sister from another mother, thirty-four, brilliant, and sharp as a tack. Catherine had loved her from the start, even when Lisa's quiet intensity sometimes felt like a wall between them. Always secretive, always calculating—but capable. Catherine trusted her, knowing her sister would catch any error before it could become a problem.

Then there was Gary Harris, leaning forward slightly, pen in hand, a faint smile tugging at the corner of his lips. Forty, caring, attentive, with a gentle, almost nerdy charm, utterly persistent without ever being intrusive. He wanted her, quietly, patiently, as if he understood she still carried shadows she wasn't ready to share.

Catherine adjusted the clicker in her hand and moved to the next slide. Her calm CEO mask never faltered, but inside, she catalogued the room: allies, confidants, observers, and the occasional unpredictable element she had learned to anticipate in a boardroom filled with ambition and ego.

She tapped the remote. "Construction bids have been reviewed, and we've shortlisted three firms for the project," she said, her voice steady. "Each meets our sustainability requirements, and all have proven track records with children's facilities. I'll be requesting final proposals by the end of the month."

A few murmurs rippled through the board. Catherine's gaze lingered on Lisa, whose expression was composed, unreadable, yet grounding. Seeing her sister's meticulous eye on every figure and forecast reminded her she had someone she could rely on completely.

Across the table, Gary scribbled notes, glancing up with a soft, knowing look that always seemed to steady her. He wasn't pushy. He didn't interrupt. He simply offered quiet reassurance—and perhaps, in his way, protection.

She cleared her throat. "We need to finalise the capital audit before the board can approve the purchase, so I expect all documentation to be submitted by next week. Any questions?"

A hand went up—Gary, of course. "Catherine, with the final audit, do you anticipate any issues with the projected budget? We want to avoid last-minute delays."

She nodded, meeting his gaze. Calm. Confident. "The figures have been double-checked, and there shouldn't be any surprises. However, we'll remain vigilant. Every penny is accounted for, and every contingency planned. That's how we protect this project—and the children it will serve."

She felt a subtle shift in the room as the board absorbed her words. Authority. Precision. Purpose. They respected it, even those who sometimes doubted. And Catherine felt a small surge of reassurance—she wasn't alone. She had allies she could trust.

Her mind drifted briefly back to the Charity Gala last Saturday. The orchestra had swelled as she excused herself to the ladies' room, and when she returned, the polished grand staircase had beckoned, its sweeping arc bathed in soft golden light—a perfect vantage over the glittering ballroom below.

Catherine had placed one hand on the railing and begun her descent, heels clicking softly, gown brushing her legs like a whisper. The chandeliers scattered tiny constellations across the crowd beneath her. For a fleeting moment, she had felt at peace—balanced, elegant, untouchable.

Then it had happened—a firm, unmistakable pressure pressing into her shoulder blades. A push.

Her heart had lurched. Adrenaline flared, but she had twisted instinctively, clutching the banister. Her body pitched forward—but didn't fall. A sharp, stuttering gasp tore from her chest as she steadied herself, fingers trembling against the cool marble.

She had spun around. Empty. The stairs gleamed in perfect, polished silence. No retreating footsteps. Only music, laughter, and that stretch of steps that suddenly felt threatening.

She had forced herself to breathe and continued downward, heels clicking with cautious confidence. Once on the ballroom floor, she'd sought out Gary and told him what happened. His concerned gaze and steady presence had made her feel safe.

Back at the boardroom table, Catherine let a small, reassuring smile touch her lips. Lisa—precise, brilliant, unwavering—handled the numbers with a care Catherine trusted implicitly. Gary, attentive and steady, added insight and quiet support. With both of them in her corner, she could lead without hesitation.

Her palms rested lightly on the polished glass. She wasn't alone. She was supported. That truth gave her strength—to lead, to protect her mother's legacy, to see the orphanage project through.

"Once the proposals are in, we'll review them and vote on the final construction company for the new orphanage."

A ripple moved through the room—murmurs, shifting chairs, pens clicking. Catherine's gaze softened at Lisa's composed smile and Gary's steady, encouraging one. Their presence mattered. More than she ever let herself admit.

She lifted her chin and addressed the board. "Before we open the floor, I want to emphasise that our priority is creating a safe, nurturing space for the children. Every detail matters—playground layout, classroom design, accessibility for children with special needs."

Hands rose. Questions came fast, focused. Catherine answered each with calm precision, her tone steady and authoritative. She caught Lisa quietly taking notes, nodding at key points. Gary leaned forward, offering gentle clarifying questions and thoughtful suggestions.

With them beside her, a quiet confidence settled over Catherine. Here, she was in command. Here, she was safe. Here, she had allies she trusted—and that made all the difference.

When the meeting finally adjourned, board members gathered their papers, talking among themselves as they filed out. Catherine exhaled a breath she hadn't realised she'd been holding. The tension eased slightly as the hum of fluorescent lights gave way to the softer sounds of the office outside.

"Catherine," a voice called from the far end of the table.

She looked up to see Lisa leaning casually against the polished surface, a slight, knowing smile on her lips.

"Lisa," Catherine said with a returning smile. Warm—but not unwary. Lisa's expression was gentle, but her eyes—green with flecks of amber—were sharp, intelligent, missing nothing. She carried herself with quiet elegance, auburn hair in loose waves, her style understated and flawless. There was an effortless precision in everything she did, one Catherine had envied as a child.

"I was wondering," Lisa said, tilting her head in that practiced, elegant way, "will you be over for dinner tonight? Father has a new chef—French–Asian fusion. He's eager for you to try it."

Catherine's smile tightened. The Grant estate had always felt more like a museum than a home—polished, curated, and cold. And her relationship with Charles… complicated didn't begin to cover it. She loved her father, of course she did, but he'd spent most of her life trying to script it for her. Appearances over connection—that was the Grant legacy.

After what happened with Ryan, she'd finally reached her breaking point and walked away. She hadn't seen her father much since. He'd made attempts to reconcile, and she appreciated that… but she wasn't ready. Not yet. And certainly not enough to step back into that house tonight.

"I'll have to pass," she said, keeping her tone polite but unmovable. "I've got work to catch up on."

Lisa's smile flickered—just for a heartbeat. A flash of something sharp crossed her face, there and gone so quickly Catherine almost doubted she'd seen it at all. Anger? Resentment? No… maybe she imagined it.

"Of course," Lisa said lightly, the smooth social veneer slipping neatly back into place. "I'll save you a place another time."

Catherine nodded, relieved. Amid board meetings, projects, and endless responsibilities, it grounded her to know she had someone she could rely on. Lisa was precise, controlling, quietly formidable—but she was family.

Lisa gathered her notes with smooth, economical movements and gave Catherine a brief nod before slipping out of the room. Catherine watched her go, a subtle exhale leaving her lungs. She loved her sister, but stepping out of the boardroom felt like escaping a weight she hadn't realised she was carrying.

Straightening her blazer, she collected her own papers and headed toward her office. The corridor was quiet, afternoon sunlight slanting through tall windows and casting long rectangles of gold across the polished floor. She moved with purpose, heels clicking softly, the weight of responsibility still there—but the strain of the meeting easing with each step.

As she reached her office door and unlocked it, she heard a soft clearing of a throat behind her.

"Catherine?"

She turned to see Gary Harris leaning casually against the doorframe. At forty, he carried a quiet, self-assured charm: dark hair touched with early silver at the temples, tailored navy suit, glasses that lent him an intellectual edge. His brown eyes held a warmth that often made her pulse beat faster, a gentle intensity that suggested he cared—not just about the charity, but about her. Catherine, however, had learned long ago to keep her heart closed since Ryan…

"I didn't mean to interrupt," he said quickly, straightening. "I just wanted to check in. How are you? Any other mishaps since Saturday?"

Catherine allowed herself a small, polite smile. "No," she said. "Everything's fine. I…maybe overreacted a bit with the stair incident at the gala." Her voice was calm, almost casual, but she could feel the faint echo of unease that still lingered.

Gary stepped fully into the office, closing the door gently behind him. "Well, you handled today's meeting beautifully," he said, his tone warm, encouraging. "I just…wanted to make sure you're taking care of yourself, too."

Catherine gave a brief nod. "I appreciate it, Gary. Truly. But I'm fine." She returned to her desk, placing her papers down carefully, keeping her focus on the work in front of her. She didn't need distraction—she didn't need the softness in his gaze, the gentle concern he offered, even if part of her felt a flicker of something she hadn't felt in two years.

Gary lingered a moment, watching her organise her documents, before stepping back. "Alright," he said with a small, respectful smile. "I'll let you get to it. But call me if anything comes up…or even if you just need someone to talk to."

Catherine nodded again, a faint trace of gratitude softening her expression, then returned to her work. The office fell quiet once more, yet the echo of Gary's concern lingered—gentle, sincere, and unrequited—a quiet reminder that some hearts were still open while hers remained firmly closed.

She guarded her feelings carefully, keeping her heartache private, but in the solitude of her thoughts, it always returned to Ryan and the life that might have been.

Chapter Two

Catherine left her office, heading down to the underground carpark. Her sleek, dark blue BMW convertible gleamed under the harsh fluorescent lights as she slid into the driver's seat. The city of Sydney stretched out before her in a blur of neon and twilight, the familiar hum of the engine beneath her hands doing little to soothe the tension coiling in her shoulders. She had left the office later than usual, despite the lengthy board meeting.

Traffic was heavier than usual for a Monday evening, cars inching forward like a line of ants in the fading light. Catherine eased the accelerator, eyes flicking to the mirrors and then back to the road. Everything felt ordinary. Routine. Safe.

Until it wasn't.

A faint grinding resistance under her right foot made her frown. She pressed the brake pedal again. Nothing. Just the same eerie resistance, as if the car had decided to ignore her entirely.

Her stomach lurched. Panic flared, sharp and visceral. Heart hammering, she pressed harder. Brake lights flickered on behind her, a sea of impatient headlights closing in.

"No, no, no," she muttered, panic sharpening her instincts.

The road sloped downhill, a ribbon of asphalt she had driven countless times. But the slope, the traffic, the speed—they were suddenly a perfect storm. Catherine's mind went into overdrive. Think. Don't panic. Hands tightening on the wheel, she shifted into a lower gear, pumping the brakes in frantic bursts. Still nothing.

A horn blared. Another car swerved. A cyclist yelped. Her pulse thundered in her ears.

Instinct and adrenaline took over. She swerved to the shoulder, tires screeching, narrowly avoiding a parked car. A sharp corner loomed ahead, and she jerked the wheel, barely keeping the car on the road, concrete barrier scraping inches from her side.

Finally, a patch of sand near the curb allowed her to bring the car to a shuddering, jerking stop. Steam hissed from the hood. Catherine's hands shook violently, leaving streaks of sweat on the steering wheel.

She sat there for a long moment, head bowed against the wheel, taking ragged breaths. Outside, the world went on: taillights flashing, distant sirens wailing, pedestrians oblivious to the near-death she had just skirted.

Her legs trembled as she opened the door. The city air was impossibly cold against her heated skin. By the time the tow truck arrived, Catherine had calmed enough to mechanically go through the motions—handing over keys, directing the driver, climbing into an Uber. The ride home was a blur of city lights and the quiet murmur of the driver's radio, every stoplight a potential threat, her fingers twitching against the seat belt.

Dusk had fallen by the time she stepped from the sleek car into the marble lobby of her penthouse building. Heels clicked softly and deliberately as she made her way past the concierge, who nodded politely. Catherine offered a faint, distracted smile, barely registering the usual scent of fresh flowers or the hum of the building's security systems.

The private elevator doors slid open with a whisper of luxury. For her, though, it felt more like a gilded cage. She pressed the top-floor button, leaning against the mirrored wall as the doors closed. The hum enveloped her, and for the first time that day, her carefully maintained mask faltered. Exhaustion stole her expression, leaving only a hint of the vulnerable woman she hid from the world.

When the doors opened, Catherine stepped into her penthouse: polished glass and steel, pale oak floors, soft cream rugs, and minimalist furniture arranged for calm and clarity. Floor-to-ceiling windows framed the harbour, the bridge glowing across the dark water—a city alive and indifferent. Everything here was curated for peace, for control. Her sanctuary.

She slipped off her heels, setting her bag and coat neatly on the marble counter. Her fingers trailed along the cool steel of the kitchen island—smooth, immaculate, almost sterile. Just the way she liked it. Cooking, even the simplest meal, grounded her. It reminded her she was alive, capable, still in control despite the exhaustion, despite the danger now threading through her days.

She headed to the bathroom, letting steaming hot water pound across her shoulders, loosening muscles wound too tight. For a few minutes, she let the warmth swallow her, letting herself feel—truly feel—how drained she was.

Wrapped in a plush towel, hair damp against her skin, she dried slowly. Back in the kitchen, she poured a glass of chilled water. A faint scent of olive oil and fresh herbs lingered from earlier cooking, blending with eucalyptus drifting from her diffuser. Comforting. Clean. Controlled.

She wandered through the penthouse, letting her gaze sweep over the clean lines, gleaming surfaces, quietly ordered rooms. Outside, the city pulsed—messy, loud, unpredictable. Inside, everything obeyed her. Every curated object, every polished surface, every glittering light beyond the glass belonged to her. Bought with her mother's inheritance, nurtured with care—just like the charity.

Finally, Catherine settled onto the sofa, shoulders slumping just slightly. She pulled a soft throw around herself, inhaling the warm mix of eucalyptus and vanilla. This was what she protected: her work, the children, her mother's legacy. All of it required focus.

Determination. Calm. And she would give it—no matter what shadows pressed against the edges of her carefully held control.

With quiet precision, she made herself a simple dinner: a lightly dressed salad, a few slices of smoked salmon, another glass of cold water. She ate at the counter, slowly, deliberately. Ritual. Grounding. A moment to reclaim herself after a day that had taken too much.

When she finished, she washed the dishes immediately, drying each one and returning it to its proper place. The kitchen gleamed once more. Restored. Order reasserted. And with it, a fragile steadiness.

She retreated to her bedroom, closing the door softly behind her—the gentle click marking the shift from duty to solitude. The space was serene, uncluttered, everything exactly where it belonged.

Catherine crossed to her bedside table and opened the top drawer. Her fingers brushed the smooth wood before closing around a small, framed photograph. She lifted it carefully, holding it as though it were made of something fragile and irreplaceable.

Because it was.

In the photograph, Ryan was lifting her off the ground, ready to spin her around, his expression full of love and joy. She looked down at him with admiration, her arms loosely around his shoulders, the connection between them undeniable. Even in the stillness of the photo, the moment was alive: laughter caught mid-breath, hearts aligned in a memory that time could never dim.

A single tear slid down her cheek. Catherine blinked it away quickly, though she allowed herself a long, steady inhale, letting the warmth of the memory fill her chest. Ryan. He had been everything—love, trust, a heartbeat that had matched hers. And though she had buried that part of herself for too long, it surfaced now, quiet, and unrelenting.

He had started working for her father as a chauffeur just before her mother's accident. Assigned to Catherine and Lisa, he drove them wherever they wanted, always with a quiet attentiveness that made him instantly likeable. Ryan was tall, broad-shouldered but not imposing, with sun-kissed skin and hair the colour of dark chestnut that caught the light when he laughed. His eyes—warm brown, always alert, with a spark of mischief—had a way of seeing her in a way no one else ever had.

At first, Catherine had simply enjoyed his company, seeking him out when she could just to talk. Laughter became a balm, a respite from the grief and weight of expectations. Slowly, those conversations blossomed into something more. When her mother passed, Ryan was the one who helped her breathe again, who reminded her that joy could exist even amid sorrow.

For months, they were just friends, talking and laughing late into the evenings. Until that night—one that would change everything. Ryan had driven her home to the Grant estate, the sky above a tapestry of stars. As he opened the car door for her, she stepped out, and he smiled, saying softly, "You're so beautiful."

Catherine had flushed and thanked him, trying to steady her racing heart. Then, hesitantly, he asked, "Can I tell you something?"

She nodded.

"I love you," he said, his voice low, steady, each word carrying the weight of a promise.

Catherine's chest fluttered with surprise, though a rush of joy surged through her. She had known for weeks that she loved him, but hearing the words aloud still made her heart leap.

When their lips met, it was gentle at first—soft, tender, a warm brush of certainty—but it deepened instantly. That first kiss was more than a kiss; it was a beginning, a vow, a quiet promise of everything to come. That night marked the start of something unshakable, something that would endure no matter what lay ahead.

From that moment, they were inseparable. Lisa had tried, at times, to monopolise his time, but Catherine and Ryan always found each other, stealing quiet moments wherever they could. That was when Catherine had purchased the penthouse— somewhere they could be together alone, free from watchful eyes. There, their love grew even stronger. Nights spent together were magical: laughter, whispered confessions, tender touches, and intimacy that left her feeling cherished and safe in ways she hadn't known she could.

But the shadow of her father loomed. One night, just after she returned to the Grant estate for bed, he cornered her. Catherine's chest tightened as she remembered his words: Ryan had asked permission to propose, and Charles had been furious. *"No daughter of mine will marry a chauffeur,"* he had said, leaving anger, disappointment, and control hanging in the room like a heavy curtain.

The next day, Ryan was gone. A car accident, the official report said—but Catherine had her doubts. She had always felt the hollow ache of injustice, the bitter absence of the man who had been her world.

She set the photograph back in the drawer with care, then reached for the letter he had written to her the day after their first night together.

Cat,

Last night was the best night of my life. Knowing that you love me as much as I love you has made me the happiest man alive.

I can still feel you—your skin, your breath, the way you whispered my name like it meant something holy. I never believed in forever until you looked at me that way. You have made my life full. You have been the only part of my world that ever felt real.

You saw me when no one else did. You made me believe I could be more than what I was.

I know you want me to quit, and I will. But I need something solid to stand on first— another job, another purpose. I know you would give me everything, but I need to know I have earned the life we will build together.

I will always love you. You deserve light, Cat. You always will.

Ryan

She placed the note alongside the photograph and closed the drawer with deliberate care. Then she climbed into bed, pulling the soft covers around her. The penthouse remained calm and orderly, the city lights twinkling through the windows, indifferent to her grief and longing. Yet, in this small, private space, Catherine allowed herself to feel—just for a moment—the love she had lost and the ache it still left behind.

She had left her father's estate immediately after Ryan's funeral, which she had arranged and paid for herself, since he had no surviving parents and his brother, Al, was uncontactable.

Everyone assumed her life had come from her father. They were wrong. Her wealth came from her mother, Evelyn Grant—the true heiress—whose grace, intelligence, and compassion had shaped Catherine into the woman she had become. Her father had tried to control her, to dictate the trajectory of her life. When her mother died, the fortune passed to Catherine. The quiet anger at that injustice still throbbed beneath her calm exterior, a tension she masked behind polite smiles and executive decisiveness.

Yet here, in the quiet of her sanctuary, she could acknowledge it fully. The penthouse was hers. Every polished surface, every curated piece of furniture, every glittering view of the city below—hers. She had earned it. She had nurtured it with care and attention, much as she had done with her mother's charity.

Catherine finally settled into bed, letting the calm of her home—and the simple act of breathing in the scent of eucalyptus and vanilla—remind her of what she was protecting. Work, the charity, the children, her mother's legacy—it all demanded focus. And she would give it willingly, even as shadows and unease lingered just beyond the edges of her carefully controlled life.

Chapter Three

Morning arrived softly, a pale wash of gold slipping between the penthouse curtains. Catherine dressed with her usual precision—a fitted navy pencil dress that hugged her waist and fell just below her knees, hair smoothed into a low twist at the nape of her neck, and makeup minimal but immaculate, accentuating the sharp planes of her face without drawing attention away from her green-gold eyes. She moved through her apartment like someone stirring from a dream she couldn't fully shake, each step deliberate, measured. The drawer she had closed the night before—the photograph of Ryan, the note he had written—hovered at the edge of her thoughts like a quiet, insistent echo, a weight of memory and longing she could neither ignore nor fully confront.

Downstairs, she ordered an Uber rather than calling her usual town car. The crisp morning air wrapped around her as she stepped outside, the city already humming with life. She passed pedestrians hurrying to work, cyclists weaving through traffic, early buses rolling past, their exhaust fumes sharp against the cool air. Sliding into the car, she allowed herself the small comfort of anonymity—no chauffeur scrutinising her reflection, no one noticing the faint tightness around her eyes or the slight tremor in her fingers as she adjusted her bag.

Traffic crawled, a slow, deliberate rhythm of red brake lights and impatient horns, but she barely noticed. Her gaze drifted over the skyline—glass towers catching the morning sun, sparkling with sharp brilliance; the harbour beyond, calm yet alive, catching the light in scattered ripples like tiny jewels. Catherine forced herself to inhale slowly, to exhale deliberately, letting the ritual of breath tether her to control. Today demanded clarity. Focus. Calm.

At the tower where she worked, she thanked the driver, straightened her shoulders, and stepped into the familiar lobby. The smell of roasted coffee and polished marble greeted her like a small, steady comfort. By eight-thirty, she was in her corner office, the city of Sydney stretched below like a glittering map. She immersed herself in emails, board reports, and schedules, letting structure steady her mind against the ghost of unease tugging at her chest.

Midmorning, she reached for her mug just as her phone rang.

Unknown number. Local.

"Catherine Grant speaking."

A man's voice answered, friendly but edged with something taut. "Morning, Ms. Grant. It's Donnie—from Precision Motors? You had your BMW towed in last night."

"Yes. Thank you for calling," Catherine said, sitting a little straighter. "Is everything okay?"

There was a pause. Paper rustled on the other end. "Well… that's what I'm ringing about. I've had a look underneath and—look, I don't want to alarm you, but it appears someone tampered with your brake lines."

The words didn't land at first. They hung in the air like smoke.

"I'm sorry," she said carefully. "No—that can't be."

"I figured you might say that," he replied. "And to be fair, I can't completely rule out wear and tear. It's always a possibility. But I'll be honest with you—I wouldn't expect it in a car as new as yours. Six months old? Those parts should be pristine."

Her heartbeat thudded once, hard.

She forced her voice to stay level. "You're certain?"

"I wouldn't ring you if I wasn't concerned," he said. "The line didn't fail on its own. It looks like it was deliberately weakened."

Deliberately.

The office suddenly felt too still, too bright. The quiet hum of the floor outside—the tapping keyboards, the distant printer—seemed to fade into nothing.

"I… see," she murmured. A breath escaped her, shaky despite her efforts. "What happens next?"

"I can repair it, no issue," Donnie said gently. "But I thought you should know. This wasn't normal."

"Thank you," Catherine managed. "Please keep me updated."

She hung up before her control could slip.

Her hand remained on the phone a moment longer, fingers tense against the cool glass. Someone had tampered with her brakes. Someone had wanted her to crash—or at the very least, not walk away cleanly.

For a heartbeat, Ryan's grave flashed through her mind—then her mother's. Two markers carved into the earth, two losses that still shaped the contours of her life. And beside them, in the quiet corner of her memory, an empty space she had never dared to acknowledge. A space that felt like a warning. A threat unspoken, unnamed.

Catherine inhaled, sharp and steady, and straightened the stack of documents in front of her.

Control. Calm. Focus.

But deep in her chest, unease curled and settled—not at the fringes of her thoughts this time, but right in the centre, heavy and insistent. She forced her gaze back to her screen, trying to fold herself into work, to bury the mechanic's words beneath emails, budgets, and schedules. She pushed the fear back—far back—where it couldn't interfere.

She had just begun reviewing a proposal when a knock sounded at her door.

"Enter," she said, crisp, professional.

The door swung open, and Gary stepped inside. His brows lifted, surprise flickering across his features.

"Oh—you are in," he said, voice warm with genuine concern. "Your car wasn't downstairs, so I thought maybe you were working from home today."

His presence softened the edges of her anxiety, a subtle warmth threading through his usually composed features. "Just wanted to check on you. And..." He hesitated, smoothing a hand down his tie, his gaze briefly locking with hers. "I was hoping you might let me take you out to dinner tonight."

Catherine blinked. The shift from fear and workplace tension to casual invitation was jarring. Dinner. Tonight. Gary—the dependable, polite, steady presence—was here, and for a fleeting moment, she allowed herself a small flutter of relief. She drew a slow, measured breath, shoulders squared, preparing to respond.

"I don't think—"

"Just as friends, Cat," he interjected gently, cutting her off with a small, reassuring smile. "I know you're not ready to... date seriously yet."

Relief softened the tension coiling in her chest. He understood without pressing, without asking more than she could give. She returned his smile, a quiet warmth spreading across her face. "In that case... yes. I'd love to."

Gary's expression brightened immediately, boyish enthusiasm flickering through his usually composed exterior. "Great. I'll pick you up at seven."

He gave her a nod before leaving, the door clicking softly behind him. Catherine exhaled slowly, letting her heartbeat settle even as the unease lingered like a shadow she could not shake.

At seven sharp, Catherine stood before the full-length mirror in her bedroom, adjusting the fall of her blouse. She'd chosen a soft, ivory silk wrap top that complimented her skin tone and paired it with tailored charcoal trousers that elongated her frame. A simple gold necklace—her mother's—rested at her collarbone, and she'd swept her hair into a low, loose twist that framed her face with effortless sophistication. Understated, polished, safe.

The intercom phone buzzed. She drew in a breath before lifting the receiver.

"Miss Grant," the concierge said, "Gary Harris is in the lobby for you."

"Thank you," Catherine replied. "I'll be right down."

She slipped into her heels, grabbed her clutch, and rode the elevator to the ground floor. As the doors parted, she spotted Gary instantly—tall, well-groomed, shifting his weight with a nervous energy he tried to hide.

The moment he saw her, his face lit up. "You look beautiful," he said, admiration softening his usually composed tone.

"Thank you," she replied, offering a small, appreciative smile.

Gary stepped forward, placing a light hand at her back as he guided her toward the waiting limousine outside. The city evening air brushed cool against her skin as the driver opened the door for them.

The ride was smooth, quiet, the city lights drifting by like scattered stars. When they arrived, the restaurant's warm glow spilled across the pavement—elegant, intimate without being romantic, exactly the kind of place Gary would choose to avoid pressuring her.

Inside, a host greeted them promptly and led them through the softly lit dining room. Crystal glasses gleamed, candles flickered, and the low hum of conversation created a comfortable undercurrent.

They were shown to a table near the window, the skyline sprawling beyond the glass like a jewelled tapestry. Catherine settled into her seat, smoothing a hand over her napkin as Gary took the one across from her.

Dinner unfolded with a surprising ease Catherine hadn't expected. The restaurant's low lighting and soft jazz made conversation feel effortless. Gary kept things light—stories from his week at the office, a funny mishap with a supplier, a disastrous attempt at baking that had ended with his smoke alarm shrieking at him. Catherine found herself laughing more than she had in days, the tightness in her chest loosening gradually with each story.

Their meals arrived—pan-seared fish for her, a rib-eye for him—and they ate in a comfortable rhythm, exchanging thoughts on the orphanage project, board politics, and even a few fond memories from university. It felt… casual. Safe. The kind of evening she could almost imagine having before her world had tilted sideways.

But midway through her tea, a thought flickered, unwanted but insistent. Catherine hesitated, tracing the rim of her cup with one finger.

"Gary," she said quietly, "something happened last night… with my car."

He looked up immediately, all warmth sharpening into focus. "What do you mean?"

"The mechanic called," she said. "He said my brake lines were… tampered with." The word felt heavy, wrong in her mouth. "He said it might be wear and tear, but the car is only six months old."

Gary froze. The casual ease from moments earlier drained from his expression. "Catherine," he said, his voice low and grave. "This is twice you've been almost seriously injured."

She swallowed. "He didn't confirm it. It could still be—"

"No." Gary leaned forward, elbows braced on the table, eyes locked on hers. "First the stairs. Now your brakes? You don't think that's random, do you?"

She tried to hold his tense gaze, trying to summon the calm she'd clung to all day, but her breath wavered.

"I don't know what to think," she admitted.

Gary exhaled slowly, visibly struggling to maintain composure. "Well, I do. And I don't like any of the possibilities."

For a long moment, silence settled between them, the hum of the restaurant fading into the background. Catherine stared down at her tea, hands trembling slightly as she gripped the cup.

She forced a small, measured smile. "I'm sure it's nothing, Gary. Maybe a freak accident… or a mistake at the mechanics. I tend to worry too much."

Gary didn't let up. He leaned back slightly, but his eyes remained fixed on her, sharp, insistent. "Cat, this isn't something to shrug off. Two incidents in the span of a week? That's not bad luck."

She gave a soft laugh, more nervous than genuine. "I handle things, Gary. I've managed the charity through far worse than a minor car problem—or a clumsy stumble on stairs. Really—I'll be fine."

"You don't understand," he said, voice low but firm, cutting through her deflection. "This isn't about fine. This is about you. You were nearly killed—twice. That's not fine." His hand hovered over the table for a fraction of a second, a subtle, grounding presence. "You need protection. Someone you can trust—someone who can make sure nothing happens when you're alone."

Catherine's throat tightened. She didn't want to admit how shaken she truly was. "I... I can be careful," she said, deliberately light, an attempt to reclaim control. "I've been careful my whole life."

Gary shook his head, frustration and concern flickering across his face. "Being careful isn't enough anymore. You can't control other people's intentions. You can't control accidents, sabotage... or worse. Not alone."

Her hands clenched around the cup. She wanted to argue, to insist she could manage it herself—but something in his intensity, in the quiet force of his gaze, made her pause. It was worry, pure and unvarnished. For her.

"I don't like the idea of being followed," she said softly.

"Cat," he replied, voice gentle but insistent, "your mother died in an accident. I can't let that happen to you."

Catherine's thoughts drifted to her mother—back to that morning, the day after she had overheard her parents arguing. She had heard Evelyn considering leaving him. And then there was Ryan, taken from her the day after he had asked for her hand in marriage. Surely, she told herself, it was all just a string of unfortunate coincidences.

Still, the weight of Gary's words pressed against the careful composure she had maintained all day. Finally, she exhaled, small and reluctant. "Maybe... maybe I should consider it."

Gary's expression softened immediately. Relief flickered in his eyes, tempered with lingering concern. "Good. I'll find the best person for the job. You shouldn't face this alone, Cat. Not ever."

She nodded, letting the words settle, the weight of reality pressing against her like a tide against the shore, relentless yet inevitable.

For the first time since the mechanic's call, she allowed herself to admit it: maybe she didn't have to be alone.

Chapter Four

Alec Cole didn't do mornings.

Not the kind with sunlight spilling over rooftops or birds chirping as if they owned the day. Not when he had spent years moving through a world where silence was survival—and every second could mean death. Morning should have been quiet, still, predictable.

Yet this one already carried a weight that pressed against his chest like a fist, heavy and unyielding.

At thirty-four, Alec Cole had lived several lifetimes already. Ex–Special Forces. Security contractor. Millionaire by thirty through a combination of grit, discipline, and an instinct for danger that refused to dull. He didn't flaunt any of it. The tailored suits, the top-floor office, the global contracts—those were tools, not trophies. He had earned every scar, every sleepless night, every hard-won instinct. Wealth was merely a side effect.

He was ruggedly handsome in a way that demanded no effort—black hair falling just slightly forward, a perpetual five-o'clock shadow darkening a jaw that could cut steel, eyes so deep and dark they almost seemed black. Eyes that had seen too much. Eyes that rarely softened. Women noticed. Men tended not to cross him. Alec cared for neither.

He dated casually, flitting from one fleeting connection to another, never allowing anyone close enough to see the parts of him that could be broken. Commitment was a word that had lost meaning for him long ago; trust was a currency he did not spend lightly. He had seen too many wives betray their vows, too many men and women crumble under the weight of temptation. The institution of marriage, in his experience, was a gilded cage built on fragile illusions. It would turn any man with eyes wide open off its constitution.

And so, Alec remained his own master, disciplined, and detached, letting desire pass through him like a current he neither captured nor pursued. He had no interest in a permanent tie, no patience for softness, and no illusions about hearts that could shatter. The first thing he noticed this morning was the scent lingering in his office: a faint tang of gun oil, sharp and metallic, woven through the subtle warmth of expensive cologne worn by his staff. It curled through the air like a thread connecting him to all the years he had survived, familiar enough to settle the constant noise in his head, unsettling enough to remind him of everything he couldn't forget.

He inhaled slowly, letting the smell anchor him—a reminder that he was awake, alive, still breathing, still capable of action. Some mornings, that was enough.

Cole Security's top-floor headquarters stretched around him—sleek, glass-lined, and modern, a fortress built on strategy, precision, and ruthless efficiency. Everything was minimalist by design, from the gunmetal-grey furniture to the clean lines of surveillance screens humming quietly in the corner. The faint scent of leather and metal lingered in the air, an olfactory signature of the company he had built with blood, sweat, and an unrelenting refusal to quit.

Alec ran a hand over the polished surface of his desk, feeling the subtle scuff marks left by years of tense palms gripping, then releasing. Control. Discipline. The only constants that had ever kept him alive—far more reliable than people, promises, or luck.

As he slid his sidearm into its concealed holster, his phone buzzed sharply against the polished surface of his desk. Alec picked it up, expecting a routine update or a scheduling note.

"Yes, Leah?" His voice was clipped, controlled.

Leah's voice came through the receiver, crisp and professional, carrying that familiar edge of curiosity he had learned to anticipate. "Another high-profile request just came through. I thought you'd want to see this one personally."

Alec's eyes narrowed. "Go on."

There was a brief pause on the line as she accessed the file on her end. "It's… Catherine Grant."

The name hit him like a physical weight, pressing against his chest with an almost tangible force. His body stiffened, muscles locking with a precision he no longer consciously controlled. For a heartbeat—just a fraction—time seemed to slow, the office fading into stillness around him.

"You interested, boss?" Leah asked, her tone light but probing.

"Yes," Alec said firmly, voice low and deliberate. "I'm interested." He hung up before another word could pass between them.

Catherine. Grant. Two names he had never expected to see together, now staring back at him from a file addressed to him. Alec froze, chest tightening as though the very air had thickened. Cole Security didn't take personal assignments lightly—and Alec didn't take assignments at all unless he wanted to. But this… this could be the opportunity he had imagined, replayed, and obsessed over for two long years.

A sharp knock at the office door pulled him back from the edge of his thoughts, reverberating through the quiet space with deliberate precision.

"Enter."

Leah Williams, his office manager, stepped inside, closing the door behind her. "Gary Harris is outside. He wants to discuss the assignment I just sent you."

Cole's mind raced. "Is he the one asking for her protection?"

"Yes," Leah said. "She doesn't want it, apparently, but he's insisting."

Alec's jaw tightened. "Send him in."

Leah inclined her head and opened the office door. "Mr. Harris, Mr. Cole will see you now."

Alec's fingers tapped a precise rhythm against the edge of his desk, each beat measured, controlled. He didn't look at the man yet. He studied his own hands, the slight tremor that only came when he was already calculating, already preparing.

The man who entered was polished to the point of arrogance—blonde, impeccably dressed, carrying the kind of confidence only money could buy. Cole rose, extended a firm handshake, and held his gaze as Leah quietly closed the door behind her.

"Please, have a seat, Mr. Harris. What can I do for you?" Alec's voice was calm but sharp, steel wrapped in velvet.

Gary eased into the chair, though the tension in his hands betrayed the smooth confidence of his posture. "A friend of mine... Catherine Grant... I believe she needs protection."

Alec's brow lifted. "And what makes you think that?"

"There have been... incidents," Gary said carefully, choosing each word as though it might explode. "Catherine insists they're nothing, but I'm not convinced. Two separate events, both too precise to ignore. I believe someone is trying to hurt her."

Alec leaned back in his chair, folding his arms across his chest. Every instinct sharpened, but so did his irritation. Privileged. Polished. Used to control. And likely oblivious to the dangers outside his insulated world.

"And why," Alec asked, voice deceptively mild, "are you so invested in her safety?"

Gary's eyes flicked to his with a flash of steel. "Catherine is very important to me."

Alec lifted an eyebrow but said nothing, letting the silence press.

Then Gary added, without hesitation, "I'm hoping Catherine will one day be my wife. I can't let anything happen to her—not if I can help it."

Alec's jaw tightened, a subtle clench he barely kept in check. Of course. Another affluent man assuming he could secure a woman's loyalty with resources, pressure, or proximity.

"I see," Alec said evenly. "Tell me exactly what has happened."

"Her brakes failed on her car. The mechanic believes it was deliberate." Gary paused, swallowing. "And there was an incident at a charity ball last Saturday. Someone tried to push her down a staircase."

Alec stilled, eyes narrowing, mind already moving into pattern analysis. "And why," he asked slowly, "do you think she'll accept our protection?"

"She knows I'm here. She's finally agreed—for my sake."

Alec's fingers froze against the desk. For his sake. That revealed more than Gary intended—and it made something tight coil low in Alec's gut.

"Alright," he said at last, voice controlled, smooth, professional. "I'll review the file and get back to you by the end of the day."

He didn't add the rest.

Because he already knew the truth:

This wasn't going to any team.

He would be taking this case himself.

"Thank you, Mr. Cole." Gary rose and extended his hand once more, locking Alec's gaze. "I need her safe. Money is no object."

"Understood," Alec said flatly, though every muscle in his body was already coiled, anticipating what was coming.

As the office door clicked shut behind Gary Harris, Alec turned to the floor-to-ceiling windows, gazing out over the city of Sydney. The harbour shimmered in the morning light, ferries cutting through the water, skyscrapers rising like glass sentinels. His reflection stared back at him—tall, broad-shouldered, dark-haired, eyes the colour of deep espresso, almost black, honed to a calculating edge. Handsome, undeniably—but he had never met a woman who had held his attention for longer than a few days. He didn't think he was built for permanence.

He studied himself in the glass, the lines at his jaw and mouth telling stories he would never share, eyes cold, alert. He looked like a man who could command a room—or silence it.

His reflection lingered, then his mind drifted—inevitable, like tide pulling at the shore—to his younger brother, Ryan. Shorter, lighter-haired, with hazel eyes and a laugh that arrived before his smile. They had been close in a way that made ordinary sibling rivalries feel trivial—an easy, dangerous loyalty that had shaped both of them.

Now Ryan was gone. For almost two years he had been missing from Alec's life.

He hadn't seen him in the year before his death. Alec had been on assignment—another dangerous mission, another place where daylight meant exposure and silence was the only currency that mattered. He had returned to a life that had kept moving without him: paperwork closed, condolences filed, the public story tidy and final. He had been told in a phone call that Ryan was dead. He had missed the funeral.

Two years. Two years that had blurred together—dust, desert heat, the relentless thrum of danger—years that had carved him into someone who moved through the world with low, constant readiness. Returning home had been like stepping into a photograph whose edges had been burned away. The official line called it a simple car accident. The file was neat, the signatures in place, the conclusions stamped and archived. But neat files could be lies wrapped in paper. Alec knew that as surely as he knew the weight of a rifle in his hands.

Ryan's face haunted him more than any firefight. Not just the image of him lying still, but the small things that broke him—an unfinished joke, a half-sent text, the way his voice used to carry when he called. Every time Alec closed his eyes, a hollow, lifeless stare played behind his lids like a loop he couldn't stop.

And now, when a name he had seen only in glossy society pages flicked across his desk—Catherine Grant—something colder than grief tightened in his chest. Fury flared behind his composure. The magazine photos showed a beautiful woman composed to perfection: poised smiles, charity galas, embroidered gowns, always on her father's arm. Alec had imagined a daughter shaped by a ruthless man—polished, controlled, distant. He resented the image before he had ever met her.

He exhaled slowly, measured, tension coiling beneath his ribs. Catherine Grant was a ghost he had never expected to touch—let alone protect. And yet here she was, threaded through his life once again because a man had walked into his office begging Alec to keep her safe.

It set his teeth on edge.

Protection wasn't his goal. Truth was. And revenge still smouldered like an ember beneath the surface of his skin.

Alec had never believed Ryan's death was merely a tragic accident. Neat. Clean. Unquestioned. Uncontested. Nothing about it had ever felt right.

Derek Samuels—a detective, Ryan's best friend since school and the only man Alec trusted with the darker corners of the truth—had shared whispered confidences: injuries that didn't match an ordinary crash, a witness who had vanished as if swallowed by the earth, paperwork looping in subtle, deliberate circles back to the same name.

Catherine's.

And then the details lodged like splinters beneath his skin. She had identified the body—because Alec had been unreachable, their parents long gone. She had paid for the funeral—every cent—quietly, without recognition, without telling anyone. And at the graveside, Derek had said, she and he were the only ones there. No press. No family. No spectacle. Just Catherine, pale and silent, standing over Ryan's coffin.

"She looked guilty," Derek had said.

Alec had clung to that. He had needed to.

So, he waited. Patient. Restrained. A hunter biding time. He would pry the truth loose when the opportunity came. He would get close, close enough to see what she was hiding, close enough to expose what had been buried.

And now her name sat on his desk like a lit fuse.

If getting close was the way in, he would go—no matter what it revealed.

If Catherine Grant thought she was untouchable, Alec thought, she had never met a man who carried his kind of grief, his kind of fury, his kind of resolve.

He let that thought settle in his chest as he stared at the glimmering sprawl of Sydney—cold, ordered, glittering. And for the first time since his brother's death, he felt an aim that belonged entirely to him.

A mission born of blood. And debt.

Chapter Five

Dusk had settled over the city by the time Catherine stepped into the private elevator. The polished doors slid shut with a whisper of luxury. She pressed the top-floor button and leaned against the mirrored wall, the soft hum enveloping her. For the first time all day, her mask faltered. Exhaustion softened her features, leaving a trace of the vulnerable woman she kept hidden.

When the doors opened, she stepped into the living room. Floor-to-ceiling windows stretched before her, framing the harbour in molten twilight, the bridge glowing like a suspended ribbon of light. She slipped off her heels, setting her bag on the marble counter with practiced precision, fingertips gliding over the cool, smooth surface—a small ritual to steady herself.

The penthouse was quiet, serene.

Then a sharp buzz from the intercom sliced through the stillness, shattering the fragile calm and pulling her abruptly from her reverie.

"Miss Grant," the concierge's voice came through, crisp, clipped. "Mr. Alec Cole is here to see you."

She exhaled softly, rolling her eyes in mild irritation. "Send him up. Thank you."

Alec Cole. She had read about him in passing—precision, skill, reputation. A former special forces operative, owner of a successful security firm, a man who commanded respect without flaunting wealth. Just a bodyguard, she reminded herself. Nothing more. And yet... her pulse quickened despite herself, a subtle flutter she immediately scolded.

The private lift chimed softly, announcing his ascent. Catherine moved toward the foyer, pulse ticking faster than she wanted to admit as she watched the numbered display glide upward. The doors slid open with a quiet hiss—and the world stopped.

He stepped out like a shadow given form.

Tall. Broad-shouldered. Every inch shaped by combat and a lifetime of discipline that turned men into weapons. Dark hair framed a chiselled jawline that looked carved from something unyielding. His eyes—deep, hard, predatory—cut across the space with the precision of a man who missed nothing and forgave even less.

There was no warmth in them. No curiosity. Only judgment. Assessment. A cold, immediate verdict of her entire being.

His stance was relaxed, but it was the kind of relaxation that came from absolute control. A man who could break someone in half without raising his voice. Power radiated from him—not charm or politeness, but something older, sharper. Something dangerous.

And her body reacted before her mind caught up.

Heat slammed low in her belly, sharp and mortifying. Her nipples tightened, breath catching in her throat. Awareness rushed across her skin, like he'd touched her—really touched her—though he hadn't moved a muscle.

Her jaw tightened.

Years. It had been years since she'd felt anything like this. Not since Ryan. Not since love had left her shattered and convinced she'd never feel attraction again.

And yet here she stood—pulse racing for a man she didn't know, didn't trust, didn't really want in her home.

Her chest constricted.

Just a man, she told herself sternly. A bodyguard. Nothing more.

"Miss Grant?"

His voice slid through the space—a low, controlled rasp that vibrated right down her spine. A voice trained to command. To warn. To claim any room he stepped into without asking permission.

God help her, she felt it in her bones.

"Yes," she managed, steadying her breath. "Please... come in."

He stepped forward, sweeping the room with a slow, methodical scan. Every glance measured. Tactical. Dismissive. When his attention returned to her, she felt the weight of it—like standing under a spotlight you'd never asked for.

"You understand I'm here at the request of Gary Harris," he said, his tone civil but edged with irritation.

"Yes. He told me." She kept her posture straight, arms folding without permission, trying to shield herself from his intensity.

"This arrangement is temporary," he continued. "My job is your safety. Nothing more."

She offered a polite smile that cost her effort. "Of course. I appreciate the professionalism."

His eyes narrowed, just slightly. Catherine had the instinctive sense he didn't believe a single word she'd said.

"How does this work, Mr. Cole?" she asked.

"I accompany you everywhere. If there's no spare room, I'll sleep on the couch."

"There is a spare room," she said quickly—too quickly.

He inclined his head. No expression. No gratitude. But there was something in the faint curl of his mouth—something that looked dangerously close to a smirk—that made her stomach tighten again.

"You'll find I prefer independence," she added lightly. "I hope that doesn't make your job difficult."

"I'm accustomed to challenges," he replied, voice smooth but heavy with insinuation. He looked at her like she was the challenge—and one he wasn't impressed by.

For a moment, neither moved. Their shared irritation charged the space between them, electric and unwelcome. She felt it. He did too—she was sure of it. His jaw ticked, just once, the only sign that the reaction in him was just as sharp and unwanted as hers.

"I'll need complete access to the apartment," he said. "Inform the concierge."

"Understood," she replied, fighting to keep her pulse from betraying her.

He took another sweep of the room, gaze dissecting exits, shadows, blind spots. When he finally looked at her again, the breath in her chest tightened.

And Alec felt it too—hit with a visceral punch he didn't want.

Up close, she was far more striking than the sanitised photographs in his file. The delicate bone structure, the fierce green eyes, the vulnerability she tried desperately to hide—it stirred something he'd thought long dead. Something he didn't welcome. Didn't trust.

Didn't want.

A low heat coiled in his stomach, sharp and infuriating. Attraction was a liability. And attraction to her—the woman tied to the destruction of his family—was unacceptable.

He shoved it down.

"I'll retrieve my bag," he said, clipped, cool. "When I return, we'll go over your schedule and my expectations."

Catherine lifted her chin, stubbornness sparking. "Respect my space while you do your job."

His lips twitched—almost a smile. Almost a challenge.

"Noted," he murmured. And the way he said it felt less like agreement… and more like a dare.

He stepped into the lift. The doors slid shut. But the tension he'd dragged in with him lingered in the room, humming under her skin.

Catherine sank onto the sofa, exhaling shakily. Her palms were damp. Her heartbeat too fast.

She needed to steady herself. To control whatever this was.

But her body, traitor that it was, thrummed with awareness.

And somewhere between the flicker of irritation in his eyes and the heat she hated feeling, Catherine Grant knew one terrible thing:

Her life had just become infinitely more complicated.

Minutes stretched, unyielding and slow. Then the private lift returned, its muted ding cutting through the open space like a warning. Catherine's spine straightened instinctively.

The doors slid open. Alec emerged, black duffel slung over his shoulder, every movement efficient, practical, predatory.

Even before he spoke, the room seemed to shrink around him.

"Thank you," she said, unsure whether she meant for his prompt return, his silent efficiency, or the low, reluctant comfort his presence brought.

He gave a curt nod. "Where's the spare room?"

"This way." She led him down the hall, aware of every measured step he took behind her—controlled, precise, utterly unconcerned with her presence except as a variable to manage.

"Here. You should have everything you need."

Alec stepped past, arm brushing lightly against hers—barely a touch, yet enough to make her pulse spike. He surveyed the room with the efficiency of a man sizing up an asset.

"It will do," he said, clipped, indifferent.

"Good." She folded her arms, bracing herself. "Now… about my schedule."

He crossed the room with slow, deliberate steps, stopping close enough that she had to lift her chin to meet his gaze. His presence was authority incarnate, a silent gravity she could not deny. And beneath it, a hard, unyielding edge—the quiet contempt of a man who suspected her, mistrusted her, and would not allow her a moment of unguarded ease.

"You'll give me a list of everywhere you plan to go each day—meetings, events, errands, social engagements—everything," he said.

She arched a brow. "And if I decide to do something spontaneous?"

His jaw tightened just enough to make her notice, eyes dark and unblinking. "Then you tell me before you leave this apartment. I'm not here to guess your movements, Miss Grant."

"That sounds more like surveillance than protection," she murmured, tone teasing lightly despite the pit of unease in her stomach.

"It's both," he said, steady and flat, calm as a predator. "I can't protect you if I don't know where you are."

She met his gaze, unwilling to yield. "I don't like being monitored."

"And I don't like unanswered questions," he replied without hesitation, his contempt clear.

The air between them thickened. Pulse quickened. Every nerve alight. His eyes flicked—once—to her mouth before snapping back to her face. She almost thought she imagined it. Almost.

She swallowed, lifting her chin. "Fine. I'll give you my schedule. But I won't have you controlling my life."

"You keep yourself safe," Alec said quietly, deliberately, "and I won't have to."

His tone—neither soft nor harsh, simply bluntly honest—made her breath hitch. For a heartbeat, she forgot why she was supposed to dislike him. But the hard edge in his eyes reminded her: he did not like her. He mistrusted her. And somehow, that mistrust was rooted deep and she could not fathom.

Alec stepped back, breaking the tension. "We'll start in the morning. For now, lock the doors. Don't go anywhere alone."

"I've lived alone for years," she shot back, voice steadier than she felt.

"And that ends tonight," he replied, deliberate pause. "Sleep well, Miss Grant."

She watched him move toward the door—broad shoulders, predatory poise, the faint scent of cologne lingering like a warning. As the door clicked shut, Catherine exhaled slowly, shaky, her calm slipping just enough to remind her of the heartbeat racing beneath it.

Her life had officially changed. And Alec Cole… well, he made sure she understood that she had stepped into a storm she could not control.

The next morning, sunlight spilled across the penthouse in soft gold sheets. Catherine entered the kitchen, her steps measured, her mind still tangled in the tension she couldn't name. Sleep had been scarce, fractured by the awareness of the stranger in the guest room—and the odd, unwelcome tug inside her chest she refused to examine.

Alec was already awake.

Of course he was.

He stood near the island, dark trousers, fitted black shirt with sleeves rolled to his forearms. A mug of coffee rested in one hand while his other hovered over his phone. Even at rest, he radiated alertness—balanced weight, squared shoulders, every line honed for action.

He looked up as she entered.

"Morning," Catherine said, voice light, carefully neutral.

"Miss Grant." His tone was clipped, professional. And yet, as his gaze swept over her, she caught the subtle edge of suspicion, the faint curl of contempt. It made her stomach tighten in ways she didn't like. She hadn't done anything—or had she?

She straightened her shoulders, masking the pull of awareness that hit her every time he looked at her. "We should go over my schedule."

He inclined his head once. "Let's sit."

The glass dining table gleamed under the morning light. She took one end, Alec beside her but keeping a deliberate distance. Still, the air felt smaller, heavier.

She opened her planner, flicking to the first page. He leaned in slightly—not touching her, but close enough that the scent of clean soap, cedar, and steel reached her. She swallowed, aware of it more than she wanted.

"So," she began, tucking a loose strand of hair behind her ear, "today is fairly simple. Nine-thirty, foundation meeting; working lunch with the board; then—"

"You'll need the addresses," he interrupted softly, precise.

She blinked, bristling. "I assumed you'd have researched where I work."

"I research everything," he said evenly. "But I need our movements exact."

Her jaw tightened. Annoyance prickled, stubbornness flaring.

"After lunch, I'm touring a potential new site for expansion. Then a donor meeting at four, back home by six-thirty."

Alec scanned her schedule like a predator charting the terrain—mapping vulnerabilities, choke points, moments where she'd be most exposed. Every entry was dissected with lethal focus, his eyes flicking over times and locations as if calculating threat probabilities in real time.

Catherine watched him, arms crossed, irritation scraping under her skin. The way he read her life—her movements, her habits—as if she were a mission instead of a person made something hot and defensive rise in her chest. She hated feeling scrutinised. Controlled.

He didn't look up when he asked, "Your driver?"

"I don't have one. I usually drive myself, or order a town car or—"

"Uber," he finished, finally lifting his head. His gaze locked onto hers, dark and unwavering. She felt the punch of it low in her stomach—unwanted, unwelcome. "Not anymore."

Her spine snapped straight. "I'm not giving up my independence, Mr. Cole."

At that, something flashed in his eyes—not amusement, but something colder, sharper. Interest, maybe. Challenge. His jaw flexed once before he set the schedule down with impossible calm.

"I'm not asking you to," he said, voice slow, deliberate, each word carrying the weight of an immovable object meeting resistance. "I'm telling you what keeps you alive."

The room seemed to tighten around them. Her pulse skipped, half outrage, half something dangerously close to awareness.

"You will not drive," he continued, his tone brooking no argument, "until I say otherwise."

Her breath caught—stubbornness flaring, pride pricking, heat unfurling under the pressure of his authority. He wasn't trying to dominate her. He simply was dominance, and her body reacted to that truth before her mind could reject it.

"Control is not protection," she said, chin lifting.

Alec leaned forward, not enough to touch her, but enough that she felt the shift in the air—heat, tension, a pull she hated herself for feeling.

"No," he said softly, his voice a low scrape of steel. "But ignorance is a threat. And I don't let threats get my clients killed."

The word clients landed like a slap. Professional. Detached. Impersonal. Yet his gaze drifted over her face—too slowly, too intensely for indifference. Something flickered behind his eyes, something he suppressed almost violently.

Neither of them liked this reaction. Neither trusted it.

But it was there, sparking between them, undeniable as a live wire.

And both of them already knew—it was only going to get worse.

"Anything else?" she asked, voice clipped.

"I'll accompany you everywhere. You don't leave a room without me knowing. You don't adjust your plans without telling me. You don't disappear into stairwells or parking garages alone."

Her pulse kicked. "I'm not a child, Mr. Cole."

A corner of his mouth twitched—not a smile, something sharper. "I know. Children are easier."

Catherine narrowed her eyes. "Is that supposed to be humour?"

"Observation."

She snapped her planner shut. "Fine. But if you're going to shadow me all day, you'll need to keep up."

Something like a spark flickered in his eyes—challenge accepted, warning implied.

"I never fall behind," he said, rising smoothly. Casual, lethal, controlled. "Finish your coffee. We leave in ten."

He strode away.

Catherine didn't move. Her heartbeat was steady but rapid, her breath shallow. And though she resented his presence, though his contempt felt unwarranted and irritating, she couldn't deny the strange, reluctant pull—an awareness she couldn't name, a tension that threaded through her chest and prickled her skin.

Today would not be simple.

Not with him.

Chapter Six

The day unfolded with the precision of a metronome, each moment accounted for, every decision deliberate. Catherine moved through it with effortless grace, her focus absolute, her purpose undeniable. But Alec's presence threaded through every second, silent, constant, a shadow she could neither see nor shake.

He followed her like a predator, half-step behind, half-step to the side. Never intrusive. Never obvious. Always observing. Always assessing. Always judging.

And he watched.

Not with idle curiosity, not with admiration, and certainly not with the casual interest most men assumed they commanded around her. He scrutinised her, cold, unflinching, uncompromising. Every smile, every tilt of her head, every carefully measured word grated against him. He saw the masks people wore. He had been trained to see them. And she wore one.

A mask of ease. Of competence. Of warmth. A mask that hid something deliberate beneath it. Something calculated. Something dangerous. Something he could not yet name—but that made every instinct in his body bristle.

At 9:30 a.m., she swept into the foundation's conference room, notes in hand, greeting staff with effortless smiles, soft hellos, charm finely tuned. Alec remained near the door, arms folded, posture taut, a shadow coiled in readiness. Every instinct screamed at him: she wasn't what she seemed. Every instinct warned him to stay sharp, to watch, to question.

He didn't speak. Didn't need to. His silence cut through the room like steel, reshaping the tempo, asserting control without a word.

He catalogued her every movement, every subtle inflection in her voice, the way she remembered names, the way she nodded at each point, guided discussions with calm authority. The precision of her gestures, the quiet intensity she carried—everything was deliberate, controlled, intentional.

And he hated it.

He had expected a gilded heiress, lazy and spoiled, performing charity as a mask to soothe a guilty conscience. What he found instead was someone meticulous, deliberate, calculating in her own right. Someone whose perfection, whose intentionality, made him distrust her. Every gesture, every smile, every nod seemed designed to mislead. Too precise. Too polished. Too controlled.

Lunch brought them to a private dining room downtown. Catherine guided conversations about budgets, audits, and strategic growth with practiced ease. Alec's attention never wavered—half on the room, half on her. Every glance she cast, every subtle shift in her expression, he catalogued and analysed.

Her fire when defending shelter expansions.

The graceful ease with which she deflected challenges.

The quiet dignity she carried—authority earned, not inherited.

It unnerved him.

How is this Henry Grant's daughter? Shaped by wealth, yet disciplined in the ways of real leadership? Polished, yes—but polished like a blade, not a bauble.

And beneath it all… what was she hiding?

He didn't trust her. Not with Ryan's death. Not with the tightening knots of inconsistencies surrounding her life. Not with anything that had the potential to cut too close to him or his team.

She was a puzzle—elegant, composed, and deliberately unreadable.

A mask made of poise and practiced graciousness.

And Alec had spent too many years sifting through lies, half-truths, and the polished performances of people who thought they could hide behind charm. Catherine Grant might fool everyone else—police, public, even the man who thought he would one day marry her—but not him.

He would peel her open.

Layer by layer.

Smile by smile.

Gesture by gesture.

He would find the truth buried under all that refinement and restraint.

She would slip—everyone eventually did—and when she did, he would be there to catch it. To catch her.

By mid-afternoon, they were standing inside the skeleton of an abandoned warehouse on the outskirts of the city. Dust drifted in slow, lazy spirals through the fractured windows, catching the harsh sun in thin, ghostly ribbons. The air smelled like rust, old concrete, and memories of things best forgotten.

Catherine moved through it with the wrong kind of grace—heels clicking over uneven floors, a vision of wealth and polish against peeling paint and corroded steel. Staff members hurried ahead, offering apologies for the state of the location, tripping over their own explanations.

She accepted it all with effortless patience, a calm smile softening the edges of the ruin around her.

Too calm.

Too measured.

Alec watched her, silent, assessing.

What kind of woman stepped through decay in designer heels without flinching?

What kind of woman didn't recoil from the shadows pooling in the corners or the echo of her own footsteps in the emptiness?

The kind who had learned to hide fear.

The kind who had learned to hide everything.

And that—more than anything—made Alec's instincts lock tight.

She was hiding something.

And he would find it.

Alec stayed close.

Too close.

His footsteps matched hers, his shadow overlapping hers, the heat of his body brushing the air at her back like a quiet, unwelcome warning. Catherine tried not to react—tried not to feel anything—but her nerves betrayed her. Every inch of her skin prickled with awareness, a subtle tightening low in her belly she despised on sight.

She hated that he affected her at all.

Hated that her body responded to a man who clearly wished he didn't have to breathe the same air she did.

Because she could feel it—his contempt. It radiated from him as strongly as heat off sun-baked pavement. The rigid set of his shoulders, the clipped cadence of his breath, the cold, measuring glances that skimmed over her like she was something sharp he didn't want to touch.

She didn't understand it.

They'd barely met, and already he looked at her as if he'd reached a verdict.

Why?

What had she done to earn that instant dislike?

What picture of her had he built in his mind before he ever stepped into her penthouse?

Her jaw clenched, the familiar burn of defensiveness threading through her chest. She kept her posture perfect, her strides steady, pretending his presence didn't rattle her equilibrium.

But she felt him.

God, she felt him.

And the worst part?

Some traitorous part of her wanted to turn, to meet that dark, scathing gaze head-on… just to see if it shook him too.

By four, they were in the office of a notoriously difficult philanthropist. Catherine handled him effortlessly, firm when needed, warm when advantageous, always commanding the room. Alec observed from the periphery, cataloguing every nuance, every tilt of her head, every flicker of fire behind her measured calm. She didn't flaunt status, didn't lean on wealth, didn't charm for attention. Yet the deliberate precision of her movements, the careful curation of every impression, sent his instincts into overdrive.

She earned respect. Too much, too fast. Too deliberate. Too calculated. And he hated it. And yet… an uncomfortable awareness prickled at the edges of his mind— admiration. A sharp, unwelcome thorn he shoved aside with force. Focus. She could not be trusted. Not with the truth. Not with him. Not with Ryan's memory.

By the time they returned to the penthouse, the city was bathed in rose-gold light. Catherine kicked off her heels, exhaling softly, unaware of the storm of observation she had left in her wake. Alec remained rigid, alert, unmoved by the fading sun. He didn't relax. Not yet. Not ever.

After a quiet dinner, the city spread beneath them like a constellation brought to earth— Sydney glittering in molten gold and silver, ferries carving slow paths across the harbour.

Catherine sank into the sofa, feeling the weight of the day settle into her bones. Every muscle ached, yet beneath the exhaustion, her nerves still hummed with keyed-up energy she couldn't shake.

Alec moved through the penthouse with mechanical precision.

Locks. Entrances. Windows. Blind spots. Shadows.

He catalogued everything with the focus of a man who expected trouble and did not intend to be surprised by it. Not one unnecessary movement. Not one moment of hesitation.

Catherine watched him, arms loosely folded—not defensive, not relaxed—something in between. A curiosity tugged at her, threaded with something warmer, something she refused to name. His presence was magnetic in the most infuriating way: disciplined, contained, a man who carried tension like it was part of his anatomy.

She needed to know.

"Have I done something to offend you, Mr. Cole?"

He paused mid-step. Turned slowly.

"Why would you think that, Miss Grant?"

"I'm not obtuse," she said softly, chin lifting. "I can feel your animosity directed at me."

His expression did not shift, but something tightened behind his eyes.

"You are my client, Miss Grant."

A non-answer. A dismissal.

And yet there it was—something sharper beneath the words. Not indifference. Not professionalism. Something personal.

Finally, Catherine rose, smoothing her skirt, fingers trailing up to twist her hair into a loose knot. "I think I should call it a night," she said, composed, polite.

Alec remained at the window, arms folded across his chest, dark eyes tracking her movements with unsettling intensity.

"Good night, Miss Grant," he said—flat, clipped—but there was an edge beneath it that made her stomach tighten. A warning. Or a promise.

She offered a weary smile as she passed him.

"Thank you for today, Mr. Cole."

He didn't respond.

He didn't even shift his stance.

He simply watched her retreat, silent and unmoving, a sentinel carved in shadow and restraint.

No one else had noticed the undercurrents around her today—but Alec had catalogued every one.

Every man who spoke to Catherine Grant registered her beauty. Some lingered too long, others straightened instinctively, interest flaring in subtle, telling ways. She could have used it. Easily. Along with her name. Her money. The effortless access both afforded her.

But she didn't.

She gave them nothing.

No indulgence.

No encouragement.

No flirtation.

Only polite distance—and a deliberate retreat behind immaculate poise.

Alec's jaw flexed.

She could have owned the room if she wanted to. Instead, she kept herself just out of reach, refusing the simplest leverage available to her. That wasn't naïveté. That was control.

And restraint always meant intent.

She hadn't cracked. Not once.

Every measured smile, every controlled gesture, every carefully constructed boundary— he recognised them. He'd seen masks like that before, worn by people with too much to protect. Across interrogation rooms. In war zones. By those who survived by never revealing where it hurt.

Catherine Grant wasn't careless. And she wasn't using what the world handed her so freely.

Which meant she was hiding something.

And Alec was going to find it.

Silent.

Patient.

Calculating.

He leaned against the back of the sofa, the city lights casting hard angles across his face, watching the hallway she had disappeared into with a predator's unwavering focus.

Tonight, she might think herself alone.

She was not.

Alec Cole wasn't just guarding her.

He was observing her.

Profiling her.

Stripping away the lies one breath at a time.

And sooner or later, her mask would slip—

and when it did, he'd be waiting.

When Catherine disappeared into her bedroom, Alec moved to the side table with quiet efficiency and retrieved his phone. Every movement was deliberate, controlled, precise. He dialled Logan Reed's number; the call connected almost instantly. Logan had been his most trusted investigator for years—a man whose loyalty and skill were beyond question.

"Logan," Alec said, voice low, clipped, urgent without panic. "I need you on two things immediately. First—track the brake tampering incident on Catherine Grant's car. Talk to the mechanic who repaired it and check any camera footage in the underground car park. I want everything: physical evidence, forensics, any trace that tells us who did it and how."

There was a pause on the other end, the familiar sound of Logan processing instructions efficiently. "Understood. Anything else?"

"Yes. Second—pull security footage from the ballroom where the charity gala was held, the night someone attempted to push Catherine Grant down the stairs. I want eyes on every angle, every potential witness." Alec's tone sharpened, every word precise, carrying the weight of both urgency and authority.

"Consider it done," Logan replied. "I'll start cross-referencing locations and timestamps immediately."

"Good. No assumptions, Logan. I want facts. Every lead, every anomaly, every connection. Bring me the truth." Alec ended the call, sliding the phone back onto the table with deliberate care, his dark eyes narrowing as he returned to his vigil by the window.

He resumed his position, gaze sweeping over the city below. Lights glittered like distant stars, oblivious to the threats he had already identified, unaware of the truths he would soon uncover. He allowed himself a brief, quiet satisfaction—Logan was on it. Soon, very soon, Alec would know exactly who had tried to harm her... and why.

For now, he waited. Watching. Calculating. Silent. And he would remain so, until the mask she wore finally slipped, and the full truth revealed itself.

The morning sunlight spilled through the office windows in soft, warm ribbons, catching on the polished steel fixtures and glass surfaces of the Grant Foundation's executive floor. Catherine moved through her routine with measured precision—emails answered, agendas finalised, staff briefed with calm authority. Everything exactly as it needed to be.

And, as he had all weekend, Alec shadowed her by a step. Silent. Focused. A presence she felt even when she wasn't looking at him.

It was just past ten on Monday morning when a knock broke the quiet rhythm of her office.

"Enter," Catherine called, lifting her gaze from the document in front of her.

The soft click of the door drew her gaze upward. Lisa Grant, her older sister, stepped inside.

"Catherine!" Lisa's voice carried her usual warmth, a hint of playfulness threading through it. "Daddy wants you to call him as soon as you can. He says he hasn't heard from you in a while and wants to know how you are."

Catherine nodded. "I'll call him soon. Thanks for letting me know."

Lisa's gaze shifted, landing on Alec, standing a quiet shadow in the corner. Curiosity lifted her brow. "And... who's this? What is he doing here?"

Catherine's jaw tightened slightly. "This is Alec Cole. He's... protecting me. A security consultant."

Lisa's expression flickered between surprise and concern. "Protecting you? From what?"

Catherine hesitated, choosing her words carefully. "Just routine precautions. Nothing to worry about."

Lisa's eyes softened, though the subtle tension in her voice remained. "I see..." She glanced at Alec again, a mischievous tilt to her lips. "Well, it's good to know you have someone watching out for you."

Before Catherine could intervene, Lisa's attention shifted fully to Alec. She stepped closer, an easy, teasing air about her. "You must spend a lot of time with her. How does she survive with someone like you following her everywhere? Sounds... intense."

Alec's eyes flicked toward her, dark and unreadable. His posture remained straight, deliberate, utterly unflinching. He didn't smile. He didn't shift. "I do my job," he said evenly, voice low and clipped, leaving no room for play. "Nothing more. Nothing less."

Lisa laughed softly, a sound meant to charm, and leaned slightly closer, tilting her head. "I've always liked strong, silent types," she said, voice flirtatious. "You must have some stories to tell. Secrets you keep tucked behind that serious face…"

Catherine's cheeks warmed, heat rising as her sister openly flirted with Alec. She cleared her throat, glancing between them. "Lisa—this isn't appropriate—"

Alec didn't look at Catherine. He never looked at her. He barely glanced at Lisa, offering only a single assessing flick of his gaze. "I'm here to protect Miss Grant, not to entertain your… amusement," he said, voice calm, measured, edged with something Catherine couldn't quite name. Disgust. Quiet, controlled, absolute.

Lisa blinked, taken slightly aback, but she didn't retreat entirely. "Well… you're very serious. I like that," she teased, a mischievous grin still in place.

Catherine groaned inwardly, wishing the floor would swallow her whole. "Lisa, please."

Alec's eyes narrowed just slightly, though his voice remained steady. "Flattery has no place here," he said, each word precise, sharp.

Lisa laughed again, brushing a strand of hair from her face, undeterred. "You two are quite the pair," she said, glancing at Catherine. "But I can see why she trusts you."

Alec's gaze returned to Catherine, and in that moment, she felt his quiet, unwavering judgment. He wasn't just ignoring Lisa's teasing—he was silently noting it, cataloguing it, evaluating it. Catherine sensed the undercurrent of his disgust, subtle but undeniable.

As Lisa finally left, blowing a quick kiss over her shoulder, Catherine sank into her chair, mortified. "I am so sorry about that," she muttered.

Alec leaned against the edge of her desk, arms folded, expression unreadable. "She's harmless," he said flatly. "Just… misjudged boundaries."

Catherine let out a long, frustrated sigh. "Harmless…?"

Alec pressed his lips into a thin line, jaw tight. "Flirting, attention-seeking, charm—it's all the same. She's predictable. You and she… are very different. It's remarkable how two sisters can be so different."

Catherine glanced at him, half amused, half exasperated. "Remarkable? She is my half-sister."

He didn't respond further, already returning his attention to the office, dark eyes scanning the room and everyone in it. Catherine, still flustered, realised again that Alec Cole was nothing if not relentless—not in protection, not in observation, and certainly not in judgment.

Chapter Seven

She had met a potential donor at the small restaurant just down the street from her apartment building and, despite Alec's quiet protest, insisted on walking afterward. The meeting had gone exceptionally well. Mr. Langford's relentless flirtation had been deflected with Catherine's practiced grace—polite, warm, immovable—and she'd still secured a generous donation for the Grant Foundation Children's Charity.

Victory buoyed her steps as her heels clicked softly against the cobblestones. The night air was cool, carrying the muted hum of the city winding down. Her phone rested inside her clutch, her thoughts replaying the conversation, the figures, the promise of what the funds would mean.

Alec walked beside her, solid and watchful, his presence a constant at her shoulder.

Then she felt it.

Not a sound at first—an awareness. A pressure at the base of her spine. The unmistakable sensation of being watched.

She tried to dismiss it. Sydney was alive at night—late diners, couples drifting home, laughter echoing down side streets. But then the footsteps registered. Too measured. Too deliberate. They matched their pace exactly.

Her stomach tightened.

Catherine subtly altered her stride, slowing for half a beat, then quickening again. The footsteps adjusted instantly, seamless, unhurried. Her pulse spiked.

Beside her, Alec's posture changed—so subtly most people would never notice. But she felt it. His shoulders squared. His attention sharpened.

A low, controlled sound slipped from him, barely audible. "Miss Grant."

The warning had barely left his mouth when he moved.

Alec stepped into the stranger's path with fluid precision, cutting him off before Catherine could even turn. One second the man was there—too close, looming—and the next he was slammed back against the brick wall of the narrow alley, Alec's grip locked around his wrist, twisting with brutal efficiency.

The man gasped, shock widening his eyes.

Catherine stumbled back instinctively, her breath catching, heart hammering so hard it felt like it might break free of her chest. She could only stare as Alec pinned the man effortlessly, his body a barrier between her and the threat.

"Who are you?" Alec demanded, his voice low, controlled—and lethal.

"I—I was just walking home," the man stammered, panic flooding his face. His gaze flicked wildly between Alec and Catherine. "I saw her leave the restaurant—I didn't mean—"

"Didn't mean to follow her?" Alec cut in, twisting his wrist another fraction. The man cried out, knees buckling. "You chose the wrong woman. And the wrong night."

"I just… wanted to meet Miss Grant," the man blurted, voice shaking.

Alec leaned in, his shadow swallowing the man whole. "You don't get to decide that."

Alec released the man suddenly, shoving him back with controlled force. "Walk away. Now. And if I ever see you near her again, you won't get a warning."

The man didn't hesitate. He fled down the alley, footsteps frantic, vanishing into the night.

Alec remained exactly where he was until the silence settled, until the city's distant hum reclaimed the space. Only then did he turn back to Catherine.

She stood rigid, pale, adrenaline still buzzing through her veins—but unharmed.

His dark gaze swept the empty alley where the stranger had disappeared, assessing, cataloguing, replaying. Every angle. Every possibility. Satisfied at last, his attention returned to her.

Catherine felt it like a physical thing—the weight of his focus, the intensity of a man who missed nothing. Her composure wavered under it. Relief surged through her chest, followed by something warmer, far more unsettling. She felt stripped bare beneath his scrutiny, as if he could see straight through the polished exterior she wore so carefully.

And yet… for the first time since the threats began, she felt safe. Undeniably. Impossibly safe.

"You have no idea how easily that could've ended differently," Alec said finally. His voice was low, even—but the restraint only sharpened the warning beneath it. "If he'd been the one targeting you… walking was a mistake. This is why you shouldn't put yourself in exposed situations. And why you should've taken the car."

The reprimand landed harder than she expected—not because it was harsh, but because it was true.

"I—" Her breath hitched, heart still racing. "Thank you."

The words came out tight, edged with adrenaline and something dangerously close to emotion.

She didn't know what unsettled her more—how close she'd come to real danger... or how much it mattered to him.

She hesitated, the instinctive defiance rising in her chest. The part of her that valued independence, that bristled at being managed, wanted to argue. But reality pressed harder. She had underestimated the risk. And she had underestimated how deeply grateful she was that Alec had been there.

His gaze held hers a second longer than necessary.

Something visceral stirred inside him—sharp, unwelcome, impossible to ignore. His chest tightened, jaw locking as instinct flared hot and primal. Protecting her hadn't been calculated. It hadn't been protocol.

It had been reflex.

And that terrified him.

He forced the sensation down with the cold discipline honed over years. He didn't want this pull. Didn't want the fierce, magnetic certainty that made every muscle coil at the thought of her being hurt.

But Catherine didn't retreat from him. She didn't flinch or bristle. She simply nodded—accepting the unspoken command, the unarguable truth—and allowed him to walk her the rest of the way home.

By the time they reached her apartment building, the city lights stretched around them like a soft, shimmering halo. Her heart still raced, adrenaline lingering, but clarity cut through the haze.

Alec wasn't optional. Not if she wanted to stay safe.

And, unsettlingly, she didn't entirely resent the idea.

Alec paused at the entrance, watching her with an intensity he didn't bother to disguise. Every instinct screamed for distance, for control—but beneath the restraint was something dangerous. Intoxicating.

He shut it down ruthlessly.

"Inside. Now," he said, voice clipped, professional.

Catherine obeyed, stepping into the building, hands trembling more than she liked. She had faced danger before—but tonight had been different. Immediate. Real.

Alec Cole had put himself between her and harm without hesitation, without thought.

And for the first time, she wasn't sure she wanted that instinct to disappear.

Catherine disappeared down the hall with a soft, exhausted goodnight, closing her bedroom door with a quiet click that seemed to echo through the apartment.

Alec stayed where he was in the living room, standing near the window, hands clasped behind his back. The city lights stretched beneath him, fractured by the glass—neat lines of order overlaying the chaos he knew simmered below. He watched them with the same relentless focus he used on everything else.

But tonight, focus felt harder to maintain.

His jaw was still tight. His breath too controlled. His skin prickled with the ghost of adrenaline from earlier—from that moment he'd seen a stranger on her tail and something violent had surged through him.

Something he didn't want to feel.

Something dangerous.

He exhaled slowly, unclenching his fists.

The phone vibrated in his pocket.

Alec answered before the second buzz ended. "Cole."

"Tell me you're not sleeping," Logan drawled. The background clatter of keys and rustling papers told Alec exactly where he was—still buried in the office.

"I don't sleep on duty," Alec replied.

"Yeah, well… you're gonna want to sit down for this one."

Alec's eyes narrowed. "Talk."

"So, I dug into the brake incident," Logan said. "You were right. It wasn't a malfunction. Someone cut them clean—professional, military-precise."

Alec's spine tightened. He'd suspected it. Hearing it confirmed sent something cold and razor-sharp sliding through his bloodstream.

"And?" Alec pushed, voice clipped.

"The cameras in the ballroom—the night someone tried to push her down the stairs—they were all shut off a couple minutes before the incident. Then switched back on fifteen minutes later."

Alec's jaw locked. He didn't speak. His gaze drifted toward Catherine's bedroom door, the faint sliver of warm light still glowing at the floor like a heartbeat.

"So," Logan continued, "this isn't random. This is targeted. Personal. And I don't like what that implies."

Alec didn't like it, either.

"Keep digging," he said, voice low and hard. "There's a pattern. We're not seeing it yet, but it's there."

A pause. Logan's tone shifted, softer but sharper. "Alec… you sound tense. Everything okay over there?"

Alec turned toward the window, the city glittering back at him. His reflection stared from the glass—sharp, controlled, unreadable. A man trained to feel nothing.

But tonight… the reflection lied.

"She was followed home," he said quietly. "And it could have ended very differently."

"You sound stressed, boss," Logan said.

Alec didn't acknowledge it. He rarely felt stress—never admitted to it—but this case was different. Too close. Too volatile.

"Just keep me updated."

"Will do."

The line went dead.

Alec lowered the phone but didn't pocket it. His pulse thudded too hard, too uneven. He looked down the hallway, his gaze catching on the closed door where she slept—or tried to.

He had promised himself he wouldn't feel this.

Wouldn't want this.

Yet his body betrayed him, feet shifting instinctively toward her room before he locked himself in place.

Protecting her had become instinct—raw, immediate, dangerously next to visceral. And that alone was a threat he couldn't afford.

He dropped onto the sofa, spine rigid, eyes fixed on the apartment's entrance. Watching. Calculating. Controlling.

He would guard her.

He would control the situation.

And he would control himself.

But each night, that resolve fractured a little more.

Because Alec wanted her. Wanted to feel her beneath his hands, taste her, pull her into him, and shoulder every fear she carried—make it his, not hers. Every night, lying in the bedroom next to hers, he imagined taking her in his arms, claiming her as his own. Madness. Pure madness.

Madness, he told himself.

He had protected beautiful women before—dozens of them—and never, not once, had he wanted to cross that line. Never had he even entertained the thought.

So why her?

Why the woman he was supposed to hate?

The woman tied—however faintly, however unfairly—to the night his brother had died?

He couldn't understand it. Didn't want to.

But the truth lodged deep and immovable in his chest, refusing to be reasoned away:

The danger outside wasn't the only thing threatening his control tonight.

A few minutes later, his phone vibrated hard against the arm of the sofa. Alec grabbed it before the second buzz finished.

"Cole."

"Alec—what the hell are you doing?"

Detective Derek Samuels. The voice was rough, urgent, brimming with disbelief.

Alec's jaw locked. "I'm doing my job."

"Catherine Grant," Derek snapped, her name thrown like an accusation. "Why are you protecting her? Tell me you're not serious. She could be responsible for your brother's death."

Alec's grip tightened, knuckles bleaching. "I know."

"She's hiding something," Derek continued, voice dropping into something cold. "I've seen the reports. And everything points to—"

"To Catherine Grant," Alec finished, tone scraping like steel on concrete. "I'm aware. So, if this is your attempt to warn me off, don't bother."

"I'm trying to make sure you haven't lost your damn mind," Derek shot back. "Ryan's death wasn't an accident. I feel it in my gut. And you—of all people—are placing yourself right in her orbit. Why? Protection?" A beat. "Or cover?"

"No," Alec said, voice tightening like a vice. "For answers."

"So, you're not just there to guard her," Derek pressed.

"That's right." Alec's voice went flat. Controlled. Deadly calm. "This assignment landed on my desk—and I took it to get close."

A tense silence followed. Static hummed between them.

Then Derek asked, "Does she know you're Ryan's brother?"

A muscle in Alec's stomach clenched. "No. And she won't. Not yet."

He hadn't meant to sound that quiet. That conflicted.

Derek exhaled. "You know her mother died in a car accident too. Six months before Ryan."

Alec stilled. "What? I didn't know that. Why didn't you tell me?"

"I wasn't part of Evelyn Grant's investigation. I only found out recently." A beat. "It could be connected."

Alec hesitated—long enough for dread to coil low and tight in his gut.

"If they are connected... I can't see Catherine wanting her mother dead."

"Maybe," Derek allowed. "But you don't know that yet. Daughters have hated their mothers before."

Alec exhaled sharply. "Yeah. True."

He scrubbed a hand over his jaw, the conflict twisting deeper. "Send everything you have to Logan. I want him to dig into it—Evelyn's accident, Ryan's... everything. See if there's any link."

"Good idea," Derek said. "Maybe we'll finally figure out what really happened to Ryan."

"That's the goal." Alec's voice dropped, roughened by something rawer than anger. "I need to know why my brother isn't here anymore."

Chapter Eight

Across the city, far from the glow of Catherine's apartment lights, Ethan Varnes stepped into the private meeting room of an exclusive, members-only club. The space was dim, walls panelled in dark wood, a single low lamp illuminating only the centre of the table—just enough light to conduct business, not enough to reveal anything that wasn't meant to be seen.

His client was already there, seated in the deepening shadows. Ethan couldn't make out a face, only the outline of a figure—still, composed, radiating a quiet, chilling authority that filled the room more effectively than any presence he'd ever known.

He closed the door behind him.

"The cut brakes didn't do the job," the client said, voice distorted by the room's acoustics, each syllable dropping like ice. "Now she has security with her."

Ethan remained standing. "She got lucky," he replied, his tone flat, detached— professional. "You wanted it to look like an accident."

A beat of silence followed. Heavy. Pensive. Sinister.

"Not anymore."

The words slithered through the space, laced with something far darker than frustration. Something decisive. Final.

"Just get the job done," the client continued, each word clipped with lethal intent. "I want her gone as soon as possible."

The shadows seemed to tighten around the edges of the room as the final command fell.

"No matter the cost."

Ethan inclined his head, his expression a perfect mask of icy obedience.

"It will be handled."

He turned and stepped back into the night, the door clicking shut behind him. A cold wind cut across the street, but it wasn't the air that made a shiver crawl beneath his skin.

This client had ice in their veins—merciless, unblinking.

And Ethan knew one thing with absolute certainty:

If you crossed them, it wasn't a mistake.

It was a death sentence.

Catherine barely slept.

Every time she closed her eyes, she imagined Alec's arms around her—solid, warm, impossibly safe. She imagined what it would be like to tilt her chin up, close that final breath of space, and feel his mouth on hers. The thought alone left her breathless.

She hadn't kissed anyone since Ryan.

She hadn't wanted to.

But Alec stirred something she thought she'd buried so deep it would never surface again. *Want. Hope. Desire.*

By the time dawn crept through the apartment windows, pale and unforgiving, she felt hollowed out by exhaustion.

She didn't bother getting dressed. She just tightened her robe around her body and forced her unsteady legs toward the kitchen. Coffee. She needed something solid to hold on to.

Alec stood at the counter, broad shoulders tense beneath a dark T-shirt, one hand wrapped around a mug like he needed it to stay anchored. His eyes lifted the moment she entered—sharp, alert, and then… softening. Concern flickered there. And something else he didn't want her to see.

She looked rumpled, fragile, shadows under her eyes.

It made his chest tighten in a way he couldn't control.

"Morning," he murmured, voice low, rough—like he hadn't slept either.

She swallowed, gripping the counter for balance. "Morning."

The scent of fresh coffee wrapped around her as she poured a cup. She stared into the dark liquid, letting its swirl become a shield. Anything was easier than meeting his eyes.

"I'm not going into the office today," she said quietly. "I'm… not feeling up to it. I'll work from home."

Alec didn't speak right away. She felt his attention on her—felt him reading every nuance she tried to hide.

"Okay," he said finally, though the single word carried a weight of worry.

She hesitated, then added, "But I still have to attend the charity gala tomorrow night."

The shift in him was subtle but unmistakable—his posture straightened, his gaze sharpening like a blade sliding into place.

"Security will be tight," he said, already calculating, already planning. "We'll take extra precautions."

He didn't ask how she felt.

He didn't ask what kept her awake.

But he saw her.

And she felt it everywhere.

Catherine stepped out of her bedroom, the soft shimmer of her champagne-coloured gown catching the light like a breath of sunrise. The fabric clung elegantly to her figure, glittering with every subtle movement. Her hair was swept up into an effortless twist; a few soft tendrils falling to frame her face and soften the refined line of her jaw. Her makeup was understated—glow on her cheeks, a hint of gold at her eyes, a whisper of rose on her lips—but it made her look impossibly poised.

She paused at the threshold, drawing in a slow, steadying breath before stepping into the living room.

Alec was already there.

The tuxedo sharpened his already imposing presence, the black fabric sculpting over broad shoulders and a body built for danger, not polishing. His usual quiet authority remained—but tonight it sat beneath a layer of formal elegance that made him look devastatingly handsome.

Catherine's pulse hitched. She forced her gaze away.

He is my bodyguard. Not a date. Not someone I'm allowed to want.

But when he turned and saw her, his reaction was unmistakable.

His breath caught—audible, sharp. His eyes swept over her once, slow, and unguarded, before he locked them down again. He knew she was beautiful—he'd known from the first moment—but tonight… tonight she was something else entirely. Luminous. Powerful. Graceful in a way that wasn't for anyone else, yet he felt it hit squarely in his chest.

He parted his lips to speak—to tell her she was stunning—but he stopped himself a heartbeat before the words slipped free.

I can't. She is my client.

He swallowed, pulse kicking hard, hands curling subtly at his sides to keep himself steady.

Catherine caught the moment—the hesitation, the way he forced himself back behind that impenetrable wall. Something warm stuttered inside her chest. She almost smiled, almost let herself enjoy the rare, unguarded look on his face.

But she tamped it down.

Don't let him see.

Don't give him anything he could use.

Don't give yourself hope.

Not tonight.

"Ready?" she asked briskly, turning toward the lift and pressing the button. Her voice was steady, but her hands trembled slightly at her sides.

Alec watched her move, muscles coiled, dark eyes tracking every subtle sway of her body. His jaw tightened, resisting the pull in his chest, the unbidden surge of something far too dangerous to admit. "Always," he said quietly—low, controlled—but the undercurrent of something unspoken carried clearly.

She glanced back at him, catching a shadow of emotion in his expression. She didn't flinch. She nodded once, resolute, and stepped into the lift. Alec followed, silent, every sense alert, every instinct on edge—not just for the gala ahead, but for the unspoken tension between them that had been building since they met.

The limousine glided up to the entrance of the Shangri-La Sydney, its grand porte-cochère glowing under the bright city lights. The red carpet had been rolled out, photographers lining the sides, flashes popping in rapid bursts. The hum of the crowd and the clicks of cameras quickened Catherine's pulse.

Alec stepped out first, tuxedo immaculate, sharp lines perfectly composed. He paused, then turned back, extending a hand toward her with the quiet authority she had come to recognise.

Catherine hesitated. She didn't want to take it—not because of him, but because of what it could do to her. She wanted to control every inch of her entrance. But the photographers' lenses swivelled toward her, hungry for the shot.

Reluctantly, she placed her hand in his. The moment their fingers touched, a current of something unspoken passed between them—tense, magnetic, grounding.

As she swung her leg out of the limousine, the slit of her gown slipped higher—just enough to reveal a long stretch of smooth, bare skin. Alec's gaze snagged on the glimpse before he could stop himself. Heat punched low and hard in his stomach—desire sharp as a blade, immediate as breath—but layered with something else. Something protective. Possessive. It made his jaw tighten until he could feel the strain in his teeth.

Catherine stepped onto the red carpet with liquid grace, shoulders back, chin lifted. Diamonds flashed at her ears, her gown shimmered under the camera lights, and she moved as though she belonged in the glow of every shutter click. Every flash. Every admiring whisper.

She didn't flinch. Didn't falter. She simply was—composed, elegant, untouchable.

Alec kept her hand clasped in his until they reached the foot of the marble steps. Only then did he force himself to release her, but he didn't—couldn't—look away. Not when she looked like this.

Strong.

Poised.

Breathtaking.

Something inside him pulled tight, a tether he hadn't realised existed until tonight. And as she glided up the steps, light catching in her hair, Alec found himself wondering—unexpectedly, uncomfortably—if he would ever get used to the sight of her like this.

Inside the ballroom, Catherine's eyes swept over the glittering space. The soft shimmer of her gown caught the golden lights above, tracing the curves of her figure with every subtle movement. Guests moved and laughed, music blending into a gentle hum that barely registered. Alec remained close behind, a shadow at her shoulder—silent, watchful, coiled with alert energy.

It didn't take long for Gary to notice her. As soon as his gaze landed on Catherine, he made his way over, a practiced grin spreading across his face.

"Catherine, you look ravishing," he said warmly, taking both her hands and holding them for just a heartbeat too long. He leaned in and pressed a quick, polite kiss to each cheek.

Catherine turned toward him gracefully, letting her gaze linger a fraction longer than necessary. "Thank you, Gary," she said, voice warm, casual, and just a hint teasing. "You look handsome as ever."

Gary's eyes lit up, delighted. "I hope you'll let me dance with you later."

"I would love to," she replied smoothly. They fell into a light conversation about the charity and other polite topics, laughter threading between them.

Alec's jaw tightened, his gaze fixed on her. Gary's easy charm, the way he looked at her—a casual, almost possessive admiration—set Alec's instincts ablaze. He remembered the words he'd muttered when he'd hired him: *'I'm hoping one day she will be my wife.'*

Alec's chest constricted at the memory. Seeing Gary smile effortlessly at her, the subtle way he lingered, the careless intimacy of his gestures, twisted that memory into a sharp edge of irritation. Every polite laugh, every tilt of her head toward Gary, every subtle smile she returned was a silent challenge—and Alec hated it.

Even as Catherine conversed effortlessly, aware of his scrutiny but unbothered, Alec's hands curled into fists at his sides. The air around them felt taut, charged with something he could neither name nor release. Protectiveness, desire, and something darker coiled within him, warning him that he didn't like this—didn't like watching anyone treat her this way, but Gary, especially, made the edge in him sharpen.

As the night stretched on, his irritation only deepened. Too many men noticed Catherine. She was graceful, poised, and charming, but she never over-encouraged them. And yet, they didn't seem to take the hint. The polite bows, the casual smiles, the subtle disengagements—none of it mattered. Their attention lingered, persistent and oblivious to the signals she sent.

What gnawed at Alec even more was that they seemed to entirely ignore that she was with him. The invisible line that should have marked her as his responsibility—his presence, his authority—was invisible to them. Each sideways glance, each lingering smile directed at her tightened the coil of unease in his chest. He wanted to move, to step in, to remind them subtly that she was not available, that she was already claimed, even if only in the quiet, protective way he had staked his claim long before anyone else could.

And Catherine, radiant and unflinching, didn't even seem to notice the growing storm in his eyes. She moved through the room with her usual elegance, laughing lightly, conversing with charm, unaware that her grace—and the way others admired it—was setting every muscle in him on edge.

Alec's jaw clenched. He couldn't tell if it was her beauty, her effortless magnetism, or the sheer audacity of the men around her that made his pulse hammer with frustration. All he knew was that by the end of the night, he would have to remind anyone who glanced too long that she wasn't theirs to notice—and perhaps, that she belonged to him in ways they would never understand.

Gary approached, extending a hand toward Catherine with that easy, confident smile that made Alec's jaw tighten instantly. "Shall we?" he asked, the promise of the dance clear in his tone.

Catherine started forward, but Alec's hand landed lightly but firmly on her arm, stopping her. She glanced up at him, eyebrow raised, a playful edge to her voice. "Surely it's fine to dance with Gary?"

Alec's gaze didn't waver, dark and unreadable. "Not without knowing it's safe," he said evenly, but there was an unspoken weight in the words.

Gary tilted his head slightly, smile still polite but firm. "Yes, don't worry. I'll look after her," he said. There was a casual assurance in his voice, but Alec felt it like a challenge.

Alec's jaw tightened, a muscle flexing along his cheek. He gave a curt nod, letting Gary lead Catherine onto the dance floor, his hand releasing her arm reluctantly.

As Gary's arm slipped around her waist, pulling her a little closer than necessary, Alec remained at the edge of the dance floor. Every subtle motion of her body, every turn of her head, every laugh—he tracked it all. His pulse thrummed low and steady, a predator watching, restrained only by the crowded room and the decorum of the gala.

Chapter Nine

Catherine moved with grace, matching Gary's steps effortlessly, but Alec felt the way she leaned into the dance just enough to amuse him, just enough to keep the men around her on edge. And he didn't like the closeness—he didn't like anyone being that close to her.

That's when a voice, smooth and measured, broke his focus.

"Finally," came a smooth voice beside him, soft as silk and just as calculated. "You're alone."

Alec's gaze slid to the right.

Lisa Grant stood there—polished, composed, every inch deliberate. She radiated intention, the kind of woman who spoke softly because she was used to being obeyed. The din of the gala dulled around her, fading beneath the quiet force of her presence.

Alec straightened, shoulders subtly squaring, though his eyes remained fixed on Catherine across the room. Something in Lisa's tone told him this wasn't an idle social call. He knew trouble when it came dressed in couture—and tonight, it wore Lisa Grant's smile.

"I would love to dance," she said, voice warm, expectant. As if she'd already granted him the privilege.

"I don't dance," Alec replied, tone clipped. "Especially when I'm working."

Lisa's brow lifted, amusement flickering like a spark. "Surely Catherine wouldn't mind," she murmured, letting her fingers brush along his forearm in a testing glide.

Alec's gaze snapped to her hand, cold and sharp.

"Move on," he said, voice low, firm, carved from steel.

Her smile faltered—just slightly—but enough. He had surprised her. Drawn a boundary she wasn't accustomed to respecting.

A flash—anger, irritation—flickered across her features before she smoothed it into a practiced, brittle pleasantness. Alec caught it instantly. He caught everything.

"What is it about you men," she said lightly, though the edge beneath the words glinted like a blade, "Catherine seems to have you all under her spell."

Alec didn't look at her. His eyes remained on Catherine—elegant, smiling, Gary holding her a shade too close.

"Your sister is my priority," Alec said calmly. "Not your ego."

Lisa's smile sharpened. Predatory now, even curious.

Her gaze slipped briefly to Catherine on the dance floor, then returned to Alec with unnerving precision.

"You watch her like she's..." She paused, considering him with a hunter's patience, "...more than a client."

A muscle in Alec's jaw tightened. Heat edged up his spine. But his posture did not break.

"I protect her," he said evenly. "Nothing more."

Lisa hummed, not buying it for an instant. "Interesting," she whispered, stepping closer so her voice reached only him. "Because I've seen men look at Catherine. And you..." Her eyes dragged slowly over his face. "...you look at her exactly the same way."

His eyes darkened, hard as obsidian.

"I watch for threats. Only."

Lisa tilted her head, studying him the way people study a locked box they want to pry open.

"Of course," she said sweetly—but her words were a blade wrapped in silk. "But tell me this... do you ever see her for who she is? Or only for what you need her to be?"

The question landed with surgical precision.

Alec's hand curled into a fist at his side.

Her implication hit deeper than she knew—or perhaps she knew exactly.

"She's not yours to question," he answered quietly, each word a warning.

Lisa's smile curled, knowing, poisonous.

Then she turned, taking one step away—but paused.

"She's not going to notice you, you know," she said softly. "She hasn't looked at another man since..."

Alec's head snapped toward her, instinct cracking through the calm.

"Since when?" hovered on his tongue—too close, too honest.

He swallowed it back.

He'd seen the way men watched Catherine.

He'd seen the way she ignored them.

But why?

Why the distance?

Why the restraint?

Why the armour?

Lisa had planted the question—and now it pulsed beneath his ribs like a heartbeat he didn't want.

With one last measuring glance, she drifted back into the crowd, smile pleasant, eyes calculating.

And Alec stood rooted, jaw tight, gaze locked on Catherine—haunted by a truth he didn't want, and a question he suddenly couldn't let go.

The music stopped, leaving a brief lull in the hum of the ballroom. Gary bowed slightly, his smile warm, sincere. "Thank you for the dance, Catherine," he said, guiding her gently back toward Alec.

As they approached, Alec's sharp eyes caught movement at the edge of his vision. Another man—one of the guests—was watching Catherine, posture open, intentions clear. He was about to ask her to dance.

Alec's jaw tightened. He didn't like it. Not one bit.

Gary guided Catherine closer, but Alec wasn't about to let another man lay even a symbolic claim on her. Before Gary's hand could close around hers, Alec stepped in— calm, decisive—and took Catherine's hand himself, leading her straight back onto the dance floor.

Catherine's brows arched, bewildered. "What are you doing?"

Alec's expression stayed carefully neutral, but something sharp flickered in his dark eyes—a warning, a decision, a line drawn. "Dancing with you," he said, voice flat, measured, but threaded with something unmistakable.

She blinked up at him, startled by the suddenness of it. He added quickly, forcing a veneer of casualness into his tone, "You clearly want to dance. And it's… easier for me to protect you this way."

Catherine let out a soft breath, part disbelief, part amusement. "Protect me?"

Her scepticism curled around the edges of her smile.

Alec's lips tugged into a half-smile—controlled, unreadable. "Exactly."

But his hand, warm around hers, betrayed him. He guided her onto the polished floor with a quiet confidence that was anything but casual. Every shift of his body shielded her, every turn placed him between her and the curious glances drifting their way. He moved like a man who had done this his entire life—not dancing but guarding.

As the music swelled again, Alec's gaze flicked to the man who had been watching her. One look—cold, territorial, unmistakably possessive—and the man faltered, then slipped away, as if Alec had drawn an invisible perimeter around her.

Catherine tilted her head, assessing him. "I didn't think you could stand being near me," she murmured, the question soft, laced with something fragile.

Alec didn't answer. Instead, he shifted her closer—too close for indifference—and kept his focus on the room, muscles coiled, vigilance honed. To him, dancing wasn't dancing. It was strategy. It was control. It was protection. And he wasn't letting anyone—not strangers, not admirers, not even Catherine herself—cross the line he'd drawn.

But the instant Catherine's body brushed his, hesitation snapped through him like a live wire. *This is a mistake*, his mind warned, his instincts snarling for distance.

Yet the moment she settled into him—soft, warm, heartbreakingly real—something in him faltered. Her body aligned with his as though it had been made to fit, and the thought shook him. Her heartbeat thudded against his chest, steady and intimate, and something primal tore through the perfectly ordered restraint he had lived inside for years.

He should pull away. He knew he should.

But his hands—firm, deliberate—held her as if letting go wasn't an option he could physically choose.

Catherine felt the tension lock his muscles and misread it instantly.

He doesn't want to be here, she thought, a quiet ache blooming beneath her ribs. *He's only doing this because he thinks he has to.*

She let the closeness soothe her anyway, even as doubt pricked at her. She didn't pull away, but she braced, certain he would if given the chance.

Alec, meanwhile, fought for composure. The gravity of her presence tugged at him, powerful and disorienting. Every instinct in him wanted to tilt the world, even briefly, so he could hold her like this without consequence, without fear.

His jaw tightened. His pulse betrayed him. His chest rose and fell with shallow control. He could feel his own restraint—stretched thin, trembling, terrifying—and it rattled him more than any threat lurking in the ballroom shadows.

Catherine had always known—somewhere deep, somewhere quiet—that if she ever allowed herself to fall fully, it would feel like this. Like belonging. Like inevitability. Like home.

Pressed against him now, it did.

She saw the tight line of his jaw, the focus in his dark gaze, and she swallowed her questions, afraid of the answers. Alec felt that hesitation in her… and without thinking, his hand slid to her waist, tightening—not in dominance, but in silent claim. In reassurance he didn't know how to voice.

For a suspended heartbeat, the world blurred out.

There was only the slow rhythm of their bodies, the press of her breath against his throat, the unspoken truth vibrating beneath their skin.

The music tapered off, leaving a lingering hum of conversation and crystal clinking around them. Alec didn't release Catherine's hand. Not even a fraction. His gaze scanned the room—sharp, precise—but even while cataloguing faces, exits, movements…

…his hold on her never loosened.

Catherine walked beside him, upright and composed, but her pulse still thrummed against the rhythm of the dance, lingering in her chest. She felt his gaze, firm and unyielding, following her every step. *Why does he look at me like that?* The thought teased at her mind, fluttering somewhere between irritation and something she didn't dare name.

Alec guided Catherine to the side of the dance floor, the music and chatter swirling around them like a muted storm. She pressed a hand to her chest, letting out a soft sigh. "I need a drink," she murmured, her voice tight with nerves.

He nodded, scanning the room. His eyes caught a waiter carrying a single flute of champagne on a tray. The man moved with purpose, ignoring the other guests who tried to catch his attention. Alec's instincts sharpened. Something was off.

He studied the waiter's uniform—the bow tie was a slightly different shade than the others he had noticed earlier in the evening. The cut of the jacket was just a touch wrong, the way it hung on his shoulders subtly different. Alec's pulse tightened.

The waiter weaved through the crowd, approaching Catherine with deliberate attention. She let out a relieved breath. "Oh, thank goodness," she said, smiling warmly at him. The man offered the flute of champagne, and she took it gracefully, murmuring a polite 'thank you'.

Alec's eyes didn't leave the man. As the waiter stepped back, his gaze flicked nervously toward Alec, a brief flash of unease in his eyes. Then he melted into the crowd.

Catherine raised the glass to her lips, the bubbles catching the light. Alec noticed a subtle, almost imperceptible film clinging to the inside of the flute. A small, reflexive alarm rang in his mind—that's not right.

His hand shot out, firm and precise, covering the rim of the glass before it could touch her lips.

"Stop," he said, low and controlled, every ounce of authority in his tone.

Catherine froze, eyes wide. "What—?"

Alec didn't answer immediately. His gaze swept the room, searching for the waiter who had offered the champagne. But he was gone, swallowed by the crowd as if he'd vanished into thin air.

"What's the problem?" Catherine asked, irritation creeping into her voice.

Alec's dark eyes returned to her, unwavering. His hand still pressed against the rim of the flute. Carefully, he lifted it to his nose, sniffing. A faint metallic tang drifted up—subtle, but unmistakably wrong.

Catherine's breath hitched as the realisation dawned. "Oh my god... it's not... is it?"

Alec didn't answer. He tipped the champagne into a nearby pot plant, the liquid disappearing silently among the leaves. His voice was quiet, almost a growl. "I think it's time we leave."

He didn't release the glass. Every movement was deliberate. He intended to take it with him—to have it tested; to confirm the suspicion he already knew in his bones: the champagne had been poisoned.

Catherine's pulse raced, the glamour of the gala fading into a blur. Every flash of light, every burst of music, seemed distant—insignificant. In that instant, she realised the truth: Alec wasn't just her protector—he was the only reason she was still alive.

He guided her toward the entrance, his movements precise and purposeful. At the valet, he ordered the car without a glance at the bustling crowd. Catherine didn't speak. She didn't acknowledge anyone. She moved like a shadow, still in shock, every step measured but hollow.

Alec helped her into the limousine. She went without complaint, sliding in quietly as if her body had already decided to follow his lead. He closed the door behind them and still held the champagne flute in his hand, inspecting it briefly even as he sat across from her.

Catherine sat rigid and silent, her hands folded neatly in her lap—the only part of her that wasn't trembling. Alec saw it in the subtle quiver of her shoulders, the way her gaze flicked to the window only to snap back again. Shock. Disbelief. The first sting of fear she hadn't had time to process.

The city lights streaked past the limousine windows in long, distorted ribbons—gold, blue, neon—but Alec barely noticed. His gaze was fixed on her, cataloguing every shallow breath, every flicker of unease, every tiny sign that she might unravel.

By the time they reached the front of her building, Catherine's composure was hanging by a thread.

Alec was out of the car before the driver could open his door. He turning to help her out with careful precision, guiding her inside with the quiet assurance of someone who had done this a thousand times—and yet, never for her. His hand hovered near the small of her back—not touching, but ready. Always ready.

The moment the penthouse lift doors shut behind them, he moved with purpose.

He crossed to the kitchen, retrieved a zip lock bag, and carefully slipped the abandoned champagne flute inside—preserving it, sealing it, setting it neatly on the marble countertop. Evidence. Proof. Something they could work with.

Then he turned to her.

Catherine stood before the floor-to-ceiling windows, staring at the glittering harbour as if it could offer answers. The city was beautiful tonight—bright, alive—but she looked impossibly small against it.

Alec approached slowly, giving her the space to breathe.

"Catherine," he said softly, "are you okay?"

She didn't turn. Didn't move. Her voice, when it came, was barely above a whisper.

"No."

A tremor.

"I can't believe someone just tried to kill me."

A single tear slid down her cheek.

Alec didn't think—didn't calculate—didn't weigh the consequences. His hand lifted on instinct. He brushed the tear away with the lightest touch, his fingertips warm against her skin.

She inhaled sharply—but she didn't pull back.

Slowly, deliberately, Alec lifted a hand to her chin, tilting her face toward his. His dark eyes held hers, unwavering, intense. "I'll keep you safe. I promise."

Her gaze locked with his, steady and unguarded, and for the first time, her voice carried no hesitation. "I… actually believe you."

The confession hung between them, fragile yet electric. Alec felt something inside him shift, a line he had sworn never to cross dissolving under the weight of truth and trust. Before his mind could catch up with his heart, he bent toward her, capturing her lips with his.

Chapter Ten

The kiss began soft, tentative, a whisper of the feelings he'd denied himself. Then Catherine responded, her lips parting, soft and willing, and the restraint that had held them both at bay shattered.

Her hands slid up his chest, gripping the broad shoulders beneath his jacket, and he tightened his arms around her, drawing her body flush against his. Every motion was a conversation—hungry, searching, fierce yet tender.

The penthouse walls seemed to vanish. The city lights outside became distant stars as heat and longing surged through them. Her pulse thudded against his chest, and his own heart answered in rhythm. Every suppressed emotion, every stolen glance, every whispered fear converged in that kiss, leaving nothing but the raw, undeniable connection between them.

When they finally pulled back, breaths mingling, foreheads resting together, Alec whispered against her lips, "Catherine… we shouldn't…"

Catherine's reply was a breathless murmur, her fingers still threaded in his hair, "Do you really want to stop?"

He looked at her, really looked at her—at the way her green eyes shimmered with unguarded vulnerability, at the curve of her lips, at the subtle tremor in her hands. She was breathtaking, luminous even in the dim light of the penthouse, and he wanted her. Desperately.

"No." The word left him low, rough, final. His lips descended on hers again, and this time there was no hesitation, no pause—only raw, unrestrained need.

The kiss deepened, urgent and consuming. Her hands moved to his chest, over the firm planes of muscle beneath his shirt, clinging, exploring. His arms wrapped around her, pulling her impossibly close, his body attuned to every shiver, every pulse beneath her skin.

Time fractured. The city outside, the lingering danger, the threats—they all disappeared, leaving only the heat, the ache, the intensity between them. Every stolen glance, every touch, every suppressed emotion surged forward, demanding release.

Alec's lips traced hers with a rough tenderness, and she responded in kind, her body leaning into him as though she could anchor herself against the storm he represented. Her breath hitched, mingling with his, each exhale a quiet surrender, each heartbeat a shared rhythm.

He lifted her slightly, tilting her so their bodies pressed even closer. A low groan escaped him, raw and unguarded, and she mirrored it, soft and breathless. They moved together instinctively, a careful chaos of desire and trust, of vulnerability and ferocity.

Finally, they parted just slightly, foreheads resting together, hearts pounding in sync. Alec's voice was a low murmur against her temple, heavy with both awe and need. He wasn't thinking about consequences. "I want you."

Her lips curved into a trembling, half-smile, half-whisper. "I want you too."

And in that suspended moment, the world outside—the danger, the chaos, the fear— vanished completely. There was only the heat of her pressed to him, the taste of her lips, the ache of longing, and the undeniable truth that nothing would ever feel the same again.

Without a word, Alec swept her up into his arms, her gasp echoing softly against his chest. He carried her across the penthouse with a predator's precision, each step measured but urgent, their bodies impossibly close. She clung to him instinctively, fingers threading through his hair, the heat radiating from him matching the fire building in her core.

He reached her bedroom and shut the door with a single, deliberate motion, the solid click of the lock echoing softly through the space. It felt final, decisive—a protective barrier sealing them off from the outside world and everything waiting beyond it. Alec set her down gently on her feet, but his hands lingered, trailing slowly along her arms and over her shoulders, memorising the softness of her skin, the warmth beneath his palms, the way she shivered at every unhurried touch.

She looked up at him, green eyes wide and luminous, filled with need, vulnerability, and a quiet, unshakeable trust. That look fractured something deep inside him. His restraint splintered. He lowered his mouth to hers again, and this time the kiss was unrelenting—claiming and possessive, a promise and a demand woven together in the press of his lips.

His hands roamed her back, slow, and deliberate, tracing the curve of her spine as though committing her to memory. When his fingers found the zipper of her dress, he paused only a heartbeat before drawing it down in one long, fluid motion. The soft whisper of fabric sliding against itself was nearly lost beneath the breathless sigh she pressed against his mouth.

The dress slipped from her shoulders and fell in a graceful pool at her feet, leaving her clad only in delicate lace panties and heels. The sight tightened his chest and sent his pulse racing, desire flaring sharp and insistent.

Alec's lips followed the elegant line of her collarbone, reverent and hungry all at once. He paused, pulling back just enough to truly see her—to take in the curve of her neck, the rise and fall of her chest, the unmistakable fire burning in her green eyes.

The words left him in a rough, awed whisper, raw with want.

"God, Catherine… you're more beautiful than I ever imagined."

She shivered beneath his gaze, every breath they shared charged with tension and longing, the air between them thick with a silent invitation for the night still unfolding.

Catherine's hands moved with deliberate intent. She slid Alec's jacket from his broad shoulders and let it fall to the floor without ceremony. Her fingers found the hem of his shirt, tugging it free from the waistband of his trousers with teasing, practiced ease.

Then, with unhurried precision, she began undoing the buttons one by one, each small movement sending a ripple of sensation through him. Alec's breath hitched, his eyes darkening as he watched her, helpless beneath her confidence. Every brush of her fingers against his skin sparked heat and anticipation.

Her hands were steady, deliberate, teasing just enough to make his pulse spike. When she eased the final button free, the fabric fell open, revealing the hard planes of his chest. Her fingers traced him lightly, following the taut lines of muscle, lingering as she revelled in the warmth beneath her touch.

Alec's hands came to her waist, fingers curling into the small of her back. He held her close—firm but careful—letting her take the lead. She leaned in, brushing her lips over the sensitive spot just below his ear, and he shivered, a low growl escaping him, betraying the restraint he so rarely lost.

Her touch was both gentle and insistent, every motion stoking the fire burning between them. She slipped her hands beneath the waistband of his trousers, tracing the line of his hips, and Alec's control wavered for the first time. He bent slightly, brushing his lips along the curve of her neck, savouring the soft gasp that trembled from her throat.

Every movement became a conversation without words—a slow, deliberate surrender to desire. The world beyond the locked door—the danger, the chaos, the constant vigilance—faded into nothing. All that remained was the heat of their bodies, the shared ache, and the intoxicating intimacy of two people finally giving in to the impossible pull that had been building since the very first night they met.

Catherine kicked off her heels, the sound soft against the floor, and stepped free of the dress already discarded. Her fingers worked deftly at his waistband, undoing it with quiet confidence. With a fluid motion, she tugged his trousers—and his underwear— down to the floor. She sank to her knees before him, her gaze never leaving his as he stood there, exposed, and unguarded, vulnerable in a way few had ever seen—and utterly irresistible.

Her hand wrapped around him slowly, carefully, as though she were memorising every inch of him by touch alone. He was thick, hard, and impossibly hot beneath her fingers, and her breath caught at the intimate reality of him. Her hand slid over him with unhurried confidence, learning his weight and shape, the subtle reactions of his body as she explored. Alec's breath hitched sharply, his entire body going taut beneath her fingertips, muscle and restraint locking tight.

When she lifted her gaze, his eyes were already fixed on her—dark, hungry, and edged with desperation.

There was something raw there, something achingly tender he couldn't hide. As if he still wasn't certain she was real. As if one wrong move might fracture the moment and send it slipping away. That look alone made her chest tighten.

Catherine leaned in, her lips parting as her tongue flicked gently over the head of his arousal. She tasted him, brushed her lips against his skin—soft, tentative, devastating in its intimacy. Alec's answering groan was low and completely unguarded, a sound torn from him that sent heat rushing through her veins and steadied her all at once.

She took him into her mouth slowly, inch by inch, unhurried, until he filled her completely, her hand stroking the rest in a slow, deliberate rhythm. Her movements were fluid and intentional, her mouth warm, her touch intoxicating, every motion designed to make him feel chosen.

"God… Catherine," he breathed, the words dragged from somewhere deep and stripped of every defence.

Whatever composure Alec usually commanded was slipping—fast. Her closeness, her deliberate intent, the way she touched him as though nothing else existed… it pushed him dangerously close to the edge of control in a way nothing ever had before.

With her free hand, she felt the unmistakable tension building low in his body—hard, urgent, and impossible for him to conceal. His reaction to her was raw, undeniable.

"Catherine… enough."

His voice wasn't firm—not the way he meant it to be. It came out rough and urgent, threaded with warning, and want tangled tightly together.

He exhaled sharply, forcing himself to steady, one hand sliding to her shoulder as if anchoring her—and himself—before he gently guided her upward. His heart was pounding so hard he wondered if she could feel it through his chest.

She rose slowly, deliberately, her body brushing along his in a way that made holding onto control feel nearly impossible. He felt every inch of her ascent—felt her intention in every breath, every subtle shift, as though she were choosing him again with each movement she made.

When she finally reached him, he framed her face in his hands and lowered his head, capturing her mouth. The kiss burned—slow, languid, unhurried, as if time itself bent around them. His fingers slid into her hair and traced the line of her spine, urging her closer. Her lips parted on a soft shiver when he deepened the kiss, guiding her, coaxing, taking command with a sensual confidence that made her melt into him.

With a low, rough sound, he gripped her shoulders and pulled her fully into his arms, his mouth plundering hers with a hunger he could no longer restrain. A soft, breathy sigh escaped her as she wrapped herself around him, holding on as though she couldn't bear even a single inch of distance between them.

Gently—reverently—Alec lifted her and lowered her onto the bed. He followed, settling beside her as she reclined against the pillows, and pressed his mouth to hers again, slower now, deeper.

His hands moved over her in unhurried exploration, stroking down the curves of her body with lingering care that made her tremble beneath his touch, every nerve ending alive and aching.

"You're so beautiful," he whispered against her skin, his voice husky, roughened by desire.

The words seared through her, almost as powerful as his hands, sinking deep and leaving her breathless, undone.

She felt rather than saw his body move closer—his muscular legs, rough with dark hair, brushing against her smooth ones in a contrast that sent a shiver racing through her.

"Catherine."

Her eyes fluttered open.

He hovered above her in the shadowed bedroom, his hard, beautiful face etched in faint light, his dark gaze burning into her like a brand. Reaching out, he smoothed her hair back from her forehead, his touch tender and possessive all at once, as though he couldn't help claiming her even in gentleness.

"You're mine," he whispered, his lips curving into a wicked, devastating smile.

His hand slid down to cup her full breasts, his fingers closing possessively around their weight. He tweaked one taut, sensitive nipple until she gasped, the sensation sharp and immediate, then softened his touch as his palm traced the curve of her waist with aching tenderness. He kissed her forehead, her eyelids, and finally her trembling lips, as though reverence guided every movement.

"Every part of you belongs to me…" he murmured against her mouth, the words a caress all their own.

In wonder, she lifted her hand to his bare chest. She marvelled at the feel of him—warm skin stretched over hard muscle; steel wrapped in satin. Her touch drifted lower, following the line of dark hair that arrowed down his abdomen, tracing it slowly, deliberately, until her fingers slipped even lower. She hesitated, breath catching—then, braver than she felt, let her hand explore.

He was enormous. Hard. Hot. Jutting from his body like a weapon forged for her alone.

A quiet groan escaped him, deep and strained, and she faltered—until reverence steadied her hand. She stroked him from the thick root to the swollen, glistening tip, her touch slow, exploratory, almost awed. A bead of pearlescent fluid gleamed there, and her breath hitched as she wrapped her small hand around him, sliding up... then down...

With a strangled sound, he caught her wrist.

"What is it?" she whispered, pulling back immediately, eyes wide with concern. "Did I do something wrong?"

"You're doing everything right." His voice was raw, thick with barely leashed desire. "I just..." He drew a breath, visibly steadying himself. "I want to make this last. I want our first time to be everything it should be." His hand slid through her dark hair, tender and sure, anchoring her. "I want this to be the night we remember."

Her response was instinctive. She slid her hands over him, tracing the hard lines of muscle along his back, feeling the powerful flex of his biceps as he gathered her close. His hands returned to her breasts, cupping their fullness in his palms. His thumbs brushed over her taut, aching nipples, teasing the sensitive blush-pink tips until her breath caught in a silent gasp. When he touched her where only one other man ever had, it was with a gentleness, a reverence, that made the moment feel entirely new.

He lowered his head, and she felt the warm brush of his breath a heartbeat before the shock of pleasure—his mouth closing over her nipple, drawing her deep into the heat of him. A low moan broke free as sensation rippled through her, sharp and sweet, racing down her spine and coiling low in her belly. The tension there tightened with every slow, deliberate pull of his mouth.

He shifted to her other breast, cupping its fullness with his large hand, stroking it as if memorising the weight of her. Then he took the aching peak between his lips, suckling her with a hunger that made her gasp. His free hand wandered in slow, reverent sweeps over her body, and she could do nothing but yield—moaning softly as he stroked her, touched her, claimed her.

When he lifted his head to capture her mouth, the kiss was deep and consuming, his tongue plundering hers as though he couldn't bear the thought of letting her go. His hands travelled down her bare shoulders, through the silky tumble of her hair against the pillow, then brushed—achingly gentle—across the soft curve of her belly.

She traced the powerful contours of his chest, the ridged strength of his abdomen, her fingertips exploring him as if she could learn him by touch alone. When she reached lower, she felt the hard length of him pressing against her, hot and urgent.

He went utterly still.

Her breath caught, cheeks heating as she looked up at him. "I...I want you so much." The confession slipped out unguarded and raw, trembling with truth.

Alec cupped her cheek, his thumb brushing her flushed skin as his dark eyes burned into hers. "I want you too," he said, his voice rough with restraint. "You're driving me mad."

He lowered his head, pressing a slow, lingering kiss to her bare shoulder, remaining there as he whispered against her skin, his voice low and rough, "Every touch of yours... it intoxicates me."

Then he moved.

His fingertips traced a feather-light path along her arms, unhurried and deliberate, gliding over the smooth plane of her belly before lingering at the narrow dip of her waist. They paused there—just long enough to steal her breath—before continuing downward, exploring the curve of her hips and the sensitive inside line of her thighs, where anticipation already pulsed and throbbed.

And then his lips followed.

He slid her panties slowly down the length of her legs, his hands reverent, unhurried, before tossing the delicate fabric aside. What came next was nothing short of worship.

One by one, he worshipped her legs—first one long, graceful limb, then the other— his mouth brushing her skin in tender, reverent kisses. He pressed a warm kiss into the hollow of one foot, then the other, and she shivered at the unexpected intimacy of it, that sensitive place igniting sparks that raced straight up her spine.

Slowly—almost torturously—he worked his way back up her legs, kissing as he ascended. The heat of his breath lingered in the hollows behind her knees, drifted higher, and settled against the delicate skin of her thighs. Each kiss stole another fragment of her composure, until her eyes squeezed shut, her fingers clutching the sheets as pleasure coiled tighter and tighter inside her.

Then he eased her thighs apart.

Deliberate. Certain.

His hand slipped between her legs, and she gasped as his fingertip found her—slick, soft, aching for him. He stroked her wet, satin-soft core with exquisite care, sliding against her, circling her, learning every response with slow, intentional precision that left her trembling.

Kneeling between her thighs, he lowered his head to where she needed him most. She felt the warm whisper of his breath against her inner thighs—soft, teasing, devastating.

He eased her legs wider.

And then he tasted her.

"God, Catherine…" he moaned against her heat, the sound vibrating through her.

Pleasure detonated inside her—fierce and blinding, a lightning strike that made her hips jolt beneath him. He held her firmly, anchoring her as his tongue swirled and stroked, learning her shape with aching precision. Tremors ripped through her in wild, uncontrollable waves. Her back arched off the bed, her breath fractured, her mouth opening on a silent, helpless cry.

His tongue shifted rhythm—broad and rough, then suddenly delicate, the soft flicker of the tip tracing slow spirals that shattered her control. Her entire body tightened, gathering into a single, trembling point of release. She arched again, shuddering violently as she broke apart, a scream tearing free before she could stop it.

"Alec."

The sound still echoed in her ears when she felt him move.

Positioning himself between her thighs, he pressed into her in one deep, claiming thrust—filling her completely, irrevocably—sealing the moment with a possession that stole what little breath she had left.

She gasped. He was suddenly everywhere, filling her completely, breathtakingly. Pleasure surged so powerfully it left her dizzy, lifted and spun by a storm of sensation. The hurricane carried her higher, higher still, until she felt lightheaded, weightless, undone.

He thrust again—slowly, deliberately—making her feel every inch of him as he slid inside her. Her breath fractured into soft, desperate pants as he filled her again and again, each measured movement lifting her closer to a place beyond thought. She lost all sense of herself, of time passing, of anything beyond the heat between them.

There was only pleasure.

Only this moment.

Only him.

Chapter Eleven

Alec had never felt anything like this. He'd nearly come three separate times already—when he'd peeled her dress from her body, when she'd wrapped her lips around him and taken his length into her mouth with reverent wonder, and when he'd tasted her sweet, responsive core for the very first time. But none of it—nothing—had prepared him for the shock of being inside her.

It was overwhelming.

Earth-shattering.

Every thrust plunged him into pleasure so fierce it stole the breath from his lungs. Her tight, wet warmth surrounded him, gripped him, drew him deeper in a way that made it feel as though this was his first time—his only time. As if every other experience in his life had been nothing more than shadows cast by something pale and incomplete. This was real. This was her. It had always been her.

From the moment he'd first seen her, he'd ached for Catherine—for her beauty, her gentleness, her quiet fire. And now she was beneath him, around him, taking him, claiming him as surely as he claimed her.

Bracing his hands against the mattress, he drove into her again—deeper—and groaned, the pleasure crashing over him in relentless waves that threatened to pull him under. He thrust again, then again, riding the edge of control by sheer will alone.

Then she cried out—a new sound, raw and exquisite—as her body clenched tightly around him. Her fingernails dug into his skin, and he froze, eyes squeezing shut as he fought desperately not to lose himself right then.

He wanted to last. God, he wanted to give her everything—wanted her to fall apart in his arms not just once or twice, but endlessly. He wanted this first night to stretch on, to linger in one perfect, unforgettable moment.

But he knew he couldn't endure much longer. Not like this. Not with her moving beneath him, hips lifting, urging him deeper with every breathless sound she made.

Abruptly, he rolled away, chest heaving.

Her eyes flew open, confusion flashing across her face—but before she could speak, he lifted her with gentle urgency and guided her astride him, settling her over his body.

She hesitated for just a heartbeat—shy, uncertain.

Then, watching his face, reading everything there, she lowered herself onto him, taking him in deeply, inch by slow, devastating inch.

And that was when everything unravelled.

He'd thought this position might help him hold on. He'd been wrong.

The sight of her above him—hair tumbling over her shoulders, breasts swaying softly as she moved—made him gasp, choking on the rush of sensation. She rode him slowly at first, tentative, then with growing confidence, building speed and rhythm as her body learned his.

Her lips parted, her expression luminous, transformed by desire. The soft light of the room kissed her skin, gilding her in a glow so breathtaking it made his chest ache.

Her head fell back, eyes closed, her face caught in an intensity that sent something primal roaring through him. She gripped his shoulders, driving herself harder, deeper, pushing them both closer to the brink.

She screamed—louder than before, raw, and beautiful.

"Alec."

The sound ripped something loose inside him. A low growl tore from his chest, rising from somewhere deep and utterly uncontrollable. Dizzy, he clutched the bed with white-knuckled hands, as if the world might spin away beneath him.

She slammed down onto him, pulling him deeper still, and his growl shattered into a hoarse, ragged cry that echoed through the room—

He broke.

The release tore through him violently, blinding in its intensity, splintering him into a thousand brilliant pieces.

Dimly, he felt her collapse onto him, breathless and trembling. Dimly, he felt his arms close around her, pulling her slick, beautiful body against his chest. They lay tangled together, limbs entwined, scarcely knowing where one ended and the other began— held in the quiet aftermath of something irrevocable.

Afterward, he drifted back to awareness slowly, as though rising from warm, fathomless depths where time had ceased to exist. His mind reassembled the world one fragment at a time. Catherine's bedroom. The muted glow of the lamp casting soft shadows across the walls. The lingering scent of her skin—warm, intimate, unmistakably hers—still clinging to him. And himself—Alec—lying beside the woman who had just undone him in every possible way.

He turned slightly and pressed a tender kiss to her temple. Her eyes were closed, lashes resting against flushed skin, her breathing slow and even. Asleep, he thought. And no wonder. He had never felt so completely spent, as though he had poured out every last reserve of strength, every ounce of desire, every guarded piece of himself he'd never intended to give to anyone. He felt emptied. Utterly done.

Or so he believed.

Because barely ten minutes later, with her delectably round backside nestled against his groin—warm, bare, and perfectly aligned with his body—something wholly unexpected happened. He stiffened. Hard. Immediate. Insistent. The shock of it shot through him. Even as a teenager, he had never felt desire rebuild so quickly, so powerfully. But Catherine… Catherine awakened a hunger in him that had no limits, no bottom.

He brushed her dark hair aside and kissed her cheek, lingering there. Then he nuzzled the soft curve of her ear, breathing her in as if he could absorb her into his bones. When his mouth grazed the tender place where her neck met her shoulder, she gave a soft, half-dreaming sigh—and pushed her bottom back against him, feeling exactly what she had stirred awake.

A low groan rumbled from deep in his chest.

His hands slid up to her glorious breasts, full and warm and exquisitely shaped. He cupped their weight, massaging gently, reverently, his fingers teasing the sensitive peaks until they tightened beneath his touch. He felt her inhale sharply, felt the subtle arch of her body as desire bloomed again, slow, and inevitable.

He couldn't stop himself. He didn't want to.

With careful, reverent strength, he lifted her thigh and guided himself into place—then slid into her from behind in a deep, claiming thrust. She gasped, fingers curling into the sheets as he filled her inch by inch, his body fitting with hers as though they'd been designed for this exact moment.

She pressed back against him, harder, deeper, her breath breaking as he moved inside her. Alec squeezed his eyes shut, overwhelmed by the sensation—by the way she surrounded him, by the way she seemed to draw him into something far beyond flesh or heat.

She filled his senses.

His blood.

His soul.

His every unspoken dream.

She was his.

And he was hers.

His mouth found her neck, heat and breath and teeth, while she tipped her head back, their bodies finding a rhythm that felt inevitable—perfect—like a truth they'd always known but only now fully understood.

"Alec…" she whispered, her voice breaking on his name.

"I know, baby," he breathed against her throat.

The words were everything at once—a promise, a surrender, a plea.

He slid out slowly, deliberately, making her feel every inch of his desire, every aching moment of absence. Then, excruciatingly, he slid back into her, deep and unhurried.

She moaned. His hand clamped around her hip, holding her steady as he drove into her again, feeling her body tighten around him in response.

And then they were falling—together—over the edge.

He thrust into her one final time, groaning her name with raw, unrestrained ecstasy as pleasure tore through him, leaving him shattered and breathless, holding her as though he never intended to let her go.

After they were spent, Catherine drifted into sleep beside him, her breath slow and even, her body warm against his. Their legs tangled beneath the sheets, as though moulded together by instinct.

Alec remained still, moving only enough to let his hand trace slow, rhythmic strokes along her side—over and over, soft, and deliberate. He wasn't trying to wake her; he simply couldn't stop memorising the feel of her like this: peaceful, unburdened, utterly his.

Careful not to disturb her, he shifted slightly and pressed a tender kiss to her temple. She murmured something incoherent against his skin, and he smiled faintly, brushing a stray lock of hair from her cheek.

"I'll never let anyone hurt you, Catherine," he whispered, low and rough with emotion.

Gently, he drew her closer. She stirred, eyes fluttering open just long enough to register his movement, then relaxed with a soft sigh, curling instinctively against him.

Alec tucked the sheet around her shoulders and wrapped her close once more, his thumb brushing slow, lazy circles along the curve of her hip as her breathing evened again. He closed his eyes, letting the quiet intimacy wash over him—her warmth, her trust, her surrender—and for a moment, the world beyond this room ceased to exist.

Alec woke to the weight of her—warm, soft, tangled against him in a way that felt both natural and dangerous. Catherine's hair lay fanned across his chest, a dark, silken spill that rose and fell with her breathing. Her breath was slow and even, the peaceful rhythm of deep sleep, and for one fleeting, treacherous moment, he wanted nothing more than to pull her closer. To wrap himself around her. To press his lips to her temple and murmur that she was safe here, cocooned in his arms.

And God help him—another urge surged beneath that tenderness.

Darker.

Hungrier.

The need to roll her beneath him, to feel her body open to him again, to drive into her until she shattered around him the way she had hours before. He wanted to feel her heat surrounding him, the way her body had gripped him without mercy, the way she had cried his name again and again last night, unrestrained and undone.

The memory alone was enough to make his muscles tense, his jaw tighten.

But he couldn't.

He shouldn't.

That way lay promises he had no right to make.

Careful not to disturb her, he shifted slowly, easing himself out from beneath her weight. His body protested, every nerve lit with restraint as he slipped from the bed. The sheets rustled softly, the faint scent of her clinging to the air—and to him—like a lingering echo.

He swallowed hard, already tasting regret, before he even reached the bathroom.

The shower ran hot, water streaming over him in relentless sheets, but it did nothing to wash away the memory of last night—the heat, the taste, the surrender. The way she had undone him. The way she had made him feel something he hadn't allowed himself to feel in years... if ever. He let his forehead rest against the cool tile, eyes closing as the weight of reality pressed down hard and unforgiving.

"What the hell did I do?" he muttered, his voice rough, nearly swallowed by the roar of the water. A bitter huff of breath followed. "You made love to her... that's what you did." The truth landed heavily. "And you enjoyed it. More than that…" His jaw tightened. "It felt right."

Frustration twisted through him, sharp and cutting. It shouldn't have. It couldn't have. She was the woman he was meant to protect, not want. Meant to shield, not touch. She might still be tied to Ryan's death—might hold answers that could destroy everything. And yet, everything he had built himself to be—controlled, disciplined, untouchable—had begun to unravel in the space of a single night.

Even now, standing beneath the spray, he wanted to go back to bed. To pull her into his arms. To lose himself again in a need so fierce and sudden he barely recognised it as his own.

He slammed his hand against the tile wall, water splashing wildly, turning scalding, then cold. "You can't…" His voice cracked with restraint. "You can't do this. Not with her. Not when there's even a chance she—"

He shook his head hard, water streaming down his face, his hair plastered to his forehead. She's alive. She's safe. That's what matters. He clung to the thought, but it did nothing to ease the ache in his chest—or silence the memory of her skin against his, the way she had trusted him without hesitation. He had crossed a line he couldn't uncross.

Stepping out of the shower, Alec wrapped a towel around his waist and stared at his reflection in the fogged mirror. Eyes hard. Jaw clenched. Control. Distance. Focus. The words formed a familiar mantra; one he'd lived by for years.

But every thought, every muscle, every pulse betrayed him.

He wanted her.

And that want was dangerous.

Dangerous—and utterly undeniable.

Morning sunlight filtered softly through the blinds, casting a pale, honeyed glow across the bedroom. Catherine's eyes fluttered open, lashes brushing her cheeks, and for a moment she simply lay there, breathing in the familiar scent of him—only to realise it wasn't there.

The space beside her was empty.

She frowned faintly, confusion stirring as she pushed herself upright. The sheets were cool where his body should have been. She swung her legs over the edge of the bed, bare feet brushing the carpet, and reached automatically for the robe draped over the chair. Wrapping it around her shoulders, she tied it tightly, as though bracing herself against a chill she couldn't quite name.

The room felt wrong.

Too quiet.

Too still.

A faint clink of ceramic and the low hum of the coffee machine drifted from the kitchen, easing some of the tension in her chest. Relief followed quickly on its heels. He was here. Of course he was.

She moved toward the sound, pausing in the doorway.

Alec stood with his back to her, broad shoulders tense beneath a plain T-shirt, his movements precise and almost rigid as he made coffee. There was nothing intimate about the way he stood there—nothing of the man who had held her through the night. His face when he turned slightly, was closed off, set in an expression she didn't recognise.

Regret.

Guilt.

Something heavier than both.

"Good morning," she said softly, her voice warm, hopeful—an offering.

He turned at the sound, offering a brief, tight smile that never reached his eyes. "Morning," he muttered, his voice low, clipped.

The word landed wrong.

Catherine's gaze lingered on him, searching. She noticed the way his jaw tightened, the way his shoulders stayed squared, guarded. Most of all, she noticed how his eyes slid past her instead of meeting hers. A distance yawned between them—sudden and sharp—and it stung more than she was prepared for.

Confusion curled in her chest.

She wanted to ask what was wrong. Wanted to step closer, to remind him—us, her mind whispered—but something in his posture stopped her. He seemed to shrink from her even as he stood only a few feet away, as though proximity itself was something he needed to avoid.

So, she stayed silent.

She watched as his hands resumed their task, the mundane ritual of coffee-making suddenly feeling absurdly important. He picked up a cup, then paused, releasing a quiet, almost inaudible sigh.

"I—uh… coffee," he said, still not looking at her, as though the words themselves required effort.

Catherine nodded, swallowing past the lump rising in her throat. The tension between them thickened, heavy with things unsaid. He was so close—close enough to touch—yet he felt farther away than anyone ever had.

He handed her a cup. Their fingers brushed briefly, and the contact sent a jolt through her that hurt more than it comforted. She leaned back against the counter, wrapping both hands around the mug for something solid to hold onto, watching him as though he might disappear if she looked away.

Then his attention shifted—to the bagged champagne flute on the counter.

"I need to get this tested," he said, his voice tightening with professional focus, retreating fully into it.

He pulled his phone from his pocket and began tapping out a number, quick and efficient, already elsewhere.

And just like that, understanding settled in her chest—cold and devastating.

Whatever had happened between them last night… whatever she'd believed it meant—

He was already walking away from it.

She said nothing.

She simply stood there, holding the cup he'd given her, feeling something inside her quietly, completely break.

"Logan," he said, low, measured, every word controlled.

"Yes, Boss," came the reply.

"I'm pretty sure someone tried to poison Miss Grant last night."

"Shit. How?"

"Champagne. Shangri-La ballroom. I need you to come get this flute—have it analysed immediately. Pull the security footage from the ballroom, too. I want a full sweep. Hopefully, you can see something I missed."

"Sure thing. Be there soon," Logan replied.

Catherine moved into the living room, her hands wrapped loosely around herself as she stared out at the harbour, the city lights flickering across the water like fragile promises. Last night pressed down on her chest, heavy and insistent, and the memory of Alec's withdrawal cut sharper than she expected. He hadn't looked at her once while speaking on the phone, the distance between them now a tangible thing. The unspoken message was clear: he wished last night had never happened.

Alec set the phone down on the coffee table and stepped toward her, his movements careful, measured. His voice softened, just enough to pierce the wall she'd built around herself. "Catherine… about last night…"

"You don't have to say it, Alec," she interrupted, voice catching, fragile. "I… I know you regret it. Forget it." Tears welled, and she pressed her hands to her face, the dam holding back all her confusion and hurt threatening to break.

"Catherine…" Alec murmured, reaching toward her, tentative, cautious.

She flinched back, a silent refusal in the sharp arch of her shoulders, keeping him at bay.

His hand dropped to his side, rigid, tense. His gaze fell to the floor for a heartbeat before returning to her, shadowed with conflict, regret, and something raw he could not name.

Then—the harsh buzz of the intercom cut through the charged silence, slicing the moment in two. Alec stepped back abruptly, his expression darkening.

He picked up the phone, voice clipped, tight, controlled. "Yes?"

"There is a Logan Reed here to see you, Mr. Cole," came the intercom.

"Send him up, please."

Alec didn't look at Catherine. Not now. The memory of last night—and the pull she had on him—made keeping control far harder than he had anticipated.

He set the phone down, taking a slow, deliberate breath to steady his pulse. His hand ran over his face, thumb brushing along the tense line of his jaw. Then, almost involuntarily, he glanced at her from the corner of his eye. She was still there, silent, quiet, eyes brimming with hurt and questions he could not answer.

He looked away immediately, forcing himself back into the rigid mask of control he always wore. Focus, he reminded himself. This is work. Nothing more.

The soft hum of the elevator announced Logan's arrival. Alec moved to the door, expression neutral, precise, measured. "Come in," he called, voice even, controlled.

Logan stepped inside, eyes immediately finding Catherine. His gaze lingered a fraction too long before he crossed the room, exuding the kind of confident ease Alec found irritating. Catherine looked up, startled for a moment, then quickly masked it with composure.

He stopped in front of her, offering a polite, practiced smile. "Miss Grant, it's a pleasure," he said, taking her hand and pressing a formal kiss to it. "I'm Logan Reed."

Catherine blinked, caught off guard by the attention. "Hello, Mr. Reed. It's… nice to meet you," she said carefully, voice steady though her pulse had picked up.

Logan's grin widened as his eyes flicked toward Alec. "Alec, you didn't tell me she was… a stunner."

"That's enough, Logan," Alec interjected, low and sharp, like steel snapping. His jaw tightened, shoulders coiling subtly. He noticed the instant stiffening in Catherine's posture—the polite smile that didn't quite reach her eyes, the tiny inward pull of her hands—and it stung him in a way he wasn't used to.

Without another word, Alec moved to the kitchen bench, picking up the champagne flute and holding it out. "Here. Take it. I need it analysed immediately."

Logan's hand closed around the flute, the confident grin flickering briefly as he caught the barely concealed warning in Alec's eyes. Catherine watched silently, her mind still whirling from last night, from Alec's retreat, from everything she hadn't yet processed. She swallowed, pressing her lips together as though sheer control could keep her from breaking.

Alec's jaw remained tight. Nothing more needed saying—the warning, the urgency, the authority—all conveyed in a single glance. Logan understood.

Then Logan's gaze returned to Catherine, a flicker of something unreadable dancing in his eyes. "Actually… there's something I need to talk to you about," he said, tone neutral, but the faint tilt of his head suggested a challenge, a curiosity that made her stomach twist.

Catherine caught the shift immediately. She straightened, forcing a polite smile. "I'll leave you two to talk," she said softly, each word careful, measured. But Alec could see the exhaustion tugging at her edges—the slight slump of her shoulders, the tension in her jaw. "It was nice to meet you, Logan."

She slipped toward her bedroom and closed the door behind her. Both men watched her go—Alec taut, conflicted, muscles coiled as if her very presence demanded restraint, Logan lingering in a curious, almost calculating silence.

Alec forced himself to look away from her door first, drawing in a slow, steadying breath. "What's up?" he asked, voice low, guarded.

Logan didn't answer immediately. He studied Alec with a flicker of amusement in his eyes, as though testing boundaries. The tight set of Alec's jaw, the barely restrained tension in his posture, spoke volumes. Finally, he lowered his voice. "Derek came to see me last night. He gave me all the information he had on Ryan's and Evelyn Grant's deaths."

"That's right. He thinks there might be a link." Alec's tone was clipped, precise, every word carrying the weight of command.

"So, you want me to keep digging?"

"Yes," Alec said immediately. "But first I want the ballroom security footage. Every angle. Every second."

"Already on it." Logan nodded once, then his gaze flicked toward the hallway where Catherine had disappeared. "Is she… okay?"

Alec didn't follow his gaze. "She will be. When we catch this guy."

But inside, he felt anything but certain. The memory of her in that quiet, controlled silence, the way she had flinched, the fragile line of her shoulders under her robe—all of it pressed against him. She was there. And yet, somehow, more distant than ever.

Chapter Twelve

Steam curled around Catherine as she stepped beneath the hot spray, letting the water pound against her skin until her muscles loosened. Her hair clung to her shoulders, droplets sliding down the curve of her spine, but nothing could wash away the hollow ache lodged deep in her chest.

Last night replayed behind her closed eyes—Alec's mouth on hers, the heat of his hands, the way he'd said her name as if it carried weight, as if it meant something. The way he'd held her afterward, warm, protective, as though the world couldn't touch her while she was in his arms.

For one brief, reckless night, she had let herself believe that he wanted her—not just to protect her, not just as part of the job—but her.

A soft, bitter laugh escaped her, barely more than a breath. God, she was foolish.

The water kept running, but her thoughts drifted to this morning: the empty space beside her, the sheets growing cold. No warm body. No whispered good morning. Just absence.

Then the kitchen—Alec standing there, shoulders tight, jaw clenched, avoiding her eyes as if looking at her might set him on fire. She'd felt the distance like a slap, felt the sharp, unspoken regret radiating off him.

He hadn't needed to say it. She'd seen it in every stiff movement, every carefully measured step.

It shouldn't have happened.

She braced one hand against the tiled wall, lowering her head as the water pounded her back, as though it could drown the ache swelling in her chest. She'd known the risk—letting herself get close, letting her guard slip for a man who had every reason to keep his firmly in place.

She wasn't naïve. Alec was holding something back, something heavier than hesitation. He looked at her like she was a puzzle he couldn't solve, a threat he couldn't ignore. And yet... she had hoped.

God, she wished she hadn't.

For so long, she had believed she would drown in guilt if she ever wanted someone after losing Ryan. Alec was the first man she had kissed since him—the first man she'd allowed close enough to touch her heart. And yet, standing here under the relentless spray, she realised with startling clarity: she didn't feel guilty.

Just broken.

The water cooled against her skin, dragging her back to herself. Catherine straightened slowly, pushing her wet hair off her face, letting a fragile thread of resolve pull taut inside her.

She would not let him see her break.

Not over this.

Not over him.

Alec could regret last night all he wanted.

She would survive it.

She had survived worse.

Catherine shut off the tap, exhaling a trembling breath, and stepped from the shower, leaving the last traces of his warmth to swirl down the drain, carrying away the fleeting illusion of what might have been.

When Catherine emerged from her bedroom after her shower, Logan was already gone.

Alec sat in his usual chair in the living room; dark eyes fixed on the silent morning news flickering across the screen. He looked impossibly composed—cold, even—as if last night hadn't happened at all. He glanced up when she entered.

Alec opened his mouth as though to speak, but before a single word could form, the sharp buzz of the intercom sliced through the quiet.

Catherine's pulse jumped. She moved to the panel, fingers fumbling slightly as she pressed the button.

"Yes?"

"Miss Grant, your father is here to see you," came the crisp, professional voice.

Her stomach tightened. She hadn't expected him. She hadn't called him—despite Lisa's urging. She loved her father, but they weren't close, and things had only grown more complicated after Ryan's death.

Catherine glanced back at Alec. He didn't move, didn't speak. Those dark eyes followed her with quiet intensity, a silent reminder that he was always watching, always assessing.

The lift dinged, and a moment later her father stepped into the penthouse. Catherine straightened, smoothing her robe before greeting him with polite, restrained warmth.

"Hello, Dad." She pressed a quick kiss to his cheek.

"Hello, sweetheart." He hugged her briefly, stepping back to study her. Concern flickered in his eyes. "Lisa told me you have a bodyguard. Why?"

His gaze shifted to Alec, who still hadn't risen, his posture controlled, alert.

"Dad, this is Alec Cole," Catherine said. Her voice was even, though her heartbeat wasn't.

Alec stood and approached, extending his hand with quiet confidence. Charles Grant shook it firmly.

"Charles Grant," he said with a nod.

He turned back to Catherine, brows tightening. "Tell me. What's going on?"

Catherine drew a slow breath and explained—her fall on the stairs, the failed brakes, the moments that had nearly cost her her life.

Alec stepped in, voice low and unflinching. "Someone tried to poison her last night."

Charles's head snapped toward him, eyes sharp with shock. "What?"

He stepped closer, gaze cutting between them. "Poison? Last night?" His voice trembled with disbelief, anger, fear.

"Yes," Alec said evenly. "At the gala. The champagne she was about to drink was tampered with."

Catherine felt her pulse quicken, though the terror of the night before seemed muted under her father's presence. She said nothing—the rigid line of Alec's jaw and the tension locked in his shoulders said enough.

Charles dragged a hand through his hair, exhaling sharply. "My God... why didn't anyone tell me sooner? Who would do something like this to you?"

"That's what we're trying to determine," Alec replied, clipped, and controlled. "The evidence is secured, and we're pulling every angle of security footage from the ballroom. Whoever did this left traces."

Charles's eyes flicked to Alec again, measuring him. "And you... you stopped it?"

"I did," Alec said simply. "That's why she's still safe."

Catherine's throat tightened. She wanted to reassure her father herself, but Alec's stance remained protective—a silent barrier she didn't push against.

Charles's expression softened as he looked at her. "Catherine... why didn't you tell me? I'm your father. I should have been there."

"We haven't exactly been close," she said quietly.

"Catherine," he murmured, regret heavy in his voice, "you know I regret what happened… every day."

"It still happened," she said gently but firmly. "And if you'd known about this, you would have tried to control everything."

"Of course I would." He stepped closer, emotion tightening his features. "You're my daughter. I love you."

Alec shifted—just enough to show he was listening, assessing, ready—but his posture softened a fraction. The tension in him wasn't aimed at Charles. It was anticipation. Protection.

Catherine took a hesitant step toward her father, closing the small distance between them. She let her hand brush his as she said, "I didn't tell you because… I didn't need you to take over the situation. I needed to handle it."

Charles's hand closed around hers, warm and grounding. "Catherine, you should never feel like you have to face danger alone. Not when I can help. Not when I love you."

She swallowed, the knot of old resentment and fear loosening slightly. "I know, Dad. But… it's complicated. I'm not the little girl you used to know."

Alec's eyes flicked between them, taking in every detail, his presence a silent reminder that while this was a father-daughter moment, the threat surrounding Catherine hadn't vanished. She felt it too—a subtle, constant tension in the air—but for the first time in years, something like normalcy brushed against her. Something like connection.

Charles leaned back slightly, offering a small, gentle smile weighted with years of regret. "I know you're not that little girl anymore. Ever since your mother died… you pulled away. I just wish I'd been there more. You need to let me in, Catherine."

Her throat tightened. She lowered her gaze, fingers twisting the edge of her robe. "I know, Dad… I just… I didn't want to be a burden. And I wasn't sure you could handle all of this."

Charles's expression softened, firm but tender. "You'll never be a burden. You're my daughter. You shouldn't have to face any of this alone. I want to be there for you—not just as someone who shows up after it's already happened."

Catherine met his eyes, vulnerability and tentative relief sliding through her. "I… I'll try," she whispered.

Alec didn't move, his posture still and protective, his dark gaze reading every nuance between them. He sensed the delicate shift—the small bridge forming—and didn't interfere. But every instinct remained alert. Catherine's safety was still his first priority.

Charles reached out, brushing a stray strand of hair from her face. The gesture was simple, tender, grounding—and for the first time in what felt like forever, Catherine felt a fragile spark of hope that maybe, just maybe, she and her father could repair what had broken between them.

Charles turned to Alec, his expression earnest. "Please… keep my daughter safe."

"I will," Alec said, voice low, steady, every word carrying unshakable certainty.

He left moments later.

Catherine sank onto the sofa, her body slumping as if the last weight of expectation had settled on her shoulders. Alec's eyes followed her, sharp and alert.

"You and your father… you're not close?" he asked, careful, measured.

"No," she said softly, the single word heavy with history.

"Can I ask why?" he pressed gently, though beneath the calm tone lay the steel of a man who needed to understand.

Catherine exhaled, fingers tracing the seam of the cushion as if the fabric could anchor her to some steadiness. "He tried to control my life. I… got tired of it. Then…" Her breath hitched, the memory leaving a bitter ache in her chest. "A boyfriend… asked my father for permission to marry me. My father was furious. He told him he wasn't good enough for me."

Alec's jaw tightened sharply, muscles clenching like iron. The unfairness of it—someone daring to question her worth—ignited something low and possessive in him, a fire he hadn't expected.

"I didn't even know he was going to see my father," she continued quietly, voice fragile yet steady. "I would've told him not to. My father… has always cared more about appearances than anything else."

Alec's voice dropped, low and reluctant, almost roughened by the ache he didn't allow himself to name. "Would you have accepted his proposal?"

Her gaze lifted, meeting his. Steady. Unflinching. "Yes."

No hesitation. No doubt.

A sharp, unwelcome stab of jealousy shot through Alec, twisting something inside him he wasn't ready to acknowledge.

"I would have married him in a heartbeat," she added softly, the words a ghost of a past love. "I loved him."

Alec's brow furrowed, the tight line of his jaw shadowing his face. "Then why didn't you? Were you worried he'd cut you off financially?"

Catherine lifted her chin, radiating quiet strength that dared him not to challenge her. "I haven't taken a penny from my father in more than two years. I live off my work—and my mother's inheritance."

Alec blinked, surprise flickering across his carefully controlled expression, and he found himself momentarily off-balance by her independence.

"That reminds me," Catherine said, voice steady, her tone leaving no room for argument. "Don't send your bill to Gary. I'll take care of it."

Alec frowned slightly. "Why?"

"Because I don't want to be indebted to any man," she said plainly, the words cutting sharp in their simplicity. "Not Gary. Not my father. No one. I stand on my own."

He didn't respond. He couldn't—not with the pull inside him tightening, deepening, becoming something dangerously close to need, something he had no right to indulge.

"I have work to do. I'll be in my study," she murmured, turning away, every movement deliberate, controlled.

Alec nodded, dark eyes following her retreat. Every step she took stirred a tension he could not shake. Even when the door closed behind her, the quiet gravity of her independence lingered in the room—along with the stark, undeniable realisation that she was slipping further under his skin, deeper than he had ever anticipated.

And then it hit him—she hadn't answered the question.

Why hadn't she married the man?

Had he run off when her father refused to bless the match? Had Catherine agreed with him, deciding her father was right? Or worse… was this the reason she had never looked at another man, the reason her sister had hinted that no one had reached her heart since?

A low, tight ache of jealousy coiled in Alec's chest. He hadn't even met the man, hadn't even seen him, and yet—something about the possibility of him, the thought that Catherine had once wanted him, made his teeth grit.

He pressed a hand to his temple, forcing his pulse down, forcing his mind to focus. He needed to know the truth. Not speculation. Not guesses. The answer, plain and unvarnished, had to come from her.

Because until he knew it, every step she took, every careful move she made, would set his blood on fire.

And he could not—would not—ignore it.

Catherine stayed in her study for the rest of the day. The door remained closed, the silence on the other side cold and deliberate. Alec checked on her a few times, but each time she dismissed him with a quiet, distant "I'm busy."

She didn't look at him.

She didn't have to.

The message was loud enough.

It was late—well past sunset—when Alec's phone buzzed on the coffee table.

He answered immediately. "Cole."

Logan's voice came through the line. "Boss, I just got the results back from the champagne flute."

Alec stood, tension snapping tight through his shoulders. "And?"

"It was definitely poison," Logan said grimly. "Aconitine. High concentration."

Alec cursed under his breath. "Damn... that'll stop a heart in minutes."

"Exactly. Whoever did this knew what they were doing. And Alec—there were no prints on the glass except yours and Miss Grant's."

Alec's jaw flexed hard. "Damn. This guy's smart."

A pause. Logan waited. Alec didn't waste any more time.

"What about the footage?" Alec's voice dropped, sharp and edged with warning.

Logan let out a long, frustrated sigh. "Nothing. Looks like he—or whoever it was—used a jammer to disable the feed. Ballroom cameras, hallway cameras... all gone."

Alec's grip tightened on the edge of the table, knuckles white. "So, he planned this. Covered every angle."

"Exactly," Logan replied. "We're blind—completely."

Alec's jaw clenched. He ran a hand over his face, his mind already racing through possibilities. Whoever had done this wasn't sloppy. They were precise, patient... and dangerous. And Catherine had been right in their crosshairs.

"We'll find him," Alec said, voice low, deadly calm. "And when we do..."

Logan didn't interrupt. He didn't need to. Alec's tone said enough.

"Does she know who you are yet?" Logan asked, voice low, cautious.

"No, Logan. She doesn't know I'm Ryan's brother."

A sharp intake of breath cut through the room. Catherine. She had been standing there, unseen, listening. The words landed like a thunderclap, and her eyes went wide, disbelief and shock flashing across her face.

"Al…?" she whispered, voice trembling, fragile.

Alec's hand tightened around the phone. Al. That's what Ryan had always called him. A single tap ended the call, and the sudden silence that followed felt deafening. His face remained carefully controlled, but his pulse hammered in his ears, raw and relentless.

"Catherine…" he said quietly, almost too low for her to hear.

Her gaze stayed locked on him, wide and searching, disbelief etched into every line of her face. "You're… Ryan's brother?"

He gave a short, sharp nod.

Her breath caught, small and uneven. "Why… why keep it a secret?"

Alec hesitated—long enough for her to see the war behind his eyes. He could lie. It would be easier. Cleaner. But he'd already done enough damage.

"I'm looking for answers about Ryan's death," he said, voice low, controlled. "I don't think it was an accident."

Catherine blinked, confusion flickering before something darker dawned. "Why not just tell me you were investigating…" Her voice faltered as the truth hit her, colour draining from her cheeks. "Oh my God." She stepped back, stunned. "You think I had something to do with it."

Alec didn't dispute her assumption. He didn't flinch.

She let out a shaky breath that was neither laugh nor sob. "You think I killed him," she whispered, voice cracking despite her desperate attempt to hold herself together.

Alec's jaw tightened, hands flexing at his sides. He didn't blink. Didn't speak. Didn't move.

"Was… sleeping with me part of the investigation?" she demanded, voice rising, brittle with disbelief and hurt.

"No."

Something fragile inside her shattered.

"You're a liar!" she shouted, voice raw and trembling. "You don't know anything! You don't get to think that about me!"

Alec's eyes narrowed, but he remained silent, letting her anger crash over him like a storm—relentless, unyielding.

Her chest heaved, fury and heartbreak tangled in every breath. "Why even protect me?" she demanded, trembling yet fierce. "If someone kills me, that would be justice, wouldn't it? That would make you happy!"

Before he could respond, she spun on her heel, storming down the hallway. Alec watched, trained and alert, yet something twisted sharply in his chest—a quiet, unfamiliar ache, deeper than jealousy, sharper than frustration.

Moments later she returned, clutching a framed photograph and a folded letter. Her hands shook violently as she thrust them into his chest, hard enough to make him stagger back half a step.

"I loved your brother," she said, tears spilling freely now. "And he loved me."

Chapter Thirteen

The words struck him like a physical blow. Alec stared at the photograph, then the letter, composure fracturing in thin, jagged cracks.

Alec's eyes darkened, a shadow of regret and longing crossing his face. He opened his mouth, then closed it. No words would undo the hurt; no explanations could erase the weight of her grief.

Catherine's shoulders trembled as she stared up at him, searching his expression, trying to read if he believed her, if he thought her innocent, if he thought her heart had been faithful. The silence stretched between them—heavy, unbearable, and aching with everything left unsaid.

Her voice rose, trembling with grief and fury. "Do you even hear what you've just accused me of?" she demanded, hands gesturing wildly, raw, and unpractised. "You think I'm a murderer! You think I killed him! How dare you look at me like that—like I'm capable of something so monstrous!"

Alec froze. Every word hit harder than any gunshot or threat he'd faced. Her eyes shimmered with pain, cheeks flushed, lips trembling. Beneath the rage was heartbreak—pure, unscripted, devastating.

"I loved him," she whispered, voice breaking, the words carved from a place deep inside. "I loved your brother. And you... you see me as a monster? After everything I've felt, everything I've lost... you dare judge me?"

She ran a trembling hand through her hair, shoulders sagging under the weight of fury, exhaustion, and years of buried grief. "You don't know anything. You don't know what love is. You don't know what loss feels like."

Alec stood motionless, absorbing every syllable. The armour he'd lived in—precise, hardened, unshakeable—shifted. Hairline fractures appeared where certainty had once been. Her grief wasn't guilt. It was devastation. Truth.

For the first time, Alec questioned everything: his instincts. His assumptions. His loyalty. His anger. His grief. His need to blame someone—anyone—for Ryan's death.

He drew in a slow, trembling breath. When he finally spoke, his voice was low, measured... softer than she had ever heard.

"You're... not what I expected."

Tears pooled in her eyes. "Then why…" Her voice faltered, but she forced it out. "Why look at me like I'm guilty? Why protect me if I'm some kind of criminal? Why make love to me? To punish me?"

He didn't answer immediately. He studied her—the shaking hands, the devastation etched into her expression, the undeniable truth in her pain. Her grief wasn't an act. Her heartbreak wasn't fabricated. Somewhere deep inside, something shifted dangerously, irrevocably.

Once again, Alec Cole wondered if he had been wrong about her all along.

Catherine didn't wait for his response. She turned sharply, chin lifted, tears blurring her vision. Her posture was fierce, unbroken, defiant. She walked to the door, leaving him standing in the quiet wreckage of the living room.

He looked down at the photograph and the folded letter in his hands—evidence of a truth he had never known existed. For the first time, Alec felt exposed. Not to danger, not to the world—but to something far more volatile, far more terrifying: the unsettling, heart-pounding possibility that the woman he had been so certain he needed to judge might, in fact, be the only one speaking the truth.

Every certainty he had clung to—the suspicions, the assumptions, the control—wavered under the weight of what he held. A cold, tight knot formed in his chest. He could have made the most reckless, irreversible mistake of his life.

The photograph weighed heavy in his hands. Ryan had Catherine lifted off the ground, ready to spin her in a circle. His expression radiated pure, unfiltered joy—love so vivid it almost glowed. Catherine's smile was soft and warm, arms draped around his shoulders, eyes shining with trust and affection. The connection between them wasn't subtle—it was blazing, alive, undeniable.

Even in stillness, the photograph throbbed with motion—laughter suspended mid-breath, a moment carved so deeply it could never fade. And yet, looking at it, Alec felt an unwelcome pang of jealousy twist through him, sharp and persistent.

He swallowed hard and unfolded the letter, the paper crackling under his fingers like something fragile and sacred. Ryan's handwriting swept across the page, intimate, confident—small glimpses of the words striking Alec with startling weight.

…last night was the best night of my life… knowing you love me as much as I love you… I never believed in forever until you looked at me that way… you deserve light, Cat…

He didn't need to read more to feel the force behind every line—the devotion, the tenderness, the plans for a future he had never imagined Catherine sharing with anyone, least of all Ryan. His jaw tightened, throat constricting, pulse hammering with a raw, relentless force.

He pressed the letter to his chest, eyes closing as a rush of emotion tore through him—anger, guilt, longing, confusion—colliding in a storm too violent to name. The world had always been simple: clean lines, sharp corners, truth and lies, threat and safety.

Now, everything blurred.

He looked back at the photograph. Ryan's radiant smile. Catherine's joy. The unmistakable intimacy between them. It wasn't speculation. It wasn't manipulation. It was truth—a truth that cut straight through him, slicing the certainty he had built around himself.

And in that truth, something dangerous unfurled—sharp, visceral, terrifying.

Protecting Catherine wasn't duty anymore.

It was personal.

It was instinct.

It was inevitable.

He lowered his head, pressing his forehead to the framed photo and letter, inhaling a shallow, ragged breath. The apartment was quiet except for the distant hum of the city—a fragile thread of normalcy that couldn't touch the war raging inside him.

Jealous.

The word scraped through him like broken glass.

Finally, he set the photo and letter on the coffee table, his dark eyes lingering as if he needed to memorise every curve, every shade, every word—before the world could rip them away the way it had taken Ryan.

Somewhere deep beneath the discipline, the steel, the control, Alec Cole admitted a truth he had buried far too long:

He didn't just want to keep Catherine safe.

He needed to.

If Ryan had loved her, if she had loved him in return, Alec would honour that love. Protecting her wasn't just survival. It was loyalty. It was respect. It was something raw, primal, and undeniable—something he didn't dare name.

Catherine barely slept. Every time she closed her eyes, she thought of Alec—the way he had held her, the way he had loved her, and then the words that cut sharper than any blade. You think I killed him. They had burned through her all night, leaving her chest hollow, raw.

By dawn, she felt drained, almost fragile. She dressed with mechanical precision, forcing her trembling legs toward the kitchen. Coffee. Distance. Anything that wasn't Alec Cole.

But he was already there.

Alec leaned against the counter, broad shoulders rigid beneath a dark T-shirt, one hand wrapped around a mug as if it anchored him. The moment she stepped inside, his dark eyes lifted—alert, assessing, unreadable.

"Morning," he murmured, voice low, rough, raw—like sleep had avoided him, too.

She swallowed and managed a clipped, "Morning."

She brushed past him, forcing her gaze away from the framed photo and letter on the coffee table—proof of everything she had lost, everything he now doubted. She couldn't let him see how much it gutted her.

But she felt his eyes, heavy, unrelenting.

The aroma of fresh coffee did nothing to soothe the tension coiling around her. Her fingers wrapped around the cup like a shield.

"I… I can get someone else," she said, voice brittle, forcing herself steady. "There are other agencies. You don't have to—" Her words faltered. "I won't keep you here."

A moment of silence stretched, too heavy, too full of unsaid words.

"No."

Her head snapped up. "No?"

Alec didn't move closer, but the air around him shifted, charged, resolute. "No," he repeated, firmer.

Catherine's brow furrowed, frustration threading through her exhaustion. "I'm giving you an out. You don't want to be here."

A subtle tightening of his jaw. His dark eyes never left hers. "You need protection."

"Why do you care?" she shot back. "You think I'm a monster."

He stiffened—not with anger, but with something far more dangerous, quickly buried.

"Catherine... I'm not leaving," he said, his voice low, steady, a pulse beneath the tension between them.

Her chest constricted, irritation flaring, relief following almost immediately—and she hated herself for it.

She gripped her mug tighter, knuckles whitening. "You... you shouldn't be here. Not after last night. If you really believe what you said..." Her voice dropped to a whisper, bitter and raw. "You should go."

He stepped closer, close enough that the heat radiating from him brushed her shoulder. He didn't touch her, but every inch of his presence was pressure, draw, insistence.

"I'm not going anywhere," he said, soft but unyielding.

Her breath hitched. Silence fell between them, heavy, electric, filled with everything neither dared voice—the unspoken need, the danger, the anger, the pull.

"Well," she said, setting her cup down with a sharp clink, "I'm ready to leave when you are."

Inside her office, they fell into routine seamlessly, as if nothing had changed. Coffee brewed, emails checked, schedules reviewed. And yet, a taut thread of tension wound itself between them. Neither acknowledged the night they'd spent together—or the fact that he'd hidden his identity as Ryan's brother. Catherine had convinced herself that burying it was safer; Alec seemed equally intent on pretending it had never happened.

The morning passed in clipped efficiency. The silence carried a weight neither dared name. Catherine focused on the numbers on her screen, while Alec lingered near the window, posture rigid, dark eyes flicking toward her with that familiar edge of vigilance.

Just after lunch, Alec's phone buzzed. He stepped aside, answering with clipped precision.

"Cole."

"Boss," Logan's voice came tight, urgent. "I've gone through the financials. It's... bad. Catherine's father—Charles Grant—there's evidence suggesting he financed the killers. Your mother, Ryan... even Catherine herself. The transfers, the accounts... it's all there."

Alec froze, the phone nearly slipping from his hand. The office seemed to constrict around him. Every instinct he'd honed over decades screamed. Fury roared beneath his calm exterior.

He hung up and turned to Catherine, voice low, sharp. "You need to know something."

She looked up, tense. "What do I need to know?"

"Logan's found evidence your father is paying someone to kill you."

Her breath caught. "I beg your pardon?"

"You heard me. It's your father."

Catherine recoiled, stunned. Her hands clutched the desk, knuckles white. "What... what are you saying?"

"That he wants you dead. He paid for your mother... for my brother... and now," Alec's jaw tightened, eyes burning, "now he wants you gone."

"No," she whispered, shaking her head, voice trembling. "I—I don't believe it. My father wouldn't... he wouldn't want me dead!"

Alec's posture stiffened, tension coiling like steel through his body. "We have proof."

Her chest constricted, betrayal twisting with disbelief. "How dare you," she said, voice rising. "You don't get to accuse my father!"

"I'm not accusing," he growled, low and controlled. "I'm telling you the truth—"

"I don't want to hear it!" she snapped, rising abruptly. Her chair scraped across the polished floor. "First you accuse me of killing your brother. Now you accuse my father of trying to kill me. It's absurd. My father may be many things, but a murderer is not one of them. You—get out. I don't want you anywhere near me."

Alec blinked, just for a fraction of a second unguarded. "I'm not leaving," he said evenly, low, and steady, but with an edge that made the words impossible to ignore.

"You are leaving," she shot back, her voice trembling, breaking. "And don't come back. I don't need you. I don't want you here."

Something inside him twisted sharply, sharper than he expected. Her words cut deeper than he'd anticipated, striking a raw nerve. He held her gaze, every second stretched tight and tense, the pull to argue, to stay, to protect her battling against the coiled intensity in his chest.

"Get out!" Catherine's voice rang out, sharp, final—each syllable a hammer strike against him. "You're fired—understand me? I don't want to lay eyes on you again."

He didn't move.

"Get. Out!" she repeated, fury blazing in her eyes, her voice carrying all the finality of a verdict.

Alec's jaw tightened. He gave her one slow, measured look—dark, unreadable, tension radiating from every line of his body. Then, with deliberate, absolute control, he pivoted and walked from the office.

The quiet click of the door behind him sounded like a final judgment, echoing in the silence she left behind.

Thirty minutes later, Alec entered his office. Logan looked up, surprise flickering across his face. "What are you doing here? Where's Miss Grant?"

"She fired me," Alec said simply, voice low, measured, each word cutting through the air like steel.

Logan's expression tightened. "Boss… she's in danger."

"Don't you think I know that?" Alec shot back, the edge in his tone unyielding. "She just doesn't want my help anymore."

He slammed the door behind him, the sharp sound echoing through the quiet office, then began to pace. She didn't want him there. She had made that abundantly clear.

The thought twisted something raw and unyielding in his chest. He had always known the dangers she faced were real—he had trained for this, lived for this—but the sting of rejection, the possibility that they might be wrong about her father's intentions, gnawed at him in a way nothing else could.

She was alive. She was safe—for now. And yet every second apart, every unspoken word, every glance she had shot his way earlier, reminded him just how fragile that safety was.

Every flicker of defiance in her eyes, every small act of independence—it tugged at him, magnetic, relentless. He clenched his fists, knuckles whitening, trying to anchor himself against the storm of emotions that had no place in his line of work.

He already cared about her. Deeply. More than he should. More than he was allowed to. He knew the rules, the boundaries—but knowing didn't stop the ache, didn't stop the protective surge that made him want to sweep her into his arms and never let go.

The office felt smaller, tighter, suffocating with the weight of his thoughts. He stopped pacing, staring out the window at the city below, oblivious to the danger that lurked just beneath the surface of her life—and to the danger that had just as much to do with his own heart.

Alec ran a hand through his hair, frustrated, furious, and uncomfortably aware. *He shouldn't feel this way. He shouldn't care this much.* But he did. And that—more than anything—terrified him.

Chapter Fourteen

In an instant, the office felt impossibly empty without him. Every corner seemed to echo with the weight of unspoken words, every heartbeat a reminder of the regret she carried—and the regret he carried too. Catherine sank into her chair, staring blankly at the polished desk. She couldn't believe it. *Her father... wanted her dead?* It didn't make sense.

The thought clawed at her chest. She had always suspected, in the shadows of her mind, that he had some role in her mother's death, Ryan's... but herself? *Why would he want her gone?* The idea was absurd, yet Alec said he had evidence—proof he had unearthed—made her stomach twist in uneasy knots.

Shaking off the thought, she forced herself to move. By the time she reached her building, the normal rhythm of her life tried to reassert itself. The concierge greeted her with his usual polite smile, though today he held a clipboard.

"Miss Grant, the gas company needed to check your lines. They were worried that there was a possible leak," he said.

Catherine gave a quick nod, brushing it off. "Thank you, I appreciate it," she said, and made her way to her penthouse, ignoring the tiny flutter of unease in her chest.

Once inside, she let the shower wash away the day—the tension with Alec, the storm of revelations about her father. Steam curled around her, warm and soothing, but it couldn't completely erase the sense of vulnerability she felt.

She dried off and settled on something simple for dinner: a salad. Her movements were automatic—chopping, tossing, plating—the rhythm grounding her, offering a fragile sense of control in a world that suddenly felt anything but safe.

She needed to find a replacement for Alec. The thought pricked at her chest, more painful than it should have. Tomorrow, she would ask Gary to help. Tonight, all she wanted was to disappear into sleep.

After dinner, she cleaned the kitchen, stacked the plates, wiped the counters. The mundane tasks—the clatter of dishes, the familiar motions—should have been comforting. Instead, a creeping light-headedness pricked at the edges of her vision. She paused, gripping the counter, forcing herself to steady against the unsteady sway of the room.

Her head spun. A sharp, disorienting tilt, and then everything lurched. She took a step toward the sofa, but the room tilted further, and the world blurred into chaos. Panic flared, sharp and immediate.

Before she could reach safety, her legs gave way, and she collapsed onto the living room floor. The last thing she registered was the cold, hard surface beneath her and the stark, sudden realisation that she was utterly, terrifyingly alone.

Alec spent the rest of the afternoon buried in his emails, the glowing screen a poor substitute for the gnawing tension in his chest. Each message, each spreadsheet, each innocuous work update blurred together, a futile attempt to keep his mind from circling Catherine. He tried to focus on numbers, on deadlines, on anything—but every glance at the clock, every ping of a new email, yanked him back to her.

The office door opened quietly, and Logan stepped in, hands clasped behind his back. Alec didn't look up immediately, as if the data could shield him from the anxiety tightening around his ribs.

"Boss," Logan said carefully, measured but edged with concern, "you sure about leaving Catherine Grant unprotected?"

Alec finally lifted his gaze, dark eyes narrowing. "She's made her choice," he said, clipped, almost too sharp. "She doesn't want my help. She knows the risks."

Logan's brow furrowed. "Knowing you're in danger and being able to prevent it are two different things. Someone tried to kill her the other night. You know how close it was. And now—after the gala, after everything with her father…" His words hung, heavy with unspoken warning.

Alec leaned back in his chair, jaw tight, hands gripping the arms of the leather seat. He didn't answer immediately. The weight of Logan's concern pressed against him, but the part of him trained to handle threats, to act decisively, rebelled against the notion of standing watch over her constantly.

"She's not a child," he said finally, voice low, controlled, though tension coiled beneath the surface like a spring. "I'm not her shadow. She has to live her life. And I—" He swallowed hard, cutting himself off, the truth lodged behind his teeth.

Logan's eyes softened slightly, but concern lingered. "Just… be careful, boss. Don't underestimate her father—or anyone else. You know how quickly things can go sideways."

Alec nodded once, curt, voice clipped. "I know."

Logan hesitated, then left, the warning lingering like a low hum in the office. Alec turned back to the screen, forcing himself to focus, but the numbers, the emails—they all blurred. The thought of Catherine alone, vulnerable, gnawed at him relentlessly.

He tried to resist it—tried to convince himself he was only her protector, nothing more—but the truth pressed against him like iron: he cared for her. More than he should. More than he had ever let himself care for anyone. The idea that she could be hurt, that she could die while he sat here pretending to focus, made his chest tighten, his stomach knot.

He couldn't sit there any longer. He stood abruptly, the chair scraping back, heart hammering. She didn't want him there; she had made that clear—but he didn't care. Not now. Not when she might be in danger. Alec moved toward the door, every muscle taut, every thought consumed by the one thing he could not control: the overwhelming, terrifying certainty that he needed her safe—and that he needed to be the one to keep her that way.

Alec grabbed his coat so fast it nearly slipped from his grip, the leather still warm from his chair as he shrugged it on. He didn't bother shutting off his computer. He didn't bother locking his office door. None of it mattered—not when every instinct in his body was screaming at him to move. *Now.*

He strode down the hallway, jaw tight, the echo of his footsteps sharp against the polished floors. In the lift, he jabbed the button for the basement before the doors had even fully closed, the small space feeling suffocating as the cabin descended.

He needed to get to her.

He needed to know she was safe.

He needed—God, he didn't even want to finish the thought.

The moment the lift doors parted, Alec was already moving. He crossed the basement car park in long, purposeful strides, his keys clenched so hard in his fist the metal bit into his skin. He unlocked his SUV, slid behind the wheel, and the engine roared to life. Tyres screeched as he shot out onto the street.

The entire drive blurred into a series of frantic glances at the clock and a mounting dread he couldn't shake. She was alone. She had pushed him away. And he had let her.

Not again.

Not tonight.

Not ever.

He pulled up to Catherine's building and barely put the vehicle in park before he was out. The concierge straightened as Alec strode past, and Alec gave a curt nod—his only acknowledgment.

Thankfully, Catherine hadn't told the staff she'd fired him. The private lift recognised him immediately, the doors sliding open with a soft chime. He stepped inside, his heart hammering in his chest.

As the lift ascended, Alec tried to steady his breathing. She's fine. She's stubborn, reckless, infuriating—but she's fine. He repeated the lie over and over, but it only twisted deeper in his gut.

The lift slowed.

The lights blinked.

A soft chime sounded as the doors slid open to the penthouse foyer.

Alec stepped out—and froze.

The wrongness hit him instantly. The air was stifling, dense and unnatural, pressing against his skin like a silent warning. No chemical tang. No burning scent. Nothing obvious for a trained nose to catch. But every instinct he trusted screamed danger.

His pulse spiked.

"Catherine?" His voice carried sharp control, but panic threaded beneath it.

Silence.

A coldness washed through him. The stillness, the heavy air, the absence of any movement—it all felt wrong.

Every muscle tightened. He surged forward, training taking over. "Catherine?" he called again, the edge in his voice cutting through the penthouse, steel barely covering the fear rising inside him.

Still nothing.

He moved deeper, steps deliberate and lethal-silent, senses locked at full alert. The air grew thicker, heavier with every breath. His instincts—the ones that had kept him alive through missions that buried lesser men—roared at him.

Scan.

Assess.

Act.

But another instinct drowned them out.

Fear.

"Catherine!" His shout cracked through the penthouse like a whip, echoing through rooms that should not have been this silent.

No response.

His eyes swept the space—fast, precise—and then he saw her.

Collapsed on the living room floor.

Alec's heart dropped, a violent, sickening free-fall.

He ran.

"Catherine—" Her name tore from his throat, raw and unrestrained.

She lay crumpled on the hardwood, body limp, hair fanned across the floor like a dark halo. Her eyes were closed, but a faint, unnatural flush tinged her cheeks—a deceptive, almost sickly pink. Her breaths came shallow and uneven, ragged little gasps that barely lifted her chest. A bluish tinge clung to the edges of her lips, and her skin was cold and clammy beneath his touch.

Alec dropped to his knees beside her, heart slamming against his ribs.

"Catherine," he hissed, voice sharp and urgent. His hands moved on instinct—one steadying her shoulders, the other sliding to her neck for a pulse.

It was there. Weak. Fluttering. Almost imperceptible, like the frantic beat of a bird trapped in a fist. Her fingers twitched but didn't curl around his. Her eyelids fluttered beneath their lashes; a faint tremor rippled along her jaw.

Alec cursed under his breath.

"Stay with me," he ordered, low, commanding, unrelenting. "Do you hear me? Stay with me."

Nothing.

He didn't waste another second.

With a controlled breath, he slid his arms under her—one beneath her knees, the other behind her back—and lifted her clean off the floor. She felt weightless. Too weightless. As if she might vanish if he wasn't holding on tightly enough.

Her head lolled against his shoulder, her breath barely warming his skin.

He pulled her closer.

"We're getting out of here," he muttered, mostly to himself. "I've got you."

He moved fast but with precision-born muscle memory, cutting straight across the apartment. He didn't risk the kitchen. Didn't touch a switch. Didn't stop. At the private lift, he hit the call button with his elbow, refusing to loosen his grip even for a heartbeat.

The doors opened with a soft chime.

He stepped inside.

Pressed the lobby button.

As the lift descended, numbers blinking past with agonising slowness, Alec kept his eyes locked on Catherine. His thumb brushed her pulse point, counting each faint flutter with rising dread.

Her breathing hitched against his chest.

Too faint.

Too fragile.

Too close to gone.

"Come on, baby," he whispered, the endearment slipping out without thought, raw and unguarded. "Stay with me."

The coil in his chest wound tighter with every floor. One arm stayed locked around her legs, the other supporting her head against his shoulder. Her breath fluttered—thin, uneven—and every second felt like it might be her last.

When the doors slid open, he didn't walk out.

He burst from the lift.

"Get an ambulance. Now!" Alec's voice cracked through the lobby like a gunshot.

The concierge, startled, scrambled to his feet the moment he saw Catherine limp in Alec's arms. "Sir—yes, of course—right away." He grabbed the phone with shaking hands, dialling emergency services as fast as he could.

Alec didn't wait. He moved toward the entrance, holding Catherine tight, lowering himself to one knee so he could support her better, his hand steady on her cheek.

"Come on, Catherine," he whispered urgently, his voice rough, fraying at the edges. "Stay with me. Don't you dare fade on me now."

Her lashes didn't flutter.

Her breath stayed shallow.

His heart hammered a brutal rhythm against his ribs.

And the terrifying truth settled over him like ice:

He had almost been too late.

Minutes stretched like hours as Alec held her, whispering to her, grounding her, fighting panic with sheer force of will. He kept two fingers pressed to her pulse, counting every faint thud like it was a lifeline. Every shallow breath she managed felt stolen, fragile—each one searing through him as if it were his own.

She shouldn't have been alone.

He should never have left.

And the knowledge clawed at him with every passing second.

"Come on, baby," he murmured, thumb brushing gently across her cheek. "Stay with me. Just stay with me."

The distant wail of sirens finally cut through the building—a bleak, haunting sound that made Alec's chest tighten. Relief didn't come. Not fully. Not when the sharper realisation settled in like ice:

He hadn't been enough to keep her safe.

But he had made it before the worst happened.

He had gotten to her.

He wasn't too late.

Her hair clung to her temple, damp from sweat, and he brushed it back with a tenderness he didn't bother hiding anymore. Holding her—keeping her anchored—felt instinctive, inevitable.

He didn't care that he'd crossed the lines he'd tried so hard to enforce. He didn't care that every second he held her only deepened something he'd been fighting since the night they first met.

Right now, there was only her.

Her breath.

Her heartbeat.

Her life in his hands.

When the paramedics burst into the lobby, rushing toward them with equipment and urgency, Alec felt the first wave of guilt crash into him—heavy, crushing—and beneath it, something even more dangerous:

The truth that he wasn't just protecting her life.

Somewhere along the way, he'd begun protecting his heart, too.

The paramedics moved quickly, expertly, lifting Catherine onto the stretcher. Alec's breath locked in his chest at the sight of her—oxygen mask secured, eyelashes still against her cheeks, completely unaware of the chaos she had left behind.

They began wheeling her toward the ambulance.

Alec moved with them.

He didn't ask permission.

He didn't look back.

He simply followed—because the idea of letting her out of his sight felt like stepping off a cliff.

"Sir, we need space to work," one of the paramedics said, trying to angle the stretcher.

"You'll have it," Alec replied, voice low, steady. "But I'm coming with you."

The paramedic started to object, then caught the look in Alec's eyes—the unyielding, protective fire burning there—and nodded once. "Fine. Stay near the back."

As they pushed through the lobby, the concierge hurried beside him, breathless.

"Mr. Cole—about the gas company—"

Alec cut him a sharp look. "What about them?"

"They came earlier today. Said they needed to check Miss Grant's gas lines. Routine maintenance." He swallowed. "They were in her penthouse for forty minutes."

Alec's blood ran cold.

He didn't slow. Didn't blink. Didn't breathe.

He just said, "Forty minutes?" in a voice so quiet it was dangerous.

"Yes, sir. He had ID, uniform—everything."

Of course he did. Professional. Planned. Calculated.

They knew how to get to her.

Chapter Fifteen

He kept pace with the stretcher, pulling out his phone with one hand as the ambulance doors opened.

He hit Logan's number. Hard.

"Boss?" Logan answered instantly.

"I need footage," Alec said, stepping up into the ambulance without hesitation. "Anyone who entered Catherine's penthouse today. Gas company, maintenance—anyone."

Logan paused. Not long. Just enough to hear the thing Alec was trying to hide.

Fear.

"Boss… what happened?"

Logan's voice crackled through the phone, tight with concern.

Alec glanced down at Catherine as the paramedics worked around her—sliding in IVs, fitting the oxygen mask over her face, placing monitors across her chest. Her skin was ashen beneath the harsh ambulance lights, her breaths shallow, her lashes unmoving against her cheeks.

"Someone tampered with her apartment," Alec said, his voice like raw steel. "I'm almost certain she was poisoned with carbon monoxide. She was unconscious when I found her."

Logan swore softly. "Is she—?"

"She's alive." Alec forced the words out, though they scraped against his throat. "But she won't be if we don't find who did this."

"I'll head to her building," Logan said immediately. "Check the heater, the vents, the roof access—everything. I'll pull footage, talk to security. I'll update you the second I know something."

Around Alec, the paramedics called out rapid instructions—

"Oxygen at eighty-five!"

"Blood pressure stabilising."

"Keep the mask sealed—CO levels are still high."

Alec braced a hand on the interior rail, fingers locking around the metal until his knuckles went white. He didn't trust himself to speak—not with the fear still thick in his chest.

Logan's voice dropped, steadier, resolute.

"I'll find them. I swear it."

The line went dead just as the ambulance doors slammed shut, sealing them in a world of sirens and fluorescent light.

Alec didn't spare a glance for the paramedics moving around him, the clipped medical jargon, or the strobe of red and blue bleeding through the back windows as the city blurred away. None of it mattered.

He looked only at Catherine.

At the faint, fragile rise of her chest beneath the oxygen mask.

At the pale curve of her cheek, still too cold.

At the woman he had carried out of a death trap minutes before she slipped beyond reach.

A woman he had almost lost.

His fingers curled tighter around the side rail of the stretcher, knuckles whitening with the effort to keep himself steady. Emotion twisted through him—raw, violent, unfiltered. Relief. Terror. Rage. And something deeper, older, truer than he had ever meant to feel.

Love.

Not the kind he'd been trained to deny.

Not the distant, disciplined kind he'd pretended it was.

But the devastating, absolute truth that hit him now with the weight of nearly losing her.

The paramedics adjusted her oxygen, running vitals, calling numbers he catalogued without meaning to. Her pulse too weak. Her breathing too shallow. Her skin still too pale.

Alec leaned in, just enough that only she could hear.

"You're not leaving me," he whispered, voice low, fierce, a promise and a plea all at once. "Do you understand? Not like this."

His world had narrowed to a single point—her.

Not the danger.

Not the killer.

Not the chaos waiting outside the ambulance.

Catherine.

The one person he couldn't fail.

The one person he would burn down cities to protect.

The one person someone had tried to take from him tonight.

He wasn't letting her out of his sight.

Not now.

Not when someone wanted her dead.

Not ever again.

Whatever line he'd once drawn—between duty and desire, between protection and something far more dangerous—had vanished the moment he found her on that floor.

And Alec knew one thing with brutal, unshakeable clarity:

Whoever had done this…

would regret not finishing the job.

Because he would not stop until Catherine was safe.

The door to the ICU room opened quietly. Alec's head barely lifted from Catherine's hand as a figure approached in scrubs. The doctor's expression was tight, professional— but the weight behind his eyes made Alec straighten instantly.

"Mr. Cole?" the doctor said, voice low. "I need to speak with you for a moment."

Alec didn't hesitate. He rose, brushing his hand over Catherine's gently, as if he could somehow anchor her even while he stepped away from her bed.

The room was stark, fluorescent lights reflecting off the polished floors. Alec's hands flexed at his sides, jaw tight.

The doctor met his gaze directly. "She's stable now," he said carefully, "but you need to understand just how serious this was. Minutes more, and she wouldn't have made it."

Alec's chest tightened, a surge of anger and fear threading through him. "How long was she exposed?"

"Long enough for carbon monoxide to reach critical levels. Her oxygen saturation dropped dangerously low. She was essentially suffocating from the inside. Your timing—arriving when you did—was the only reason we were able to reverse the immediate damage."

Alec's fingers curled into a fist at his side. "And her brain? Any lasting damage?"

The doctor shook his head slowly. "Right now, it's too early to tell definitively. CO poisoning can cause neurological damage—but at this point, she's breathing on supplemental oxygen, her vitals are stabilising, and she hasn't exhibited any immediate deficits. We'll need to monitor her closely for the next 24 to 48 hours."

Alec's shoulders slumped slightly. Relief washed over him, but it was brittle, edged with lingering fear. He didn't say anything. Couldn't.

The doctor added gently, "As you can see, she's still unconscious. That's normal for this level of exposure. The sedation also helps prevent any stress on her heart while her body recovers."

Alec's eyes shot back toward where Catherine lay, pale and fragile beneath the hospital blankets, tubes and monitors keeping her alive. His chest tightened at the sight, every instinct screaming at him to stay right there, to never let her out of his sight.

"How long before she wakes?" Alec asked, voice rough, taut with barely contained fear.

"Could be hours. Could be overnight. We just don't know yet. But she's alive, and that's the critical part. That's what matters right now," the doctor replied, measured but firm.

Alec swallowed hard. "Alive," he repeated, like a mantra, the single word carrying all the relief, guilt, and terror he'd felt since finding her slumped in her apartment.

The doctor hesitated, then added, "We've contacted her father. He's on his way."

Alec's stomach twisted into a knot so sharp he almost doubled over. His mind raced. Her father—the man he suspected had orchestrated the hit on her, on her mother, on Ryan—now on his way to see her. Every muscle in Alec's body tensed, instincts screaming that he could not allow that to happen.

He forced himself to nod, but it was mechanical, cold, deliberate. He refused to show the panic clawing at his chest.

Turning back to Catherine, he pressed a finger gently to her hand. Her eyelids fluttered, almost imperceptibly, as if sensing him there.

"Hang on, Catherine," he whispered, voice low and fierce, every syllable a promise. "I'm not going anywhere. Not now. Not ever."

The doctor stepped back silently, leaving Alec alone with her fragile form, the monitors beeping softly. Each second stretched endlessly, a reminder of just how close she had come to death—and of the dangerous truths lurking behind every person she trusted.

Alec's gaze hardened, dark and unyielding, as he silently vowed: if her father—or anyone—so much as thought to harm her again, they would answer to him. No excuses. No mercy.

The door to the hospital room slammed open, crashing against the wall.

Alec's head snapped toward the sound, his hands instinctively tightening around Catherine's.

"Catherine!"

Charles Grant stumbled inside, breath ragged, eyes wild with panic. His face was ashen, drawn tight with fear. He nearly tripped in his rush to reach her bedside, gripping the rail so hard his knuckles blanched. His hands shook violently as he leaned over his daughter.

"Oh—God." His voice cracked. "Catherine… sweetheart…" He brushed trembling fingers across her hair, whispering her name over and over—each repetition raw, desperate, pleading.

Alec straightened, every protective instinct flaring. He angled himself subtly forward, alert, evaluating. Watching.

But what he saw made him pause.

There was no calculation in Charles's expression. No forced grief. No hidden agenda.

The man in front of him was shattered. Terrified. Barely holding himself together.

And every instinct Alec possessed—the ones trained to read liars, manipulators, killers—told him one truth with absolute clarity:

Charles Grant was not acting.

He loved his daughter.

He was breaking right in front of him.

Alec's jaw tightened, the ground shifting beneath him. The suspicion he'd carried—the certainty that Charles had ordered the attacks—wavered, fractured. *Had they been wrong?*

Finally, Charles looked up, eyes glassy with fear. "Please… what happened? How did she end up like this?" His voice broke. "Who would do this to her?"

Alec forced his tone steady. "We don't know yet. But it was carbon monoxide poisoning. My man is investigating her apartment now."

Charles swallowed, shoulders shaking. "You… you saved her." His gaze locked with Alec's, unguarded and sincere. "Thank you."

Alec felt something twist painfully in his chest. He didn't respond—couldn't. The moment was too raw, too complicated, too dangerous in its own way.

Charles sank into the chair beside the bed, burying his face in his hands. He looked smaller. Older. Devastated.

Maybe… just maybe… they had been wrong about him.

But Alec's resolve didn't waver.

He laid a steady hand on Catherine's shoulder, never taking his eyes off her. Whether Charles was innocent or not, one truth remained unchanged: danger still circled her, closer than ever.

And Alec would not let it near her again.

Silent.

Vigilant.

Unyielding.

He stayed by her side—because whatever had brought Catherine here tonight, he would damn well make sure it never happened again.

Catherine surfaced slowly, as if swimming upward through heavy, murky water. Voices drifted around her—low, urgent murmurs—then the steady beeping of a monitor pulled her fully awake.

Light. A ceiling she didn't recognise. The faint antiseptic scent of a hospital.

Her hands were warm, solid in the grip of two people. She blinked and realised Alec was on her right, his fingers curled around hers, thumb brushing in slow, steady circles. On her left, her father held her hand, his expression taut with fear and relief.

She tried to sit up, but a wave of dizziness pinned her back against the pillows. "Wh-what… what happened?" Her voice was hoarse, shaky.

Her father's voice cracked. "Sweetheart… you collapsed in your apartment. We think it was carbon monoxide. You barely made it out."

Alec's dark eyes never left her face. "I found you just in time. You were not breathing properly. You were lucky." His voice was low, raw with concern, and the tight set of his jaw revealed just how scared he had been.

Catherine's pulse quickened. "Carbon monoxide…? How…?"

"We're looking into it," Alec said. "We should know more soon."

Her father shook his head; helplessness etched in every line of his face. "You're safe now. That's what matters."

Alec leaned closer, his gaze fixed on her like he was afraid she might vanish again. "You've been out for twelve hours," he said quietly. "Your oxygen levels were dangerously low."

Twelve hours.

The number sank into her chest like a weight.

Catherine's gaze flicked between them, memories of Alec's words about her father and the earlier confrontation stirring unease. She tried to withdraw her hand from Alec's.

But he tightened his grip instinctively, grounding her, refusing to let go.

She didn't try again. She didn't have the strength, and she didn't want to discuss Alec's suspicions in front of her father. So, she did the only thing she could—she thanked him.

"Thank you… for saving me."

"You don't have to thank me. But you scared the hell out of me." His thumb brushed slowly over her knuckles, steadying her.

Her father lingered a little longer but was soon called away on business. He bent to kiss Catherine on the forehead. "I'll see you soon," he murmured, before shaking Alec's hand firmly and thanking him again for saving his daughter's life.

He looked ten years older than he had yesterday, the strain etched into every line of his face. Alec studied him carefully, noting the raw, unfeigned worry in his eyes. If this was genuine concern… then Charles had nothing to do with the attempt on his daughter's life.

Chapter Sixteen

When her father left, Alec reached for Catherine's hand again, but she pulled away.

"Why are you here? I thought we already said everything we needed to," she asked, voice low but firm.

"Catherine… I'm not going anywhere. No matter what you say." His voice was calm, resolute. He wanted to tell her how much he cared—more than she realised, more than he should—but he held back, waiting until she was stronger, until the storm inside her had quieted.

She lay back, closing her eyes. The steady beep of the monitor was the only sound in the room, rhythmic and unnervingly constant.

Not long after, there was a knock at the door. It opened, and Logan stepped in, Detective Derek Samuels trailing behind. Alec released Catherine's hand and stood.

Catherine opened her eyes. Logan spoke first. "How are you feeling?"

Catherine tried a small smile. "Okay, I think… still a bit fuzzy."

Alec's voice cut in. "What did you find?"

Derek hesitated. "Maybe we should talk outside?"

"No," Catherine said firmly. "I want to know what's going on. All of it." She looked at Derek. "You… you were at Ryan's funeral."

"Yes. Detective Derek Samuels. I'm glad you're okay." His tone lacked sincerity, but Catherine let it go.

Alec noticed her glance and interjected. "Before we talk about that, you both need to know something." He paused, letting the weight settle. "Ryan and Catherine were in love."

Derek blinked, stunned. "What? Seriously?" He turned to Catherine.

"Yes." Alec nodded once. "She showed me proof."

"Holy hell," Derek breathed. "How serious was it?"

Catherine opened her mouth to speak, but Alec's jaw flexed, his voice cutting in first. He had already pieced it together—the man who had asked Charles Grant for permission to marry Catherine had to be Ryan. The realisation pressed like a stone in his chest.

"He was going to marry her," Alec said quietly, keeping any trace of jealousy carefully masked.

"Shit." Derek dragged a hand over the back of his neck. "I was Ryan's best friend, and I had no idea. He mentioned he'd met someone, but he never said who—or how serious it was."

Catherine's gaze hardened. "He probably didn't tell you because my father didn't approve."

Derek looked remorseful. "I'm sorry… Miss Grant… I had no idea… I thought—"

"I know what you thought," Catherine interrupted, voice steady but edged with pain. "You thought I had something to do with his death. I didn't. I loved him, and he loved me."

A heavy silence fell over the room, the weight of her words lingering, undeniable.

Alec broke it, voice low, tight. "Tell me you found something."

Logan exhaled—frustration, not relief. "Yeah, I found something. But you're not gonna like it."

Alec stiffened, tension crawling up his spine. "Logan."

"The guy who came earlier—the one claiming to be from the gas company?" Logan said. "He knew where every camera in that building was. Walked the blind spots like he'd memorised them. Kept his hat low, head down. Never gave the lenses a clean angle."

Alec's jaw clenched. "Any footage at all?"

"Nothing useful," Logan replied. "Not even half a face."

A slow, cold fury ignited in Alec's chest.

"And the source?" he asked, already bracing.

"That's the worst part," Logan said grimly. "I checked the service room. The central heating unit was deliberately tampered with. Vents partially blocked, airflow restricted, fuel mix altered so it burned dirty and pumped CO straight into her apartment."

Alec closed his eyes for a moment, letting the words land like a physical blow.

"This wasn't a malfunction," Logan continued. "This was engineered. Someone set that place up to kill her before anyone even knew something was wrong."

Alec glanced at Catherine—pale, still weak. Something twisted in him, sharp and devastating.

"The doctors said if I had been ten minutes later…" His voice cracked, barely audible.

"Holy hell," Logan breathed. "Alec—if you hadn't gone back—"

"Don't." Alec cut him off, low and lethal. He forced a slow, controlled breath. The alternative was something he couldn't allow himself to picture. "We need to find him."

"We will," Logan said. Then, quieter: "And Alec… this wasn't amateur work. The guy's a pro. He knew exactly what he was doing."

Alec's gaze hardened on Catherine, a fierce, protective heat settling deep in his chest like armour.

Derek spoke softly, almost regretfully. "Which means he'll try again."

Alec and Logan didn't need words. The silence between them was enough—grim, certain.

"Why is someone doing this?" Catherine whispered. "It doesn't make sense. I don't think I've hurt anyone to warrant this."

"Murder rarely makes sense, Miss Grant," Derek said calmly.

She turned to Alec, eyes searching. "Do you still think it's my father?"

Derek's eyes narrowed. "You don't think Charles Grant had something to do with Ryan's death?"

Alec shook his head, slow and deliberate. "I don't think so. He was here—and he wasn't faking his concern for her." His gaze drifted back to Catherine, pale against the hospital sheets, shaken but listening. "There's something else at play. I can feel it."

Logan cleared his throat. "Oh—about that."

Alec looked up sharply. "What?"

Logan's voice lowered, steady and all business, though Alec could hear the tension threading beneath it.

"Okay, here's what we've got," Logan began. "Three separate transfers—each for three hundred grand. One payment dated two weeks before Evelyn Grant's death, another on the day of Ryan's, and the last one three weeks ago. I'm assuming that one was for Miss Grant's hit. All of them move through the same shell corporation—Northstar Consultancy. On paper? A legit firm out of Singapore. In reality? A ghost. No employees. No clients. Just a name and a bank account."

Alec's jaw locked. "Who sent the money?"

"That's where it gets… tricky," Logan said. "The transfers originate from accounts tied to Charles Grant. Two are business accounts—mixed in with routine vendor payments. Disguised well. The third comes from his private trust."

Alec's breath stilled. "Meaning he authorised it."

Catherine's breath hitched, though she stayed silent.

"That's what it looks like," Logan said. "But—" He hesitated. "The authorisation codes were entered digitally. Could be him. Could be someone with access."

Alec frowned. "How many people have access?"

"Officially? Just Charles. Unofficially?" Logan exhaled. "Anyone who's been in his home office. Anyone who's seen his passwords or biometric setup. It's sloppy. Way too sloppy for a man like him."

Alec's gaze sharpened with dawning clarity. "So, you're saying it could be a setup."

"I'm saying," Logan replied carefully, "that the trail points to him, but it's not ironclad. The pattern suggests intent. The timing matches the deaths. The amounts match professional contract work. But the transfers weren't done from his device. They were approved through a mirrored login."

Derek stiffened. "Meaning someone duplicated his authorisation."

"Exactly," Logan said quietly. "Whoever did this wanted it to look like Charles. They didn't hide the money completely… but they hid just enough to keep the trail muddy."

A cold, slow fury unfurled in Alec's chest, tightening every muscle.

"What about the shell company?"

"That's the kicker," Logan said. "Northstar's been the middleman for at least five contract hits—three in Europe, two in the U.S. Same playbook. High-paying clients, but no direct links. Burn accounts. Rotating logins. Very professional operation."

Derek let out a low breath. "So, Charles is connected. But that's all we've got. Connection."

"Connected," Logan agreed. "Not confirmed."

Derek folded his arms. "So, someone wants Miss Grant out of the way. And they're in a hurry."

Alec's fury crystallised into something lethal.

"Keep digging," he said.

"You got it." Logan glanced at Catherine, softening. "We'll work this out. Don't you worry."

"Thank you, Logan," she whispered. She looked at each of them. "Thank you… all of you."

Catherine was released from the hospital the next morning.

Alec hadn't had much of a chance to talk to her about what had happened between them. Between her sister's tearful visit and her father hovering anxiously for hours, Catherine was utterly drained by the time the room finally quieted. Even Gary had shown up briefly, and Alec's jaw had tightened the moment he saw him—if Gary still imagined Catherine would one day be his wife, Alec was certain he was sorely mistaken. *Over his dead body.*

Yet no matter who had come or gone, Alec found himself drawn back to her bedside, as if pulled by some unshakable instinct. Each time, he took her hand again, steadying her—and, in some quiet, unspoken way, grounding himself too.

At first, she'd gone still, uncertain. But she no longer tried to pull away.

By the time dawn crept in through the blinds, something between them had shifted. Her fingers curled around his just as often as his curled around hers—soft, steady, as if she'd finally stopped fighting the one place she felt safe.

And when the nurse came in to discharge her, Alec realised Catherine hadn't let go of his hand once.

Alec made a conscious effort not to reveal the exact details of the attempt on Catherine's life to her sister, Lisa, or her father, Charles. Until they knew precisely who they were dealing with, that information would remain tightly controlled.

Once the doctors signed her discharge papers and she was deemed ready to leave, Alec suggested, his voice steady, "We shouldn't go back to the apartment just yet. Not until we know exactly what we're dealing with."

Catherine nodded, still pale but alert, trusting him without question. The drive away from the hospital felt heavy with unsaid truths, but Alec's grip on her hand never wavered, a quiet promise that he wouldn't let anything—or anyone—hurt her again.

They ended up at The Langham, Sydney, a discreet suite tucked away on one of the upper floors, offering privacy and security. Alec had one other bodyguard stationed at the suite door and another downstairs, ensuring that no one could approach unnoticed. Derek and Logan had been busy, chasing down every lead they could uncover while Catherine was being settled.

As soon as they entered the suite, Alec guided Catherine to a plush armchair near the window. He made sure she was settled, a glass of water placed on the side table.

He took a slow breath, meeting her eyes. "We should talk."

"About what?" Catherine asked, uncertainty flickering across her face.

Alec's dark gaze held hers, steady and unflinching. "About us."

She blinked, a faint incredulity crossing her expression. "Is there an us?"

"Professionally, there shouldn't be," he admitted, a sigh slipping out of him. "But I can't pretend anymore."

He ran a hand through his hair, tension pulling at his shoulders. "I care about you, Catherine... more than you know. I know I kept my identity secret, and I thought—"

"It's okay," she interrupted softly, her voice gentler than he expected. "You didn't know what Ryan and I had. And... I know you just want to find the truth about what happened to him. I want that too." Her words faltered, the weight of everything unsaid settling between them.

He dropped to his knees in front of her, taking her hands carefully in his. "When I saw you on the floor of your apartment... it broke me. It was my fault you were nearly killed."

Her fingers lifted to his face, cupping his cheek with tender insistence. "No... it wasn't. It was mine. I never should've fired you, told you to leave. That was my mistake."

He leaned into her touch, eyes closing briefly. "I understand why you did it. No one wants to believe their own family could be involved in something like this."

Their gazes met again, heavy with unspoken pain, relief, and the weight of everything they'd endured. For a moment, the chaos of the world outside the hospital walls seemed to fade, leaving only the quiet intensity between them.

Catherine's chest tightened. She had only ever felt this connected to one other man—Ryan. And yet, the memory of Alec—how he had touched her, how he had made her feel—refused to be ignored. Her voice came out small, tentative, edged with vulnerability. "Do you... really regret what happened between us that night?"

Alec's dark eyes held hers, raw and steady. He had never felt like this before—not about a client, not about anyone. Desire. Longing. Something deeper he hadn't dared claim until now. With Catherine, it wasn't about control anymore. It was about need. About wanting.

"No," he said, low and unflinching.

"Why…"

He cut her off gently, leaning closer, the intensity in his gaze almost tangible. "Because… I shouldn't have done what I did. You're my client, Catherine. I know that. But I can't stop wanting you."

Her breath caught, the confession hanging between them, dangerous and electric. A truth neither had planned to face, but both silently acknowledged.

He stayed kneeling, hands holding hers as if letting go might make her disappear. His voice came out low, stripped bare. "I… I know you loved Ryan. God, I'm glad he had you. But… could you ever—one day—look at me that way?"

Catherine's chest ached, a mix of grief, guilt, and something warm and unfamiliar rising inside her. She studied him—the vulnerability in his eyes, the way his fingers held hers without pressure, the raw honesty he didn't try to hide.

"I…" She swallowed, her voice trembling. "I don't know if I can forget everything that's happened. But… I can't deny how I feel about you. You're the first man I've even kissed since Ryan. I never thought I would feel this way again."

Alec's chest tightened at her words, his dark eyes searching hers for any hesitation. There was none. Only truth, fragile and glowing in the space between them.

He leaned forward slowly, giving her time to pull away if she wanted. When she didn't, his hands tightened slightly around hers, anchoring them both.

Alec closed the distance, his forehead resting lightly against hers for a heartbeat, letting the moment linger. Then, ever so gently, he pressed his lips to hers.

It was soft at first, tentative—a careful exploration, a question asked without words. Catherine responded, leaning into him, her fingers threading into the back of his hair. The kiss deepened, slow and searching, carrying everything they'd both been holding back: longing, fear, relief, and a fragile hope.

Alec's phone buzzed in his pocket. He swore softly, standing to pull it out. "Cole."

It was Derek. "One of my informants just called. He wants to meet. I put feelers out for a contract killer in town, and he says he has information for me."

"That someone you can trust?" Alec asked.

"Yeah, he always has been. Says it's big."

"Take Logan with you. Let me know as soon as you can."

He ended the call and turned to Catherine's expectant look. "Derek thinks one of his informants has a lead."

"That's good," she said, a flicker of hope in her voice.

"I'll make some coffee." Alec moved to the kitchen. When he returned, Catherine had fallen asleep. She still looked fragile. He picked up the throw from the sofa and gently draped it over her, tucking it around her shoulders. He pressed a soft kiss to her forehead and then simply waited.

Chapter Seventeen

It was an hour before Derek and Logan knocked on the suite door. Alec went and opened it, letting them in. As they stepped into the living area, Catherine stirred awake, blinking against the light.

Both men looked grim—faces carved with tension, eyes sharp with something darker than concern. Logan's jaw was clenched so tightly a muscle ticked in his cheek. Derek's expression carried the weight of someone who had just glimpsed into the heart of something rotten.

Alec's instincts kicked in immediately. "Tell me," he demanded. "What did you find?"

Derek's gaze was stern. Logan settled on the sofa, placing his laptop on the coffee table in front of him.

"My informant said there's a hitman in town," Derek said, voice tight. "Name's Ethan Varnes."

Logan opened his laptop, scanning the screen before speaking, his tone low and precise. "Ethan Varnes. Ex-military, dishonourable discharge. Vanished from all official records around three years ago. He's off the grid, but I traced his activity through old deployment files and contractor records. I'm almost positive he was the one hired for all three hits—he was in the country at the time of the other two, and he's here now."

Derek continued, "My informant said he's met Varnes, and he's pissed that he keeps missing. Apparently, even Varnes thinks the person who hired him has ice running through their veins."

"That's saying something," Logan muttered.

"Does he know where he is?" Alec asked, his dark eyes narrowing.

"No," Derek said. "He only bumped into him by accident through other people. He didn't know anything about Mrs. Grant or Ryan's 'accidents,' but it's definitely the one targeting Catherine."

Catherine's breath caught, a chill crawling up her spine. Her hands trembled as she gripped the edge of the armchair, eyes wide and unblinking. "This is a nightmare," she whispered, the room suddenly feeling too small, too exposed.

Alec's hand moved instinctively to cover hers, grounding her even as his own jaw tightened. "I know," he said quietly. "But we'll handle this. He's not getting near you."

Derek exhaled slowly. "We need to flush him out."

Logan nodded. "Agreed. He's too careful to slip on his own. We need to force his hand."

Alec turned to them sharply, disbelief flashing across his face. "You're not seriously thinking about using her as bait."

Derek held his gaze. "It might be the only way to catch him."

Catherine swallowed hard, steadied herself, and lifted her chin. "I'll do it."

"No, you won't."

Alec's voice cut through the room like a crack of thunder—low, sharp, and shaking with a protective fury that left no room for doubt. He stepped closer, his grip tightening around her hand as if sheer will could keep her safe. "I'm not risking you like that. Not ever."

Catherine met his stare, unflinching. "I can't live like this anymore, Alec. Looking over my shoulder… waiting for the next attempt. If this is the only way to stop him—then I'll do it. It's not your decision."

Across the room, Logan and Derek exchanged a glance—half tension, half respect—neither daring to step between them.

Alec shook his head, jaw clenched. "Catherine, it's too dangerous. Varnes isn't just some thug. He's a professional. A ghost."

Her voice cracked, but her resolve didn't. "Don't you think I know that? I'm the one he's tried to kill—four times. Four."

She took a shaky breath, eyes shining with fear and fire. "It has to stop. I can't keep pretending I'm safe when I'm not."

Her words hit the room like a final verdict—quiet, but indisputable. Alec closed his eyes briefly, fighting the instinct to lock her away somewhere the world couldn't touch her. When he opened them again, the conflict in his gaze was unmistakable: fear, anger… and the kind of devotion that made surrender inevitable.

The trap was set.

No one knew if Ethan would take the bait tonight—or wait until tomorrow. Every precaution had been taken, every detail planned to make Catherine look vulnerable.

Catherine, Derek, Logan, and Alec had made it clear to anyone who might listen that she had fired Alec and his team. The message was simple, consistent, and believable: *Catherine was on her own.*

Derek had fed the same story to his informant. In her office, Catherine had casually told everyone she would be working from home—no protection, no bodyguards, nothing.

As far as the outside world was concerned, she was alone.

Inside, she sat quietly in the penthouse, Alec's presence hidden but reassuring, Logan monitoring every camera, Derek stationed nearby. Her heart raced with a mix of fear and determination. She was bait, yes—but she was also ready.

Tonight, they would see if Ethan Varnes would bite.

Logan and Derek were in position. Logan stationed himself in the private elevator shaft, fingers poised over the manual override. Hidden cameras dotted the building, each equipped with motion sensors ready to trip if anyone entered the lifts or stairwells. Derek waited in the spare bedroom, eyes sharp, every muscle coiled for action.

Alec took his place in a shadowed alcove just inside the penthouse foyer, disappearing into the shadows. Before settling in, he checked Catherine's comm one last time.

"You stay where I can see you," he instructed, his voice low, firm.

Catherine met his gaze, nodding once. "I trust you."

Alec's jaw flexed, tension crawling through him. Then, almost instinctively, he pulled her close, pressing a quick, hard, desperate kiss to her lips.

"God help him if he touches you," he murmured against her mouth, voice raw.

Catherine's hands clutched at his shirt, holding on as if anchoring both of them against the storm they were about to face.

The room seemed to shrink, the city below fading into insignificance. All that existed in that moment was them—and the dangerous game they had to play to catch the man who was coming for her.

It had been over two hours, the tension in the penthouse building like a coiled spring. Just before midnight, Logan's voice crackled over the comms.

"The fire alarm was just disabled," he reported, calm but urgent.

"Heat signature just tripped on the fire escape stairwell," Derek whispered from one floor below. "One subject ascending fast. Height matches. Gait is aggressive. That's him, Alec."

Alec exhaled once, slow and controlled, though the chill crawling up his spine told him otherwise. Catherine sat on the sofa, tense but trying to appear calm, waiting for this nightmare to end.

Alec's blood ran cold at the thought of Ethan Varnes climbing toward the woman he loved. Every instinct screamed at him.

Then he heard it—the sharp, metallic scrape of tools against the fire escape door.

He flexed his fingers around the comm, eyes narrowing in the shadows. "Stay down," he murmured into Catherine's earpiece, voice low, lethal.

Her fingers tightened around her own hands, the sound of the lock's resistance echoing through the penthouse. Every second stretched, heavy with the weight of what was coming.

The lock gave a final, metallic click. Alec's eyes snapped to the fire escape door as it creaked open.

Ethan Varnes stepped into the foyer, hood shadowing his face, movements precise and predatory. A small knife glinted in the moonlight—he had taken the bait.

"Stay calm," Catherine whispered into the comms, more to herself than anyone else.

Alec melted into the shadows, keeping her in his sight, framing her without her realising how exposed—or how protected—she truly was.

Catherine's heart hammered, every nerve on fire, but she stayed seated, feigning sleep on the sofa. Her eyes were half-closed, tracking the intruder.

Ethan's gaze swept the room, then fixed on the "sleeping" figure. He advanced slowly, deliberate, knife poised.

Alec counted his steps, memorised his angles, and waited for the perfect moment.

"Now," Derek whispered through the comms.

Alec exploded from the alcove, movement lethal, precise. "Freeze!" His voice cut through the tension like a blade.

Ethan spun, startled, but Alec was faster. A practiced disarm, a sharp twist, and the knife clattered to the floor.

Derek stormed in from the spare room, gun raised, while Logan moved to lock down every possible exit. Every route was blocked. Every move anticipated. Ethan realised too late he had walked straight into a trap.

He struggled in Alec's grip, fury flashing in his eyes, but Derek was on him in an instant. Handcuffs snapped around his wrists, arms twisted firmly behind his back.

"You have the right to remain silent," Derek said, voice calm but sharp, "anything you say can and will be used against you in a court of law."

Ethan's jaw clenched, eyes darting frantically around the room—trapped, cornered, defeated.

Alec's gaze swept to Catherine. She was on her feet now, moving cautiously but instinctively away from Derek as he secured Ethan's hands in handcuffs. Alec let out a low, controlled breath, tightening his grip on his gun, every muscle coiled and alert.

Derek steered Ethan toward the private elevator. The lift chimed and slid open smoothly, Logan already inside, watching with a satisfied gleam in his eyes.

"We got the bastard," Logan said, voice sharp with triumph.

Alec's eyes lingered on Catherine for a heartbeat longer, letting her see that she was truly safe before he finally allowed himself to relax—just slightly.

Derek and Logan left with Ethan. Logan needed to get all the footage logged into evidence, while Derek had to interrogate Ethan and, hopefully, uncover who had hired him.

When the suite finally fell silent, Alec turned to Catherine. Without a word, he scooped her into his arms as if she might vanish if he didn't hold her. He nuzzled into her hair, voice low and raw with relief. "Thank God you're okay. Don't ever put yourself in danger again."

Pulling back just enough to see her face, his dark eyes locked with hers. Then he kissed her—hard, urgent, and consuming, the pent-up fear and relief pouring into the heat of the moment.

Catherine sank against Alec, letting herself finally feel the weight of relief that had been coiled tight inside her chest for hours. Her hands pressed into his shoulders, then slid along his back, memorising the strength she had always found so grounding.

Alec held her as if she might vanish if he loosened his grip, but there was no urgency— just an intensity born of fear, relief, and unspoken longing. His lips hovered near hers for a heartbeat, then brushed against her mouth softly, testing, asking for permission in every careful touch.

Catherine responded instantly, leaning into him, her fingers sliding into his hair and tightening as though she'd been waiting hours—years—for this moment. Their kiss deepened without thought, slow but consuming, layered with the hunger and connection that had never truly faded. Alec's hand curved around her waist, drawing her flush against him until their heartbeats collided in one urgent rhythm. Catherine's breath caught, a shiver lighting through her spine as she pressed closer, letting herself be anchored, protected, and wanted with a fierceness that stole her breath.

"God, Catherine…" Alec murmured against her lips, his voice low, rough, unsteady. "I was so fucking worried… I can't lose you. Not now."

She clung to him harder, the tremor in her hands exposing everything she felt. "You won't," she whispered, her lips brushing his. "I'm here. I'm not going anywhere."

They moved as if guided by instinct, by memory, by the desperate pull that had always lived between them. His hands traced familiar curves; hers mapped the lines of his shoulders and chest. Their mouths found each other again and again, each kiss deeper, needier, answering every unspoken fear.

It wasn't careful—it was urgent, deliberate, a second chance neither of them was willing to waste. Every touch spoke of the nights they'd spent apart, the danger she'd faced tonight, the raw relief of finding one another alive, whole, here.

Clothes were tugged free between kisses, falling in a scattered trail behind them as Alec backed her toward the bedroom, their bodies never breaking contact. Catherine's gasp mixed with his low groan as fingers fumbled with fabric, pushing, pulling, needing.

By the time they reached the bed, they were tangled together—breathless, half undressed, utterly lost in each other. Alec guided her down with him, their bodies finding the same fierce urgency as they fell onto the mattress, the world narrowing to nothing but the heat between them and the certainty that tonight, neither of them would let go.

Alec's breath tore from him in a low, guttural sound, something raw and uncontrollable. "God, Catherine..." he whispered against her mouth, his voice rough with need. "I want you so much it terrifies me."

Her fingers curled around his shoulders, pulling him closer, her own breath shaking. "Alec..." she gasped, every word trembling with wanting. "Please... I want you too."

His hands moved over her with a kind of desperate reverence, as if memorising the shape of her, grounding himself in the proof that she was alive and in his arms. Every soft sound she made, every shift of her body, pushed him closer to the edge of control.

When he lowered his head and his mouth replaced the brush of his fingers, teasing along her skin, she gasped—her back arching, a helpless cry slipping out before she could stop it.

First teasing her nipples with the flat of his tongue, then he moved lower, licking a path down her trembling stomach, until he reached the place, she was hot and slick with need. When his tongue found her, a broken sound escaped her, sharp and breathless, her body tightening instinctively beneath his touch. She couldn't stay still—her muscles shivering, her legs unsteady as she arched toward him, overwhelmed by the rush of feeling he pulled from her so effortlessly.

"Alec..." Her voice was wrecked. "Please."

"God Catherine…," he murmured, voice hoarse and reverent. Then he lost himself in her, every stroke, every suck designed to push her higher. She writhed beneath him, gasping his name, until she shattered against his mouth with a cry that made his blood burn.

He kissed his way back up her body—slow, deliberate—his mouth lingering over every inch until she trembled beneath him. By the time he settled between her thighs, her breath was already fractured, her fingers clenched in the sheets. The blunt tip of him brushed her entrance, sending a shock of heat through them both.

He kissed her then—deep, hungry, claiming—his tongue sweeping into her mouth with a demand that made her gasp. She tasted herself on his lips, felt the shudder in his muscles as he fought, barely, to hold on to the last thread of restraint.

Then, with one long, controlled thrust, he entered her.

Catherine's cry tore softly from her throat as her back arched, her body tightening around him like she never wanted to let him go. The sound undid him.

"Catherine…" he groaned, her name rough and reverent in the same breath.

He began to move—slow at first, savouring every slick, perfect inch of her wrapped around him—but control was a fragile, doomed thing. It lasted only heartbeats. Need surged through him, primal and overwhelming. His rhythm deepened, quickened, his hips driving harder as the pleasure crashed through him in relentless waves.

She clung to him, nails sinking into his shoulders as she matched him, thrust for thrust, her breath breaking on every movement. His mouth found hers again, swallowing her moans in frantic, consuming kisses.

Their bodies found a devastating rhythm. Her soft, desperate sounds filled the air. His breath grew ragged. He pushed deeper, harder, chasing that razor-edge of bliss.

Then she cried out—a raw, exquisite sound—as her body clenched around him, tight and trembling.

He felt her climax hit, felt her pulse around him, and it snapped the last of his restraint. He thrust again, then again—and followed her over the edge with a harsh, choked groan, her name ripped from him like a vow.

Afterward, he drew in a shaking breath and shifted onto his back, but he didn't release her. Not even a little. Catherine melted against him, fitting perfectly along his body, her cheek resting over his heartbeat—still wild, still echoing everything they'd just shared.

Her fingers brushed the scar at his neck, that faint line no one ever asked about. She touched it gently, tracing it as though memorising him, piece by piece. Something tightened deep in his chest—pain, affection, devotion all tangled together.

Alec lowered his head and pressed a slow, lingering kiss into her hair. His voice when it came, was low and rough, edged with something fierce and absolute.

"I'm not letting anyone get near you again. Do you hear me? Catherine—I swear it. I'll burn the world down before I let anyone touch you."

She didn't answer with words. She didn't have to. Instead, she curled into him, strong despite her exhaustion, her hands clutching him like he was the only safe place she had left. And that quiet, instinctive trust told him everything she couldn't say aloud.

He wanted to speak the rest—the truth tugging at his ribs.

That he loved her.

That losing her had nearly broken him.

That he couldn't imagine a life without her again.

But for now, holding her was enough.

Wrapped around each other, their breaths slowly fell into sync. Fear loosened. Tension unknotted. Exhaustion finally dragged them under.

They slept tangled together—two hearts still pounding with the echo of everything they'd almost lost… and everything they'd finally found again.

But sleep didn't hold them for long.

In the soft hush of early morning, golden sunlight spilled through the curtains, draping the room in a warm, forgiving glow. Alec stirred first, his breath brushing her skin before his lips followed—pressing a tender kiss to Catherine's shoulder, lingering as though afraid to break the fragile peace settling around them.

Catherine shifted in his arms, her lashes fluttering before her gaze lifted to his. Her eyes were heavy—not with sleep, but with something far deeper, something she hadn't dared to feel in years. Love. Gratitude. Relief. A quiet joy she had never expected to find again.

She wanted to tell him—wanted to say the words beating inside her chest. That it wasn't merely desire anchoring her to him anymore. That she loved him. Fully. Fiercely. That after Ryan's death, she had believed her heart would remain fractured beyond repair… but Alec, impossibly, had gathered the broken pieces and made her whole.

But she didn't speak. She didn't need to.

Resting in his arms, feeling the steady rise and fall of his breathing, the security of his hold, was enough. Her heart swelled softly, steadying itself against his, tethering to him with a certainty she hadn't felt in years.

When they made love again, it wasn't frantic or charged with the fear of losing one another.

It was reverent. Intentional. Sacred.

Alec's hands traced her curves like a blessing, his fingertips memorising her body with a tenderness that stole her breath. Each touch was a vow. Each kiss, a quiet promise. His lips trailed across her throat, her collarbone, the gentle slope of her shoulder—not simply seeking her body, but her soul.

They faced each other, bodies aligned, breaths mingling. And when he could no longer restrain himself, he lifted her leg over his hip and thrust into her with a deep, consuming hunger—as though the brief separation had been unbearable.

Catherine arched into him, offering herself with quiet reverence. She opened to him completely—no fear, no walls, trusting him not just with her body, but with every tender, still-healing part of her heart.

He moved inside her slow and steady, fingers intertwined with hers, their gazes locked in a silent conversation more intimate than any words. Every glide of his body within hers, every whispered sigh, every soft murmur of her name wrapped around them like silk—gentle, binding, unbreakable.

And when their pleasure crested, it wasn't with helpless cries, but with trembling breaths, shuddering releases, and tears neither of them tried to hide.

It was more than desire.

More than need.

It was love—deep, irrevocable, and everlasting.

Chapter Eighteen

When they surfaced again, Alec's lips found the tip of her nose, slow and teasing. "I need to go to the office for a little while. Check on Logan… and a few other things. You'll be alright here? One of my men is still downstairs—I can have him come up and stay with you."

Catherine melted against him, body pressing into his, her hands roaming lightly over his chest. She let out a soft laugh as he groaned low, clearly affected. "No, I'll be fine," she murmured, letting her warmth tease him.

"You're trying to kill me, aren't you?" His hand clenched around her waist, pulling her impossibly closer.

She tilted her head, lips curving in a sultry smirk. "I don't know what you're talking about."

He caught her mouth in a heated, lingering kiss, his hands roaming, holding her as if he could anchor himself in her. When he finally pulled back, his dark eyes were heavy with need. "I better go… before I change my mind," he murmured, voice thick with frustration.

Catherine's fingers traced lightly down his chest, her lips brushing the corner of his mouth. "Spoil sport," she whispered, breathless, the unspoken promise between them lingering.

Alec gathered his scattered clothes from the living room floor, moving toward the bedroom to dress.

"Actually, I should go to the office," Catherine said, tilting her head with a playful glint in her eyes. "I've been neglecting work… need to sort a few things out. I need my laptop."

Alec paused, his gaze softening. "I can pick it up on the way back, if you like."

Her lips curved into a warm, mischievous smile. "Could you?"

He nodded, a faint smile tugging at his lips.

"Thank you," she added, her voice soft and reassuring, and he felt a tug at his chest he couldn't ignore.

Before leaving, he bent down and pressed another slow, lingering kiss to her lips, letting the moment stretch between them. Then, reluctantly, he pulled back and went to get ready, while Catherine watched him go, a small shiver running through her as she rose to take a shower.

Derek slammed the file onto the metal table, the sound cracking through the interrogation room like a gunshot. Ethan didn't flinch—but the tightness in his jaw gave him away.

"We've been here for hours," Derek said, voice low, dangerous. "And you're running out of time to stop being stupid."

Ethan glared, arms crossed, shoulders tight with defiance. "I told you already. I'm not saying a damn thing."

Derek leaned in, palms flat on the table, his stare drilling into him. "You walked into a baited trap like an amateur, and now you're sitting in federal custody. You think the person who hired you gives a shit about you?"

A muscle twitched in Ethan's cheek. Something cracked—subtle, but Derek saw it.

Finally, Ethan let out a harsh breath. "You don't get it." He shook his head, voice rough. "The woman who hired me... she's got ice in her veins. Cold. Calculating. Nothing rattles her."

Derek's eyes sharpened. There it is.

He straightened slowly, folding his arms. "Ice in her veins, huh?" His tone shifted—deadly calm. "Tell me something, Ethan... if she's that calculating, that untouchable—"

He leaned down again, lowering his voice to a razor's edge.

"—how long do you think you're going to live once she finds out you failed?"

Ethan's breath hitched. The first real crack. Sweat beaded along his temple.

Derek pressed harder, voice quiet and merciless. "She's not going to bail you out. She's going to erase you. Because that's what people like her do when liabilities arise."

Ethan swallowed, throat bobbing.

Derek held his stare, unblinking. "So, decide: do you want to end up in a grave dug by the same icy bitch you're protecting... or do you want to walk out of here alive?"

Silence. Thick. Suffocating.

Ethan finally exhaled, the fight draining from his shoulders. "Fine." His voice was barely a rasp. "It was Lisa Grant. She hired me."

Derek didn't move. Didn't blink. Didn't give Ethan the satisfaction of a reaction.

He simply stared at him—cold, steady, dangerous.

"Are you telling me," Derek said slowly, "that Catherine Grant's *own sister* wants her dead?"

Ethan huffed out a bitter laugh. "Yeah. That's exactly what I'm telling you. She's cold, that one. Ice in her veins. She had me take out her stepmother just because she didn't like the woman."

Derek's jaw clenched, but his voice stayed flat, controlled. "Go on."

Ethan shifted, eyes dark. "What about Ryan Cole?" Derek pressed.

"Oh, I didn't kill him." Ethan shrugged, almost casual. "*She* did."

Derek straightened, disbelief flashing across his face. "She did?"

"Yeah," Ethan said, leaning back. "Bashed his head in with one of those marble statues. Lost it because he loved her sister and not her. Then she hired me to get rid of the body—to make it look like a car accident."

Silence cracked open between them.

Derek's mind raced. The autopsy inconsistencies. The bruising that didn't match the crash patterns. The unexplained timeline gaps. The uneasy instincts he'd dismissed.

Every piece slammed into place with brutal clarity.

Lisa Grant wasn't just unstable.

She was a murderer.

Derek stepped out of the interrogation room, jaw tight, icy determination settling into his bones. He pulled out his phone, needing to get the news to Alec immediately.

He tapped Alec's number. The phone rang—once, twice, three times. Still no answer.

"Come on, Alec," he growled, teeth clenched. "Pick up. Now."

Alec never took this long. Derek's patience snapped. He ended the call and quickly dialled Catherine's number.

No answer. His stomach tightened. Something was wrong.

He dialled Logan. The phone clicked on the second ring.

"Derek? Everything…" Logan began, concern threading his voice.

Derek cut him off sharply. "Where's Alec?"

"He left about twenty minutes ago. Said he needed to pick up Catherine's laptop," Logan replied.

"Is anyone with her?"

"Not that I know of," Logan said quickly. "Why?"

"It was Lisa Grant," Derek blurted, urgency raw in his voice.

Logan froze. "What? Her sister?"

"Yes. That's who hired Varnes—Lisa Grant."

A stunned silence hung between them, heavy and suffocating.

Logan swore under his breath. "Fuck. If she knows Varnes has been caught, she could do anything."

"That's exactly what I'm thinking," Derek said grimly. "Catherine would never suspect her sister… she's the one who killed Ryan."

"Fuck. I'm going there now," Logan said, voice sharp.

"I'll meet you there," Derek replied.

The call disconnected.

The intercom buzzed. Catherine picked up the phone.

"Miss Grant, your sister… Lisa Grant is here to see you," the concierge said.

Catherine's lips curved into a polite smile. "Oh, send her up."

She waited by the private elevator, eyes flicking to the floor numbers as it ascended. When the doors opened, Lisa stepped out. She didn't smile. Her gaze was sharp, calculating, and for a fleeting moment, Catherine felt a chill she couldn't explain.

"Lisa… what's wrong? You look upset," Catherine asked, trying to mask the unease creeping into her voice.

Lisa's lips pressed into a thin line. "I heard Alec caught the person who was trying to hurt you."

Catherine stepped toward the living area, relief softening her features. "Yes… thank goodness."

Lisa's eyes tracked her every move, unblinking. For a heartbeat, a chill radiated from her, a coldness Catherine couldn't place—but it made her stomach tighten.

"Where is Alec?" Lisa asked, her voice deceptively calm. "Why isn't he here to protect you?"

There was a subtle, cutting edge to the question, the kind that suggested she already knew far too much. Catherine hesitated, a cold knot forming in her stomach, unaware that Lisa had already pieced together part of the truth—Varnes hadn't made it to their scheduled meeting, and Alec must have intercepted him. He wouldn't have left Catherine unprotected, and now Lisa's knowledge hinted at a deeper, more dangerous understanding of events than Catherine could have imagined.

Lisa began prowling the living room, keeping unnervingly close to Catherine. "You know," she said, voice low and sharp, "I never understood why Ryan loved you... and not me."

Catherine froze; shock etched across her face. "What? How... how did you know that?"

Lisa smirked, sarcastic and bitter. "Oh, I knew about you and him... getting it on."

A shiver of unease ran through Catherine. "Did you...?"

"Yes. I loved him, Catherine. And you... you took him from me."

"Were you two—?"

Lisa laughed, a sharp, humourless sound. "No. You swooped in before I could. But I did tell him... the night he died."

Catherine's heart stuttered. "What are you saying, Lisa?"

Ignoring Catherine's words, Lisa began circling slowly, her eyes never leaving her sister, a predator sizing up its prey. Each step was deliberate, measured, deliberate, until she stopped just a foot away, leaning in slightly as if to invade Catherine's space without touching her.

"You know what he said..." Lisa's voice was low, dangerous, every syllable dripping with venom. "He told me you were the only one he could love. That he never gave me any encouragement."

Catherine's stomach knotted. She instinctively stepped back, her hands rising slightly as if to shield herself.

"That was a lie!" Lisa spat, her tone trembling with barely restrained rage, eyes narrowing, a sharp glint of obsession in them.

"What's going on, Lisa? Why are you telling me this?" Catherine asked, her voice shaky, trying to keep calm despite the chill creeping through her.

Lisa ignored her, tilting her head slightly, a cruel smile playing across her lips. "If that wasn't bad enough… daddy keeps asking me to get you to call him, always comparing you to me… as if *I* am not good enough." Her gaze bore into Catherine's, sharp and cold, every word a threat wrapped in venom.

Catherine's chest tightened, every instinct screaming at her to get away, but Lisa's movements were fluid, blocking her retreat without ever touching her—like a cat circling a cornered mouse.

"You think I don't notice, Catherine?" Lisa hissed, voice low and dangerous. "You get all the praise, all the attention, and I… I get nothing." She stepped closer, closing the space between them, her hand twitching at her side as if testing her own strength.

Catherine stumbled back, nearly tripping over the edge of the sofa. "Lisa… please… this isn't you…"

Lisa's smile twisted, sharp and predatory. "Oh, but it is me. Your mother knew what I was capable of. That's why I had to get rid of her."

Catherine's eyes widened in horror. "What?"

Lisa sneered, advancing closer. "That's why your mother threatened to leave Daddy… because she said if he didn't get me help, she'd take you with her. Evelyn thought I was… unstable. Can you believe it?"

"Are you saying… you had my mother killed? And Ryan?" Catherine's voice wavered, terror taking hold.

"Oh, I killed Ryan," Lisa said, her tone casual, as if discussing the weather. "An accident, of course."

Catherine's knees buckled, her breath catching in her throat. "You… you killed Ryan?" she whispered, disbelief making her voice tremble.

Lisa's eyes glittered with venom, a cruel smile twisting her lips. "I wouldn't have done it on purpose… but when he told me he'd never love me because of you, I snapped. I hit him with a statue. I didn't mean to kill him. I loved him."

Catherine tried to back away, but the back of her knees struck the sofa, and she collapsed to the floor.

In an instant, Lisa pounced. Her hands shot out, gripping Catherine's throat with alarming force. Panic and disbelief flared in Catherine's eyes as she struggled against her sister's iron grip.

"Lisa… stop! Please!" she gasped, clawing at the hands around her neck.

Lisa's eyes glittered with fury and envy, her body pressing against Catherine's as she tightened her hold. "You always had everything! My life, my family… and Ryan! You think you deserve it all!"

Catherine's vision blurred at the edges, her heart hammering wildly, breaths shallow and ragged. Her hands fumbled for leverage, weakened from the carbon monoxide poisoning, desperately trying to pry Lisa's fingers from her throat.

Lisa leaned in, voice venomous, each word slicing into Catherine like a blade. "Everything was fine until your mother came along and ruined my life. Every man I ever wanted noticed you first. Even Alec… he wouldn't look at me the way he looked at you at the Charity Gala. He wouldn't even dance with me, but he danced with you. It was sickening."

Catherine's strength faltered. Her hands clawed at her sister's iron grip, fingers sliding uselessly over unyielding skin. Her head spun, lungs burning, chest heaving with shallow, ragged breaths. She kicked, she thrashed, tried to push Lisa away, but her sister's weight pinned her mercilessly to the floor. Panic surged through her, icy and unrelenting—she couldn't breathe, she couldn't scream—and a suffocating, helpless dread seeped into her bones. Darkness crept at the edges of her vision, and all she could think of was Alec… how she hadn't told him how she felt. *She loved him—and he would never know.*

Chapter Nineteen

Alec was leaving Catherine's office with her laptop tucked under his arm, moving fast. He needed to get back to her—needed to tell her how he felt. He should've told her that morning. He should've told her days ago.

He nearly collided with Gary in the hallway.

"Mr. Cole—how is Catherine?" Gary asked, then frowned. "Wait... where is Catherine?"

"She's at home resting," Alec replied. "We caught the hired killer last night."

Gary let out a long breath. "Thank God. Is he in custody?"

Alec gave a single, clipped nod. "Yes."

"That's wonderful. Lisa will be relieved too. She was telling me this morning how the killer tampered with the central heating to cause the carbon monoxide poisoning. I had no idea something like that was even possible."

Alec froze. The world seemed to lurch sideways.

"I'm sorry—what did you just say?" His voice was low, sharp. "Lisa told you that?"

"Yes," Gary said, oblivious. "We were both worried, we were talking about it earlier."

Alec's pulse slammed against his ribs, panic burning up his throat. "Where is Lisa now?"

"Oh—she went to see Catherine," Gary said lightly, as though it were the most ordinary thing in the world.

Alec didn't even respond. "I have to go," he snapped, already moving. He bolted for the exit; the laptop clutched in his hand as he sprinted toward his car.

Something was wrong. Terribly wrong.

He had deliberately kept the details of Catherine's poisoning from everyone except the investigators. Only a handful of people knew the carbon monoxide had been engineered through a tampered heating system.

So how did Lisa know?

The only way she could know is if...

Alec's chest tightened. Ice flooded his veins.

She was involved.

Alec tore across the carpark and slid behind the wheel, jamming the laptop onto the passenger seat. He fired up the engine and shot out onto the main road—only to slam on the brakes moments later.

A line of cars stretched ahead, unmoving. Horns blared. People leaned out of windows, shouting. Up ahead, flashing lights strobed against the buildings—an accident had completely choked the intersection.

No. Not now.

Alec gripped the steering wheel so hard his knuckles blanched, his pulse thundering in his ears. Every stalled second felt like it was being carved out of him. Catherine was alone. With Lisa.

He couldn't sit here. A run to Catherine's building would take fifteen minutes—maybe less if he pushed himself—but sitting trapped in traffic? It could take forever.

"Dammit," he breathed, already moving.

He killed the engine, left the keys in the ignition, flung the door wide, and bolted. No phone. No plan. Just pure, blistering urgency.

He tore down the footpath, weaving through startled pedestrians, lungs searing as he forced his legs faster, faster. His heartbeat was a frantic drum, each thud a countdown he couldn't afford.

Catherine's building burst into view just as two black SUVs screeched to the curb, tyres spitting heat across the asphalt.

Derek and Logan spilled out, weapons concealed but ready.

"Lisa—" Derek began.

"I know," Alec barked, not slowing. "She's with Catherine now!"

They stormed into the lobby together. The concierge jumped to his feet, but Alec didn't give him a glance. They headed straight for the private lift, swiping access.

The doors slid shut. The lift began to rise.

Too slowly. Far too slowly.

Alec could feel the seconds dragging like weights around his throat. His pulse was a roar in his ears, hands clenched so tight they shook.

Hold on, Catherine. Hold on. I'm coming.

The elevator finally dinged.

Alec shot out of it—then stopped dead, breath ripping from his lungs.

Catherine lay on the floor, limp, unmoving. Lisa straddled her, fingers locked viciously around her throat, eyes wild with murderous intent.

Alec's blood turned to ice.

He didn't think—he *couldn't*. A raw sound tore out of him, something primal and feral, and he sprinted across the room. He seized Lisa by the shoulders and ripped her backward, so violently her hands were wrenched from Catherine's throat.

He hurled her onto the sofa—the impact sharp, brutal.

Then Alec dropped to his knees beside Catherine, terror gripping him harder than any chokehold ever could.

His hands hovered over her trembling frame. "Catherine... please—please be okay," he begged, voice torn and shaking.

Catherine's body convulsed as air finally surged past her crushed throat.

A brutal cough tore out of her, then another—raw, scraping, agonising.

Alec gathered her into his arms, cradling her head, his other hand braced firmly around her shoulder.

"Catherine—sweetheart—come on. Breathe for me. Please."

His voice shook so badly it barely sounded like his.

Her fingers twitched on the floor, then curled weakly into his shirt as another coughing fit racked her. Her eyes fluttered, unfocused, glassy.

"That's it... that's it." He swept her hair from her damp forehead, every touch desperate, terrified. "I've got you. You're safe now. Just breathe."

She dragged in a shuddering gasp—thin, wheezing, barely there—but it was breath. Her chest rose, fell, then rose again, slower, steadier.

Her voice was a broken rasp. "A... Alec..."

His heart broke open. "I'm here. I'm right here."

He pressed a shaking kiss to her temple, holding her as if releasing her wasn't an option.

Catherine blinked, vision wavering, tears slipping free—reflex, not emotion. Alec wiped them away with a gentle sweep of his thumb.

"Hurts..." she whispered, fingers drifting to her throat.

"I know," he murmured, voice thick with anguish. "I know, sweetheart. You're okay. Just keep breathing."

Behind them, Derek and Logan struggled to pin down a snarling, unhinged Lisa, but Alec barely heard the chaos—the world had narrowed to the fragile rise and fall of Catherine's breath.

She swallowed with a wince, her voice trembling. "I… thought…"

Alec pulled her closer, forehead pressed to hers. "No. Don't. I've got you. You're safe. I'm here."

Her body trembled violently—shock, fear, the sting of survival—and Alec wrapped himself around her, shielding her completely. Her fingers curled around his wrist, weak but trying, holding on.

"Alec…" she whispered, hoarse but alive.

He closed his eyes, relief nearly buckling him.

"I've got you, Catherine," he whispered, fiercely, fiercely gentle. "I'm not letting go."

Lisa thrashed on the carpet, wild, snarling, spitting curses. Derek moved fast, pinning one wrist to the floor with a sharp twist. Logan grabbed the other, forcing her arms behind her back despite her feral struggle.

"Lisa Grant," Derek ground out, breath harsh, "you're under arrest for the attempted murder of Catherine Grant—and for the murders of Ryan Cole and Evelyn Grant."

Lisa screamed—a high, jagged, unhinged sound—but Derek snapped the cuffs onto her wrists with a decisive click. Logan hauled her upright just long enough for Derek to shove her back onto the sofa, securing her legs with a firm knee until she stopped fighting.

"Get off me! She ruined everything!" Lisa shrieked, thrashing.

Derek didn't even look at her. His eyes had already shifted across the room—to Alec and Catherine.

Alec was cradling her on the floor; his entire body curved protectively around her trembling form. His hands shook where they held her, one against the back of her head, the other gripping her shoulder as if she were the only thing keeping him breathing. His forehead rested against hers, murmuring soft, frantic reassurances just to keep her conscious.

Catherine's breaths came shallow and fragile, each one making Alec's jaw clench with fear.

Logan exhaled slowly, a tight, low sound. "Jesus… I've never seen him like that."

"Yeah," Derek murmured, swallowing hard. "Me neither."

Alec Cole—strategic, razor-focused, unbreakable—looked like a man on the edge of losing everything. The toughest son of a bitch either of them knew, brought to his knees by the sheer terror of almost losing one woman.

His voice trembled as he whispered to her. "Stay with me, sweetheart… please. I've got you."

Catherine's fingers curled around his wrist, weak but clinging. Alec's breath hitched—raw, unguarded. Nothing about him was composed. Nothing held back.

Logan looked from the trembling woman in Alec's arms to the handcuffed monster on the sofa, then back to Alec again.

"He cares about her," Logan said quietly. "More than I realised."

Derek nodded once, eyes softening.

"Yeah," he said quietly. "That's not a man protecting a witness."

They watched him hold her—watched the silent terror, the fierce relief, the way he wrapped himself around her like he'd shield her from the world before letting it touch her again.

"That's a man who almost lost the woman he…" Derek didn't finish it. He didn't need to.

Alec's voice cracked softly as he pressed another kiss to Catherine's forehead.

Logan's jaw tightened.

"We should give him a minute," he said quietly.

Derek nodded, standing guard between the handcuffed killer and the man who would happily tear the world apart for the shaking woman in his arms.

Because one thing was brutally clear—

Alec Cole wasn't just shaken.

He was in love.

The ding of the elevator announced the paramedics' arrival. They burst into the living room, calm but urgent.

"Get her on the stretcher, quickly," one said, kneeling beside Catherine. Alec didn't move.

"Sir, we need to move her," another said, glancing at him.

"I'm not leaving her," Alec snapped, voice low and sharp. His dark eyes pinned them in place, leaving no room for argument.

Behind him, Lisa continued to struggle, spitting venom and rage, but Derek and Logan held her firmly, blocking her view of Catherine, ensuring she had nowhere to run.

Alec let the paramedics carefully lift Catherine onto the stretcher, but he stayed right beside her, hands gripping hers, eyes never leaving her pale, trembling face.

"Just breathe, Catherine," he whispered, voice thick with fear. "I'm right here. You're going to be okay."

Her fingers twitched weakly around his wrist, and a shudder ran through her. "A... Alec..." she rasped.

"I'm here. Don't try to speak," he murmured, pressing a tender kiss to her damp hair.

As the paramedics wheeled her toward the elevator, Alec fell into step beside the stretcher, unyielding and protective. Derek gave him a brief, knowing look. "She's in good hands," he said softly, though Alec barely registered the words.

Lisa screamed behind them, the sound abruptly cut off as the elevator doors closed, sealing away the last trace of danger. Alec held Catherine's hand as if letting go for even a second might undo everything.

Through the quiet hum of the elevator, Alec remained vigilant, every ounce of his focus on her. She was alive, and he would never let anyone—or anything—harm her again.

The hospital room smelled faintly of antiseptic, sharp and sterile. Catherine lay in the bed, pale and fragile, her fingers loosely clutching the edge of the blanket. Tubes and monitors beeped softly, a quiet rhythm against the pounding of Alec's heart. He hadn't left her side since the paramedics wheeled her in, his hand wrapped around hers, thumb tracing circles over her knuckles.

Catherine's eyes fluttered open, groggy, and she tried to lift a weak smile. "A... Alec..."

"I'm here," he murmured, brushing damp hair from her forehead. "Right here. You're safe."

She gave a faint squeeze of his hand before letting her eyelids fall again.

A soft knock interrupted the quiet. A doctor stepped into the room, clipboard in hand, his expression calm but serious. Alec's hand tightened around Catherine's.

"Mr. Cole?" the doctor asked, glancing at Alec.

"Yes. That's me," Alec replied, his voice steady but tense, eyes never leaving Catherine's face.

The doctor nodded. "Miss Grant—she's lucky. The strangulation caused significant oxygen deprivation, and she's extremely weak, but she's stable for now. We need to monitor her for at least twenty-four hours. There may be some lingering effects—light-headedness, fatigue, even memory gaps—but nothing permanent is evident at this point."

Alec's jaw tightened. "What does she need? What do I do?"

"Right now, rest. Fluids. Oxygen if necessary. She should remain in bed, minimal stimulation, and no visitors except those she trusts. If she experiences chest pain, dizziness, or shortness of breath, call us immediately." The doctor paused, looking at Alec seriously. "And keep her calm. Emotional stress can exacerbate her recovery."

Alec nodded sharply, his hand squeezing hers. "I'll stay. I won't leave her."

The doctor gave a small, reassuring nod. "Good. She needs to feel safe right now.'

As the doctor left, Alec leaned closer, pressing his forehead to Catherine's. "I'm not going anywhere. Not for a second. You hear me? You're going to get through this, and I'm going to be right here the whole time."

Catherine's eyes, still half-lidded, met his, a mixture of gratitude, relief, and trust shining through. She weakly squeezed his hand again, letting herself rest in his presence.

And for the first time since the attack, Alec allowed himself to breathe—just a little— knowing she was alive and, for now, safe in his arms.

Chapter Twenty

The next morning, the soft hum of the hospital was punctuated by the quiet footsteps of two detectives as they entered Catherine's room. Sunlight filtered through the blinds, casting pale stripes across the bed where she lay, still fragile but awake. Her voice was soft, raspy from the ordeal, each word seeming to cost her effort.

"Catherine, we just need to ask you some questions about yesterday," one detective said gently, sitting in the chair beside her bed.

She nodded faintly, adjusting herself against the pillows. "I… I'll do my best," she whispered, her throat still sore from Lisa's attack.

The detectives asked methodical questions, and Catherine answered carefully, recounting the events with as much clarity as she could manage. Her hand rested lightly in Alec's, who sat nearby, dark eyes flicking between her and the detectives, protective and alert.

When the questioning finally ended and the detectives slipped out, Catherine sagged back against the pillows, exhausted. A moment later, the door opened again—slowly, quietly.

Her father stepped inside.

He looked older than she remembered. Not just tired—worn. Guilt sat heavily on his shoulders, and grief clung to the lines around his eyes. He paused at the foot of her bed, his gaze first meeting Alec's.

"Mr. Cole," Charles said, voice thick. "I… I can't thank you enough. You saved her again."

Alec's expression softened, but only slightly; vigilance never fully left him. "She's safe now, sir."

Charles let out a shaky breath and turned to his daughter. "Your mother… Evelyn told me Lisa carried darkness in her, but I didn't listen." He swallowed, voice cracking. "And it cost her her life. That's on me."

He rubbed a trembling hand over his face. "I never believed Lisa could do something like this. I thought I understood the shadows in her, but… seeing what she's done… knowing she went this far…" He shook his head, defeated. "You're lucky, Catherine. Very lucky to have Alec watching over you."

Catherine's eyes filled, and she offered a small, aching smile. "I know, Dad. I know."

Beside her, Alec squeezed her hand gently—solid, steady—silently promising he wasn't going anywhere.

Charles moved to the chair and sat heavily, taking Catherine's free hand in both of his own. "Catherine… we've both lost so much. I can't lose you too." His voice wavered. "Can you find it in your heart to forgive me?"

Alec remained quiet but attentive, a silent presence at her side.

Catherine studied her father, her voice soft but firm. "I love you, Dad… but you can't try to control my life."

"I know," he whispered, eyes shining. "I know. The night we spoke about Ryan's proposal… when you reacted the way you did… I realised I was wrong. I had no right to stand in the way of someone you loved." His breath hitched. "I was going to talk to him the next day. To tell him I'd changed my mind."

Catherine's lips parted, tears slipping over her cheeks. "Were you… truly?"

"Yes," he said, his voice breaking. "I swear it. When I saw how much you loved him, everything became clear. And I regret—every day—that I didn't tell him sooner. You started pulling away after your mother's death, but after Ryan…" His voice faltered. "I felt like I lost you completely."

Emotion swelled thick in the room—regret, grief, and the fragile beginnings of healing—as Catherine squeezed her father's hand, a small but undeniable bridge across years of distance.

"I want to try," she whispered, voice soft and raspy, her throat still raw. "But I'm an adult now, Dad. You need to respect my decisions."

Charles nodded quickly—almost desperately. "I will," he said, hope flickering through his tired gaze. "I promise. I love you, Catherine."

He rose slowly, then leaned down to press a gentle kiss to her forehead.

"I love you too," she murmured, her voice barely above breath.

As he stepped back, Catherine watched him—saw the remorse, the love, the effort—and for the first time in years, she felt a path opening between them. A way back. A way forward.

Her father left soon after, promising to return the next day. At the door, he paused and extended his hand to Alec.

"I see you care about my daughter," he said quietly.

Alec didn't hesitate. "I do."

Charles glanced between the two of them, something settling in his expression—acceptance, maybe even relief. "Just treat her right," he said gently. "And we'll get along fine."

Alec gave a small nod, steady and certain. "I intend to."

When the door closed behind her father, Alec returned to Catherine's side. He sank into the chair, fingers instinctively finding hers again, thumb brushing lightly over her knuckles.

"How are you feeling?" he asked, voice soft but threaded with concern.

She gave a faint smile. "My throat is still sore… but I feel better."

Alec exhaled, a quiet breath of relief, his thumb continuing its slow, reassuring sweep over her hand. His gaze dropped to the bruising along her throat—dark, angry fingerprints marring the soft skin he had kissed so gently just hours before. An icy shiver tore through him, lodging deep in his chest, and he tightened his grip on her hand instinctively.

A knock at the door broke the tense silence. Logan and Derek stepped inside. Alec didn't let go of Catherine's hand; he didn't care who saw how fiercely he cared for her.

Logan's eyes softened as he noticed, offering a small, reassuring smile. "How are you, Catherine?"

"Better," she rasped, her voice hoarse but steady.

Derek's expression darkened slightly, the weight of the news pressing in. "I thought you should know—both Ethan Varnes and your sister, Lisa, have been charged."

"Ethan's already singing like a bird," Derek continued. "Hoping for a reduced sentence if he comes clean. Doesn't seem likely."

Logan's tone was measured but firm. "Lisa used your father's accounts to pay for the hits. She tried to make it look like he was involved, but we confirmed he wasn't."

Catherine shook her head, disbelief, and sorrow warring in her eyes. "I just… I can't believe she hated me that much. I loved her."

Derek's jaw tightened, voice low and steady. "She was consumed by jealousy—of your relationships with Ryan, and even with your father. Your mother threatened to leave your father if he didn't get her help. Evelyn saw how seriously off she was… but no one could have imagined she'd go this far."

Catherine swallowed hard, the weight pressing down on her chest. "I never thought she could do something like this…"

Logan exchanged a brief glance with Derek, both men grim. "Most people wouldn't have. That's why it caught everyone off guard."

Catherine's fingers trembled slightly as she held Alec's hand, thankful for the anchor she desperately needed. "I just... I just can't believe it."

Derek gave a curt nod. "It's over now."

Catherine's chest tightened, a mix of relief and lingering sadness washing over her. "I'm just glad it's all over," she said softly, glancing at Alec, Logan, and Derek. "Thank you... all of you."

Alec's thumb brushed gently over her hand, a silent vow. "You don't have to thank us," he murmured, voice low and fierce. "You're safe now. That's enough."

Her eyes met his, and in that moment the bruises and fear seemed to fall away, replaced by the quiet strength of being held, protected, and finally—truly cared for.

Logan and Derek left soon after, the door clicking shut behind them and leaving Alec and Catherine alone at last.

"I nearly lost you again," Alec whispered, his voice cracking under the strain of everything he'd been holding back. "I feel like I failed you."

Catherine's eyes widened. "Alec... don't be silly. You saved me. Again."

"I shouldn't have left you," he murmured, jaw tight, guilt carving tension into every line of him.

"No one suspected Lisa," she said softly, brushing her thumb over the back of his hand. "I would never have believed it."

He lifted his gaze—and something in him simply broke open. The fear. The relief. The weeks of holding himself in check. It all crashed to the surface. After nearly losing her in his arms, he couldn't hide behind restraint anymore.

Alec leaned in, voice low and rough. "Catherine... I never thought I would find someone I cared this deeply for. I always believed I wasn't built for permanence." He drew a shaky breath. "You don't have to say anything. Not yet. But I need you to know—I love you."

The memory of finding her on her living room floor flashed in his eyes—her skin pale, her breaths shallow, the apartment thick with carbon monoxide. It was a ghost that still haunted him.

"I think I've loved you from the moment I met you," he whispered. "I just... didn't realise it until the day you fired me and I found you there, barely breathing."

Her breath hitched. Tears filled her eyes, shimmering like glass. His confession settled between them—warm, trembling, undeniable.

"Alec…" Her voice broke. "I love you too."

For a heartbeat he went completely still. Then joy—raw, fierce, and overwhelming—lit his face. He stood, cupped her carefully, and drew her into his arms, holding her as though he needed to feel the proof of her pulse beneath his hands.

"Do you?" he asked, pulling back just enough to see her eyes, needing to hear it again—needing the certainty.

She reached up, fingertips brushing along his jaw. "Yes, Alec. I love you."

A shy flush warmed her cheeks. "I would never have slept with you that first time if I didn't."

Alec let out a shuddering breath, a sound of relief and love twisted together. He leaned his forehead gently against hers, careful of the bruises marking her skin.

"God, Catherine…" he whispered. "You have no idea what that means to me."

Her fingers threaded through his dark hair, tentative and trembling, anchoring herself to him as if he were her lifeline. "I never thought I would feel like this again," she murmured, voice thick with emotion. "After Ryan died, I thought something in me died too. But you… you pulled me back into the living." Her words softened, fragile with gratitude. "Thank you."

"You don't have to thank me… just keep on loving me," Alec whispered, his voice low, raw, and heavy with emotion.

He lowered his head slowly, giving her the tiniest moment to breathe him in before his lips met hers. The kiss was everything—long, deep, and trembling with a lifetime of longing and relief. His mouth moulded to hers as though memorising her, tasting her, making up for every moment he had ever feared losing her. Each press of his lips spoke of desperate protectiveness, of love clawed back from the edge of despair, of an unspoken promise to never let her go.

Catherine melted into him, her own lips responding in kind, hands clutching at his shoulders, pulling him closer, needing the warmth, the grounding, the undeniable connection. It was slow, tender, and fierce all at once—full of the relief that she was alive, that he was here, that they were finally together again without fear.

When they finally parted, just enough to breathe, their foreheads rested together, breaths mingling, hearts hammering in unison. Alec's gaze searched hers, dark and intense. "You're mine," he murmured, voice breaking slightly. "Only mine."

Catherine's lips quirked into a soft, tearful smile. "And you're mine."

The kiss had said everything words couldn't. It was love, longing, relief, and a promise—sealed in the quiet aftermath of chaos, in the safety of being finally, irrevocably together.

Epilogue

Twelve months later…

The grand doors of the new children's orphanage swung open, sunlight spilling across the steps as guests mingled, laughter and soft chatter carrying on the spring air. Alec's hand was warm around Catherine's as he guided her down the red-carpeted walkway. Her eyes sparkled with quiet pride, the culmination of months of planning and tireless work finally taking shape before her.

"Catherine, this is incredible," her father said, stepping forward to embrace her. There was a lightness in his eyes, a softness that hadn't been there for years. "I'm so proud of you."

Catherine smiled, squeezing his hand. "Thank you, Dad. For everything… and for being here."

Alec's gaze swept over Charles Grant, noting the genuine warmth between father and daughter. His own presence seemed to have earned the man's respect; Charles's approving nod and subtle smile toward him didn't go unnoticed. Alec returned it with a faint, confident smile of his own, slipping seamlessly into the moment without overshadowing Catherine.

Throughout the day, Catherine moved effortlessly from donor to child, shaking hands, offering soft words, and sharing laughter that lit up every corner of the orphanage. Alec stayed close, a silent sentinel at her side, his steady presence and quiet support a grounding force for her. When her father joined them for a brief tour of the building, he exchanged a few easy, familiar words with Alec. For the first time, Alec felt a genuine sense of acceptance, a quiet camaraderie that surprised and pleased him.

The previous evening, Alec had shared a serious conversation with Charles Grant—a rare moment that had tested even his usually unshakable nerves. He wasn't often uneasy, but this was important: he was asking for Catherine's hand in marriage. They discussed boundaries, responsibilities, and the future, the conversation tense at first, each word weighed carefully. Yet, through mutual respect and steady understanding, the tension gradually eased. By the end, Alec felt a quiet satisfaction settle over him—trust had been acknowledged, and a delicate, yet real, bridge had formed between him and her father.

Now, standing beside Catherine at the orphanage, watching her move among the children with warmth and grace, Alec felt an overwhelming surge of gratitude. This woman—brave, kind, and unshakeably strong—was his. He silently vowed never to take her for granted, never to let her feel unsafe or alone again.

His thoughts drifted to their frequent visits to Ryan's grave. The last time they had been there, he had lingered by the headstone, Catherine leaving him behind for a moment as she walked toward the car. Alec had stayed, staring down at the small plaque, and in the hushed reverence of that moment he had whispered, almost like a prayer, "Thank you for bringing us together, little brother. I will love her forever—and I'll always keep her in the light, just like you wanted." The memory settled in him, a quiet, steady flame. Watching Catherine now, surrounded by the children's laughter and the glow of the evening sun, Alec felt the weight of that promise pulse in his chest. She was alive, thriving, radiant—and he would guard that light with every fibre of himself.

As the evening drew to a close and the last of the guests departed, Alec and Catherine lingered on the steps, taking in the sight of children pressing faces to the windows, their small hands waving goodbye. She leaned into him, warmth radiating from her, and Alec wrapped an arm around her shoulders, savouring the simple, unspoken joy of this day— a day built on hope, healing, and the promise of the future they would face together.

"I can't believe how far we've come," Catherine whispered, leaning against him.

Alec tightened his arm around her. "Neither can I," he admitted. "You've done something extraordinary here… you've changed lives."

Catherine lifted her face to him, eyes catching the last glow of sunset. "I couldn't have done it without you. You've been my rock."

"I always will be," Alec murmured, slipping her hand into his as he helped her into the waiting limousine. He settled beside her, thumb brushing over her knuckles in that quiet, grounding way he always did.

The ride passed in a comfortable silence, city lights streaking past the tinted windows as the limousine carried them toward his penthouse. They entered the lobby and waited for the private elevator. When the doors opened, Alec pulled Catherine close, pressing his lips to hers the moment they stepped inside.

As his mouth drifted to her neck, Catherine's breath hitched, a soft, playful sound escaping her. "What are you trying to do—seduce me in an elevator?"

Alec's grin was teasing, dark, and irresistible. "Could I?"

She giggled, her tension melting. "You know you could."

The lift doors slid open, and Catherine stepped into the penthouse—only to be met with a wall of perfume and a riot of colour. The living room was a sea of flowers, every vase catching the soft glow of the lamps, petals trembling in the light. Her eyes went wide. "What… what's all this?"

Alec chuckled, brushing a stray lock of hair from her face. "I wanted tonight to be special."

Catherine melted into his arms. "I think every day with you is special, you know that."

He guided her to the centre of the living room, surrounded by the intoxicating scent and beauty of the flowers. Taking both her hands in his, he looked into her eyes, voice low and full of raw honesty. "I never thought in a million years I'd find someone like you… and love you as much as I do. But I thank God every day that we found each other."

"I do too," Catherine whispered, her smile radiant.

Alec dropped to one knee, and Catherine's breath caught. He opened a small box to reveal a solitaire diamond that sparkled like a captured star. "Catherine… I love you, and I can't imagine my life without you. Will you make me the luckiest man alive and marry me?"

Tears welled in her eyes, and words failed her. She simply nodded. "Yes. God… yes."

He slid the ring onto her finger, stood, and lifted her into his arms, pressing his lips to hers in a kiss that was tender, fierce, and infinitely full of love—a promise of forever.

The skyline stretched endlessly before them, but Alec's focus was only on her. Every danger, every loss had led to this moment. Their fight was done. Their bond unbreakable. The Blood Debt had been settled, and their future was theirs.

The End

Wife in Name Only

Alison Reid

A complete standalone romance

Previously published individually

Chapter One

The smell of old books and stronger medicines hung heavy in Henry Fitzgerald's study, wrapping around Renee like a shroud. The scent of aged leather bindings and antiseptic mingled in the air, a cruel reminder of time slipping away. The fire crackled behind the grate, casting golden shadows across the mahogany-panelled walls, but its warmth didn't touch her.

She sat upright in the armchair across from her grandfather, hands folded tightly in her lap, knuckles bloodless. Her pulse beat a steady, anxious rhythm against her ribs—warning, warning, warning—like her body already knew what her mind refused to guess.

Henry's once-booming voice had softened over the last year, thinned by chemotherapy and the truth they all tried to deny. But tonight, it carried a sharp edge of clarity. The same voice that once brokered million-dollar acquisitions now sliced through the silence like a verdict.

"I need you to marry Hudson."

The words landed like a slap.

Renee blinked.

"Excuse me?"

Henry leaned back in his chair, his posture still commanding despite the fragility creeping into his frame. His once-black hair had turned almost entirely silver, and his hands trembled slightly where they rested on the armrests. But his eyes—steel-grey and unyielding—locked onto hers with quiet determination.

"I'm dying, sweetheart." No euphemisms. No softening. "No treatments. No miracles. No second chances. I need to know you'll be safe when I'm gone… and that the company will be in the right hands."

A thousand thoughts screamed in her mind, but all she could manage was a brittle whisper.

"I don't need a man to be safe, Granddad."

"I know you don't." His tone gentled, but the weight behind it never lessened. "But the world still acts like you do. You're young. Brilliant. Loyal. But you give too much, and you trust too easily. I won't always be here to protect you… or this company. Hudson's solid. Strategic. He'll guard Fitzgerald Enterprises like it's his own."

Renee's spine stiffened. She kept her expression neutral—years of business meetings had taught her how to mask emotion—but inside, she flinched.

Hudson Waterford.

The name alone stirred a familiar ache. He'd been her grandfather's protégé, a golden boy with a sharp mind and a gaze that always seemed to look through her instead of at her. She'd fallen for him when she was nineteen, working internships in the corporate offices, desperate to impress both the man she admired and the one she adored in silence.

Hudson had never seen her. Not really. Not as a woman. Just as Henry's serious granddaughter, good with numbers and better with restraint.

And now Henry wanted to hand her to him like a peace offering. Or worse—a contingency plan.

"I know it's asking a lot," Henry added softly, watching her closely. "But I need this, Renee. I need to know that everything I built, everything your father would've protected if he'd lived… will be guarded after I'm gone."

Her throat tightened at the mention of her father. The pain of his sudden death—the car accident, the empty chair at birthdays, the way Henry had stepped in like a fortress around her after—still lived quietly in the corners of her heart.

Henry had been her rock. Her anchor. When her world fractured at thirteen, it was he who dried her tears and taught her to fight with her brain, not her heart. He'd been more father than grandfather ever since.

And now… he was asking her to give him peace in return.

"I don't want to force this," Henry continued, his voice quieter now, threaded with fatigue. "But time is slipping through my fingers, and I can't leave everything to chance."

She looked at him—the man who had sacrificed so much for her, who'd taught her to stand tall in boardrooms full of wolves, who had given her a name and a legacy.

"I love you, Granddad," she said softly, her voice catching. "You know that."

His lips curved into a faint smile. "I do. That's why I trust you to do this."

Renee stared into the fire, its flames dancing and cracking like her certainty. She didn't know if she could stomach the arrangement, if she could walk into a cold marriage with the one man she had never truly gotten over.

But she knew one thing for sure: she couldn't say no to the man who had never once said no to her.

After leaving her grandfather's estate, Renee didn't drive straight home.

She couldn't.

The silence of her apartment would echo too loudly with everything left unsaid—the weight of Henry's request, the finality in his eyes, the choice that wasn't really a choice at all.

Instead, she headed uptown, threading through the city like a ghost behind the wheel. The familiar buzz of Manhattan was little more than background noise as she crossed into the Upper West Side, past warm-lit cafés, and old brownstones, until she reached the place where she could breathe.

Vivian's apartment.

Vivian, her best friend since their college days at NYU. The only person who didn't see Renee Fitzgerald—the heiress, the executive, the polished product of privilege— but simply Renee. The girl who'd cried over midterms and carried granola bars in her purse for homeless vets.

By the time she reached the building, her hands were cold around the steering wheel. She didn't remember where she'd parked or how she'd buzzed in—only that moments later, Vivian was there, opening the door in a silk robe and fuzzy slippers, eyebrows lifting the second she saw her face.

"Ren?" she said gently, stepping aside. "Come in."

Renee walked in without a word and dropped her coat over the arm of the couch. The dam didn't break right away. It never did with her. But Vivian handed her a glass of wine without asking, and that was all the invitation she needed.

She exhaled, slow and shaky, and said in a voice that barely sounded like her own—

"He wants me to marry Hudson."

The scent of bergamot and baked brie filled the air, but nothing about the kitchen felt warm tonight. Vivian paced in her silk robe the colour of wine, her arms crossed tight under her chest. Her gold hoop earrings swayed with every turn she made.

At the counter, Renee sat on a barstool, turning a stemless wine glass between her fingers. She hadn't taken a sip.

"Are you seriously considering this?" Vivian asked, stopping mid-pace to stare at her.

Renee sighed. "I don't know."

Vivian narrowed her eyes. "You do. You just don't want to say it out loud."

"I'm giving my grandfather peace," Renee said, quieter this time. "That's all that matters."

"No." Vivian stepped closer. "That's not all that matters. What about your peace? Your happiness? You're giving up your life for an obligation."

"It's not just an obligation," Renee said, voice thin but steady. "It's gratitude. It's love."

"Love?" Vivian scoffed. "You're about to marry a man who doesn't even like you, let alone love you."

Renee flinched but didn't argue.

Vivian's tone softened. "Renee… you're a beautiful woman. You're intelligent beyond your years. You've built your own reputation apart from Fitzgerald. You could have anyone you want. So why him?"

Renee's eyes dropped to the wine glass. Her thumb traced the rim, over and over like a mantra.

"I'm not asking for love," she whispered.

Vivian stood in front of her, her voice gentler now, full of a tenderness that had no sharp edges.

"That doesn't mean you don't deserve it."

Renee's throat tightened.

Vivian tucked a strand of hair behind Renee's ear. "You've spent your whole life being the strong one. The logical one. But I see you. I see how lonely you are. How long you've loved him in silence."

Renee blinked, and her eyes shimmered with unshed tears. "It doesn't matter. He'll never love me back."

"Then don't marry him hoping he will."

"I'm not," Renee said quickly, then paused, her voice cracking. "I'm not that naive anymore."

Vivian stepped back slowly, brushing invisible lint from her robe. "Then you better prepare yourself, Ren. Because once you say, 'I do,' there's no room for wanting more."

Renee didn't respond. She just stared into the glass, her reflection warping in the curve of the wine.

She was marrying him for logic. For legacy. For love that wasn't hers to receive.

Rain skidded across the floor-to-ceiling windows, softening the glitter of Manhattan's skyline into a blur of golds and silvers. The city pulsed below, electric, and oblivious. Inside, the penthouse was all cool lines and quiet luxury—concrete, glass, and understated power.

"You'd finally be CEO," Helen said, swirling dark red wine in her glass before refilling it.

Hudson stood by the window, shoulders squared, one hand braced against the glass as he looked out over the city like it was a chessboard.

He didn't answer right away. His silence had a weight to it, a stillness that Helen knew not to fill too quickly.

"All you have to do," she added, voice smooth as the Merlot, "is marry her."

He turned then, the edge of his profile cast in shadow.

"It's not exactly the proposal I imagined."

Helen smirked faintly. "Since when has love ever factored into corporate succession?"

"Since never." He glanced down at the glass in his hand but didn't drink. "It's cold, even for Henry."

"Maybe." Helen crossed her legs, her tone deliberately casual. "But he's dying. Men get sentimental about legacy when the clock starts ticking."

"And what if she says no?"

Helen tilted her head, as if amused by the question.

"She won't. Henry's her Achilles' heel."

Hudson's jaw flexed.

He hadn't thought about Renee Fitzgerald in years—not beyond the occasional boardroom encounter or distant mention in quarterly reports. She'd always been there, orbiting just outside the centre of power. Quiet. Controlled. Good with numbers. He remembered once hearing her debate a CFO twice her age into a corner over a projected earnings dip. Her voice had been calm, precise—but there'd been fire in her eyes. Passion for the numbers, for the legacy her grandfather had built.

Eyes that flicked away the second he met them.

He remembered that, too.

She was beautiful. Unobtrusively so. Tall, elegant, with a grace that didn't announce itself. The kind of woman who didn't know how much space she took up in a room until you couldn't stop watching her.

Sexy in a way that snuck up on you—like realising too late you'd misjudged a storm.

And now?

Now, she was the price of a title he'd worked toward for ten years.

"She's not a fool," he muttered.

"No," Helen agreed. "But she's Henry's granddaughter through and through. Duty runs thicker than blood for that girl. And she'd do anything for him... even marry a man who sees her as a business transaction."

Hudson looked away again. His reflection stared back at him in the glass—sharp suit, sharper ambition, and a flicker of something he didn't want to name.

This wasn't love. This wasn't personal.

It was leverage. Strategy. A means to an end.

And yet...

Something about her name, the way it settled in his chest, made him feel like this deal might be more complicated than any merger he'd ever negotiated.

Hudson drained his glass in one long sip.

The same fire that had cast dancing shadows on Renee's face now crackled behind Hudson Waterford, throwing heat against a wall of cold intentions.

Henry Fitzgerald sat behind his desk like a fading monarch—thinner than Hudson remembered, paler, but still with that razor focus behind pale blue eyes.

"I appreciate you coming," Henry said, his voice raspier than usual.

Hudson took the seat across from him, posture perfectly straight. "You asked for a meeting. I assumed it wasn't social."

Henry offered a dry smile. "It's always business, isn't it?"

Hudson didn't blink. "Especially with you."

The old man gave a short cough—painful, from the sound of it—but waved off concern. "I'll spare you the grand speeches. You know what I'm asking."

"To marry your granddaughter," Hudson said flatly.

"To ensure she's looked after when I'm gone," Henry corrected. "You'll become CEO of Fitzgerald Enterprises, effective immediately following the wedding."

Hudson's gaze didn't waver. "You really think she'll agree?"

"She already has," Henry said, with that same, terrifying confidence that once closed multi-billion-dollar deals in a single phone call.

A beat passed. Hudson leaned back slightly, surprised despite himself.

"She said yes?"

"She said she would—for me. You have no idea what she's giving up."

Hudson exhaled through his nose, jaw tightening. "She's smart. She'll resent this."

"Eventually," Henry agreed. "But by then, you'll have earned her trust. Maybe even her respect."

"And if I don't?" Hudson asked, the challenge sharp in his tone.

Henry met his eyes dead on. "Then you'll have no one to blame but yourself."

There was no affection in the old man's voice, no pretence of romance. This was legacy. Strategy. And for the first time, Hudson felt the slightest sting of guilt curl in the pit of his stomach.

He nodded once. "You'll have your arrangement."

Henry closed his eyes briefly in relief, though his face remained unreadable. "Then we begin the paperwork."

As Hudson stood to leave, Henry added quietly, "Take care of her, Hudson. Whether she ever asks you to or not."

Hudson paused at the door, jaw clenched, something unnameable tightening behind his ribs.

Then he left.

It had been four years ago. Maybe five.

A quarterly strategy session had run late. The boardroom was nearly empty, leftover coffee cooling beside half-eaten fruit trays.

Hudson had been reviewing notes on projected losses when she walked in—Renee, fresh from grad school, barely twenty-one, in a sleek black dress and heels too high for comfort.

"I thought the room was empty," she said, pausing by the door.

He looked up, ready to dismiss whoever had wandered in—until he saw it was her.

"Come in," he said, more curious than polite.

She did. With quiet confidence. Sat two chairs down and pulled out a binder so thick it made him arch a brow.

"Cash flow discrepancies in the Q2 report," she said. "The growth model's skewed by short-term supplier overpayments."

Hudson blinked. "You're not on the audit team."

"I know." She flipped the binder open, eyes focused. "But I noticed something when I was running numbers for the annual report."

She explained, clearly and cleanly, breaking down a million-dollar oversight with calm precision. By the time she finished, he was staring.

Not at the numbers. At her.

The way her mind worked. The glow in her eyes when she solved a problem. The breathless little pause she made before delivering the final conclusion—like even she couldn't believe she'd gotten there first.

He'd said something dismissive, he remembered. Something about her being "thorough for an intern."

She'd smiled, thanked him anyway, and walked out.

He never forgot it.

And tonight, as he prepared to marry her for ambition's sake, that memory slid under his skin like a warning.

She wasn't a pawn. She never had been.

Two days later in Henry's study, the contract lay between them like a living thing—quiet, pulsing, final.

Renee picked up the pen first.

Her fingers curled around it with elegant precision, but her hand only stayed steady because she forced it to. Her signature flowed in graceful script across the bottom of the page—an act of love disguised as legal consent.

She didn't look up.

Hudson took the pen next. His fingers brushed the edge of the paper before he began to write, each stroke deliberate, measured. His name—Hudson James Waterford—sealed beneath hers in thick black ink. The final signature on an agreement neither of them truly understood the cost of yet.

One glance passed between them when he set the pen down.

Neutral. Civil. As sterile as the paper they'd just signed.

Henry exhaled like a man who'd been holding his breath for months. He sank back into his leather chair, his face drawn with fatigue, but his eyes—still sharp behind the wear of illness—shone with quiet relief.

"Thank you," he murmured, voice thin but steady. "You've given me peace. More than I ever hoped for."

Renee offered him a smile. It was soft, practiced, but didn't quite reach her eyes.

She would have done anything to give him this—this final sense of security. Even if it broke her.

Hudson nodded, hands clasped on the table before him, a portrait of composed professionalism. "You can focus on your health now," he said carefully. "We'll handle everything else."

Henry gave a ghost of a nod, leaning his head back against the chair, the colour in his cheeks already fading as the moment took its toll.

There was silence.

Then, Hudson stood and extended his hand toward Renee.

She hesitated for half a beat before rising. Her palm met his. A handshake—cool, brief, and devastatingly impersonal. Her engagement ring, newly slipped onto her finger, glinted under the chandelier light, a hollow echo of what it should have meant.

Their fingers parted.

It was done.

No fireworks. No vows. Just two signatures and a grandfather's legacy binding them together.

Renee turned to her grandfather, leaning down to kiss his cheek gently. "Get some rest, Granddad."

Henry patted her hand, eyes half-lidded, already slipping into the kind of exhaustion only illness brings.

Hudson followed her silently to the door. Neither spoke.

Outside, the hallway seemed colder than when they entered.

Chapter Two

The Fitzgerald rooftop garden had never looked so elegant—or so hollow.

Twinkle lights shimmered above like captive stars, strung in meticulous lines around the pergola. White roses curled over the trellises, scenting the dusk air with a sweetness that didn't quite reach the heart. A string quartet played in the corner, their music soft and classical, as if rehearsed more for a gala than a wedding. Below them, the skyline of Manhattan glittered like a stage set for a story that didn't belong to her.

It was perfect.

And yet, it felt like a merger.

Renee stood beneath the archway, her ivory dress draping her body like a whisper. It was sleek, minimal, elegant—but devoid of fantasy. No veil. No lace. No sparkle. She'd chosen her gown like she chose her quarterly budgets: with logic. Not dreams.

Once, when she was sixteen, she'd clipped a page from a bridal magazine—an off-the-shoulder gown with layers of soft tulle and embroidered stars, like a fairytale come to life. She'd tucked it inside a notebook, never daring to show anyone. Not even Vivian.

She hadn't thought about that dress in years.

Until now.

And standing here in ivory silk, elegant and calculated, Renee realised—she hadn't just let go of the dress. She'd let go of the girl who believed she'd ever wear it for love.

Hudson stood beside her, straight and composed in a charcoal suit, a man carved from ambition. He looked every inch the CEO he was about to become. Measured. Unreadable.

He didn't smile.

His fingers were cool when they took hers.

The officiant read the vows. There were no stumbles. No emotion.

Renee said, I do.

Hudson said, I do.

They did not kiss.

There was polite applause. Someone—probably Helen—offered a delicate, lone whistle that didn't quite earn its place.

Vivian, seated toward the front in a bottle green silk dress and diamond studs, leaned toward the guest beside her and muttered, "Is this a wedding or a quarterly board meeting?"

Renee caught the flicker of her best friend's expression—and almost laughed. Almost. But it caught in her throat, like everything else had lately.

Instead, she smiled for the crowd. The small, handpicked group of board members, legal representatives, elite family friends. All of them clapping politely, none of them believing for a second this was a love match.

Henry sat in a carved velvet chair near the front, too frail now to stand, his face slack with exhaustion but eyes alight with relief. He was the only one beaming. The only one who looked like today meant something.

And maybe, Renee thought, that was all that mattered.

She moved through the rooftop reception like a hostess at a formal charity gala. She greeted guests, accepted their congratulations with grace, and posed for photographs beside Hudson like they were two executives launching a partnership.

In some ways, they were.

There were no lingering glances. No whispered jokes. No touches that lingered.

Once, she brushed Hudson's arm as they stood side by side. He didn't flinch. But he didn't move closer either.

She stepped away, spine straightening.

Vivian found her by the hors d'oeuvres table. "If I see one more botoxed smile, I'm going to stab myself with a cocktail fork."

Renee gave a soft laugh that didn't reach her eyes. "It's fine."

Vivian studied her. "Is it?"

Renee shrugged, looking out at the glittering skyline. "It's just a lot."

"It's a lie," Vivian snapped. "You deserve someone who looks at you like you're made of wildfire and mystery. Not someone who only notices your financial forecasting skills."

Renee's mouth twisted. "He's not a bad man."

"No," Vivian said gently. "But he's not your man. Not really. And if he doesn't realise what he has… someone else will."

Renee didn't respond.

Across the rooftop, Hudson stood with Helen, speaking in low, calculated tones. He hadn't sought her out once since the vows.

They were married.

But no one would have guessed it.

Renee stood at the railing, her gaze skimming the skyline without really seeing it.

Behind her, heels clicked on the flagstone.

"Hiding already?" came Helen Waterford's smooth, amused voice.

Renee turned, managing a faint smile. "Avoiding. It's not quite hiding yet."

Helen stepped up beside her, dressed in her signature sharp heels and silk. She held out a glass of champagne. "To last-minute peace and the illusion of choice."

Renee took it, clinking her glass lightly. "Is that what this is?"

Helen studied her for a moment—always too perceptive for comfort. "You don't strike me as the kind of woman who folds easily."

Renee sipped, eyes back on the skyline. "I didn't fold. I made a decision."

Helen tilted her head. "For Henry."

"For Henry," Renee confirmed, her voice soft but steady.

Silence stretched between them for a beat.

Then Helen asked, lightly, "And Hudson?"

Renee's throat tightened. She kept her expression unreadable. "He's getting what he wants. CEO status. A company he respects. I don't expect anything else."

Helen didn't respond immediately. She was watching Renee closely now, her polished exterior betraying the flicker of something deeper. Maybe curiosity. Maybe concern.

"You know," Helen said, sipping her drink, "I've never seen him agree to something he couldn't control."

Renee turned to face her, brows lifting. "And this—marrying me—is control?"

"No," Helen said, lips curving into a faint smile. "This? This is a variable. You are a variable."

Renee blinked. "That sounds like a threat."

"It's not." Helen looked genuinely amused. "It's admiration. And a warning."

Renee narrowed her eyes. "Warning me about what?"

"That he might not know what he's gotten himself into," Helen said. "And you... might not know what you mean to him."

Renee's breath caught slightly.

Helen leaned in a little closer, voice lower now, more intimate. "He's a cold strategist, yes. But even cold men can burn if something gets under their skin."

Renee scoffed, but it sounded forced. "Hudson sees me as an obligation."

Helen smiled slyly. "Are you sure?"

Renee turned back to the skyline, heart suddenly racing.

Helen gave her a beat of silence before stepping back. "Just don't be too quick to assume his silence means nothing. Sometimes it means everything."

She walked off, heels clicking again into the distance.

Renee stayed at the railing, the city lights blurring into stars. Her fingers tightened around the stem of the champagne flute.

For the first time, she wondered if her grandfather wasn't the only one trying to manipulate the pieces on this board.

Hudson's penthouse was elegant, quiet, and impossibly vast. Expansive windows offered a glittering view of the Manhattan skyline, but the space itself felt hollow—like a high-end hotel suite designed for show, not for living. Everything was polished and perfect, down to the imported marble and curated art. Cold beauty.

It didn't feel like home.

Not for her.

Not for them.

Renee had moved into the guest wing the moment they arrived—by mutual, unspoken agreement. No argument. No protest. Just silence. The kind that filled all the empty spaces between two people who weren't supposed to be strangers—but somehow were.

She closed the door to her suite with a soft click.

Her dress was still flawless. Her hair hadn't moved. Her makeup remained untouched, her lips still bearing the faintest trace of a smile she'd forced hours earlier.

To anyone else, she looked like the picture of calm elegance. A composed bride.

Inside, something had died quietly and been buried in her chest.

Hudson hadn't followed her.

There'd been no mention of a honeymoon. No shared itinerary. No awkward conversation about what came next.

Just silence.

They were legally husband and wife.

But the quiet between them held more weight than any vow spoken aloud. It was dense. Inescapable. A language of its own.

Renee sat on the edge of the bed, spine straight, eyes blank.

She reached for the wedding ring on her finger—cool metal against warm skin—and slid it off without hesitation. Not out of anger. Not even sorrow. Just... necessity. Practicality.

She placed it gently in the porcelain dish beside the lamp.

It wasn't symbolic.

It was a reflection of what this union had become: functional. Clean. Defined by mutual benefit.

Like everything else about this day.

But beneath all the reason, all the logic she'd tried to armour herself with—there was a truth. One she'd hidden from even herself for weeks now.

She loved him.

She had for five years.

She remembered the moment it started—she'd been nineteen, a summer intern at Fitzgerald Enterprises, nervous and eager, buried in spreadsheets, when he'd paused behind her desk and asked a sharp question about cash flow analysis. She'd answered with more confidence than she felt. He'd looked at her, not like she was a kid playing grown-up, but like someone worth listening to.

And just like that, her world had shifted.

He was older, focused, intense—but something in his presence lit a fire beneath her ambition. He never noticed, of course. Not really. To him, she was just Henry Fitzgerald's too-serious granddaughter. A junior analyst. Later, the company's rising CFO. Always intelligent. Always capable. Always... untouchable.

She had buried her feelings beneath long hours, promotions, carefully constructed emotional detachment. But they'd never left her.

And now, she was married to him. Married—but not his.

Not in any real sense.

The irony tasted bitter.

She had given her heart years ago—and today, she'd given her name.

But she couldn't give him what he didn't want.

She lay back slowly against the crisp, expensive sheets and stared at the ceiling, her chest rising and falling with shallow breaths.

No one had asked if she wanted this.

She'd done it for Henry.

For the company.

For duty.

And somehow, in the quiet aftermath of the most important day of her life, it was clearer than ever:

She had never felt more alone.

Hudson stood at the bar in the corner of his private study, turning a glass of scotch in his hand without drinking it. The liquor caught the light like amber, smooth and deceptive.

Just like today had been.

The wedding was done. The deal had been sealed. And yet, he couldn't shake the feeling that something irrevocable had been set in motion—and not just in terms of the company.

Renee was in the guest wing. The door had closed behind her an hour ago with a soft click he'd heard all the way down the hall.

She hadn't expected him to follow. And he hadn't.

Not because he didn't think he should.

But because he didn't know what he would say if he did.

He set the glass down without drinking and braced both hands on the edge of the marble countertop, jaw tense.

This wasn't how he imagined any of it.

Not the marriage.

Not the company.

Not her.

For years, Renee had been in the periphery of his vision—brilliant, disciplined, intimidatingly competent. But always reserved. Always distant. It wasn't until Henry had laid out the terms of the deal that he'd been forced to truly see her.

And what he'd seen had caught him off guard.

Not just her elegance or her intelligence—but her strength. Her quiet loyalty. Her refusal to look away when others flinched. She wasn't a child or a pawn. She was a force.

And now she was his wife.

On paper.

But tonight, when she said I do, there'd been something in her eyes—a flicker he couldn't name. Not cold. Not afraid. Just… closed. Like she'd already locked the door behind some part of herself he wasn't allowed to see.

He hated how much that bothered him.

Hudson loosened his tie and sat in the leather chair by the window. The city pulsed below—alive, ambitious, relentless. It looked like everything he'd always wanted.

So why did it feel like nothing?

He rubbed a hand over the back of his neck, then leaned forward, elbows on his knees.

She hadn't smiled once—not really.

She hadn't cried, hadn't protested. Hadn't demanded a thing.

And somehow, that quiet surrender unsettled him more than outrage ever could have.

She'd walked into this marriage with grace, with dignity. And without illusion.

He should have felt victorious. Everything had gone to plan—every line of the contract, every clause, every silent concession. But what unsettled him most wasn't what she said.

It was what she didn't.

Hudson could predict markets, restructure entire divisions, and neutralise hostile boardroom tactics. But Renee?

He couldn't read her.

Couldn't move her.

And for the first time in his life, he understood what real risk looked like: not in numbers or negotiations, but in silence.

In the way her eyes never once looked at him like she used to.

And in the haunting suspicion that somewhere deep inside, she'd already let him go.

Which made him the fool.

Because something in her silence made him feel like he'd already lost something he hadn't even known he was trying to keep.

He remembered the day he realised that Renee was more than just Henry's granddaughter, three years ago. The boardroom was emptying out slowly, the usual rustle of papers and polite murmurs trailing in the wake of a long quarterly review. Hudson had already gathered his laptop and notepad, but something made him linger near the head of the table.

That's when he heard her voice.

"Actually, if we reroute the surplus through the mid-year discretionary budget, we won't have to cut research spending at all."

He glanced back.

Renee Fitzgerald was still seated two chairs down, her slender fingers tapping on the keyboard of a silver laptop. Her brow was slightly furrowed, her mouth moving in rhythm with thoughts she seemed to be articulating mostly for herself.

"No offence, but I don't think anyone wants to present another three-year plan with backloaded growth projections," she added, half to the CFO, half into the air. "If we're not aggressive with capital now, we'll lose momentum."

Hudson frowned slightly.

He had known Renee—Henry's granddaughter, the financial analyst he'd plucked straight out of her MBA and given a real role before anyone thought she was ready. She was rarely vocal in meetings, more likely to work behind the scenes with spreadsheets and silence. Until now.

She looked up then, sensing eyes on her.

Her gaze met his—and just for a second, it startled him.

Not because of the way she looked, though she was striking in a clean, understated way that didn't try to impress, but because of the intensity in her eyes. Focused. Fierce. Unapologetically smart.

She blinked quickly and looked back at her screen, clearly uncomfortable with the sudden attention. A faint flush rose along her cheekbones.

The CFO beside her chuckled. "Remind me not to underestimate you again, Renee."

She shrugged, trying to brush it off. "I just like solving puzzles."

Hudson watched her a beat longer.

There was something about the way she sat—poised, quietly confident, not looking for approval but not afraid of disagreement either. Something in her tone, in the quick-fire clarity of her analysis, in the steel beneath her calm exterior.

She didn't defer.

She didn't pretend to be less than what she was.

And that—that—was the first time Hudson Waterford saw her as more than Henry Fitzgerald's granddaughter.

More than a junior staffer.

More than a cog in the company machine.

That day, she became a presence he couldn't quite ignore.

He didn't know her story.

Didn't know the depth of her loyalty.

Didn't know she watched him when he wasn't looking.

But something shifted.

And now, sitting alone in his penthouse study, he remembered that exact look in her eyes—burning with vision, with challenge—and realised how long she had been right in front of him.

And how long he had been blind.

Chapter Three

The next morning the scent of French roast and toasted brioche drifted through the open breakfast room, mingling with early light filtering through the floor-to-ceiling windows. The view was spectacular—Central Park kissed with morning fog, city traffic just beginning to hum to life.

But none of it touched the silence at the table.

Renee sat with a steaming cup of coffee cradled between both hands, dressed in a slate-grey cashmere wrap and fitted slacks. Her hair was twisted into a low knot, and she looked composed, efficient. A CFO, not a newlywed.

Across the table, Hudson turned a page of the Wall Street Journal, his custom-tailored shirt crisp, tie already in place.

They hadn't spoken since the rooftop reception. Not a single word.

Renee glanced at him over the rim of her cup. "The board approved the Paris expansion budget?"

Hudson didn't look up. "Yes. Late last night."

She nodded, trying not to feel the sting at how easily this could have been an email. "Congratulations. That was in the pipeline for a year."

He finally folded the paper and met her eyes. "You were right to push for early investment. Your analysis made the case airtight."

A polite compliment. Respectful. Impersonal.

"Thank you," she said evenly. "I'll adjust the liquidity report accordingly."

A long pause. Their coffee cups clinked faintly against their saucers.

Hudson studied her then—closer, more carefully than he intended. She looked... exactly as she always had at the office. Polished. Prepared. But there was something different in her eyes this morning. Quieter. Heavier.

"Did you sleep well?" he asked, surprising even himself.

She blinked. "Well enough."

He hesitated. "The suite is comfortable?"

"Yes," she said, with a tight, courteous smile. "You didn't have to go to the trouble."

"I didn't," he said. "It was already prepared."

Of course it was.

Prepared. Like the marriage. Like the contract. Like the future they'd agreed to live beside one another, not with.

Renee placed her napkin on the table, rising. "I have an early call with Zurich. I'll see you at the 10 a.m. revenue review."

Hudson stood as well, reflexively. "Of course."

She moved past him—graceful, calm—but just as she reached the doorway, she paused.

"Hudson," she said quietly, still not facing him.

He straightened. "Yes?"

She turned her head slightly, her voice barely above a whisper. "This arrangement… you don't have to pretend. I understand what it is. What it isn't."

Her words lingered like frost on the air.

Before he could respond, she disappeared down the hallway, leaving behind only the scent of her perfume—and something like regret.

Hudson stood alone in the silence of their marriage.

A man who had everything he'd asked for.

And suddenly, it didn't feel like enough.

Hudson's penthouse was immaculate, silent, and cold. It functioned like a museum—beautiful, ordered, and devoid of intimacy. Six months had passed since the wedding, and Renee and Hudson lived like polite strangers. Business partners. Roommates. Ghosts in designer clothing.

Each morning began the same.

Renee would rise early, make coffee she didn't drink, and sit in the breakfast nook reviewing market reports until Hudson emerged from his wing. They'd exchange greetings—never more than a few words—and part ways before the sun was fully up. No shared meals. No late-night conversations. Nothing personal.

She had tried, in the beginning. Subtle gestures. Light conversation. Invitations to dinner, to walk in the park, to share a moment. Each attempt was met with a polite but firm deflection.

Hudson was always "too busy." Meetings. Strategy calls. Deadlines.

Eventually, she stopped asking.

Instead, she buried herself in work. As CFO, she helped bring Fitzgerald Enterprises into one of its most profitable quarters. Numbers became her armour. Financial forecasts and acquisition reports were her distraction from the quiet ache that never left her.

At night, she returned to the guest suite and tried not to imagine what it would feel like if he opened her door. If he cared enough to ask how her day had really gone. If he remembered that once, long ago, she had mattered to him. Even a little.

But that door never opened.

Only one place brought her comfort now—her grandfather's estate, Fitzgerald Hall. She visited twice a week, sometimes more, bringing tea and reports and the warmth of her presence.

Henry's health was fading. He was thinner now, and his eyes tired faster, but his mind was still sharp, and his heart—always sharpest of all—was watching her closely.

One afternoon, he set down his teacup with a clink and studied her over his glasses.

"You're not happy," he said simply.

Renee glanced down at the cookie she'd been crumbling between her fingers. "I'm fine, Granddad."

"No," he said. "You're managing. There's a difference."

She looked up. "It's only been six months."

"I didn't expect fireworks. But I didn't expect… frostbite either."

She smiled faintly, but it didn't reach her eyes.

He leaned forward. "You love him."

She froze. "Granddad—"

"I may be old, but I'm not blind. I saw the way you looked at him when you thought no one else noticed."

Her throat tightened. "It doesn't matter."

"Yes," Henry said softly. "It does."

She stood and walked to the window, folding her arms. "He doesn't feel the same. This was always about the company. About you."

Henry let silence fall between them like a thick, weighted curtain. The ticking of the mantel clock filled the space, louder than before.

Finally, he said quietly, "You're worth more than any company, Renee. I asked you to marry him because I thought he could protect you. Because I trusted his mind. His loyalty. But I didn't realise…" He paused, voice tightening with regret. "I didn't realise he'd be the one to hurt you."

Renee turned from the window, her eyes bright with unshed tears, but her voice remained calm—measured, like she'd practiced it a dozen times before. "He hasn't hurt me. Not really. He just…" She swallowed. "He doesn't see me. Not as a woman. Not as someone he could ever want."

Henry leaned back slowly in his chair, gaze never leaving her. "Then make him see you."

She gave a soft, tired laugh that didn't hold any amusement. "I've tried."

Henry's eyes narrowed—not in anger, but in recognition. He saw what it had cost her to say that. What it had cost her to hope.

"I've tried in all the ways that count," she continued, her voice quieter now. "I've been patient. I've been kind. I've supported him, never stood in his way. And all I've gotten in return is polite distance and professional courtesy. Like I'm a secretary he feels vaguely indebted to."

Her hands tightened in her lap.

"I married a man who doesn't want a wife," she said. "He wants a company. A title. A future on his terms. And I… I just happen to be part of the packaging."

Henry's jaw tightened, his heart cracking behind his stern composure. "He's a fool."

"No," she whispered, shaking her head. "He's just focused. The same way you've always respected in him."

"But focus isn't an excuse to be blind."

Renee gave a small, brittle smile. "Maybe not. But it makes it easier to forget who's hurting in the shadows."

Henry looked at her for a long moment, his eyes misted with a grief that was more than illness—it was guilt.

"I thought I was giving you protection," he murmured. "What I gave you was silence in a suit."

Renee moved to him then, kneeling beside his chair, taking his hand in hers. "You gave me everything you could, Granddad. And I don't regret marrying him. I regret… hoping for more."

It wasn't bitterness. It was truth—quiet and worn, like a stone polished smooth by disappointment.

Henry squeezed her hand gently, a whisper of strength in his fading grasp. "Then don't give up yet. Sometimes the blind don't see until they're afraid of losing something."

She didn't answer.

But deep in her chest, something shifted.

Not hope.

Not yet.

But something close enough to hurt.

Later that same week, Hudson found himself in the Fitzgerald boardroom alone with Henry for one of their quarterly reviews. The room was filled with charts, numbers, growth models—but Henry's attention was somewhere else.

"You've done well," Henry said after Hudson's summary. "Better than I expected."

Hudson inclined his head. "I'm grateful for the trust."

Henry studied him with the sharp gaze of a man who'd built empires. "But I wonder, Hudson… What exactly have you been building?"

Hudson blinked. "I'm not sure I understand."

"You have the company. The title. The power. But you've lost something, haven't you?"

Hudson didn't answer.

Henry tapped a knuckle on the table. "Don't let ambition cost you what really matters."

Hudson stared at him, expression unreadable. "Is this about Renee?"

Henry didn't flinch. "It's always been about her. She's the legacy. Not the company. Not the brand. Her."

Hudson exhaled slowly. "She deserves more than what I can give her."

"Then grow into a man who can," Henry said, his voice thin but fierce. "Before she realises, she doesn't need you at all."

The penthouse was silent, save for the hum of the city just beyond the glass. Midtown glittered like a kingdom he owned but never touched. Hudson sat alone in the darkened office, tie loosened, sleeves rolled to his elbows. The light from the city painted harsh lines across his face, catching on the untouched scotch at his elbow. His reflection in the window stared back—impeccably dressed, perfectly groomed.

A man who had everything.

Except her.

And for the first time, that felt like the only thing that mattered.

He didn't hear the door open. Only the soft click of heels on polished floors alerted him. He didn't need to look.

"Mother," he said.

Helen Waterford stepped into the room like she owned it, her presence as sharp as her signature silk coat. "I knocked. You didn't answer."

"I wasn't taking visitors."

"That never stopped me."

She crossed the room to the bar, poured herself a generous glass of wine, and settled into the leather chair across from his desk—the one she always took, like it was made for her brand of elegant judgment.

She studied him. He looked up finally, brow raised.

"You look like hell," she said, voice light but eyes shrewd.

Hudson took a slow sip, then set his glass down. "You came all the way uptown to insult me?"

"No. That was just a bonus."

He exhaled through his nose. "Then what?"

Helen didn't answer right away. She just watched him, her expression unreadable. "How long are you going to keep pretending this is what you wanted?"

Hudson turned back to the window. "I wanted the company. I got it."

"And the girl who came with it? She was just part of the acquisition package?"

He didn't respond.

"I've watched you close billion-dollar deals," she said. "But you've never looked more uncertain than you do now. Hudson, what are you doing?"

He looked down, hands braced on the edge of the desk. "I'm keeping my promise. To Henry. To myself."

"And in the process," she said softly, "you're pushing away the one thing that wasn't a transaction."

Hudson's throat worked. "You think I don't know that?"

Helen rose slowly, wineglass in hand. She circled the desk until she stood beside him, gaze angled toward the skyline.

"She loves you," she said quietly.

Hudson didn't answer.

"She's been in love with you for years. I knew the moment she walked into a boardroom and couldn't look at you for more than five seconds without blushing. But you—" Helen's eyes narrowed slightly. "You've spent six months pretending she's just furniture. Do you really not care, or are you just afraid of what happens if you do?"

He met her eyes then. And for the first time in years, Helen saw her son uncertain. Vulnerable.

"I'm not afraid," he said finally.

"Then prove it," she challenged. "Before she realises, she doesn't need you anymore."

She placed a hand on his shoulder—a rare gesture—and left the room in silence, the scent of her perfume lingering like a warning.

Hudson stayed where he was, staring at the place where she'd stood.

In the window, his reflection watched him with empty eyes.

And all he could think was: You're losing her. And you're too damn proud to stop it.

A few days later, Henry's condition worsened suddenly.

The call came just after lunch. Renee abandoned her spreadsheets, caught a car service, and arrived at the estate before the rain started.

She found him sitting in the sunroom, pale and drawn, wrapped in his favourite blanket. He looked small, as if the illness had begun stealing him inch by inch.

Hudson was already there.

He stood when she entered, moving aside so she could kneel beside her grandfather.

"Hey, Granddad," she whispered, taking his hand.

He smiled faintly. "Always beautiful. Always in control."

"Don't you start," she warned gently, brushing a curl from her face.

Henry coughed lightly, and his hand tightened on hers. "You two—you're doing okay?"

Renee hesitated.

Hudson answered first. "We're managing."

It wasn't a lie. But it wasn't truth either.

Henry's gaze flickered between them. "Heard what matters most is respect in a marriage. Trust. If love comes later... well, that's just a blessing."

Renee lowered her eyes.

Hudson shifted behind her. She could feel the tension coming off him in waves.

Henry closed his eyes briefly. "Just... take care of each other."

After a while, he drifted off. His breath was shallow but steady.

Renee stood, brushing her hands down her coat, heart aching. "He's fading fast."

Hudson nodded once. "I know."

Something cracked in her voice. "He's the only real parent I've had since I was thirteen. And now he's dying... and I feel like I've lost everything already."

Hudson's expression changed—just slightly. He took a step closer.

"You haven't lost everything," he said quietly.

She looked up at him, eyes burning. "Haven't I?"

Their gazes locked. His jaw flexed, but no words came. Whatever he felt—regret, sympathy, something more—it stayed buried.

Renee blinked, broke the moment, and turned away.

"I'll be working remotely for the rest of the week. I want to be here."

Hudson nodded but didn't move. He stayed behind as she stepped back into the house.

Chapter Four

The rain came softly that morning, as if the city itself knew to grieve.

Renee sat beside her grandfather's bed, one hand wrapped around his frail fingers, the other holding a cup of untouched tea. The sunroom was dim, overcast light filtering through gauzy curtains, the same way it had for weeks. But today, the stillness was different. Too quiet. Too final.

Henry's breaths had grown shallower by the hour. Each one a whisper. A fading thread.

"I'm here," she said softly, voice trembling. "You're not alone."

He didn't respond, but his fingers twitched in hers.

She laid her head gently against the back of his hand, tears sliding soundlessly down her cheek.

"I love you," she whispered.

A long, ragged breath. Then… stillness.

Renee didn't move at first. She stayed with him, forehead resting against his knuckles, letting the silence settle. Letting her heart break.

It was ten minutes before she reached for her phone. And when she did, she didn't call Hudson.

She called Vivian.

The line barely rang once before her best friend picked up. "Renee?"

Her voice cracked. "He's gone."

"Oh, honey." Vivian's voice filled the silence like a balm. "I'm coming."

By the time Hudson arrived—two hours later, pressed and composed in a tailored black suit—the estate was already filled with quiet visitors, murmuring condolences. A family doctor had come and gone. Arrangements were being made. Renee was in the sunroom still, curled on the settee with a blanket around her shoulders, eyes red, hands folded tightly in her lap. Vivian sat beside her; one arm draped protectively around her back.

Hudson stopped in the doorway, gaze settling on the two women. On the way Renee leaned into Vivian's shoulder. On the fact that she hadn't called him.

He hadn't known Henry was gone until his assistant forwarded a message from the house staff. Not from his wife.

That hit harder than he expected.

He cleared his throat softly.

Renee looked up, expression unreadable. "You came."

"Of course I did," he said. "I'm... sorry, Renee. I know how much he meant to you."

She nodded, but her eyes flicked away. "He didn't suffer."

Vivian stood, brushing off her jeans. "I'll give you both a minute."

She touched Renee's arm gently, then shot Hudson a brief, measuring look as she passed. One that said I'm watching you.

He waited until she was gone before speaking. "Everything is being handled. I've contacted the funeral director, and the board is drafting a formal statement. I've asked our legal team to begin executing the trust directives."

She stared at him. "You didn't have to do all of that."

"Yes, I did." He paused. "He would have wanted it done right."

Renee looked down. "It's not about doing it right, Hudson. It's about doing it together."

He had no answer for that.

The funeral was held three days later at St. Bartholomew's; the same cathedral Henry had once taken Renee to as a child for Christmas Mass. It was filled with mourners—colleagues, dignitaries, old friends from the firm, even a few rivals who came to pay respect to the legend who'd outlasted them all.

Hudson stood at the front, straight-backed, dignified. The face of Fitzgerald Enterprises.

Helen stood beside him, chin lifted proudly, eyes dry and appraising.

"Look at him," she whispered, barely audible. "Not a step out of place. Just like his father."

But Renee didn't see pride when she looked at Hudson.

She saw distance.

He was flawless, yes. In control. But every word of his eulogy had felt like a press release. Polished. Safe. Painfully impersonal.

She stood between Vivian and the casket; fingers curled tightly around a handkerchief that still carried the faintest trace of Henry's cologne.

Vivian squeezed her hand. "You don't have to hold it in."

Renee blinked. "I can't fall apart. Not here."

"Why not?"

Her eyes flicked to Hudson. "Because he isn't."

Vivian's voice sharpened. "Don't use him as your measuring stick."

A pause.

"You've already lost your grandfather. Don't lose yourself too."

Renee looked at the casket.

And knew—Vivian was right.

Fitzgerald Hall had never felt so crowded—or so cold.

Renee moved through the maze of black suits and whispered condolences like a ghost. Faces blurred. Names slipped past. Grief muffled everything.

The grand foyer was filled with mourners holding champagne flutes, soft jazz playing in the background—per Henry's request. He'd hated sombre affairs. Said if people had to cry, they should at least do it with a glass of good scotch in their hand.

Renee had tried to stay downstairs, to be gracious, to smile and nod and accept people's kind, empty words. But after an hour, her throat ached from saying "Thank you for coming." Her face hurt from pretending.

She needed air. Or quiet. Or just… less.

She slipped away from the main hall, heels echoing against the marble floor as she walked towards the stairs to the east wing. Her old bedroom was up there, untouched since college—one of the few places that still felt like hers.

But as she passed the sunroom, she stopped.

Voices.

Low. Familiar.

She took a slow step closer, drawn by instinct, by the gravity of hearing his voice.

Hudson.

She paused just outside the half-closed French doors.

"…It's not that I don't care about her," he was saying. "I just—damn it, Marcus. I wish I hadn't married her."

Renee froze, one hand catching the edge of the doorframe to steady herself. The cool glass pressed against her fingertips, grounding her even as the floor beneath her seemed to tilt.

Her heart stopped.

Inside, Hudson stood near the window, one hand gripping a tumbler of bourbon, the other clenched at his side. His tie was loose, jacket gone. For once, he didn't look perfect. He looked… tired.

Marcus Blackwell sat on the arm of the nearby chair, nursing his own drink. "That's a hell of a thing to say, man."

Hudson ran a hand through his hair. "I know. But this marriage—it was never supposed to be this. It was a transaction. A merger. I gave my word to Henry. She agreed. But now she's… grieving. Hurting. And I don't know how to be what she needs."

"She's your wife."

"She's a stranger I happen to live with."

Renee's breath caught in her throat.

Marcus was quiet for a beat. "So, you regret it?"

Hudson turned back toward the window. "I regret that she looks at me like I broke her. Like I'm supposed to be something I never promised to be. I regret that I'm tied to someone who deserves more than I have to give."

Silence.

Renee stepped back, careful not to let the floor creak.

Her fingers were numb, her chest hollow.

She should've turned away. Gone back down. But her feet wouldn't move.

Marcus's voice came again, softer this time. "You ever think maybe she doesn't want anything from you? Maybe she's just grieving her grandfather, not trying to make you, her saviour?"

"I don't know," Hudson said. "All I know is, I'm not who she needs. I'm not who she wants. And I never should've let Henry talk me into this."

Something broke inside her then.

She stepped away, turning quickly, her breath unsteady. She didn't cry—not yet. Not until she reached the staircase. Not until the hush of the sunroom gave way to the swell of voices below.

Only then did it strike her.

He hadn't said her name. Not once.

The steady murmur of conversation drifted through Fitzgerald Hall, softened by candlelight and the low hum of mourning. Servers glided past with trays of wine and canapés no one touched. Grief hung in the air, dressed in black silk, and tailored suits, perfumed with sympathy and quiet ambition.

Renee stood at the edge of it all, near the grand staircase, her fingers wrapped loosely around a glass of champagne she hadn't tasted. Her gaze was vacant, her spine stiff, as though holding herself upright was the only thing keeping her from splintering.

She couldn't feel her feet. Or her hands. Just the hollow pressure in her chest—a deep, aching absence where her grandfather's voice used to be.

Without a word, she turned and slipped away down the rear corridor, her heels whispering against the marble floor, vanishing into the quiet like smoke.

By the time she reached Vivian's brownstone, the night air had turned cold.

Vivian answered the door in a sweatshirt and leggings, her dark curls pulled into a high, messy bun. "Ren?"

"I needed to get out," Renee said quietly, stepping inside.

Vivian didn't ask questions. She just pulled her in and shut the door behind them.

They sat on the couch, the city a faint glow through the window. Renee stared down at her hands for a long moment before speaking.

"I was looking for Hudson to let him know I was going upstairs…," she said. "I needed a minute."

Vivian waited.

"He was in the sunroom," Renee continued, voice flat. "With Marcus. I didn't mean to listen, I swear."

"What did he say?" Vivian asked gently.

Renee looked up, her eyes hollow. "He said, 'I wish I hadn't married her.' Just like that. Like I was a mistake he couldn't take back."

Vivian's expression darkened. "That son of a—"

"It's okay," Renee interrupted softly. "It's not like I didn't already know."

"No," Vivian said sharply, her voice cutting through the quiet like glass. "No, it's not okay. You've been trying, Ren. You've given him space, respect, grace—and he treats you like a merger document that got misfiled in a cabinet somewhere?"

Renee's lips parted, but the words didn't come easily. "I don't know what to do."

"Divorce him," Vivian snapped. "Take your heart back before he forgets you ever had one."

Renee shook her head, voice low. "I don't need a divorce."

Vivian narrowed her eyes. "What does that mean?"

"It means…" Renee exhaled slowly, her smile bitter. "It was never consummated. I can file for an annulment."

Vivian froze. "Wait—what?"

Renee gave a soft, hollow laugh. "He's never touched me, Viv."

Vivian stared at her, the silence stretching with disbelief. "You mean like… not even—"

"Not even once," Renee said, voice flat now. "Six months of marriage. Not a kiss. Not a hand on my back. Not a single moment where I wondered if maybe he felt something more."

Vivian's face twisted in outrage. "You've been living in that palace with him like two strangers on opposite ends of a business trip?"

Renee nodded. "It was always about the company. About my grandfather. I was just… part of the deal."

Vivian sat back, stunned, her jaw clenched. "Unbelievable."

Renee looked down at her hands. "I'll call my lawyer in the morning. The paperwork's easy. All I have to do now is leave."

Vivian reached across the couch, her grip warm and fierce. "When?"

Renee met her eyes, calm and certain for the first time in weeks. "Tonight."

Vivian helped her pack in silence. They moved like ghosts through the immaculate apartment—packing boxes in the walk-in closet, slipping dresses into garment bags, and folding up her grandmother's quilt.

Renee moved through the space without looking at anything too long.

"He's still at the wake," Vivian murmured.

"Good."

The last thing Renee placed into her duffel was a small photo of her and Henry, taken years ago on the porch of his estate. He was smiling. She was laughing.

She paused, fingers brushing the frame, then zipped the bag shut.

No goodbye note. No dramatic confrontation.

Just absence.

The penthouse doors opened with its usual soft chime.

Hudson stepped inside, loosening his tie, the echo of hushed condolences still clinging to him like the scent of lilies and cold stone. The apartment greeted him with dim lighting and an unnatural silence—too still, too clean.

He set his keys in the dish by the door and paused.

The thought he'd been shoving down since Henry's death pushed to the surface again, sharper now.

She'd called Vivian.

Not him.

She'd needed someone. And he hadn't even occurred to her.

His jaw tightened as he stepped into the living room. No coat tossed over the arm of the sofa. No heels kicked off near the door. He moved toward the kitchen—spotless. Undisturbed.

Something was wrong.

His pace quickened down the hallway. Her suite door stood open, the room beyond too dark, too still. He crossed the threshold, pulse ticking up.

Drawers: empty.

Shelves: bare.

Her signature floral perfume still lingered—but faint, already vanishing.

He turned toward the closet. Half the hangers were bare. No silk scarves. No shoes lined up like soldiers. Just space. Hollow, waiting space.

Then he saw it.

The nightstand.

Henry's framed photo—gone. Not knocked over. Removed. Deliberate. Like a piece lifted from a puzzle, leaving nothing but the absence.

A cold chill coiled around his spine.

She was gone.

Hudson stood motionless in the doorway, the silence of the penthouse now deafening. The kind of silence that screamed.

And for the first time since the day they said, "I do," the truth landed like a gut punch.

He hadn't just lost her.

He thought of her laughing once—really laughing—barefoot in the kitchen with a spoonful of frosting, icing cupcakes for the office staff because "the board could use some sugar."

He'd never really had her at all.

Chapter Five

The door to Renee's office burst open with a sharp, echoing crack. Hudson strode in, his presence a storm barely contained. His tie hung askew, collar unbuttoned, the picture of a man unravelling. Anger burned behind his eyes, but beneath it, something more fragile simmered—disbelief.

Renee looked up, her pen still hovering over a legal pad. She didn't flinch, though tension coiled in her shoulders like a spring drawn tight. She said nothing.

Hudson didn't bother with preamble. "You filed for an annulment?"

He tossed the envelope onto her desk. It landed with a dull, accusing thud. "You couldn't talk to me first? Just go behind my back and make this kind of decision?"

His pacing began—erratic, restless. "I came home from the funeral expecting to find you there. You were gone. No note. No call. Just… gone."

Renee folded her hands—calm on the outside, cold as frost beneath. "There wasn't much left to say."

He stopped, staring at her like he couldn't believe she was serious. "You don't just walk away from something like this. From me. Not without a conversation."

At that, Renee stood—slowly, deliberately—and stepped around the desk. She closed the distance between them until they stood inches apart. Her voice was soft, but it sliced clean through the room.

"You already had the conversation, Hudson. Just not with me."

Hudson froze. His breath caught as the realisation flickered behind his eyes.

"You said," she continued, gaze unwavering, "that you wished you hadn't married me. That I was a stranger you happened to live with. That I was nothing more than a transaction. A merger."

She took one more step, each word landing like a blow. "You said I meant nothing."

Colour drained from his face. "You—you heard that?"

Renee nodded once. "Every word."

Regret hit him visibly, like gravity pulling him into himself. "Renee, I didn't mean it. I was tired—angry—Marcus was pushing, and I just… I wasn't thinking straight."

"Don't." Her hand came up, silencing him. "Don't excuse it. People don't say things like that unless some part of them believes it."

"I didn't know you were there. I never wanted you to hear that." His voice cracked, raw now. "I was venting. I was a damn fool. I'm sorry—I didn't mean to hurt you."

"But you did." Her voice wavered for half a second before hardening again. "And the worst part is—you didn't even realise it."

She took a breath, steadying herself. "I came into this marriage with hope, Hudson. Hope that maybe, one day, you'd see me. And every time you passed me in that penthouse like I was invisible, I told myself to be patient. That it would get better."

Her voice dipped lower, grief threaded through every syllable. "But it never did. I wasn't your wife—I was a condition. A clause in a contract. A means to your end."

His eyes filled, but he didn't speak.

"You think this is unfair?" she continued. "What's unfair is how long I waited for you to care. How I smiled through board meetings and photo ops, pretending our marriage was real, while you couldn't even pretend to look at me like I mattered."

"I know I failed you," he whispered, voice fraying. "But we can fix this—please, don't walk away like this."

Renee shook her head, her expression resolute. "There was never a 'we,' Hudson. That's the problem."

He stepped back, like her words had knocked the air from his lungs. "So that's it? You're really going through with it?"

"Yes," she said, voice clear. "I am."

"I'll contest it."

She gave him a long, cool look—then turned, collected her things, and walked past him.

"Try," she said, without looking back.

And then she was gone, leaving Hudson alone in the silence she left behind.

Two days after the funeral, they sat across from each other again—not as spouses, but as adversaries.

The conference room of Int. Fitzgerald & Associates - Law Office was draped in sombre elegance. Heavy mahogany furniture. Dark velvet drapes. The scent of old books and stronger grief clung to the air.

Renee sat upright at the long conference table, her hands clasped in her lap, face composed but pale. She hadn't slept. Across from her, Hudson leaned back in his chair, jaw clenched, arms folded tightly over his chest.

Mr. Alcott, Henry Fitzgerald's long-time attorney, cleared his throat. "Thank you both for coming. Your grandfather prepared this will personally with me three months ago. There have been no recent amendments."

He placed a small recorder on the table and pressed play. Henry's voice, low and gravelly, filled the room.

"If you're hearing this, it means I've finally gone and left Renee to clean up after me. Darling girl… everything I ever built was for you. I leave Fitzgerald Enterprises in your capable hands—full ownership, voting shares, and the title of Chairwoman. Fitzgerald Hall, the trusts, all assets—are yours. You are the future of this family."

Renee blinked. Her breath hitched—quiet, but sharp. Across the table, Hudson sat forward.

"To Hudson Waterford," Henry's voice continued, "I thank you for stepping in when I needed you to. You have a sharp mind and strong ambition. I know you'll find your own way."

Click. Silence dropped heavy in the room.

Renee stared at the table, as though she could still hear her grandfather's voice lingering in the grain of the wood.

Hudson's chair scraped violently as he stood. "You knew."

Renee looked up slowly. "What?"

"You knew this was coming," he snapped. "That he was leaving everything to you."

"I didn't," she said, barely above a whisper.

"You expect me to believe that?" He leaned on the table, his hands braced wide, staring her down. "You filed for an annulment the day after his funeral. And now—now we find out you're the sole beneficiary of everything?"

Her spine straightened. "I didn't know, Hudson. I would never—"

"Don't," he cut in. "Don't pretend you didn't see this as an opportunity. Henry's gone. You don't need me anymore. Isn't that the truth?"

Renee stood, quietly, with purpose. "You think I did this for control?"

He stepped back, his voice bitter. "Didn't you?"

She stared at him; wounded disbelief etched across her face. "You think this is about power?"

"I think the second you realised you could run this company without me; you made your move."

Renee's expression hardened. "No. I made my move the second I realised you'd never stand beside me—only in front of me. You don't get to accuse me of playing games when you were the one who treated our marriage like a strategy meeting."

Hudson shook his head, almost laughing, but there was no humour in it. "Unbelievable."

Mr. Alcott quietly cleared his throat. "Perhaps we should reconvene another time."

"No," Renee said, gaze locked with Hudson's. "We're done here."

She turned to leave, her steps measured and unshaken—every inch the woman who had borne grief with grace but refused to shoulder betrayal.

At the doorway, she paused, glancing back over her shoulder at Hudson. Her voice was calm but laced with quiet fire.

"It's a good thing we won't be married much longer," she said, her gaze steady. "Because if you truly believe I'm as cold-hearted as you are… then you never knew me at all."

She didn't wait for a response. She simply turned and walked away, spine straight, head high.

And this time, Hudson let her go.

But he looked at the empty chair she left behind like it was something that used to matter—before he let it all slip through his hands.

A cold dawn bled into the skyline, grey and unwelcoming. The silence in Hudson's office was louder than any boardroom argument. The skyline behind him was washed in dull grey light, the kind that matched the unrest in his chest. His suit jacket was off, his sleeves rolled up, but his usual polished confidence was nowhere in sight.

A knock at the door.

Before he could answer, the door opened, and Renee stepped in.

She was dressed in sleek navy slacks and a cream blouse, her hair pulled back, minimal makeup—but her poise was unshakable. There was no hesitation in her steps, no bitterness in her expression.

Just quiet resolve.

She placed a folder on his desk and slid it toward him.

Hudson stared at it. "What's this?"

"A signed executive order," she said evenly. "Effective immediately, you are reinstated as CEO. For the foreseeable future."

He looked up at her, stunned. "What?"

"You heard me."

He opened the folder, reading the official letterhead, the legal language, her signature at the bottom. It was real. And binding.

"I thought you wanted me out," he said cautiously.

She met his gaze. "I never wanted you out. Not from the company."

His brow furrowed.

"I didn't know about my grandfather's will," she said, clearly and without defensiveness. "I was just as shocked as you were. If I had known, I would've told you. He didn't confide in me."

Hudson remained silent, watching her like he wasn't sure if he believed her—but hoping he could.

"You've always been the best person to run this company," she continued. "My grandfather knew that. I know that. You built this with him. You earned it."

He started to speak, but she held up a hand—firm but calm.

"I'll stay on as CFO. That's where I belong."

He studied her, his voice low. "Then why file for the annulment?"

Her expression softened, but she didn't flinch. "Because we don't work, Hudson. And this—" she gestured around the office "—isn't about us. It never should've been."

A long pause. His throat worked like he wanted to say something but couldn't find the words.

"I'm not here to punish you," she said gently. "And I'm not here to prove a point. I'm here because the company matters to me. The people in it matter. And I believe in what we built, even if we couldn't last."

Hudson looked down at the signed papers again, then back at her. "You're really walking away from all of it?"

"Not all of it," she said with a hint of a smile. "Just the part that was never real."

She turned to leave.

At the doorway, she paused without turning back. "This isn't revenge, Hudson. It's peace. For both of us."

And with that, she walked out, head held high, leaving him sitting in the office he now owned again—but suddenly unsure of what any of it was worth.

Hudson didn't move for a long moment after the door clicked shut.

The office felt bigger now. Emptier.

His gaze dropped to the folder again, to the signature at the bottom of the executive order. Renee Waterford.

He ran his thumb over the curve of her signature, the familiar slant of her handwriting suddenly achingly personal.

This wasn't just ink on a page. It was her—measured, resolute, gone.

He leaned back slowly in his chair, staring at the door she'd just walked through. Not with anger. Not even with regret.

With longing.

City lights spilled through the towering windows of the penthouse, scattering fractured reflections across the dark hardwood floor. Hudson sat hunched on the edge of the couch, a half-empty tumbler of scotch dangling from his fingers, his sleeves rolled up and tie abandoned hours ago.

Marcus entered from the kitchen, holding a beer, eyebrows raised. "You look like hell."

Hudson didn't glance up. "Thanks."

Marcus dropped into the armchair across from him. "So? What happened? You look like someone kicked your soul in."

A pause.

Hudson stared at the scotch, then finally said, "She heard me."

Marcus blinked. "Who? Renee?"

Hudson gave a bitter laugh. "At the wake. When I was talking to you."

Marcus sat forward slowly, the weight of understanding settling in. "She heard all of it?"

Hudson nodded once. "Every word. About how I regretted marrying her. How it was just a business move. That she was a stranger."

Marcus winced. "Damn."

"She left that night," Hudson added. "Filed for an annulment the next morning. Served me at the office."

Marcus exhaled. "Well, I'd say she had a reason."

There was silence between them, stretching like a wound.

Hudson finally spoke again. "Then came the will."

Marcus looked over, confused. "What about it?"

"She inherited everything. The shares, the assets, the controlling interest. All of it." He took a sip of his drink, jaw tight. "Fitzgerald Enterprises is hers."

Marcus let out a low whistle. "Damn. So, she really didn't need you anymore."

Hudson shook his head slowly. "That's what I thought. That she was cutting me out—for good."

Marcus frowned. "And?"

Hudson set the glass down on the table. "She came to my office today. With a signed executive order. Gave me back the CEO position. Said I was the best person to run the company."

Marcus blinked. "She what?"

"She said she didn't know about the will," Hudson said. "Told me straight to my face. And I believed her." He rubbed a hand over his face, suddenly weary. "She's staying on as CFO. Said the annulment had nothing to do with business."

Marcus leaned back, his gaze sharp now. "So, she didn't leave to get rid of you… from the company."

"No."

Another pause.

Marcus tilted his head slightly. "Then let me ask you something. And don't give me that CEO poker face."

Hudson looked at him.

Marcus asked, quiet but serious, "Are you sure you're not in love with her?"

Hudson didn't answer. He didn't need to.

Silence spoke the truth he wasn't ready to say.

Marcus nodded slowly, took a swig of his beer, then leaned back again. "Yeah. That's what I thought."

The soft amber glow of a floor lamp bathed the room in warmth. A half-empty pizza box sat open on the coffee table, flanked by two wine glasses, within easy reach. Renee was curled up on the couch in leggings and an oversized sweater, barefoot, a fleece blanket draped over her legs like armour she didn't know she needed.

Vivian sat cross-legged across from her, wine glass in hand, cradling it like a truth serum.

"So…" Vivian tilted her head, one brow arched. "You going to tell me what really happened? Because I know a PR pivot when I see one—and you, my friend, have been dodging headlines and feelings like a pro."

Renee let out a slow breath, fingers idly tracing the rim of her glass.

"He showed up at my office," she said quietly. "Right after he got the annulment papers. I told him I heard him that night. He said he was sorry. I said I wasn't interested."

Vivian's jaw tensed. "What an idiot."

Renee gave a tired shrug. "It's not like I didn't already know. But hearing him say it… it still cut."

Vivian leaned forward, eyes softening. "You loved him."

"I did." Renee nodded, voice barely above a whisper. "And I still don't know what that says about me."

"It says you're human. And brave. And loyal—even when someone doesn't deserve it."

Renee offered a faint smile, but it didn't quite reach her eyes.

"Then the will was read," she went on. "Turns out everything—Fitzgerald Enterprises, the estate, the shares—was left to me. Not a single mention of him. Just a thank-you in the letter."

Vivian's mouth fell open. "Wait. What?"

"Yeah," Renee said dryly. "He thought I knew. Thought I was setting him up. Accused me of using the annulment to push him out."

Vivian blinked. "Please tell me you slapped him. Or at least threw something expensive and breakable."

"I wanted to. God, I wanted to. But instead, I gave him the CEO title back."

Vivian stared at her like she'd grown a second head. "You… gave it back?"

Renee nodded. "He's the right person to run the company. He cares about it. And I realised… I need to stop choosing people who never really choose me back."

Vivian reached over and squeezed her hand, her voice gentling. "You didn't deserve any of that."

"No," Renee said softly, the truth finally sitting comfortably on her tongue. "I didn't."

A beat of silence passed. Not heavy this time—just full.

Then Vivian broke it with a smirk. "Okay, but I still wish you'd ruined one of his thousand-dollar suits. Like, full red wine massacre."

That pulled a breath of laughter from Renee—quick and unexpected. She clapped a hand over her mouth, surprised.

Vivian's eyes lit up. "There she is."

Renee blinked. "What?"

"That laugh." Vivian smiled. "God, it's good to hear you laugh again."

Renee looked down, her smile lingering this time. "Yeah… it felt kind of good."

Vivian raised her glass. "I've missed you. Not the CFO. Not the PR-perfect wife. You. The girl who used to eat strawberry Pop-Tarts at midnight and dance in her pyjamas."

"I still do that," Renee said with a smirk.

Vivian gasped theatrically. "And you didn't invite me?"

Renee laughed again—richer this time, like something inside her had finally cracked open in a good way. "You're invited. Pyjamas mandatory."

Vivian lifted her glass. "To Pop-Tarts, pyjama dancing, and never letting a man tell you who you are."

They clinked glasses.

"You're coming to my boutique opening on Saturday night," Vivian added.

Renee smiled. "I wouldn't miss it for the world."

And for the first time in weeks, Renee didn't feel like she was pretending to be okay. For the first time… she believed she might be.

Chapter Six

The glass-walled mediation room was sleek and sterile—exactly the kind of neutral territory suited for unravelling a life built on paper.

Renee sat on one side of the long table, composed, and poised. Untouchable.

Her lawyer was beside her, calm and silent.

Across from them, Hudson sat with his attorney, tension coiled tight in his jaw, fingers steepled as if he could pray the outcome into something else. His eyes flicked to her, then quickly away.

Renee folded her hands in her lap to keep them from trembling.

Not from fear. She wasn't afraid anymore.

She'd simply spent too many nights trying to hold on to a marriage that had never truly begun.

And now, for the first time in six months, she looked at Hudson and saw a man not in control.

He wasn't angry.

He was rattled.

The mediator cleared her throat. "Mr. Waterford, you've contested the annulment. Can you state your reasons?"

Hudson's voice was gruff. "I believe our marriage can be salvaged."

Renee's lawyer responded smoothly, "My client maintains the marriage is not salvageable."

Hudson turned toward her, his tone more urgent now. "Why? We can try."

Because I begged with my heart in silence—and you never noticed.

Because I loved you. And you treated me like a transaction.

Renee looked him dead in the eye. Her voice was quiet but edged in steel.

"Because I deserve more than a man who married me for a title and never once tried to be my husband."

His jaw tightened. "You agreed to this. Don't act like you were tricked."

"I was willing to make it work. Really work, Hudson." Her words were calm, measured. "You never even looked at me long enough to see it."

Then she turned to the mediator, her voice steady.

"If you need proof that our marriage was never consummated, I'm willing to undergo a medical examination. I have nothing to hide."

Hudson's breath caught.

The words hit like a slap.

She was still—

God.

She was untouched.

Six months of silence. Of absence. Of all the things he should've said and never did.

She'd tried.

He hadn't.

He had treated her like a legal formality. A convenience. A bridge to power.

And now that truth stood naked in the centre of the room, unforgiving and cold.

His voice, when it came, was barely more than a whisper. "You don't have to do that."

"I'm not doing it for you," she said, without blinking.

The mediator cleared her throat again. "We'll allow a brief recess while both parties consider mediation alternatives."

Hudson's attorney leaned in, voice low but clear. "We'll advise our client to reconsider his contest."

Renee stood slowly, gathering her coat with practiced grace. Her hands didn't shake anymore.

She looked at Hudson one last time—not with bitterness, but with the calm of someone who had already walked through the fire and come out whole on the other side.

"Goodbye, Hudson."

This time, she didn't wait to see if he followed.

Later that night, across town, Marcus was halfway through a steak and an overpriced bottle of red when the knock came. He padded barefoot across the hardwood floor, wineglass still in hand, and opened the door.

Hudson stood there like grief dressed in a suit—creased shirt, tie loosened, skin pale beneath the city lights. His jaw was clenched, but his eyes were the real giveaway. They looked empty. No fire. Just ruin.

Marcus raised a brow. "Did someone die, or are you just dressed like heartbreak tonight?"

Hudson didn't answer. Just said, voice low and raw, "Can I come in?"

Marcus stepped back without another word. When a man like Hudson Waterford came to your door looking like he'd been gutted, you didn't joke. Not really.

Hudson walked in, mechanical, like his body had shown up ahead of his mind. He didn't sit. Didn't speak. Just started pacing—back and forth across the loft's open expanse, his movements tight, restrained, like he was trying not to break something. Or someone.

He hadn't stopped moving since Renee walked out of that hearing.

No—since she'd looked him in the eye and offered to prove their marriage had never been real. Never touched.

God, he could still hear her voice. Calm. Cold.

"I have nothing to hide."

She was still a virgin.

His twenty-five-year-old wife. Six months married. Untouched.

And now?

Now someone else would have the right.

Marcus watched him with growing concern, wineglass forgotten on the counter. "You want a drink or a sedative?"

Hudson turned sharply. "She's still a virgin."

Marcus blinked. "Okay… that wasn't on my Bingo card tonight."

"She said it to the mediator," Hudson rasped. "Said she'd do a medical exam if that's what it took to finalise the annulment. She didn't even flinch, Marcus."

Marcus's brow furrowed. "Wait—Renee? Renee *Renee*?"

Hudson nodded, sinking onto the edge of the coffee table like his knees had finally given out.

"Six months," he murmured. "We've been married six months."

Marcus let out a low whistle and lowered himself onto the couch. "And you didn't touch her? Not once? Are you—" He cut himself off, shook his head. "You had to have known. The way she looked at you. That girl was gone over you."

Hudson's voice was barely audible. "It wasn't supposed to be that kind of marriage."

Marcus stared at him. "Jesus, man. You really thought you could lock her into a contract and keep it clinical?"

"I thought I was protecting us both," Hudson said. "Keeping it clean. Simple."

"Yeah, well, look around." Marcus gestured vaguely to the air between them. "How's that working out?"

Silence stretched, heavy and unforgiving.

"I bet she walked into that hearing like she was made of steel," Marcus said quietly. "Calm. Controlled. Like she'd finally figured out she didn't need you to validate her worth."

Hudson leaned forward, elbows on his knees, rubbing a hand down his face.

"She didn't even look back," he whispered.

"Would you?" Marcus asked. "After the way you treated her? She married you out of love, man. Love. And you treated her like a goddamn promotion."

Hudson's throat tightened. He couldn't argue. There was no defence left.

"She was willing to prove it," he said, more to himself than to Marcus. "Just to get away from me."

Marcus leaned forward, voice soft but firm.

"Then the real question is, Hudson—what are you willing to do to get her back?"

The city was alive outside his floor-to-ceiling windows, a blur of headlights and neon streaking through the dark. But up here, in the stillness of glass and stone, Hudson felt nothing but silence.

He poured a drink he wouldn't finish. Whiskey—single malt, thirty years aged. The kind of drink meant to be savoured.

It tasted like ash.

The hearing replayed on a loop in his mind. Renee's voice, calm and steady. Her spine straight as steel. That quiet fire in her eyes when she said:

"I deserve more than a man who married me for a title and never once tried to be my husband."

He hadn't flinched then. Hadn't said a word. Just sat there like the coward he now realised he was.

He hadn't just let her down.

He'd never shown up.

Hudson set the glass down untouched and moved through the room like it wasn't his. Like the penthouse, the title, the view—none of it mattered now. Not really.

The office across the hall still held her things. A scarf on the back of the chair. A planner with her handwriting, neat and purposeful. He hadn't had the heart to move it.

And suddenly, he didn't want to leave it untouched. He didn't want to pretend anymore that this was what he wanted.

Because for the first time in years, he was sure of something.

He wanted her.

Not the convenience. Not the legacy. Her.

Renee.

The woman who'd loved him in silence. Who married him without demands. Who walked away with her pride intact, even when he'd given her every reason to fall apart.

She deserved more.

And if he wanted even a chance to be that man—the man who saw her, chose her, fought for her—he would have to earn it.

Hudson sat at his desk and pulled out the annulment papers. Her signature stared back at him like a confession.

He reached for a pen—and for a long time, just stared at it.

Then slowly, deliberately, he signed his name again.

Not to finalise the ending.

To start over.

To give her everything she'd deserved the first time.

This time, on her terms.

This time, with nothing held back.

The envelope was heavier than it should've been.

No return address. Just her name, handwritten in a familiar scrawl that made her heart stutter before she could remind it not to.

Renee closed the apartment door behind her with a soft click, the world outside fading as she crossed to the kitchen, envelope clutched in her hand like it might disappear if she loosened her grip.

She didn't open it right away.

She set it down on the counter. Made tea. Let the kettle scream longer than necessary.

She'd waited six months to feel seen. She could wait another five minutes to open a piece of paper.

Still, when she finally slit the envelope open, her fingers trembled.

The annulment agreement stared back at her, clean and final.

His signature was there. Inked in bold strokes, just below hers.

Hudson James Waterford.

A name that had once sounded like a promise.

Now it was just ink.

She sat down, the stool cool beneath her legs and let the moment settle. She didn't cry. She didn't smile, either. She just breathed.

He'd let her go.

After all the silence, the coldness, the distance—he'd finally let her go.

She should've felt victorious.

She'd won.

Freedom.

Clarity.

Peace.

And yet… something ached. Not like regret, but something quieter. A hollow sort of knowing.

Because even now—even now—a part of her had wondered if he'd fight.

If the man who'd married her for a title would, in the end, finally choose her.

But maybe that was the cruellest part of hope. It didn't die with logic. It burned, even in the ruins.

Renee folded the papers, slid them back into the envelope, and stood. Her tea had gone cold. Her heart hadn't.

She walked to the window, letting the city fill her eyes.

She was free.

The boutique was lit like a dream—soft gold lighting casting a warm glow on polished marble floors and sleek glass displays. Laughter, the clink of champagne flutes, and flashes from camera phones filled the air as New York's elite mingled around Vivian's newest venture.

Hudson hadn't planned to come.

He'd told himself it didn't matter, that it was just a boutique opening, just another party. But somehow, he was there—shoulders stiff in a charcoal suit, jaw tight as he scanned the crowd.

And then he saw her.

Renee.

His breath stalled.

She stood near the back of the boutique, framed by racks of elegant gowns and sparkling accessories. The red silk gown she wore skimmed her figure like liquid fire—floor-length, backless, daring and devastating. Her honey-brown hair spilled in soft waves down her spine, the colour catching the light like warm whiskey.

She laughed at something her companion said.

Hudson's stomach dropped.

The man beside her was tall, athletic. Asian American, with close-cropped black hair and an easy, confident presence. He wore a navy suit that fit too well to be off the rack and stood close—closer than Hudson liked—with the air of someone who belonged beside her.

"Dr. Elias Chen," someone murmured nearby. "He's a trauma surgeon at Lenox Hill. Brilliant. Single."

Hudson didn't realise he was staring until Marcus appeared at his side, holding two glasses of champagne.

"Careful," Marcus said dryly, handing him one. "You're looking like a man two seconds from committing a felony."

Hudson didn't answer. His gaze was locked on Renee.

Her hand brushed Elias's arm lightly as she leaned in to say something. Her eyes sparkled. She looked... free.

Alive.

Different.

"You didn't think she'd wait around, did you?" Marcus said, watching him from the corner of his eye. "You signed the annulment. You let her go. Now someone else gets to see what you were too blind to appreciate."

Hudson's grip tightened around the glass. "Who is he?"

"Elias Chen. Trauma surgeon. Smart, kind, family money. The kind of guy your mother would call safe and strategic."

Hudson's jaw clenched.

"Ironic," Marcus added. "You finally see her. And she finally sees someone else."

Across the room, Renee glanced up—and for a heartbeat, her eyes met Hudson's.

She didn't look away.

She didn't smile, either.

Just one quiet, unreadable moment. Then she turned back to Elias and laughed at something he said.

Hudson felt the world tilt slightly off centre.

He had signed the papers.

But standing here now, watching Renee shimmer in silk and sunlight and something close to happiness, he realised with slow-burning certainty—

He'd made the biggest mistake of his life.

Chapter Seven

Hudson stood at the window, mug in hand, untouched coffee gone cold hours ago. He hadn't slept—not really. Not after watching Renee glide across Vivian's boutique in that backless red silk gown, her honey-brown hair cascading like something out of a dream he didn't deserve to have.

She had laughed. Not politely. Not carefully. But fully—head tilted back, lips parted.

At him.

Dr. Elias Chen. Trauma surgeon. Tall, smart, charming. The kind of man who probably knew how to touch a woman and not break her spirit in the process.

Hudson's jaw flexed. He needed to talk to her. See her. Just to make sure… she wasn't falling for a polished stranger with perfect teeth and an Ivy League pedigree.

Just to see.

Footsteps padded across the hardwood.

"You look like hell," Marcus said, shirtless, yawning, sipping from his own mug like he hadn't been watching Hudson pace since dawn. "Let me guess—still thinking about Dr. Tall, Dark, and Scalpel?"

Hudson didn't answer. He didn't need to.

"You're not seriously thinking of showing up at her apartment, are you?" Marcus asked, already bracing for the answer.

"I just want to talk to her," Hudson muttered, setting his mug down with a quiet clink. "Get a feel for this guy."

Marcus raised a brow. "Right. 'Talk to her.' That why your fists were clenched every time he so much as looked at her?"

Hudson looked away. "I just want to know what she's doing with him."

Marcus set his mug down beside Hudson's with deliberate slowness.

"She's living. That's what she's doing. Living the life, you handed back to her in a signed envelope."

Hudson flinched.

"I know," he said, voice low. "I know I screwed it up."

Marcus crossed his arms, voice softening just slightly. "Then don't make it worse. Don't show up with jealousy dripping off you like cologne. She doesn't owe you anything— not even an explanation."

"I'm not trying to win her back—"

"Bullshit," Marcus cut in, calmly. "You're not ready to say it out loud, but that's exactly what you want. And if you go charging in now, acting territorial, you'll prove her right for walking away."

Silence stretched between them.

Hudson leaned against the glass, staring at the skyline. The weight in his chest wasn't rage anymore. It was regret. And maybe… something worse.

"I just want to know if she's happy," he said quietly.

"Then let her be," Marcus replied. "If she is… you don't get to be the reason that changes."

Renee glanced up from her laptop at the knock.

Before she could answer, the door opened with the breezy entitlement of someone who never needed an invitation.

Vivian strolled in wearing oversized sunglasses and the satisfied smirk of a woman who came with both gossip and intention.

"Well, well," Vivian said, peeling the glasses off. "You look criminally composed for someone who spent last night being eye-devoured by Hudson Waterford and Dr. Dreamy McScalpel."

Renee blinked, bemused. "Hello to you too."

Vivian dropped onto the visitor's chair, crossing her legs like she was settling in for tea. "So, tell me. Was that chemistry with Elias Chen, or was I just drunk on champagne and fantasy?"

Renee gave a soft laugh, pushing a strand of hair behind her ear. "He's…nice."

Vivian blinked. "Nice? Renee, that man could read your EKG just by looking at you. Nice doesn't begin to cover it."

Before Renee could respond, her assistant tapped on the door and stepped inside, holding a sleek black box tied with a crimson ribbon.

"These just came for you," she said, setting them on the desk before slipping back out.

Vivian sat up. "Ooooh. Do not tell me those are from—"

Renee opened the box to reveal a lush bouquet of white peonies, her favourite. Nestled between the blooms was a handwritten card.

Vivian leaned in, unapologetically nosy. "Well? From Elias?"

Renee read the card silently, her expression unreadable. Then she smiled—gently, almost sadly—and set it aside.

Before Vivian could press further, the door opened again.

Hudson.

He stopped just inside the threshold, eyes cutting to the flowers, then to Vivian, then settling on Renee with a flicker of something he tried—and failed—to hide.

Vivian stood slowly, her presence suddenly feeling very intentional.

"Well, this got interesting," she murmured under her breath.

Hudson cleared his throat. "I hope I'm not interrupting."

"You are," Vivian said sweetly. "But don't let that stop you."

Renee, calm as ever, gestured toward the other chair. "Did you need something, Hudson?"

He walked further into the office, stiff, eyes returning to the flowers like they might explode.

"Just wanted to follow up on the board memo," he said, voice too casual.

Vivian stepped aside, moving toward the door. "I'll just…give you two a moment." She paused next to Hudson on her way out, leaned close, and said under her breath, "Don't trip over your ego. It's showing."

She slipped out, the door clicking shut behind her.

Silence.

Hudson stared at the flowers again. "Your favourite?"

"Yes," Renee said simply.

"Do you like them?"

Renee tilted her head. "Why do you care?"

"I don't," he said too quickly.

Renee leaned back in her chair, the edge of a smile playing at her lips.

"Then why are your fists clenched?"

Hudson looked down. Released his grip. Said nothing.

She let the silence stretch.

Hudson stood there, motionless, except for the slow rise and fall of his chest. When he finally looked up, her gaze was cool, steady. Detached in the way only a woman who had once loved too hard could be.

"You don't get to act like you care, Hudson."

Her voice was soft, but final.

And just like that, the balance shifted again.

He exhaled slowly, his composure cracking. A flicker of vulnerability crossed his face—one she'd never seen during their entire marriage.

"Renee," he said quietly, almost like her name hurt to say. "Can we try?"

She blinked.

Not because she hadn't heard him.

But because it was the last thing she expected.

"Try?"

He stepped closer, just enough to close some of the distance, but not enough to break her space. "I didn't get it before. I—I was so focused on what I thought I needed that I never saw what I already had."

She studied him, her face unreadable.

"You mean me," she said.

He nodded once. "I mean you."

Renee didn't respond right away. She let the words hang between them like mist—visible, fragile, waiting to either evaporate or settle.

Finally, she stood, smoothing her hands down the front of her dress.

"Now you want to try," she said, more to herself than to him. "After I walked away. After we signed the papers. After I gave up waiting for you to see me."

"I see you now."

She met his eyes. "Do you? Or do you just see someone else standing beside me?"

That landed. His mouth opened, but no defence came out.

She took a breath, not out of emotion—but strength.

"I'm not the woman who waited anymore, Hudson. So, if you want a chance, it won't be on your terms. It won't be out of guilt or jealousy. And it damn sure won't be easy."

His jaw tightened, but this time, it wasn't out of pride. It was out of hope.

"Then make me work for it," he said. "But don't shut the door."

Renee paused. Then picked up the card from the bouquet and held it between her fingers.

"I didn't shut the door, Hudson," she said, voice steady. "I just stopped holding it open."

And this time, she was the one who walked away, heels quiet against the polished floor, leaving him standing in the centre of her office—silent, stunned, and very much alone.

A soft knock tapped against the doorframe. Vivian poked her head in, her eyes sliding from Hudson's frozen stance to Renee's retreating back.

"Is he done, or do I need to bring security?" she asked, only half-kidding. "Because I am starving, and you promised me pasta and details."

Renee didn't look back. She simply set the card down on her desk, her fingers lingering for half a second.

Vivian crossed the room and plucked up the small square envelope with a dramatic flourish. "Oooh, mystery flowers. Did Elias send these, or are we dealing with a late-blooming ex-husband?"

Hudson's posture stiffened, but he didn't speak.

Renee slid her purse onto her shoulder, her tone breezy but unreadable. "Read it if you want. I haven't decided if it's sweet... or strategy."

Vivian raised an eyebrow, then flipped open the card.

Three simple words stared back at her, scrawled in Hudson's bold, unmistakable handwriting:

'I see you.'

Vivian's lips pressed into a line. "Well. Damn."

She glanced at Renee. "So… are we ordering wine with lunch, or many wines?"

Renee let out a small breath—half sigh, half laugh. "Many."

Behind them, Hudson was still standing there. But this time, he wasn't trying to stop her.

She didn't look back.

And for the first time, he really watched her go.

The little Italian place Vivian insisted on had red leather booths, soft jazz playing overhead, and the comforting scent of garlic, butter, and ambition.

Renee swirled the wine in her glass, her untouched plate of linguine cooling slowly in front of her. Vivian, on the other hand, was already halfway through her puttanesca and completely unrepentant about it.

"So," Vivian said, leaning forward with a twinkle in her eye, "we're just gonna skip right over the fact that Hudson showed up at your office looking like regret in designer shoes?"

Renee raised a brow. "I wasn't aware regret came in Tom Ford."

Vivian smirked. "Everything comes in Tom Ford if you're rich enough. Don't deflect."

"I wasn't deflecting," Renee said, setting her wine down. "I was… processing."

"Oh, honey. You were doing that thing where you get real calm, and real pretty, and emotionally nuke a man with a single sentence."

Renee tilted her head. "He asked if we could try again."

Vivian nearly dropped her fork. "Wait, what?"

Renee nodded. "Just… stood there in my office, after months of silence and red tape, and asked if we could try."

Vivian stared, wide-eyed. "And you said…?"

"I told him," Renee said evenly, "he doesn't get to ask questions like that anymore."

Vivian leaned back slowly, impressed. "You're getting scary good at this whole 'self-worth' thing. I'm proud. And a little afraid."

Renee gave a small, tired smile. "I'm tired of loving him quietly. I'm tired of feeling like I have to prove I'm worth the effort."

Vivian reached across the table, her voice gentler. "You never had to prove it. You were always worth the effort, Renee. He was just too blind to see it."

Renee exhaled, then tapped the edge of her wineglass. "He sent flowers. The card said, 'I see you.'"

Vivian made a face. "Ugh. That's either incredibly romantic or suspiciously vague. What does that even mean?"

"I don't know," Renee admitted. "But for once, I didn't read it twice. I didn't spin it in my head and twist it into something it wasn't."

Vivian raised her glass. "To letting him do the spinning for once."

They clinked glasses.

Renee smiled, real this time. "To stopping the wait."

Vivian's grin widened. "And maybe… to Dr. Dreamy and red silk gowns?"

Renee laughed—warm, open, almost weightless.

"Maybe."

The fundraiser gala was in full swing at the Met—the kind of event where diamonds sparkled under chandeliers and old money moved through the room like perfume.

Hudson stood near the bar, untouched drink in hand, watching Renee across the room before he realised he was doing it. Again.

She looked breathtaking—no, dangerous—in deep emerald satin, her hair pinned up in soft waves that framed her neck, that was adorned with a diamond necklace. Elias stood beside her in a sharp tuxedo, relaxed, confident, leaning in just slightly as she laughed.

She was laughing. Laughing.

Hudson hadn't heard her laugh like that in… God, had he ever?

Elias said something, and Renee touched his arm as she responded—easy, instinctive. Her eyes sparkled with something Hudson used to think was his to earn. Now it was just… gone. Given elsewhere.

He didn't realise he'd tensed until Marcus appeared beside him with a low whistle.

"She looks good," Marcus said, sipping his scotch. "Not that I'm surprised, she was always a stunner. Dr. Elias Chen seems to have noticed."

Hudson's jaw clenched. "It's not serious."

Marcus raised a brow. "That sounds like hope or denial?"

Hudson didn't answer. His gaze stayed fixed on the pair across the room. Elias leaned in, whispering something that made Renee tilt her head back and laugh again, full-bodied this time.

And it gutted him.

Because he'd never seen her that unguarded. Not with him. Not like this.

Hudson stood frozen near the edge of the room, watching Renee laugh—really laugh—with Elias Chen, her hand resting lightly on the man's arm, her eyes bright and unburdened.

"She looks happy," Marcus said beside him, voice low.

Hudson didn't answer.

"You should leave," Marcus added gently.

"I'm not going to cause a scene."

"I'm not worried about that," Marcus said. "I'm worried about you standing here looking like heartbreak in a tux while she finally remembers what it feels like to be seen."

Hudson's jaw flexed. He looked away. "I asked her if we could try."

Marcus turned to him fully. "And?"

"She said she never shut the door," Hudson said, voice rough. "She's just not holding it open anymore."

For a beat, neither of them spoke.

Then Marcus sighed. "Well... you'd better figure out if you're ready to knock. And this time, don't expect her to answer just because you're standing there."

Hudson didn't reply.

He turned his head slowly, gaze pulling back to the dance floor like a tide he couldn't resist.

Renee was there—glowing.

In Elias's arms.

Too close.

Her head tilted back in laughter, her hand resting confidently against the man's chest. She didn't look like a woman waiting for anything. She looked like a woman who had finally stopped hoping—and started choosing.

A flicker of something hot and bitter twisted in Hudson's gut.

It was time.

Time to stop standing on the sidelines of the life he wanted.

Time to make a move—before someone else made it permanent.

The fundraiser had started to wind down, the string quartets tempo softening, laughter fading into the hum of late-night conversation. Hudson stepped out onto the rooftop terrace, needing air, needing space.

And found Elias already there.

The trauma surgeon stood by the railing, tuxedo jacket unbuttoned, tie loosened, a half-empty glass of champagne dangling from his fingers. The city lights reflected in the dark sheen of his eyes. He didn't turn around.

"I figured you'd follow her out," Elias said, voice calm.

Hudson stilled. "She's not out here."

"I know," Elias replied, finally turning. "But you still looked like you needed to breathe."

Hudson stepped closer, slow, measured. "You two seem…close."

Elias gave a small smile. "We're getting there."

A silence stretched between them—cool, tense, male.

Hudson's jaw shifted. "What do you want from her?"

Elias tilted his head. "That supposed to be a warning?"

"It's a question."

Elias studied him for a long beat. When he answered, his tone was steady, unshaken. "Exactly what any man with eyes and a working heart would want from Renee—her time. Her laughter. Her trust. Her love."

Something coiled tight in Hudson's chest. "You don't even know her."

"I'm getting to," Elias said without missing a beat. "And I hear you didn't—and you were married to her."

Hudson's eyes narrowed. "That a dig?"

Elias shrugged. "Just an observation. One I've seen too many times in trauma rooms. People don't realise what they've lost until they're bleeding out from it."

He took a sip of champagne, then met Hudson's gaze again—calm, controlled.

"I'm not looking to compete with you, Hudson. That's not how I move. But I won't step aside just because you've suddenly remembered she's worth fighting for."

Hudson's voice dropped, tight. "You think I don't know I blew it?"

"I think knowing it and fixing it are two very different things." Elias stepped closer now, just enough. "She doesn't need someone who just regrets losing her. She needs someone who knows how to keep her—and is willing to do what it takes."

Hudson didn't reply. Couldn't.

Elias let the silence hang, then softened his voice. "And if that's not you… do her the kindness of stepping aside for someone who will."

With that, Elias gave a quiet, respectful nod and walked past him, back into the warmth of the party, leaving Hudson standing in the cool glow of the city skyline—surrounded by noise but overcome by silence, and his own unravelling certainty.

Chapter Eight

The black town car eased to a stop in front of Renee's building, its sleek frame catching the last glimmers of city light. Elias moved quickly around to open the door, ever the gentleman, hand extended.

Renee stepped out carefully, gown gathered at her side, heels clicking softly on the pavement.

"You didn't have to walk me up," she said with a small smile, warmth in her voice. "I'm perfectly capable of handling a lobby."

"I know," Elias said, his gaze steady. "But a night like this shouldn't end at a car door."

Renee's smile deepened. "Thank you."

They walked in step toward the front door. Inside, the concierge nodded them through, and the elevator carried them in quiet ease to her floor.

When the doors slid open, they stepped out into the still corridor. Renee paused at her door, pulling her keys from her clutch.

"Well," she said, turning toward him.

Elias looked at her for a moment—really looked—and then gently brushed a strand of hair from her cheek. "You shine, you know that?" he said softly. "And not just in designer gowns."

Renee's breath caught for half a second, but she kept her tone light. "You've got a way with words, Dr. Chen."

"Only when it matters."

He leaned in then, not abrupt or demanding, but sure. His lips touched hers—soft, respectful, a promise of interest, not a claim of possession.

Renee let it happen. Didn't pull away. But when it ended, she stepped back with a small, grateful breath.

"Goodnight, Elias."

He nodded, accepting her quiet boundaries with grace. "Goodnight, Renee."

He walked down the hallway and disappeared into the elevator. The moment the doors shut, a figure stepped out of the shadows near the stairwell.

Hudson.

Jaw tight, hands buried in the pockets of his coat, he exhaled for what felt like the first time in hours. Relief. Sharp and unspoken.

She hadn't invited Elias in.

He hadn't kissed her like he already belonged there.

But he had kissed her. And she'd let him.

Hudson stared at the door for a long moment. He didn't want to be the man who showed up unannounced, again. But he couldn't leave. Not without trying.

Not this time.

He walked up and knocked—twice, firm but not loud.

From inside, muffled footsteps.

The door opened.

Renee stood there, still in the emerald gown, barefoot now, earrings off, hair beginning to fall from its pins. She blinked when she saw him.

"Did you forget something?" she asked, brow furrowed.

Hudson's mouth twitched—half a smile, all nerves. "Not exactly."

Recognition dawned. Surprise faded into something else—something guarded.

"Hudson," she said evenly. "What are you doing here?"

He looked at her for a long beat, then cleared his throat, voice low. "Can we talk?"

She didn't move, didn't open the door wider.

"About what?" she asked.

He swallowed. "About everything."

Silence stretched.

Finally, Renee stepped back just enough to let the door open.

"Five minutes," she said. "That's all you get."

Hudson stepped inside.

She closed the door behind him, the soft click echoing louder than it should have in the quiet space. When she turned, he was watching her—his expression unreadable, but his eyes blazing.

He took a step toward her.

She stood her ground. "Why are you here, Hudson?"

Another step.

"Because," he said, voice low and rough, "when I saw you tonight, I wanted to do this."

He closed the space between them, his hands lifting to cup her face as he bent his head. He kissed her—raw, hungry, unguarded. Nothing polite. Nothing patient.

Renee gasped against his lips, but then she melted into it. Her hands clutched at his lapels, pulling him closer as his arms wrapped around her, one hand sliding into her hair, the other pressing against the small of her back.

He kissed her like he was starving. Like he'd been holding back for years and couldn't do it one second longer. His mouth moved over hers with urgency, and hers answered in kind—matching him, meeting him, losing herself in him.

Heat sparked and surged, dizzying, and overwhelming. She could feel every beat of his heart, every shuddered breath, every unspoken thing he was pouring into her with that kiss.

But then—clarity.

Like cold water doused her.

She pulled back with a sharp inhale, pressing both hands to his chest and shoving him away—not harshly, but firmly enough to make him stop.

Breathless. Flushed. Her lips still tingling.

His eyes searched hers, wide and uncertain. "Renee," he whispered.

She stepped back, her breath still ragged. "Why," she said, voice unsteady. "Why did you… kiss me?"

He looked at her, something raw flickering across his face—guilt, longing, desperation.

"I can't stop thinking about you," he said, his voice rough with emotion. "Every day since you left, it's been you. In every room. In every silence. I wanted to convince myself I made the right choice… but I didn't. I want a second chance."

Her arms tightened around herself as if she could somehow hold her heart in place. Her gaze dropped for a moment, then lifted to meet his. "Now?" she whispered. "Now you want a second chance. After everything?"

"I know I don't deserve it," he said. "But I had to try. Seeing you tonight—smiling, laughing—I wanted it to be me. God, I hated that it wasn't."

She blinked hard, trying to stop the tears gathering in her eyes. "You only want me because someone else does."

"No," he said, stepping forward, gentler now. "I want you because I was a fool not to fight for you when I had the chance. Because I've already lost you once and I don't think I can survive doing it again."

Renee's heart pounded, torn between everything she still felt for him and everything she'd learned to guard against.

She shook her head slowly. "You don't get to say that. Not when you're the one who made me feel like I was nothing more than a business transaction."

"I know," he said. "And I'll regret it for the rest of my life. But I'm here now, Renee. I'm not here for the company, or for appearances. I'm here for you."

Renee opened her mouth to tell him to leave. To tell him he was too late. That her heart had already mended—without him.

But the words wouldn't come.

Because even now, with her pride bruised and her trust shaken, her heart still beat faster when he looked at her like that. Like she was the only thing that mattered.

"I want to hate you," she whispered, her voice cracking. "I've tried. God knows I've tried."

Hudson stepped closer, careful not to touch her this time. His eyes never left hers. "I wouldn't blame you if you did."

"I wake up some mornings and I almost forget," she said, tears stinging her eyes. "And then I remember. What you said. What you did. And it breaks me all over again."

He looked stricken. "Renee—"

"I needed you," she said, the emotion rising now, barely contained. "When my grandfather died, when the world was falling apart, I needed you. And you weren't there. You were never really there."

He exhaled like the weight of her words was too much. "I know. I was too focused on what I thought I needed—what I thought we needed. But I see it now. None of it matters without you."

She closed her eyes for a second, trying to steady herself, to build the walls back up before it was too late. But his voice kept breaking through them.

"I love you, Renee," he said, quietly, earnestly. "And I'll spend every day proving it to you, if you'll let me."

Her breath hitched. She wanted to believe him. God, she wanted to fall into him and pretend the past hadn't happened.

But she couldn't. Not yet.

Still, she didn't ask him to leave. Didn't push him away again.

And that silence—that long, aching silence between them—was louder than any answer she could give.

Hudson stepped closer. Too close. She could feel the heat of him, the pull that had always existed between them, stronger now, more dangerous.

His hand came up slowly, fingers brushing her jaw, then sliding along her cheekbone with the gentlest touch. His thumb lingered just beneath her eye, a stroke full of reverence and something else—something deeper.

"Let me try," he said, voice husky, eyes locked on hers. "Really try."

He bent his head slowly, giving her time to pull away. A moment of grace, of choice.

She didn't move.

His lips met hers—soft at first, searching, and then suddenly, it was like the dam broke.

The kiss deepened in a heartbeat. His mouth claimed hers with a hunger that stole her breath, like he'd been starving for her. And maybe she had been starving too—because she kissed him back just as fiercely. Her hands fisted in his shirt, pulling him closer as his body pressed hers gently, insistently, against the door.

His hands slid to her waist, then up her back, anchoring her to him, possessive, and tender all at once. His kiss was heat and ache and longing, full of all the things they'd never said, all the time they'd wasted.

She moaned softly against his mouth, fingers sliding into his hair, her heart pounding so hard she could barely think. He kissed her like a man drowning, like she was the only thing that could save him.

And for one reckless, breathless moment, she let herself forget.

She let herself feel.

The door at her back was cool, but his body was fire—his lips, his hands, the way he said her name between kisses like a prayer he didn't deserve to speak.

Renee clung to him, lost in the tide.

But even in the haze, a voice whispered in her mind. You can't trust him. Not yet.

Still, she didn't stop. Not yet.

Hudson's mouth trailed from her lips to her jaw, then down the side of her neck, each kiss igniting sparks that made her knees weak. Renee gasped, her head tilting to give him more, hands slipping under the hem of his shirt to feel the heat of his skin.

He groaned softly at her touch, lips returning to hers in a kiss that was deeper now—possessive, raw, desperate. His hands found her hips, fingers digging in as if he was afraid, she might disappear again. He pressed her harder against the door, his body a perfect fit against hers, all strength, desire, and tension barely held in check.

She was drowning in him.

All the pain, the longing, the what-ifs—they blurred into this moment, into the taste of him, the feel of his hands, the way he kissed her like he needed her more than air.

His fingers bunched up the fabric of her dress, inching it higher until it was at her hip, brushing over the soft, heated skin of her thigh. She arched into him, breath catching, mind spinning. Her hands slid under his shirt, palms roaming the hard planes of his back, needing more—needing him.

"God, Renee," he breathed against her mouth, his voice rough with want. "I want you."

She couldn't speak. Could barely think. Words would shatter the fragile, burning world they'd fallen into. And she didn't want to leave it. Not yet.

His hand moved to her back, found the zipper of her dress, and slowly began to slide it down. Her breath hitched, anticipation curling low and hot in her belly. Every nerve ending sparked alive, trembling with the weight of everything they hadn't said—everything they still felt.

Then—

A knock.

Sharp. Sudden. Jarring.

They froze.

Renee's eyes flew open. Her chest heaved, lips swollen, skin flushed. Hudson's gaze locked with hers—dark, dazed, thunderstruck. He stepped back slowly, as though waking from a dream he wasn't ready to leave.

Another knock, louder this time.

Reality crashed back, brutal, and cold.

"Renee?" A voice called from the other side of the door.

Vivian.

Renee's stomach dropped.

Renee yanked her zipper back up with shaking fingers, trying to smooth her dress as her heartbeat thundered in her ears. Her lips still tingled, her skin burned where Hudson had touched her. She spun around, eyes wide with panic, chest still heaving.

"Renee, I know you're in there!" Vivian's voice rang out again from the other side of the door. "I saw Hudson's car outside!"

Renee met Hudson's gaze—his hair tousled, shirt half-untucked, chest rising and falling like he'd just come out of a dream. Her own dream. Or nightmare. She didn't know anymore.

There was no time to think.

She turned on her heel, reached for the handle, and opened the door.

Vivian stood in the hallway, arms crossed, brows raised, one hip cocked with suspicious precision. Her gaze slid past Renee instantly, narrowing.

"Oh," she said, stepping inside. "So, I wasn't hallucinating."

Renee barely had time to move before Vivian swept past her, eyes locking directly on Hudson. Her mouth parted slightly in shock—then curved into something dangerously close to amusement.

Hudson had straightened, but the tension in his body betrayed him. He nodded once in silent greeting.

Renee stepped back from the door, shoulders stiff. "You should go."

Hudson hesitated, jaw clenched like the words hurt more than he'd expected. But after a beat, he nodded—slowly, reluctantly—and slipped past Vivian with a final glance at Renee. Then he was gone.

Vivian stepped inside and closed the door behind her with a soft click. She turned to Renee, arms crossed, expression sharp. "Seriously?"

"Vivian—" Renee started, but her voice broke on the word. Her chest still heaved from the adrenaline, her lips felt swollen, and the memory of Hudson's touch clung to her like smoke. She folded her arms, as if she could somehow hold herself together that way.

"I wasn't expecting company," she added, weakly.

Vivian's eyes scanned her, taking in the tousled hair, the flush on her cheeks, the dress clinging to her hips like it had been hastily adjusted. Her brow arched. "Yeah. No kidding."

She turned her gaze toward the door. "Do we need to have a talk, or should I let you keep self-destructing in peace?"

Hudson's absence still echoed in the room. But his presence lingered, too—everywhere.

Renee winced. "Viv—don't."

"I'm serious," Vivian said, voice sharp. "You're letting the man who shattered you back in like he never walked away."

"He didn't—" Renee stopped. The words felt false even in her own mouth. She shook her head, voice hoarse. "This isn't… anything. Not tonight."

Vivian looked at her for a long moment, and then her tone softened. "Then why do you look like he just kissed the air back into your lungs?"

Renee flinched. Her throat tightened. Because he did. God help her, he did.

But she couldn't say that. Not out loud. Not yet.

She looked away. "I'm fine."

Vivian didn't believe her. It was all over her face. But she didn't push. Not now.

"Okay," she said finally, her voice quiet. "I'll go. But you and I, we're talking tomorrow. And you better be ready for honesty."

She moved to the door, then paused, her hand on the knob. Glancing back, she fixed Renee with a stare—then shifted it toward the hallway beyond.

"If he hurts you again," she said, cold steel in her voice, "I don't care how powerful or charming or sorry he is—I'll bury him myself."

Then she left.

The door closed behind her, and silence fell like a shroud.

Renee stood frozen, breath uneven, hands trembling. Her heart—stubborn, traitorous—ached with both want and warning.

And under all of it… something that felt like hope.

But she wasn't ready to believe in it. Not yet.

Chapter Nine

The soft click of the door echoed in Hudson's ears like a gunshot.

He stood there in the hallway, still breathing hard, still tasting her on his lips, the scent of her clinging to his skin like a memory he hadn't earned.

His hand twitched at his side, like it wanted to knock again—one more try, one more plea—but he didn't. Couldn't. Not with her best friend standing between them like a line he'd already crossed.

He turned and walked slowly toward the elevator, each step heavier than the last. His reflection caught in the sleek brass panelling of the doors—shirt wrinkled, hair mussed, lips still parted slightly like they couldn't quite let go of her.

The doors opened. He stepped inside.

And only then—only in the boxed-in silence of the lift—did he let himself exhale. A sound half-laugh, half-choke, his hands dragging through his hair like he could shake loose the feeling of her, the fire of her kiss.

Jesus.

He'd never kissed her before. Not even at their wedding.

Their first kiss.

Their first real anything.

After all this time—after the cold arrangement, the hollow vows, the distance, the silence—he had been the one to finally cross that invisible line he'd drawn on their wedding day.

He hadn't seen her.

Not really.

He saw the name. The legacy. The advantage. The woman who was convenient and gracious and beautiful in a way that made sense on paper. She was a solution, not a spark.

But tonight—God help him—tonight he felt the wildfire.

The elevator doors opened to the lobby. He stepped out like a man half-asleep, the polished floors beneath his feet grounding him just enough to keep walking. Outside, the city buzzed around him, but none of it broke through the haze of her.

That kiss had undone him.

It wasn't just passion—it was revelation. Every second her mouth had moved against his, every sound she'd made, every tremble in her breath—it all screamed of a woman he hadn't deserved. And now? Now he ached with the weight of what he'd missed. What he'd wasted.

How the hell had he missed it?

The fire. The softness. The steel beneath the grace. She wasn't just beautiful. She was brilliant. She was fierce. She was loyal in a way that could destroy a lesser man—and he'd taken it for granted.

He reached his car but didn't open the door. Just stood there with the handle under his palm, staring down the street like maybe if he looked hard enough, he could see who he was supposed to be. Who she needed him to be.

Because what kind of idiot never kisses his wife? What kind of man got a second chance after throwing the first away like it didn't matter?

The kind standing here with her taste on his lips and her voice echoing in his head like a promise wrapped in regret.

He closed his eyes, jaw tight. He couldn't go back. Couldn't undo the things he'd said. The way he'd made her feel. The cold, clinical way he'd treated the one person who might have loved him before he'd earned it.

And why did he suddenly feel like a man who'd spent months ignoring a treasure he'd been too blind, too proud, or too stupid to claim?

But he could try now.

He had to.

Because tonight, for the first time, he didn't see her as the heiress. Or the leverage. Or the woman he'd married for the company.

Tonight, he saw Renee.

And he'd never wanted anything more in his life.

A sharp knock echoed through the apartment, followed by the sound of the doorknob jiggling.

"Renee! I know you're in there," Vivian called. "Don't make me use the spare key you gave me."

Renee groaned from her spot on the couch, still wrapped in the oversized hoodie she'd thrown on after tossing and turning most of the night. Her hair was a mess, her eyes puffy, and her heart—still an unsteady thud behind her ribs.

She opened the door reluctantly.

Vivian didn't wait for an invitation. She stepped inside with the kind of righteous energy only a best friend could summon after witnessing your emotional breakdown in real time.

"Coffee?" Renee mumbled.

Vivian waved her off. "Nope. Not until we talk about him."

Renee sank back into the couch. "There's nothing to talk about."

Vivian arched an eyebrow. "You mean besides the part where Hudson Waterford kissed you like a man who just realised, he's been in love with you this whole damn time?"

Renee's face flushed. "It wasn't—he didn't—it was a mistake."

Vivian flopped down beside her. "Renee, no. Don't do that. Don't go rewriting it in your head to protect yourself. I saw him. I saw you. That kiss wasn't casual. It sure as hell wasn't meaningless."

Renee hugged a pillow to her chest, her voice quiet. "It doesn't change anything."

Vivian gave her a look. "Are you kidding me? Of course it changes things! The man you've loved since college, the same man who married you for power and then treated you like an afterthought, just kissed you like he's drowning and you're air."

Renee didn't respond. Her silence said enough.

Vivian softened, but her voice remained firm. "I'm not saying he didn't feel something last night. I'm saying you can't afford to go down that road again unless you're sure he's changed. Really changed."

"I know," Renee whispered.

"Do you?" Vivian asked gently. "Because last time, you let him break your heart so quietly, you didn't even fight back. You just… disappeared. Filed for an annulment and vanished. That's not healing, Ren. That's hiding."

Renee blinked back tears.

"I'm not trying to be harsh," Vivian added. "But I love you. And I saw what it did to you, loving someone who only saw you as convenient."

"I thought I could be okay with it," Renee admitted, her voice cracking. "But I wasn't."

Vivian reached over and took her hand. "Then don't settle for halfway again. If he wants you back, he better come with more than kisses. He better come with honesty. With apology. With proof."

Renee nodded slowly.

Vivian squeezed her hand. "And until then? You keep choosing you. Because you're not the same girl who married him out of duty to your grandfather. You're wiser now. Stronger. And you deserve someone who sees that—not just your last name."

A pause stretched between them, heavy with unsaid things. Then Renee let out a shaky laugh.

"I really should've made you coffee first."

Vivian grinned. "Damn right you should've. I just delivered a full TED Talk on emotional resilience and toxic men, and I'm running on half a granola bar."

They both laughed, and for the first time since the night before, some of the pressure in Renee's chest eased. Just a little.

Vivian collapsed onto the couch, legs tucked beneath her, scrolling through her phone. Renee leaned against the kitchen counter, nursing her mug of tea. The silence was comfortable but charged—like they were waiting for the next storm cloud to break.

"So," Vivian said without looking up, "what's the game plan for today? We crying, cleansing, or committing petty revenge?"

Before Renee could answer, a knock sounded at the door.

She froze. "If that's Hudson, I'm pretending not to be home."

Vivian perked up. "Say the word and I'll handle it. I've got a very satisfying door-slam locked and loaded for his smug CEO face."

But when Renee opened it, it wasn't Hudson.

It was Elias.

Casual in jeans and a button-up, sleeves rolled, smile easy. He radiated calm, like a breeze on a too-warm day.

"Hey," he said. "Sorry to drop in unannounced. I was nearby and figured I'd check in."

Vivian leaned around Renee, eyes lighting up. "Well, well. If it isn't Dr. Tall, Dark, and Scalpel."

Elias laughed. "Still calling me that?"

"Until you legally change your name, yeah."

Renee shot Vivian a look but stepped aside. "Come in."

Elias entered, his eyes settling on Renee. "You look… better."

She nodded, heart ticking a little faster at how gently he said it.

"She's healing," Vivian said, flopping back onto the couch. "Mostly thanks to people whose names don't rhyme with Judson."

Elias gave a quiet smile. "I'm glad. Actually"—he turned to Renee— "I was wondering if you'd like to grab dinner tonight. Casual. No expectations. Just food and maybe a little fun conversation."

Renee blinked. "Dinner?"

Vivian sat up straight. "She'd love to."

"Viv—"

"Nope," Vivian said, waving her off. "You need a night out. Preferably with someone who doesn't come with emotional booby traps. And you—" she jabbed a finger at Elias, "—are emotionally stable, attractive, and own a stethoscope. Honestly, it's basic science."

Elias chuckled. "So… I'll take that as a yes?"

He stood there—solid, warm, uncomplicated—and for a second, she wondered what it would be like to fall for someone who didn't come with warning labels.

Renee glanced at Vivian, then back at Elias. "I'd like that," she said softly. "Dinner sounds nice."

Elias smiled. "Perfect. I'll text you the details."

As the door closed behind him, Renee turned to Vivian, arms crossed but brow raised.

"You really think I should go?"

Vivian's teasing fell away. "Yes. Because Hudson doesn't get to be the only one who changes the story. You deserve a fresh start—with someone who sees you. Not someone who had to lose you to realise your worth."

Renee considered that.

"Really?"

Vivian gave her a dry look. "Girl, it's time you stopped writing sonnets for men who needs flashcards to understand your value. Try a chapter where you win."

Renee laughed—and this time, it reached her eyes.

Hudson stared at the untouched cup of coffee in front of him, the steam curling upward before disappearing into the quiet morning air.

Sleep had been useless.

His mind had replayed that kiss on a loop—her soft gasp, the way she clutched his shirt like she didn't know whether to pull him closer or push him away, the tremble in her breath afterward when she whispered, "This changes nothing."

The hell it didn't.

Hudson pushed back from the counter and paced toward the floor-to-ceiling windows overlooking the city. It was a perfect spring morning—blue skies, sunlight dancing off the rooftops. But all he could see was her.

Renee.

The woman he married for strategy and security.

The woman who walked away from him with nothing but her pride.

The woman he kissed like a starving man, only to realise too late just how much she meant to him.

He dragged a hand through his hair.

He'd thought he was doing the right thing. Keeping it business. Keeping it simple. She was elegant, dangerous in a way that got under his skin and made him hesitate—feel too much.

And he didn't hesitate. Not in business. Not in life.

Until her.

Now, everything was unravelling. His carefully controlled world, the mask he wore, the plan he'd stuck to so ruthlessly—it all felt hollow.

Because the truth hit him like a freight train:

He didn't want to run the company without her.

Didn't want the title, the power, or the legacy if it meant going home to silence and sleeping alone in that cold, oversized bed.

He'd hurt her. Maybe worse than he even realised.

The way she'd looked at him before he'd left last night—like she was bracing for impact—like she'd seen it coming all along…

Damn it.

He turned back toward the kitchen, grabbed his phone, and opened his calendar. Back-to-back meetings, board prep, investor calls. All of it could wait.

If he wanted to win her back, he had to do more than say sorry.

He had to prove she mattered. That this mattered.

He needed a plan. Not a business strategy. A Renee strategy.

First: show her he was listening.

Second: undo the damage. Not just with flowers and hollow words—but with real, vulnerable honesty, the kind he avoided like the plague.

And third… if she let him get that far, fight for her the way she deserved.

Hudson exhaled and stared at his reflection in the dark glass of the window.

"Time to stop being a coward, Waterford," he muttered. "You want her back? Then be the man she needed you to be the first time."

He didn't know if it would be enough.

But he was damn well going to try.

Hudson didn't know what he expected when he showed up at Renee's apartment that evening—but it definitely wasn't Vivian opening the door.

She leaned against the frame like a bouncer outside a velvet rope, arms crossed, sweatshirt sleeves pushed up like she meant business. Her expression could've curdled wine.

"Well," she drawled, "if it isn't the man formerly known as Renee's husband."

Hudson exhaled through his nose. "Is she here?"

"Nope." Vivian popped the P like a punctuation mark. "And even if she was, you'd be the last person she'd want to see."

He kept his tone even. "Vivian, I'm not here to fight."

"Then this is going to be a short visit," she said, unmoved. "Because whatever grand, sweeping apology you've got loaded in that sleek CEO brain of yours? It's about six months and one heartbreak too late."

His jaw tensed. "I just want to talk to her."

Vivian paused, studying him. For a flicker of a second, something behind her eyes shifted—maybe doubt, maybe reluctant recognition—but then it was gone, replaced by that same unreadable smirk.

"Well," she said, "you missed your window. She's got dinner plans."

Hudson's brow pulled. "With who?"

Vivian's smile was slow and deliberate. "Elias."

His chest went still. "Dr. Elias Chen?"

"The one and only," she said sweetly. "You know—tall, kind, listens when women speak? A doctor who doesn't treat love like a hostile takeover?"

Something unravelled inside him—cold, green, unreasoning. His brain told him Renee was free to do whatever she wanted. That this shouldn't matter.

But it did.

It mattered more than he was prepared for.

"She said yes?" he asked quietly.

Vivian's stance softened—just barely. "Yeah. She did. Because he sees her, Hudson. From the start. Not just when it's convenient."

Hudson swallowed hard, guilt and jealousy clashing in his chest. "Where are they going?"

Vivian raised a brow. "So, you can crash the date and win her back with a grand gesture?"

"No," he said, shaking his head. "So I don't."

That made her pause. She tilted her head slightly, reading him like a puzzle she didn't trust.

Hudson took a breath. "Vivian… I know I messed up. I know I hurt her. I didn't even realise how much until it was too late. But I'm not here to manipulate her. I'm not here for power plays or second chances on my terms."

He met her gaze. "I just want to make it right. I love her. And for the first time, I'm ready to show up the way she deserved from the beginning."

Vivian stared at him for a long moment, her expression unreadable. Then she nodded once, slow, and sceptical.

"Good," she said. "Because if you hurt her again? She won't be the only one slamming a door in your face."

And with that, she shut the door, leaving Hudson alone in the hallway—heart pounding, mind racing, and one step closer to realising just how much he had to lose.

Chapter Ten

The restaurant was tucked into a quiet corner of the city, dimly lit and humming with soft conversation. A string of Edison bulbs glowed overhead, casting golden light across the reclaimed wood tables. It was the kind of place people found by accident and returned to on purpose.

Renee arrived first, nerves a fluttering mess beneath her calm exterior. She smoothed her dress—simple, navy, not trying too hard—and glanced toward the door just as Elias walked in.

Jeans. Rolled sleeves. That easy confidence that didn't try too hard—just like him.

He spotted her and smiled.

"Hey," he said as he slid into the seat across from her. "You look… like you've slept more than three hours. I'll take that as progress."

Renee laughed softly. "Barely. But I appreciate the optimism."

He nodded toward the menu. "Anything look good?"

She pretended to study it, though she barely registered the words. Her mind still buzzed from last night. From Hudson. From that kiss. And now, here she was—sitting across from a man who made her feel… safe.

He didn't push. Didn't prod. Just waited while she tried to breathe like a normal person.

"You know," Elias said, setting his menu down, "I wasn't sure you'd say yes."

Renee looked up. "Why?"

He shrugged, candid. "Because you've had your heart handed back to you in pieces. And because the last guy you dated came with a castle, a boardroom, and a tragic inability to communicate."

She smiled, despite herself. "I didn't realise you'd been briefed on my romantic history."

"I work in surgery," he said with a wink. "I'm good with scars."

Renee's smile faltered—just a little—and Elias noticed. His expression softened.

"Too much?" he asked.

She shook her head. "No. Just… honest."

They placed their orders, the conversation drifting into lighter topics—college stories, embarrassing first jobs, the weirdest things patients had ever said under anaesthesia. Elias was funny in a quiet, self-aware way. Thoughtful. Grounded.

But part of her mind kept splitting off—drifting back to Hudson. To the way her skin still remembered his touch, even when her heart warned her to forget.

"Can I ask you something?" Elias said, bringing her back to the present.

"Sure."

"Why did you say yes to tonight?"

She hesitated, fingers curling around her water glass.

"Because I needed to remind myself that not every man, I care about is going to hurt me," she said quietly. "Because you're kind. And easy to be around. And... because I don't know what happens next, but I didn't want to be afraid of trying."

Elias's gaze didn't waver. "That's a good answer."

Renee exhaled, relieved. "I'm not ready for anything serious."

"I didn't ask for serious," he said gently. "I asked for dinner."

Their meals arrived, giving her a moment to collect herself. The food was good—she barely tasted it. But the company? The company made her feel like she wasn't unravelling.

As they finished, Elias leaned back in his chair and studied her with that same steady calm.

"I like you, Renee," he said. "But I'm not here to compete. I know there's someone else still in your head."

Her throat tightened.

"I just want you to know that if you ever decide you want a different kind of love— one that's calm, and clear, and not built on regret—I'm here."

It wasn't pressure. It wasn't a proposition. It was just... a door, left open.

And for the first time in a long time, Renee didn't feel trapped.

He hadn't meant to see her.

Hudson had come to the restaurant for a business dinner, a routine meeting with a supplier who was running late. He stepped inside, glanced around for the host—and then he saw her.

Renee.

Her back was to him, shoulders relaxed, hair swept into a low, elegant twist he remembered tugging free with his hands. She was laughing. Not the polite kind she gave in boardrooms or at society events—but real laughter, the kind that crinkled her eyes and made her whole face glow.

And sitting across from her… was him.

Elias.

Hudson froze, half-shadowed in the corner of the restaurant as a wave of something bitter and unfamiliar crept up his spine. Hudson wasn't used to jealousy—not like this. But seeing Renee—his wife, even if only technically—leaning toward another man, smiling like her heart wasn't in pieces…

It gutted him.

She looked different. Lighter. Like the storm she'd carried inside her chest had finally passed.

Elias was talking, his voice low and calm. Hudson couldn't hear the words, but he didn't need to. The way Renee looked at him—curious, open, present—was enough.

She never looked at him that way. Not until it was too late.

A waiter passed between them, blocking his view for a second. When Hudson looked back, Elias reached across the table and brushed a crumb from Renee's cheek. It was a small gesture—insignificant to anyone else. But it hit like a hammer.

Hudson turned away.

He should leave.

He should forget what he saw and pretend it didn't gut him.

But his feet wouldn't move.

What the hell was he expecting? That she'd sit at home pining for him while he tried to figure out how he felt?

She was moving on. She deserved to move on.

Still, something primal burned behind his ribs.

This wasn't just jealousy. This was fear. Fear that she might stop loving him altogether. And for the first time, that possibility felt real.

That was new.

The host finally approached, but Hudson barely registered the man's voice. He nodded absently, muttered something about rescheduling, and walked out into the night.

As he stepped onto the sidewalk, the cold air hit him like a slap. He stood there, hands clenched, jaw tight, mind full of the woman he'd taken for granted—

And the man who hadn't.

The knock came to his study door just as Hudson was pouring his third drink of the night.

He ignored it at first, thinking it was the doorman or a delivery. But it came again— louder this time, more familiar.

Marcus opened the door then leaned against the frame, casual in jeans and a Henley, a six-pack in one hand and that unreadable look on his face.

"Was in the neighbourhood," Marcus said. "Figured I'd check on the king of self-sabotage."

Hudson turned to face him, wordless.

Marcus strolled in, set the beer on the desk, and scanned the room. "Jesus, you really are spiralling. This place looks like a Restoration Hardware ad for loneliness."

Hudson tossed back the rest of his scotch. "Don't start."

"Too late," Marcus replied, grabbing a bottle for himself. "Word travels fast. You showed up at her place?"

Hudson didn't answer.

"And she's out with Elias."

Still nothing.

Marcus whistled low. "Damn. So, this is what losing your mind looks like in a penthouse suite."

Hudson finally turned, voice tight. "She said yes to him. Just like that."

Marcus raised a brow. "You're surprised?"

"She's my wife."

Marcus took a sip of beer. "Correction—she was your wife. And even when she was, you barely acted like it mattered."

Hudson flinched. "You think I don't know that?"

"I think you know it now," Marcus said, levelling him with a stare. "But back then? You treated her like a strategic asset. A stepping stone. Hell, man, she's not even in the building anymore and I can still feel the cold in here."

Hudson rubbed his face, exhaustion and frustration clawing at him. "I didn't mean to hurt her."

"But you did," Marcus said. "You hurt her because you never let her in. You wanted the title, the power, the image—but not the risk that comes with feeling something."

"I do feel something," Hudson snapped. "I can't stop feeling it."

"Well," Marcus said, "welcome to the human race. We've got beer and bad timing."

Hudson walked past him into the living area and sank onto the edge of the couch, shoulders hunched, staring at the glass in his hand like it might offer clarity.

"I kissed her, Marcus. Really kissed her. And it was like the whole damn world shifted underneath me."

Marcus sat across from him, sprawled in the leather armchair like he owned the place, though his voice was gentler than usual. "And now she's kissing someone else."

Hudson's head snapped up, jaw tight.

Marcus held up his hands. "Don't look at me like that. I'm not trying to be cruel. I'm saying—it's not too late. But it will be if you keep standing still."

Silence stretched between them, thick with everything Hudson didn't want to say out loud. He stared at the drink in his hand like the answers might float to the surface.

Marcus leaned forward, eyes steady. "Do you love her?"

Hudson's shoulders dropped, the question hitting like a sucker punch he didn't even try to dodge. "More than I ever thought I could," he said quietly. "More than makes sense."

He let out a breath, long and frayed. "I don't know when it happened. Maybe it was always there, and I just refused to see it. Or maybe it crept in slow—through all the moments I ignored, all the chances I wasted."

Marcus nodded once, thoughtful. "So, what the hell are you going to do about it?"

Hudson dragged a hand down his face. "I don't know. I screwed it up. Badly. She left for a reason."

"Then give her a reason to come back."

Hudson looked up, doubtful. "What? Show up with flowers? Grand speech? Apologise in a press release?"

"No," Marcus said, firm now. "Be honest. Not strategic. Not polished. Honest. Tell her you were wrong. Admit you didn't see her—really see her—until it was almost too late. Tell her she's not the heiress anymore, not the deal you thought you were making—she's the woman you love."

Hudson swallowed hard, throat tight.

"And if she doesn't want you back?" Marcus shrugged. "Then at least you gave her the truth. And maybe—just maybe—you'll stop living like a man trying to win a boardroom and start living like one trying to win a heart."

The words landed like stones in water, rippling through the silence that followed.

Hudson leaned back, staring at the ceiling like it held some kind of map he could follow. But there was no roadmap for this. No quarterly projections. Just regret, and hope, and a woman who'd once loved him enough to marry him for nothing more than a promise—and who'd walked away when he failed to keep it.

"I don't deserve her," he muttered.

Marcus stood, finishing his drink. "Probably not. But that's never been the question, has it?"

Hudson looked up at him.

Marcus gave him a nod. "The question is—are you finally going to be the man who tries anyway?"

Then he was gone, the elevator doors shutting behind him with a quiet ding that echoed louder than it should have.

And Hudson was alone again—with his guilt, his love, and a choice he couldn't afford to keep avoiding.

Two hours later, across town, Renee just finished a long video meeting and was halfway into a bowl of leftover soup when there was a knock at her door.

She wasn't expecting anyone.

She frowned, wiped her hands on a towel, and walked to the door.

"Hudson?"

He stood in the doorway—not in a suit, not guarded. Just jeans, a navy sweater, and that unmistakable tension in his jaw when he was nervous but trying to hide it.

"I didn't come to fight," he said softly. "And I'm not here to convince you of anything. I just… wanted to give you something."

She raised a brow. "You brought a gift?"

"No. Not exactly."

He stepped forward and handed her a manila envelope.

She opened it cautiously, expecting legal papers or some kind of business damage control. Instead, she pulled out several sheets of paper—handwritten. His handwriting.

"What is this?" she asked.

"My resignation letter."

She blinked. "From Fitzgerald Enterprises?"

He nodded. "It's not dated. I didn't submit it. But I wrote it—fully. And if you tell me that me being CEO still feels like a leash around your neck, I'll sign it and walk away. You deserve to know I'm not staying because of power or legacy. I'll leave tomorrow Renee."

Her breath caught in her throat. He wasn't bluffing. There was no performance in his eyes, no smug grin.

"I told myself I wanted the company more than I wanted you," he said. "But that was a lie. A stupid one. I want you. Not the arrangement. Not the contract. You."

She looked down at the letter again, the edges trembling in her hand.

"I'm not asking for anything from you," he continued. "Not today. I know I've hurt you. I know I don't deserve another chance just because I finally figured it out. But I had to show you that I'm done choosing strategy over heart."

Renee didn't answer right away.

Hudson turned to leave, giving her one last glance over his shoulder. "Keep it. Do whatever you want with it. I just wanted you to have the choice this time."

He turned to go. For a second, she opened her mouth—then closed it again.

The door clicked shut behind him.

Renee stood frozen, staring at the letter—the ultimate symbol of power—and realising for the first time, he might finally understand what love really meant.

Her fingers curled around the paper, the edges soft from where he'd handled it. And for once, the power in her hands didn't feel like a burden. It felt like a beginning.

Monday morning, the rain tapped softly against the floor-to-ceiling windows, the city blurred behind the droplets like a half-forgotten painting. Renee sat at her desk, reviewing the third-quarter financials for the upcoming board meeting. Her head was pounding, but she powered through.

A knock sounded.

She didn't look up. "Come in."

The door opened, and Hudson stepped inside—no assistant, no preamble. Just him, looking like tension carved in human form.

Renee tensed instinctively, though she kept her expression neutral. "Is there something you need?"

"I wanted to go over the projected cash flow variance for Q4," he said, closing the door behind him. "The new expansion strategy—if we move the timeline up—we'll need to reallocate reserves."

She leaned back in her chair. "We already reviewed that last week. You signed off."

"I know. I just…" He trailed off, his jaw tightening. "I needed to see the numbers again. With you."

Renee narrowed her eyes. "Is this about numbers or something else?"

He stepped closer, stopping just short of her desk. "It's about both."

She rose slowly, her chair sliding back with a whisper. "I don't have time for games, Hudson."

"No games," he said, voice quiet but insistent. "Just a conversation."

She exhaled, arms crossed. "Fine. Here's the forecast." She handed him a folder, their fingers brushing—barely—but it was enough to charge the space between them.

He didn't look at the folder. "Renee…"

Her name in his voice did something to her. Unravelled threads she'd spent weeks trying to hold together.

He stepped around the desk, closing the last bit of distance. "I can't stop thinking about that kiss."

Her breath caught.

"I came in here telling myself I needed your insight on projections," he said. "But the truth? I needed to see your face. Hear your voice. Remind myself what I'm actually fighting for."

She tried to hold her ground, but emotion cracked through her calm. "Hudson, don't—"

"Tell me to stop and I will," he said, voice low. "But don't lie to me. Don't pretend you didn't feel it, too."

She looked up at him—really looked—and all the walls she'd built started shaking.

He was standing so close now, their breath mingling. Her heart thundered in her chest.

"I told myself I wouldn't do this again," she whispered.

"So did I."

His hand lifted—hovering for a beat—before brushing a strand of hair from her cheek with a touch so careful it nearly broke her.

She didn't move. Didn't breathe.

His face tilted closer, slowly, as if giving her time to stop him. She didn't. Couldn't.

His lips hovered a breath from hers, the space between them charged and trembling.

And then—

She surged forward and kissed him.

It wasn't soft. It wasn't cautious. It was full of all the things she'd bitten back for months—anger and ache and the kind of longing that bloomed in the hollow places people couldn't see. Her hands gripped the front of his shirt, pulling him closer, needing the weight of him, the heat of him, as if that might somehow undo the nights, she cried herself to sleep or the mornings she woke up alone.

His mouth answered hers with the same hungry, reckless desperation. A groan rumbled low in his throat as one hand slid to her waist, the other to the back of her neck, anchoring her like he'd finally stopped running.

Everything else disappeared—the city behind the glass, the spreadsheet still glowing on her monitor, the fragile peace she'd been trying to build without him.

There was only this.

Only him.

Only the taste of a truth they'd both ignored for too long.

When he finally broke the kiss, it was only to rest his forehead against hers, his breath uneven, warm against her skin.

"I've missed you in every room I walk into," he whispered.

Renee's eyes fluttered shut. Her heart felt like it was trying to tear free from her chest. She wanted to say something—anything—but all that came out was a soft breath of air, a sound that tasted like surrender.

Then came the knock.

It was sharp. Jarring. Real.

She pulled back like she'd been burned, the spell broken. Her lips still tingled, and her mind scrambled to catch up with her body.

Hudson swore under his breath, low and vicious.

She swallowed hard, smoothing her blouse, willing her pulse to calm.

"Come in," she said, the words steady—too steady—as if they hadn't just torn each other open in the middle of a Monday morning.

Hudson stepped back as the door creaked open, but his mind stayed exactly where she was—pressed against him, lips warm and urgent, her hands fisting his shirt like she couldn't bear to let go.

He barely registered the assistant who walked in with a file and a question. Renee answered, her voice even, but Hudson didn't hear a word. His heart was still thundering in his chest, like it hadn't gotten the message that the moment had passed.

His gaze stayed on her—on the flush still high on her cheeks, the way she tucked a loose strand of hair behind her ear with trembling fingers. She didn't look at him, not even once.

Because she couldn't.

Because if she did, he might kiss her again, and this time he wouldn't stop.

He took a breath. It didn't help. The taste of her was still on his lips—like memory and hope and every stupid, selfish reason he'd told himself he could keep her at arm's length.

But he couldn't anymore.

That kiss had cracked something open inside him. Not just want—though God, he wanted her—but something deeper. Something terrifying.

It was how she'd kissed him back. Like she'd been holding it in just as long. Like it hurt to touch him, but it hurt more not to.

He clenched his jaw, trying to stay upright, composed, the way he always had in boardrooms and crisis calls and family wars. But this—Renee—she was not a line item he could manage. She was fire. And all he'd done was try to contain her, structure her, control the narrative so he didn't have to face what he felt.

And now?

Now, he couldn't remember why he ever thought distance was safer. Because the second her lips touched his, he knew—he could burn for the rest of his life and still call it worth it.

When the assistant left, closing the door with a soft click, the silence returned.

So did the weight of everything unsaid.

She still hadn't looked at him.

Hudson swallowed hard. "Renee—"

"Don't," she said quietly, eyes still fixed on her screen. "Not right now."

He nodded slowly, though his whole body screamed to stay, to fight, to speak.

But he left.

Not because he didn't care.

But because for the first time in his life, he was starting to understand that loving her meant giving her space—even when it hurt like hell.

Chapter Eleven

They only saw each other in the boardroom on Wednesday. Just a few tense glances across polished mahogany, a clipped exchange about Q4 projections, and then nothing. Cold professionalism where there used to be heat.

Now it was Friday. And Hudson couldn't do this anymore.

He needed to see her. For real. No boardroom table. No titles. Just her.

He stood outside her office door, fists flexing at his sides, heart thudding like a war drum. Then he knocked—twice, sharp, and clear.

Renee looked up from her screen, startled. Her expression shifted when she saw him. Wariness first. Then something softer. But it disappeared almost as quickly.

"Hudson," she said, setting her pen down. "Is there something you need?"

"Yeah," he said, stepping inside without waiting for an invitation. "Dinner."

Her brows drew together. "Excuse me?"

"Dinner," he repeated. "With me. Tonight."

She blinked. "Is this a business meeting or—?"

"No," he said gently, but firmly. "Not business."

She leaned back in her chair, arms folding across her chest. "Why now?"

He exhaled, steadying himself. "Because waiting hasn't made any of this easier. And because I'm tired of pretending like I don't want to spend time with you outside of fluorescent lights and quarterly reports."

She looked at him—really looked at him—for the first time in days. "I don't know if I'm ready."

"I'll pick you up at seven," he said, offering a small smile. "You've got a couple hours to decide."

Her lips parted, probably to protest again, but he was already turning for the door. He paused, just briefly, his hand on the handle.

"I hope you say yes," he said, glancing over his shoulder. "But either way... I'm showing up."

Then he left, leaving her with nothing but the quiet hum of her office, the scent of his cologne lingering in the air, and a racing heart that betrayed how unsure she really was.

Hudson adjusted the cuffs of his jacket as he stood outside Renee's door, the weight of the moment pressing down on him harder than any boardroom negotiation ever had. He could deliver billion-dollar pitches without breaking a sweat—but this? This was different.

This was her.

He lifted his hand to knock when the door opened before he could.

And for a second—he forgot how to breathe.

Renee stood there, dressed in a deep emerald green that made her skin glow, and her eyes look like secrets. Her hair was swept off her neck, soft waves cascading over one shoulder. She wasn't wearing much makeup—she never needed to—but her lips were painted a subtle rose, the same shade that used to stain his thoughts at night.

"Hi, you're right on time," she said, her voice quieter than usual, like she wasn't sure this was real.

Hudson blinked, then swallowed hard. "You look… incredible."

She glanced down, almost self-conscious, then met his gaze again. "Thanks. You clean up pretty well yourself."

He let out a soft laugh, the tension in his shoulders easing just slightly. "I was afraid you wouldn't come."

"I almost didn't," she admitted, stepping aside to let him in.

He entered slowly, like one wrong move might send the whole moment crashing down. Her apartment was tidy, elegant—much like her—but there was a new candle burning on the console table by the door. Lavender and sandalwood. Soft. Intimate.

"You ready?" he asked.

Renee hesitated, then nodded. "Yeah. I think I am."

They rode the elevator in silence, the tension electric but not hostile—just charged, like something waiting to happen.

When they reached his car, Hudson held the door open for her, and for a heartbeat, their hands brushed. She froze. So did he.

"Sorry," she murmured, pulling back.

"Don't be," he said gently. "I've missed you."

The words hung between them, daring her to answer, but she just looked out the window as he closed the door.

As they drove, the city lights reflected in her eyes, and Hudson risked a glance at her every few moments, wondering if tonight could be the beginning of something neither of them was ready to name—but both of them had already started to feel.

The restaurant was quiet and dim, tucked into a side street in Midtown like a secret. It wasn't flashy—no valet, no neon. Just warm lighting, hushed voices, and the scent of garlic and rosemary lingering in the air.

Hudson sat across from her, struck silent for the third time since she'd stepped out of her apartment.

Renee wore deep emerald tonight, the kind of green that made her eyes glow like a forest after rain. Her hair was swept to one side, soft curls brushing her bare shoulder. She didn't try. That's what always got him. She never tried to be stunning.

She just was.

"I've never been here before," she said, glancing around as she unfolded her napkin.

"I know," he said softly.

She raised an eyebrow, amused. "You keeping tabs on my restaurant history now?"

He smiled faintly, but his mind wasn't on her question.

It had drifted—without permission—to a memory he hadn't touched in years.

It was spring. Maybe five, six years ago. A Fitzgerald gala at the estate. Renee was still in grad school then, not quite polished, but already impossible to ignore. He'd come out onto the terrace to take a call, irritated by something board related. And there she was—curled on a bench under the rose trellis, shoes off, a glass of champagne forgotten beside her, reading a novel. Completely unbothered by the chaos of suits and social climbing behind her.

She hadn't noticed him. But he'd watched her for longer than he should have.

That was the moment. The one he never admitted to anyone. Not even himself.

The moment he realised she was different.

That she saw the world in a way he didn't. That she felt things deeply—quietly, fiercely.

That he might already be in trouble.

"You're quiet," Renee said now, her voice cutting into his thoughts.

Hudson blinked, pulled back to the present. "Just thinking."

"About what?"

He debated lying. Dodging. But this wasn't a night for armour.

"About the first time I saw you," he said. "Really saw you."

Her expression shifted, curious. "When?"

"A night on the terrace. You were reading under the roses. Everyone else was inside pretending to be important. But not you."

A flush crept into her cheeks. "I didn't even know you noticed me back then."

"I did," he said. "Too much."

Their eyes locked, candlelight flickering between them like some unspoken promise. The moment stretched, thick with what might've been—and what still could be.

The waiter appeared, quiet and discreet. They ordered without looking at the menu. Neither broke the gaze for long.

"You've been avoiding me," Hudson said, once they were alone again.

She hesitated, then gave a slight nod. "I needed space. Time to think."

He nodded. "Did it help?"

"Yes," she said. Then after a beat: "But I don't know what to do with the answers."

Hudson leaned in. "Tell me what they are, and we'll figure it out together."

Renee looked down at her wine, swirling it slowly. "I'm afraid. Not of you exactly. Just… of getting hurt again. Of being convenient instead of chosen."

Hudson swallowed hard. "You were never convenient, Renee."

She met his gaze again, and this time it lingered.

"You said you regretted marrying me."

"I said that when I was scared and stupid and trying to protect myself," he said. "But I've burned every day since."

Her eyes shimmered—whether from the candlelight or something else, he didn't know.

"I ordered the scallops," she said quietly, shifting the mood.

He gave her a crooked smile. "I was definitely planning to steal some."

And just like that, the tension eased. The air around them softened.

They ate slowly, conversation meandering through books, travel, shared memories that suddenly felt less painful and more… precious. He watched her laugh—really laugh—and his chest ached with how badly he wanted to keep that sound in his life.

By dessert, her hand rested near his on the table. He didn't reach for it.

But when his fingers brushed hers, she didn't pull away.

The ride back to Renee's apartment was quiet, but not awkward. It was the kind of silence that wrapped around them like a familiar blanket—soft, weighted with meaning, neither of them in a rush to break it.

Outside, the city blurred past in streaks of gold and red. Hudson glanced at her as his car turned down her street. Her head rested lightly against the window, the delicate curve of her neck visible in the low light.

He remembered the way she'd smiled when he handed her the dessert spoon first. The way her voice had gone quiet when she talked about Henry. The way her fingers lingered when they brushed his on the table.

He wanted to reach for her hand again.

He didn't.

When they reached her building, she turned to him. "Do you want to come up?"

There was no flirtation in her tone. No seduction.

Just honesty. A thread of hope. A quiet invitation to something unfinished.

Hudson nodded once. "Yes."

They didn't speak as they rode the elevator—words felt too fragile, too heavy. The silence between them wasn't tense, only charged with everything they hadn't yet said. Her fingers fidgeted with her keys; his hands were buried in his pockets, clenched against the urge to reach for her.

When they reached her floor, she moved ahead, unlocking the door with a soft click. She stepped inside and turned back, holding it open for him.

He followed.

The apartment smelled like vanilla and cedarwood—warm, clean, familiar. Like her. It wrapped around him the moment he crossed the threshold, settling in his chest and behind his ribs.

She kicked off her heels with a quiet sigh and padded toward the kitchen, the soft thud of her footsteps muffled against the hardwood floors. A warm glow from the floor lamp spilled golden light across her shoulders, casting long, delicate shadows that danced with her every movement.

Hudson paused in the entryway, watching her. Taking her in.

She moved through the space with an unconscious grace, the kind that came from belonging. From comfort. From being wholly herself. There was something magnetic in it—something he doubted she even realised she possessed.

"My feet are killing me," she muttered, half to herself.

Hudson smiled, loosening his tie. "Fashion demands sacrifices, apparently."

She glanced back with a faint smirk but didn't reply. Instead, she moved into the kitchen. "Coffee?"

"Please."

She poured two cups, the clink of mugs and gentle pour of liquid filling the silence between them. When she handed him one, their fingers brushed. Neither of them commented.

They settled on the couch, side by side but not quite touching. The silence lingered, dense but not uncomfortable. They sipped slowly, the bitter warmth grounding them.

Then Hudson set his cup down and looked at her.

"I want you back, Renee."

Her breath hitched just slightly.

"I know I said and did some really stupid things," he continued, voice low but steady. "But I was scared. I felt like I was failing you—and I didn't know how to fix it. I thought keeping some distance, not dragging you into my mess, was protecting you. Protecting us."

He shook his head, eyes never leaving hers.

"I see now... all I really did was shut you out. And that's what broke us."

Her fingers tightened around her mug, but she didn't speak. Not yet.

So, he kept going—softly, honestly.

"I miss you. Not just the idea of you. You. Every day."

Her fingers tightened slightly around the mug, but she said nothing.

The silence stretched—not cold, not angry, but thick with emotion. With everything she might say, and everything she wasn't ready to.

Hudson didn't rush her. Didn't reach for her. He just sat there, his heart thudding hard in his chest, watching the way her gaze dropped to the coffee in her hands. The way her bottom lip trembled for just a second before she pressed it into a firm line.

A minute passed. Maybe two. Long enough for the ache in his chest to sharpen into something raw and exposed.

But still, he waited.

Because for once, Hudson Waterford wasn't trying to control the outcome.

He was just… here. Honest. Open.

Renee finally exhaled—a long, quiet breath that trembled at the edges. She set her mug on the table and leaned back against the couch cushions, eyes still focused straight ahead.

And then, softly—barely louder than a whisper—she said, "I didn't stop loving you, you know."

Her voice cracked on the last word.

Hudson closed his eyes for a heartbeat.

Then he turned to her. "Say that again."

She looked at him then—really looked at him. Her eyes were glassy, full of all the feelings she'd kept buried. Vulnerable. Strong. Shining.

"I never stopped," she said softly. "I couldn't. I tried."

Hudson's breath hitched. His voice came low, thick. "I didn't realise how much I loved you until you were gone."

A beat passed.

She held his gaze, and when she spoke again, her voice trembled. "I'm scared you won't be there when it matters. That when it counts—when I need you—you'll shut down again. Disappear."

His jaw tightened, and for once, there was no defence. Just truth.

"I was scared," he admitted. "Scared of failing you. Of not being enough. But I'm not going to make the same mistakes, Renee. I love you. And now—I know what that means. I know what you mean to me. I should have known from the start, but I was too blind to see it."

He leaned in, his fingers brushing against hers on the couch.

"But I see it now. I see you. And I'm not walking away. I need you to trust me." His voice was raw, steady. "I know I haven't given you much reason to—but I won't fail you again. Not ever."

For a long beat, she didn't move.

Then slowly, she turned her hand over in his, palm to palm. The contact was simple, but it felt like everything.

He held it—just held it—for a moment longer. Then gently, deliberately, he tugged her closer.

She didn't resist. She came to him like a tide returning to shore.

His forehead touched hers, his breath warm between them.

"I want you back," he whispered.

Her voice was a thread of air. "I want to believe you."

And then his lips met hers.

Softly at first—sweet, searching, reverent. Like a man trying to remember something precious. Like he'd waited years just to taste this moment.

She melted into him, one hand lifting to rest lightly against his chest, and the ache between them broke open.

The kiss deepened. Grew urgent.

He slipped his arm around her waist and pulled her onto his lap, the motion fluid, instinctive. She settled against him without hesitation, her fingers tangling in his hair as their mouths met again and again—slow, then hungry, then something almost desperate.

The kind of kiss that says I missed you.

The kind that says I'm still yours.

The kind that leaves no space for doubt—only feeling. Only heat. Only them.

Chapter Twelve

Hudson's arms wrapped tightly around her, anchoring her to him as their mouths moved together with growing urgency. The world beyond her apartment dissolved—no boardrooms, no regrets—only the shared warmth of breath and skin, of two people trying to find their way back.

His hands moved carefully, reverently, exploring the curves of her silk-draped body with a restraint that only deepened the intensity between them. Every glide of his fingers spoke of memory and wonder, of rediscovery. He touched her like she was both sacred and familiar.

And Renee… she leaned into it.

She tilted her face to his, breath shallow and eyes half-lidded with something raw and tender. "Hudson," she whispered, her voice trembling, "touch me."

Something in his chest cracked wide open.

His hand slid up slowly, gently cupping her breast through the silk. He was cautious—watching her, reading every breath, every shift of her body—but she didn't pull away. She sighed instead, soft and wanting, her lips parting on a quiet moan that only made his name fall from her lips again.

"Renee," he breathed, rough and devoted.

The sound of it—her name in that low, husky tone—sent a shiver skittering down her spine. She arched into his touch, pressing more firmly into his palm, her desire no longer hidden, no longer guarded.

Hudson's hand slid slowly along her thigh, the silk of her dress bunching beneath his fingers as he revealed her inch by aching inch.

His hand slipped beneath the fabric, gliding up the smooth curve of her leg. He moved with excruciating patience, savouring the heat of her skin, the shape of her hip, the sharp hitch in her breath when his fingers brushed the inside of her thigh.

"Please…" she whispered, soft but desperate, her voice trembling with need. "Yes."

She could feel him—hard and straining—through the fabric of his slacks, the weight and pressure of him pressing into her leg. The knowledge of how much he wanted her made her pulse race. It made her ache deeper. Every nerve was lit with the same aching hunger. Her body trembled, not from fear, but from the sheer intensity of wanting him.

Of still wanting this. Wanting him.

Hudson stilled, his hand resting against her thigh as his gaze lifted to hers.

"Are you sure?" he asked, voice tight with restraint. "Because if we do this… I need to know it's not out of hope. You have to want this—for you. You have to want me."

Renee's breath caught, her eyes searching his, her fingers curling into the front of his shirt like she needed something to hold on to.

"I do," she whispered, voice trembling. "I want you."

His expression shifted—heat giving way to something tender, something deeper.

"I want you too," he groaned, his forehead resting briefly against hers.

Emotion flickered across his face—raw, unguarded. He looked at her like he was holding something rare and fragile in his hands. He exhaled a breath that felt like it came from the centre of him.

"You tell me to stop," he said gently, brushing the back of his fingers against her cheek. "At any moment, Renee. I mean it."

But she didn't want him to stop.

Instead, she pulled him down into another kiss—slow, certain, full of unspoken trust.

Hudson scooped her into his arms, lifting her with effortless strength, and carried her to the bedroom. He set her gently on her feet beside the bed, his hands lingering at her waist.

He kissed her again, slower now, with the reverence of a man touching something sacred. Every stroke of his fingers, every graze of his lips, was a question she answered with the soft curve of her body into his, a sigh, a whispered yes.

He peeled the dress from her shoulders one inch at a time, watching her, giving her space. His eyes never left hers.

When the fabric fell to the floor, pooling at her feet, Hudson looked at her like she was made of light and wonder—like this moment was something he'd never forget.

"You're so beautiful," he said, the words slipping out rough and quiet, like they'd been torn from somewhere deep.

He hadn't meant to say it. But he meant it—every word.

Her skin warmed beneath his gaze, but she didn't turn away. Not this time. Not with him.

When he touched her again, there was no urgency—only reverence. A slow, deliberate exploration of skin and sensation, of breath and heartbeat. He laid her gently on the bed, as if afraid she might disappear.

He stripped off his clothes in a swift motion, but when he returned to her, his movements slowed again—his body following the curve of hers like he was memorising her with every inch of himself.

The heat between them built steadily, but so did something deeper. Trust. Emotion. A silent understanding that this wasn't just about desire—it was about love. Unspoken, yes, but present in every breath, every look, every touch.

His hands roamed her body with patient care, achingly gentle in their exploration. When his fingers brushed her breasts, she groaned, arching into the touch as his thumb circled her nipple, teasing it to a hardened peak. Then his mouth followed, lips closing around her with warmth and hunger. He licked and sucked until she was breathing in broken gasps, her fingers tangling in his hair.

He kissed his way down her body—slowly, like each inch of her deserved its own moment—until he reached the centre of her. When his tongue slid through her slick folds, Renee cried out, her hips lifting, her hands tightening in his hair like it was the only thing tethering her to the earth.

"God, Renee..." Hudson groaned against her, his voice rough with awe and hunger.

He licked her with a devastating mix of tenderness and skill, his mouth worshipping her until she was writhing, moaning his name— "Hudson!"—as she came undone, the orgasm crashing over her in waves of pleasure so intense it stole her breath.

He didn't stop until the last tremor faded. Only then did he rise, sliding up her body with soft kisses along her skin, his hands gentle on her hips. He settled over her, his weight supported by trembling arms, his breath ragged.

When he entered her, it was with exquisite care—his body shaking with restraint, every movement cautious. Her fingers clutched his shoulders; her eyes locked on his.

It hurt—just a little. A brief sting, sharp but fleeting. But it was nothing compared to the way he looked at her, held her, moved inside her like she was something precious.

He paused, letting her adjust, giving her time. Letting her lead.

"You feel... incredible," he whispered, voice hoarse, forehead pressed to hers.

They began to move together slowly, tentatively—each movement a question, each answer given in soft moans and whispered names. There was no urgency. Only connection. Only them.

Renee clung to him, overwhelmed not just by sensation—but by feeling. The fullness of him. The closeness. The way her body opened for him and her heart followed.

Because it wasn't just the physical—it was Hudson. With her. In her. Real.

Her chest ached with unsaid love, too fragile to speak but burning in her gaze, in her touch, in every whispered breath.

"Hudson…" she breathed again.

He kissed her like he heard it all—like he felt it too.

She shattered again, the pleasure ripping through her with breathtaking intensity—like coming undone and becoming whole all at once. Hudson followed with a low, primal groan, his release wracking through him as he buried his face in her neck, his body trembling with the force of it.

When his breathing finally steadied, he shifted carefully, rolling onto his back and bringing her with him. She curled against his chest, her cheek resting over his heart as his arms wrapped around her protectively—possessively. Like she belonged there.

Soon, her breathing slowed. She drifted to sleep, a faint, contented smile curving her lips.

Hudson stayed wide awake, staring at the ceiling, his hand brushing gently along her bare back, barely breathing. Six months married to her, and he'd never touched her like this. Was he Insane.

It felt insane now. Impossible.

No one had ever made him feel the way Renee did. No one had slipped past his defences so effortlessly—softly, quietly, completely—until she was part of him in ways he hadn't even noticed happening.

And now that he knew, he also knew this: he would never be the same again.

They woke just before dawn, the early light painting the room in soft gold. When he reached for her, she came to him without hesitation—no words, just a shared understanding in the silence between them.

And once more, they came together.

This time was slower, deeper—a devout echo of the night before. Not driven by urgency, but by need. Not just for touch, but for closeness. For connection. For each other.

The soft light of morning filtered through the curtains, casting golden streaks across the sheets. Hudson stirred first, his arm still wrapped around Renee's waist. Her bare skin was warm against his, her breathing even, peaceful. For a moment, he just lay there—

watching her, memorising the curve of her lips, the flutter of her lashes, the way she looked in the quiet after everything had changed.

When she stirred and turned to face him, her sleepy eyes met his, and something unspoken passed between them—soft, tentative, real.

Neither of them said a word.

Instead, he leaned in and kissed her gently. She responded, her hand sliding to his chest. What began as tenderness became heat again, a slow burning need that pulled them from the bed and into the bathroom, limbs tangled, laughter low and breathless.

The shower was warm and misty, steam curling around them like a cocoon. Water cascaded over their bodies as they moved together—not hurried, but slow and intimate, each touch deliberate, each kiss deep and lingering.

His hands explored her slick, glistening skin with reverence, mapping every familiar curve as if rediscovering her for the first time. He slid his hands to the backs of her thighs and lifted her effortlessly, her legs wrapping around him in a fluid, instinctive motion.

Her fingers tangled in his damp hair, then slid to the nape of his neck as he pressed her gently against the cool tile. The contrast of heat and chill made her shiver—but it was his touch, his presence, that made her tremble.

Their mouths met again—hungry, consuming, tender.

When he finally entered her, it was with a low, ragged groan, his eyes locked on hers like she was the only thing anchoring him. It felt like everything had led to this—this moment of complete surrender, of love laid bare between them.

Like he couldn't believe she was his.

And she was—at least for this moment.

They made love again, wrapped in steam and silence and whispered names. And when it was over, he held her beneath the water, her head resting on his chest, both of them breathing in sync.

Later, wrapped in robes and barefoot, they made breakfast together—eggs, toast, fruit. It was domestic, easy. Renee sat on the counter, sipping coffee while Hudson cooked, stealing glances at her like he couldn't believe she was still here. She smiled at him once, a small, private smile that felt like sunlight. But beneath it, she was turning something over inside her.

After they ate, she set her cup down and looked at him with clear, searching eyes.

"Hudson," she said quietly.

He turned, instantly alert.

"I meant what I said last night. I don't regret it. Not any of it." She swallowed, her fingers curling around the edge of the table. "But I still need time."

His expression tightened. "Time?"

She nodded slowly. "To be sure. To trust that this version of you—the one who looks at me like I matter, like I'm not just some responsibility or... obligation—won't disappear. I need to know you won't let me down again."

He didn't speak for a moment, jaw tensing, hurt flickering behind his eyes. But then he stepped closer, his voice low and rough.

"I don't like it," he admitted. "I want you now. I want us now." He cupped her face in both hands, gently, reverently. "But if time is what you need, I'll give it to you."

Then, after a breath, his voice softened further. "Just know this—I can't let you go again, Renee. You and I... we belong together. Whether you're ready to believe it or not, I already know it's true."

Her eyes shimmered, not with tears but with the weight of everything unsaid.

"I just need to be sure," she whispered.

He brushed his thumb along her cheek, then leaned in and kissed her forehead.

"Then I'll spend every day making sure you are."

The days passed quietly, each one folding into the next with a strange sense of stillness. Hudson had returned to his apartment, giving Renee the space she needed—to hopefully gain clarity. But even with the space, Hudson hadn't disappeared.

He didn't crowd her. He didn't show up uninvited or push her for more than she could give. Instead, he did exactly what he'd said he would: he showed up in the little ways.

Every morning, just after sunrise, her phone would buzz with his call.

"Good morning, beautiful," he'd say, his voice still rough from sleep. "I just wanted to hear your voice. I love you."

It was never a long call. Sometimes she was still in bed, sometimes halfway through her first coffee. But no matter what, she always answered. And every time she hung up, her chest ached a little more—not with pain, but with the unfamiliar weight of hope.

Each night, just before ten, her phone lit up with a message.

Goodnight, Renee. I love you. Sweet dreams.

Simple. Uncomplicated. But steady. Every single night.

And slowly, the walls she'd built—stone by careful stone—began to feel less like protection and more like a prison.

She hadn't expected him to mean it when he said he'd wait. She hadn't expected him to be patient. To be kind. To love her in a way that didn't demand anything in return.

But he was. And he did.

Renee found herself thinking about him at odd times—in the grocery store when she passed his favourite coffee, in the evening when she heard a song that reminded her of the way he'd looked at her that morning in the shower, that morning over breakfast. She caught herself smiling at her phone, rereading his messages, hearing his voice echoing in her head.

She hadn't told him yet. Not that she was softening. Not that the doubt was slowly being replaced by something quieter, warmer.

But maybe… just maybe… he had changed.

And maybe, just maybe, he really did love her.

On Thursday afternoon, a soft knock at the door pulled Renee's attention from her laptop.

"Come in," she called, expecting her assistant—or maybe the delivery she was waiting on.

But when the door opened and Elias stepped inside, her breath caught just a little.

He smiled in that familiar, warm way—the kind that had always made her feel safe. "Hey. I was in the neighbourhood and thought I'd stop by."

She stood, smoothing her hands over her skirt more out of nerves than necessity. "Elias. I wasn't expecting you."

"I know," he said, his tone gentle as he slipped his hands into his pockets. "But if I didn't come, I think I'd always wonder."

She nodded slowly, then gestured toward the chairs. "Do you want to sit?"

He shook his head. "No need. I won't stay long."

A quiet pause settled between them before she spoke. "I should tell you… Hudson and I are trying again. We're seeing where it goes."

For a split second, something flickered in Elias's eyes—disappointment, maybe—but he recovered quickly, offering a soft, knowing smile.

"I figured," he said. "Even when you tried not to talk about him, it was obvious he had your heart."

Renee lowered her gaze. "I never wanted to lead you on."

"You didn't." His voice was kind, steady. "You were honest with me from the beginning. You were just trying to figure out what you needed. There's nothing wrong with that."

She looked up and met his eyes. "You're a good man, Elias."

He smiled, though this one was tinged with goodbye. "And you're a remarkable woman. I hope Hudson knows what he has."

He turned to leave, but as he reached for the door, it opened—and Hudson stood there, clearly not expecting the scene in front of him.

"Dr. Chen," Hudson said, eyes narrowing just slightly. "Didn't expect to see you here."

"Neither did I," Elias replied, extending his hand without hesitation. "But I'm glad I did."

There was a beat of silence—a brief, electric second—before Hudson shook his hand.

"You're a lucky man," Elias said, holding Hudson's gaze with quiet sincerity.

Hudson didn't miss a beat. "I know."

Elias gave Renee one last look—respectful, final—and stepped past Hudson, disappearing down the hall, the sound of his footsteps fading behind him.

Hudson closed the door with a soft click, then turned to her, one brow raised.

"You told him."

"I did," she said, nodding. "I thought he deserved to hear it from me."

He stepped closer, taking her hand in his. "Thank you for that."

She gave a small, wry smile. "Don't thank me yet."

"I will," he murmured, brushing a kiss across her knuckles. "Eventually."

She tilted her head. "What brings you by?"

Hudson exhaled and gave a crooked smile. "I'm going out of my mind. Can I see you this weekend?"

“Not tomorrow,” she said with a sigh. “I'll be working late on the Worthington contracts.”

“Saturday?”

“I'd like that.”

He stepped closer, pulling her gently into his arms, and kissed her—slow and sure, as if reminding them both exactly where they stood.

Chapter Thirteen

It was nine thirty, the office was quiet, save for the faint hum of her desk lamp and the steady clack of Renee's keyboard. Most of the building had emptied hours ago, the city outside dark and glittering, casting a soft glow through the floor-to-ceiling windows.

She paused, stretching her fingers and rolling her shoulders. A smile tugged at the corner of her lips as her thoughts drifted to earlier in the evening—Hudson showing up at her office door with a crooked smile and two cups of coffee.

Just to say goodnight.

No pressure. No demands. Just him. Gentle. Intentional.

"I'll let you get back to it," he'd said, brushing a kiss to her forehead before leaving. "But I can't wait to see you tomorrow."

He'd looked at her like he meant it, like he really was looking forward to simply being with her. Not as part of some obligation or plan, but as a man who was falling—and maybe already fallen—in love.

Her chest warmed at the memory.

She turned back to her laptop, determined to wrap up the Worthington contract notes before midnight. She was deep into the financial projections when something flickered in the corner of her eye.

She glanced down.

A thin curl of smoke was drifting under the door to her office.

Renee blinked, confused.

Was that…?

She stood slowly, heart beginning to thump harder. There were no alarms blaring. No flashing lights. No automated voice over the intercom telling her to evacuate.

But that was definitely smoke.

She crossed the room cautiously, grabbing her phone from the desk on instinct. Her heels echoed lightly against the polished wood floor as she approached the door. The air had shifted. Heavier. Thicker.

She crouched slightly, reaching toward the thin gap beneath the doorframe—and recoiled immediately.

The smoke was warm.

"Okay, what the hell…" she murmured, stepping back, pulse spiking now.

Still no alarms. No sprinklers. Nothing.

She dialled building security with one hand and reached for her purse with the other, just as another, darker plume began to curl in under the door—thicker this time.

The call rang. Once. Twice. Then straight to voicemail.

That was not right.

She hung up, heart pounding, and moved to grab her coat, glancing again at the door.

A sudden, muffled thud from the hallway made her flinch.

Then silence.

Her fingers fumbled over her phone, hands trembling as she tapped Hudson's name.

It rang once, twice—

"Renee?" His voice came through, light and laughing, like he'd just heard something funny. He must still be with Marcus.

"There's smoke in the building," she said, urgency tightening her voice. "It's coming under my office door. There's no alarm, no announcements—security isn't answering."

Silence on the other end for half a heartbeat.

Then, sharp and alert: "Where exactly are you?"

"My office. 18th floor."

"I'm calling 911," he said immediately. "Don't open that door. Go to the window. Stay low if the smoke gets thicker. I'm coming."

"Hudson—"

"Stay on the line with me," he cut in, voice sharp now, all laughter gone. "I'm on my way."

As she backed toward the windows, trying to keep her breath steady, her eyes swept the room.

And for the first time, the silence didn't feel peaceful anymore.

It felt wrong.

Something wasn't just off—it was deliberate.

And suddenly, she wasn't just afraid of fire.

She was afraid of why no one else seemed to know it had started.

The phone was still pressed to his ear as he grabbed his keys off the table, striding toward the elevator with Marcus trailing behind him.

"What's going on?" Marcus asked, his easy smile fading the second he saw Hudson's face.

"There's smoke in her office," Hudson said tightly. "No alarms. No security response."

Marcus blinked, confusion flashing across his face. "That doesn't make any sense—"

"I know," Hudson snapped, already striding toward the elevator. His voice dropped to a mutter, more instinct than thought. "Something's wrong. I can feel it."

He shoved through the lobby doors; the phone still clutched in a white-knuckled grip.

"Marcus—call 911," he barked without looking back. "Eighteenth floor, east side. Tell them there's smoke and no alarms."

Marcus didn't hesitate. He was already pulling out his phone, his usual calm replaced by grim focus.

"Got it," he said, dialling fast. "Go. I'll handle this."

"Renee, talk to me," he said, breathless now. "What can you see?"

There was a pause on the line. A short, shuddering inhale.

"It's getting thicker," she said quietly. "And I still don't hear anyone else."

His chest constricted. Every instinct in him screamed that this wasn't just a malfunction or an isolated fire.

This was intentional.

And whoever had started it… hadn't planned for her to make it out.

"Hang on," he said, teeth clenched as he slid behind the wheel. "I'm coming. Just hold on, Renee. I'm coming for you."

The smoke was thicker now, curling under the door in slow, sinister tendrils. It crept along the floor and began to climb the walls, painting everything in a ghostly haze.

Renee coughed, backing away until the backs of her knees hit her desk. She dropped to her knees, remembering from somewhere—school, maybe—that the air was cleaner down low. But it didn't help much. Her eyes were burning, her throat raw.

"Come on, come on," she whispered, clutching the phone like it was a lifeline. Hudson was still on the line, his voice low and urgent in her ear, telling her to hold on, that he was almost there.

But the fear was growing—sharp and fast, like a tide rising in her chest.

No alarms. No voices in the hallway. No footsteps. Just smoke and silence.

Her heart thudded, frantic. This wasn't an accident. It didn't feel like an accident. It felt like something else—calculated. Targeted.

And she was alone.

She pressed a hand over her mouth to muffle a sob, her eyes darting around the office. No sprinklers. No water. The window wouldn't open—it was sealed shut like every damn window in this building. She thought about breaking it, but the only thing near enough to throw was a paperweight that wouldn't scratch tempered glass.

A bitter wave of helplessness surged in her chest.

She tried the door once more, yanking hard.

Still locked. Still no answer from security. Still nothing.

The smoke was creeping closer now, hungry, and thick. Her chest burned with each breath, her vision blurring at the edges.

Her knees gave out.

She sank to the floor, one arm pressed tightly over her mouth, the other still clutching her phone.

"H-Hudson," she choked out, her voice barely more than a whisper. "I don't think I'm getting out."

"Don't say that," he snapped, panic bleeding into his voice. "You are getting out, Renee. I'm almost there. Just… just hang on. Please."

She tried to answer, but a harsh coughing fit stole her breath. Her head drooped to rest against her knees, dizziness creeping in like a shadow.

She'd never been this scared before. Not when her grandfather died. Not even when she had walked away from Hudson.

This was different. Cold. Final.

And beneath the fear, one desperate thought kept looping like a prayer: Please let me see him again.

Another cough racked her body, harsher this time. Her voice came out ragged but clear.

"Hudson… I love you."

"No, don't say that," he pleaded, voice thick with urgency. "You're going to be okay. I'm coming for you."

"I'm sorry…" She started to sway, dizziness overwhelming her.

"Renee? Renee! Don't—stay with me! Please!"

Hudson threw his car door open, barely pausing to park properly. He sprinted toward the building, heart hammering in his chest. Inside, he dashed to the elevator and slammed the button for the 18th floor.

When the doors slid open, a wall of smoke hit him instantly—thick, acrid, burning his lungs before he even moved.

His eyes locked on the flames, licking fiercely at the front of her office door—only her door. No other fires.

Every step up the hall felt like thunder in his chest, but he didn't falter.

Firefighters stormed in just behind him, radios crackling, boots thundering against the floor. But Hudson barely registered them. He pushed forward, eyes wild with panic and purpose.

He had to find her.

"Renee!" he shouted, his voice cracking under the weight of desperation. "Don't you give up—do you hear me? You have to marry me again. I love you. Please, God…"

Only silence answered. No cough. No cry. Just a stillness so heavy, it crushed the air from his lungs.

No. No. She was in there. She had to be.

With a strangled cry, Hudson hurled his phone to the floor and tore the fire extinguisher from the wall.

Smoke stung his eyes, heat blistered the air, but he didn't hesitate. The extinguisher hissed violently as he battled the flames devouring her door.

Firefighters closed in, barking instructions, moving with precision—but Hudson didn't move aside. Not for anyone.

He wasn't leaving without her.

As the fire finally gave way, he tossed the extinguisher aside and lunged for the door handle. The metal seared his palm, and he bit back a cry of pain—but didn't stop. He grabbed the handle again, wrenched it. It was locked.

He didn't care.

He slammed his shoulder into it once. Twice. A third time.

"Renee!" he roared. "I'm here! I'm not leaving you!"

His burnt hand throbbed, smoke clouded his vision—but nothing could stop him now.

Not when the woman he loved was on the other side.

With a guttural roar, Hudson slammed his shoulder into the door again. The frame groaned but held. He stepped back, sucked in a scorched breath, then charged.

This time, the lock gave way with a splintering crack.

The door burst open, releasing a wave of dense, choking smoke. He stumbled in, coughing, eyes scanning wildly.

And then he saw her.

Renee was collapsed on the far end of the room near the window, her body crumpled like a rag doll, one arm curled around herself, the other limp at her side. Her phone was still clutched in her hand. Her face was pale beneath the smudges of soot. She wasn't moving.

"Renee!" he choked, stumbling through the haze toward her. "No, no, no—"

He dropped to his knees beside her, gathering her into his arms, cradling her head to his chest. Her body was terrifyingly still.

"Come on, sweetheart, don't do this to me," he whispered, brushing the hair from her face with shaking fingers. "Please... breathe. Just breathe..."

The firefighters burst into the room behind him, barking commands and scanning for danger—but Hudson didn't move. Didn't flinch. He clutched Renee to his chest like she was the only thing keeping him breathing.

He wasn't leaving without her. Not now. Not ever.

Cradling her carefully, he rose to his feet and carried her through the smoke-thick hallway and out into the clearer air of the foyer. His eyes never left her face, not even when his vision blurred from pain and exhaustion.

The paramedics rushed in, and only then—only when they surrounded her with urgent hands and medical equipment—did Hudson finally let go.

Barely.

He hovered at her side, muscles tense, eyes locked on her pale face as they eased her onto a stretcher. One of them fitted an oxygen mask over her mouth and nose. Another checked her pulse.

"Pulse is faint but present," someone said. "We've got her. Let's move."

Hudson nodded stiffly, but he didn't take a step back.

Couldn't.

Because until Renee opened her eyes, nothing felt certain. Not even hope.

The paramedics wheeled her into the elevator, oxygen mask still pressed to her face, vitals being shouted between them. One of them glanced at Hudson's hand—raw, blistered, bleeding.

"You're burned," the paramedic said as they moved, already reaching for supplies. Hudson barely heard him.

"I'm fine," he muttered, eyes locked on Renee. "Just take care of her."

But once inside the ambulance, there was no escaping the pain in his hand. The paramedic dressed the burn quickly, efficiently, but Hudson didn't even flinch. His gaze stayed glued to Renee, every bump in the road making his jaw clench tighter.

She hadn't stirred. Not once.

When they reached the hospital, the ER doors flew open. A trauma team was waiting. They pulled the stretcher out with swift precision, voices calling out vitals and administering care before Hudson could even step down from the vehicle.

He moved to follow, but a nurse intercepted him. "Sir—your hand. We need to treat it properly."

"I said I'm fine—"

"She wouldn't want you losing it because you were too stubborn to get help," the nurse said gently, guiding him toward a side area. "Let us take care of you. Just for a minute."

Reluctantly, Hudson allowed it. He sat still while they cleaned, numbed, and dressed the angry red burns, every second away from Renee stretching like an eternity.

The moment they were done, he was back on his feet, pacing the waiting room, heart hammering against his ribs.

And then—finally—a doctor stepped into the waiting room. She was petite, mid-forties, with a calm expression and soot smudged on her scrubs.

"Hudson Waterford?"

He stood so fast the chair behind him scraped against the floor. "Yes. Is she okay?"

The doctor gave a tired, reassuring smile. "I'm Dr. Lin. Renee is stable. She has mild burns and smoke inhalation, but we got to her in time. She's breathing on her own now. She's going to be okay."

Hudson's knees nearly gave out.

He exhaled a breath he hadn't realised he'd been holding. A shaky, broken sound escaped him—half relief, half prayer.

"Can I see her?"

The doctor nodded. "She's asking for you."

Chapter Fourteen

The hospital hallway was quiet, save for the soft hum of machines and the distant murmur of nurses at the station. Hudson walked slowly, each step weighted with emotion. His hand, freshly bandaged and aching, hung at his side, but he barely felt it.

He reached the door and paused, gripping the frame like he needed it to stay upright. For a moment, he just looked at her.

Renee lay in the hospital bed, pale but alive. The oxygen mask had been removed, a nasal cannula in its place. Her hair was a little singed at the ends, and there was a faint bruise on her forehead, but her chest rose and fell in soft, steady breaths.

His heart clenched.

He stepped inside.

Her eyes fluttered open at the sound of his footsteps, and when they met his, something in Hudson shattered.

"Hey," her voice was weak, raspy, but it was hers.

He sank into the chair beside her bed, brushing a strand of hair from her face, his hand trembling. "You scared the hell out of me."

"You're one to talk," Renee whispered, her voice raspy but teasing. Her gaze dropped to his bandaged hand, her smile faltering. "You ran into a burning building."

Hudson followed her eyes, then shrugged like it was nothing. "I'd do it again," he said softly. "A thousand times, if it meant getting to you. You're all that matters, Renee."

Tears welled in her eyes again, glistening against the soot on her lashes. "I thought... I wasn't going to see you again."

His breath hitched. He leaned in slowly, resting his forehead gently against hers, careful not to jostle the oxygen tube or brush against the tender skin near her temple.

"You almost didn't," he whispered. "And I—I can't lose you, Renee. I need you to hear this, even if you're not ready to say anything back."

She nodded once, her fingers brushing lightly over his uninjured hand.

"I'm listening."

"I love you," he said softly. "Not because of the company or the arrangement or anything else. Just you. The way you fight, the way you care, the way you never gave up on people, even when we didn't deserve it."

Tears slipped down her cheeks. "You mean it?"

"With everything I am." He reached for her hand, gently lacing their fingers together. "So please. Get better. Come home. And when you're ready… marry me again."

Her lips trembled, a single laugh breaking through her tears. "You're not proposing to me in a hospital room, are you?"

His smile returned—crooked, boyish, and full of love. "It's not how I planned it, but I figured I shouldn't wait."

She gave his hand a gentle squeeze, her voice still soft but sure. "Okay. Yes. Just… maybe give me a few days before we walk down the aisle."

Hudson let out a shaky laugh and lifted her hand to his lips, pressing a kiss to her knuckles. "Take all the time you need," he said, his voice rough with emotion. "I'm not going anywhere."

He stayed with her a while longer, watching her drift into a peaceful sleep, soothed by the steady rhythm of the heart monitor and the soft rise and fall of her chest. Eventually, a nurse gently urged him to get some rest. With great reluctance, he left—his hand lingering on hers just a moment longer before he slipped out into the hall.

The next morning, sunlight filtered through the hospital window, casting pale stripes across the crisp white sheets. Renee was sitting up when two uniformed officers stepped into her room, their expressions professional but concerned.

"Miss Fitzgerald," one began, flipping open a small notebook. "We're with the city's arson investigation unit. We have some updates about the fire in your office."

Renee tensed, setting her water cup aside. "Go ahead."

"The fire inspector confirmed it was arson," the officer said gravely. "Accelerants were used. And the building's sprinkler system had been deliberately disabled—wired to prevent them from activating. Whoever did this didn't just want to scare you. They wanted to trap you."

Renee's stomach turned. "Oh my God…"

"We need to ask—do you know anyone who might want to harm you? Anyone with a grudge? Personal or professional?"

She opened her mouth, but before she could answer, the door swung open.

Hudson stepped inside, his expression tight with concern. He glanced from the officers to Renee and immediately crossed the room.

"What's going on?" he asked, voice low and clipped as he reached for her hand.

The officer straightened, offering a measured nod. "Mr. Waterford. We were just updating Miss Fitzgerald. The fire was ruled arson. Accelerants were used, and the sprinkler system was tampered with. It appears someone deliberately disabled it to prevent it from responding."

Hudson's grip on Renee's hand tightened. "You're saying someone tried to kill her."

The second officer, a woman with sharp eyes and a calm demeanour, stepped forward. "We're not jumping to conclusions, sir. But the facts do indicate the fire was set with intent. Miss Fitzgerald could've died."

Hudson's jaw clenched. "She almost did."

The first officer turned back to Renee. "We need to ask, Miss Fitzgerald—do you have any enemies? Anyone who might want to hurt you, or hurt someone close to you through you?"

Renee's brow furrowed. "I… no. I mean, not that I know of. I've had disagreements with vendors and former employees over the years, but nothing remotely personal. No threats. No strange messages. Nothing."

"Any recent arguments?" the female officer asked. "Changes in business deals? Anything unusual at all?"

Renee glanced at Hudson, then back to the officers. "There was tension with one of our acquisition candidates—Worthington Tech. We passed on a merger a few weeks ago, and the CEO, Damian Worthington, wasn't thrilled. But it was strictly business. He was… pushy, but not dangerous."

Hudson's expression darkened. "I never liked him."

The officers exchanged a glance. "We'll look into him. Anyone else come to mind? A rival? A former employee who left on bad terms?"

Renee thought for a moment, the weight of the question pressing on her. "We had a facilities manager quit unexpectedly a few months ago. He was reprimanded after a security breach—nothing major, but he left angry. I can't even remember his last name. Just… Thomas?"

The officer jotted it down. "We'll find him."

Hudson's eyes hadn't left Renee. His voice was quiet, but tight with barely restrained emotion. "You said the sprinklers were disabled. That means someone planned this. They waited until she was alone."

"Yes," the officer replied grimly. "They knew the schedule, the security gaps, and how to bypass the alarm system. This wasn't random."

Hudson turned toward the window, jaw tight, then back to the officers. "I want a full security detail on her. Until you figure out who did this."

"We'll coordinate with building security and your private team," the officer assured him. "We're treating this as a high-priority investigation."

The officers handed Renee a card and a small list. "These are just a few follow-up questions we may have. If anything—or anyone—comes to mind, please call us. Day or night."

Renee nodded, fingers clutched around the card. "I will."

They thanked her and left, quietly promising to keep her updated.

As soon as the door closed, Hudson turned back to her, sinking into the chair by her side, his hand still wrapped around hers.

His voice was raw. "They planned it. Someone planned it, Renee. And if you hadn't called me when you did—" He stopped, swallowing hard. "I wouldn't have gotten to you in time."

"You did," she said gently, squeezing his hand. "You got to me."

Hudson's eyes shimmered, but he didn't look away. "And I swear to you—I'm going to find out who did this. I don't care what it takes. No one gets to hurt you and walk away."

For a long beat, neither of them spoke. The hum of machines filled the silence between heartbeats.

Then Renee spoke, her voice steady despite the weight in her chest.

"Hudson?"

"Yeah?"

"When they find out who did it… promise me something."

He leaned closer, brushing her knuckles with his lips. "Anything."

"Don't let anger turn you into someone you're not. We'll face it together. But I need you to come back to me whole."

His throat worked as he nodded, eyes locked on hers.

"I promise."

Hudson leaned in slowly, brushing his lips against Renee's—soft, reverent, as if still afraid she might vanish. Her eyes fluttered shut, her fingers tightening around his. The kiss was brief, but it held all the words they hadn't yet said aloud.

The door burst open.

"Renee!"

Vivian skidded to a stop just inside the room, her eyes widening at the sight of them— Renee pale but smiling, Hudson close beside her, lips just parting from hers.

She blinked. "Oh."

Renee flushed, her fingers still entwined with Hudson's.

Vivian hesitated only a second before hurrying forward and throwing her arms around Hudson. "Thank God, you saved her."

Hudson stiffened, surprised, then let out a shaky breath and hugged her back. "Marcus told you?"

"He called me this morning. I dropped everything." She pulled back, eyes brimming with emotion as she turned to Renee. "You scared the hell out of me."

Renee gave her a weak smile. "It scared the hell out of me."

Vivian leaned over and hugged her, careful not to disturb the IV line or the bandages. "Don't ever do that again."

"I'll try not to," Renee whispered.

Vivian turned back to Hudson. "You—you went in after her?"

He nodded quietly, the memory flashing behind his eyes. "I didn't think. I just had to get to her."

Vivian's voice broke. "You really love her."

He met her eyes. "Yeah. I do."

Vivian nodded slowly, a small, knowing smile tugging at her lips. "Good. Took you long enough."

She sat down on the other side of Renee's bed, her expression softening. "I'll let you have your moment again in a minute. I just needed to see her with my own eyes."

Renee laughed faintly, squeezing both their hands. "I'm glad you're here."

Hudson reached for the water cup and offered it to her. As she sipped, Vivian watched them with a protective yet satisfied gaze.

"I'll let Marcus know you're okay," Vivian said, already pulling out her phone. "He's been worried sick all night. He told me you called Hudson when you saw the smoke—he's been trying to reach him ever since, but apparently it keeps going to voicemail."

Hudson rubbed the back of his neck. "Yeah… my phone's still at the office."

Renee turned to him, brows knitting. "Why is it at the office?"

He shrugged, a small smile tugging at his lips. "I left it. I was a little… preoccupied."

Vivian arched an eyebrow. "Preoccupied, huh?" She waved her phone like a flag. "You two and your heart eyes—honestly. I love you both, but I can only take so much goggly-eyed nonsense before I start gagging."

Renee laughed softly, the sound raspy but warm. "Sorry. We'll try to tone down the near-death romance."

"Please do," Vivian said dryly, settling back in her chair with a teasing smirk. "Some of us are single and barely hanging on."

They all chuckled, the mood light for just a moment—until Renee's laughter gave way to a rough cough. She pressed a hand to her chest, wincing.

Vivian's smile softened with concern. "Still sore?"

Renee nodded. "Yeah. Breathing feels like sandpaper, but I'm okay."

Vivian hesitated, then glanced between them. "So… how did this even happen? I mean, what actually caused the fire?"

The question dropped like a stone in the room.

Hudson's expression darkened, the warmth draining from his features. He sat forward, voice low and tight. "It wasn't an accident. The fire department confirmed it this morning—it was arson. Set intentionally. Accelerant was used. And the sprinklers were disabled."

Vivian blinked. "Wait—what?"

"They think someone tried to kill her," Hudson said, his jaw clenched. "This wasn't random."

Vivian stared at him, stunned. "Oh my God…"

The weight of Hudson's words settled over them, suffocating the room in a thick, uneasy silence. The earlier laughter felt like a distant echo. Hudson reached for Renee's hand again, his grip gentle but steady—anchoring them both against the fear that had crept in like smoke under a door.

The door swung open, and Marcus stepped inside, slightly breathless.

"I was driving past when I got Vivian's text," he said, eyes scanning the room. Then he paused, his gaze sharpening as he caught the tension in their faces. "What happened? Is it that bad?"

Hudson stood slowly, his expression grim. "The police think someone tried to kill Renee."

Marcus froze. "What?"

"Arson," Hudson continued, his voice low but controlled. "Accelerant. Disabled sprinklers. It wasn't just a fire—it was a setup."

Marcus's brows furrowed, disbelief flashing across his face. Then his jaw tightened. "Jesus… Who would do something like that?"

"That's what they're trying to figure out," Hudson said, glancing toward Renee, his hand still wrapped around hers. "But whoever it was knew what they were doing."

Renee looked down, her voice barely above a whisper. "They didn't want me to make it out."

The words hung in the air like smoke, curling around them with cold finality. No one spoke for a long moment.

Eventually, they talked—quiet, uneasy theories passed between them—but no one could name a single person who might want Renee dead. Business rivals? Old grudges? It all felt too extreme. Too personal.

When visiting hours ended, Vivian and Marcus both leaned in to hug her tightly.

"Get better, okay?" Vivian said, kissing her cheek. "We've got way too much gossip to catch up on."

Marcus added, "And I want answers—after rest, of course." He gave her a gentle smile, then turned to Hudson. "You did good, man."

Hudson gave a grateful nod; his hand still curled protectively around Renee's.

After they left, the room grew quiet again. A few minutes later, the door opened, and Dr. Keller stepped inside.

"You're lucky," he said with a warm smile. "You're healing well. Barring any complications overnight, you'll be discharged in the morning."

"Thank you," Renee said, managing a tired smile.

As soon as the door closed behind him, Hudson turned to her. "You're not going back to your apartment."

Renee raised a brow. "Hudson—"

"I'm serious," he said gently, but firmly. "You're coming to the penthouse. Just until we know more. The security's better, and I'll sleep outside your door if I have to."

She opened her mouth to protest, but the look in his eyes stopped her—protective, earnest, and just a little bit afraid.

"I almost lost you," Hudson said quietly. "Please… let me keep you safe."

Her resolve melted under the weight of his words. After a moment, she nodded.

"Okay," she murmured. "But no sleeping outside the door."

He started to speak, but she added, softer still, "I'd rather have you in the bed with me."

Hudson's smile broke slowly across his face—full of love, relief, and something deeper.

He reached for her hand again, his voice soft and steady. "Deal."

And for the first time in days, the future didn't feel so far away.

Chapter Fifteen

The morning sun filtered through the blinds, casting soft golden light across the hospital room. Renee sat on the edge of the bed, dressed in a comfortable pair of leggings and an oversized cardigan, her hair brushed but still slightly damp from a gentle sponge bath administered by a kind nurse.

Hudson appeared in the doorway, a takeaway coffee in one hand, a small paper bag in the other. His suit jacket was slung over one arm, sleeves rolled up, his tie loosened like he'd only just remembered to throw it on.

"You ready, Mrs. Almost-Again-Waterford?" he teased, his voice soft but bright with relief.

Renee looked up, a smile tugging at her lips. "Do I look ready?"

He crossed the room in a few strides and leaned in to kiss her forehead, careful to avoid her healing bruise. "You look like the bravest woman I've ever seen."

Just then, Dr. Keller stepped inside, clipboard in hand and a friendly smile on his face. "Morning. How's our patient?"

"Sore, but ready to escape," Renee said, adjusting the sleeve of her cardigan.

Hudson chuckled. "That sounds like a yes."

Dr. Keller nodded approvingly, then looked at Hudson. "She's medically cleared, but I need you to keep a close eye on her. She shouldn't be working, answering emails, or lifting anything heavier than a coffee cup for at least a week. Rest is non-negotiable."

Hudson gave a crisp, almost military nod. "Got it. She'll rest."

"I'm in the room, you know," Renee muttered with a hint of dry amusement.

Dr. Keller smirked. "And I'm trusting him to be the enforcer." He handed Hudson a folder. "Instructions, prescriptions, and my personal cell if you have questions. No stress, no exertion, and no skipping meals."

Hudson took the folder and shook the doctor's hand. "Thank you—for everything."

With a final smile, Dr. Keller exited the room.

Hudson turned back to Renee. "You heard the man. Doctor's orders. No playing CFO, no climbing stairs, and absolutely no stubborn independence."

Renee arched a brow. "You're enjoying this a little too much."

He grinned. "Not even pretending to hide it."

She shook her head with a soft laugh. "Okay, fine. I'll be good. But I swear, if you try to spoon-feed me soup or tuck me in like a toddler—"

"Noted," he said, raising his hand in mock surrender. "But fair warning, there may be fuzzy socks involved."

She narrowed her eyes. "I don't wear fuzzy socks."

"You do now," he said with a wink, then offered his arm. "Shall we?"

She looped her arm through his and let him help her up slowly. "Where are we going? I assume not back to my apartment?"

He paused for a beat, then glanced down at her, his tone gentler. "Vivian dropped by last night after you fell asleep. Brought some of your clothes, toiletries, and a few things she thought you'd need."

Renee blinked. "She did?"

"She was halfway through reorganising my closet when I got back," Hudson said dryly. "Your things are in my room... but if you want to stay in the guest room. Just let me know."

A flicker of emotion passed across her face, too swift to name.

"And don't worry," he added, voice softer, "you can have space if you need it. Privacy, if you want it. But I meant what I said—I want you safe. And until we know more, the penthouse is the safest place you can be."

She looked up at him, lips parted in quiet gratitude. "Hudson..."

"I know," he murmured. "We'll figure the rest out later. Right now, you just need to heal."

She nodded, a lump rising in her throat. "Okay. Home it is."

"Home," he echoed, letting the word settle between them.

Then he guided her toward the door, matching her pace, his hand steady at her back.

Outside, a sleek black car waited at the curb, its windows tinted, the driver already holding the door open.

Hudson helped her inside, tucking the blanket over her lap and passing her the coffee from earlier. Once he slid in beside her, she leaned her head against his shoulder with a tired sigh.

The soft rustle of sheets and the filtered grey light of a cloudy morning filled the bedroom. Hudson stood at the edge of the bed, buttoning the cuffs of his crisp white shirt, his tie draped around his neck, forgotten for the moment.

In the centre of the rumpled king-sized bed, Renee lay curled under the covers, hair tousled, skin glowing with the aftershocks of a very satisfying morning. Her lips curled into a smug, sleepy smile as she watched him dress.

"You should call in sick," she murmured, stretching languidly against the pillows. "Or fire someone so you can stay in bed longer."

Hudson chuckled, shaking his head as he crossed to the dresser to retrieve his watch. "Tempting. But I have a board meeting at ten and a mountain of emails waiting."

Renee sighed dramatically. "Fine. Leave me here. Abandoned. Unloved."

Hudson turned, arching a brow. "You didn't seem unloved ten minutes ago."

She grinned shamelessly, tugging the comforter a little higher. "That's fair."

He walked back to the bed and leaned down; one hand braced on the mattress beside her. "You are not to get out of this bed today," he said firmly, his voice low and authoritative, but with a teasing edge.

She fluttered her lashes at him. "Only if I get rewarded when you get home."

His eyes darkened, and a slow, wicked smile tugged at his mouth. "Deal."

He dipped his head and kissed her—deep and lingering, his hand cupping her jaw, thumb brushing her cheek. When he finally pulled back, her eyes were half-lidded, her smile lazy and satisfied.

"I'll have someone bring you lunch around noon," he murmured. "And Vivian said she's stopping by later to harass you into doing nothing."

Renee groaned. "She'll bring magazines, won't she?"

"Probably ten."

He leaned in again, brushing his lips against her temple this time. "Rest. Heal. I'll be home before dinner."

She gave him a sleepy little salute. "Yes, boss."

As he walked to the door, she called out, "Hey, Hudson?"

He turned, hand on the doorframe. "Yeah?"

"I like our bed."

His expression softened. "Me too."

Then he was gone, and she let herself sink into the pillows, his scent still clinging to the sheets, her heart full and her body humming.

The elevator doors opened with a soft chime, and Hudson strode out, his expression sharp and focused. He adjusted the cuff of his suit jacket over the bandage on his hand, the memory of the fire—and Renee's unconscious form in his arms—still a vivid echo in his chest.

Ava Sinclair, his personal assistant, looked up from her desk the moment she heard him. A polished blonde with flawless makeup and a wardrobe that always hovered just on the edge of professional, she stood quickly, concern flickering across her carefully composed features.

Hudson barely paused, offering a curt nod. Even after six months, he still found himself missing Penny—his former assistant who had retired with grace and a tin of homemade cookies on her last day. Penny had been dependable, discreet, and unflinchingly loyal. She'd known how to anticipate his needs before he even voiced them, never once overstepping.

Ava… was different.

Capable, yes—but her energy was sharper, more calculated. Her attention, though meticulous, often felt a little too fixed on him.

He kept walking, pushing the thought aside.

"Hudson, we heard about Renee," she said, her voice soft but urgent. "Is she… alright?"

"Yes," he said with a nod, his tone clipped but sincere. "Thank God."

Her eyes dropped, narrowing slightly when she caught sight of the white gauze peeking from beneath his cuff. Without hesitation, she rounded her desk.

"You're hurt," she murmured, reaching for his hand before he could react. Her fingers closed around his wrist—cool, careful, and too familiar. She turned it slightly, inspecting the burn like it was something precious.

"It's nothing," Hudson said quickly, pulling back. Her touch lingered a beat too long, the warmth of her skin still ghosting against his as he withdrew.

There was something in her gaze—soft, almost reverent—but too focused. Too personal.

He gave a tight smile to mask his discomfort. "Just a burn. I've had worse shaving."

Ava's brow furrowed. "It was heroic. Still… you shouldn't be throwing yourself into fires. That kind of recklessness…"

She trailed off, biting her lip as if the emotion were too much to finish the thought. It wasn't grief—it was closer to frustration.

Hudson gave a dry chuckle and stepped around her, making for his office. "Wasn't exactly planned. I wasn't about to leave her in there."

She followed at a measured pace, stopping just at the threshold. "Of course. It's… admirable. Most people wouldn't risk that much."

He paused, hand on the door, glancing back.

"Thanks, Ava," he said, voice cool but polite. "Hold my calls for the next half hour, will you?"

She nodded, her smile small and oddly tender. "Of course. Let me know if you need anything."

He gave a faint nod and closed the door behind him.

Inside, silence greeted him. He leaned against the frame and stared at his bandaged hand. Heroic? No.

He hadn't been thinking about bravery or risk. He'd been thinking about her.

Because when you love someone, you don't hesitate. You run into fire.

Ten quiet minutes passed, filled only with the occasional sound of Hudson's fingers tapping against the glass of his desk. His thoughts were already drifting back to Renee— curled up in his bed, her hair wild on his pillow, a satisfied smile still haunting his memory.

His phone buzzed.

Ava's voice came over the speaker, "Hudson, Marcus Blackwell is here to see you."

He smirked, knowing Marcus never waited long when he had something on his mind.

He pressed the intercom. "Send him in."

The door swung open a moment later, and Marcus stepped in, closing it with a firm click behind him.

"When did she start calling you Hudson?" he asked without preamble, heading straight for one of the leather chairs opposite the desk.

Hudson leaned back, folding his arms. "Not sure. But it's... off. Too familiar. Makes my skin crawl a little."

Marcus arched a brow. "She's acting like you're dating, not drafting quarterly reports."

Hudson's jaw ticked. "We're not. And we never will be."

Marcus's expression didn't shift, but the gleam in his eye sharpened. "Just checking. She watches you like she's already picking out china patterns."

Hudson sat forward, voice clipped. "Don't start that rumour."

"I'm not the one acting like she's got your name monogrammed on her towels."

Hudson rubbed a hand over his jaw, irritation creeping in. "The last thing I need is Renee hearing any of this and thinking there's something going on. There isn't."

Marcus studied him for a beat, then nodded slowly. "You really don't want to mess this up."

Hudson's gaze drifted to the skyline beyond his office window, but in his mind, he saw only Renee—her smile, her fire, her trust hard-won and too precious to risk.

"No," he said quietly. "I don't."

Marcus leaned back in his chair. "Then you need to set boundaries. Because your assistant? She's not subtle."

Hudson let out a quiet groan. "Yeah. I've noticed. I've been trying to ignore it, hoping she'd get the message."

Marcus gave him a look. "You know better than that."

Hudson nodded. "You're right. I'll deal with it. But not today. Today I'm clearing my schedule and getting home to Renee."

Marcus stood, adjusting his jacket with a grin. "Smart man. Go remind her exactly who you come home to."

Hudson cracked a rare smile. "I intend to."

He paused at the door. "For the record, I like you better with Renee. She makes you... less of a jackass."

Hudson rolled his eyes. "Get out."

Marcus grinned. "Gladly."

The door shut behind him, and Hudson looked back down at his bandaged hand.

Less of a jackass, huh?

He could live with that.

Hudson moved efficiently through the day. After clearing out a full inbox of emails, he sat through a two-hour board meeting where his focus only occasionally drifted to the image of Renee curled up in his sheets that morning.

When the meeting turned to updates on department performance, he cleared his throat.

"I want to inform the board that Renee Fitzgerald will be out for the remainder of the week recovering from the incident."

A hush fell briefly over the room, followed by a murmur of concern.

"Is she alright?" one of the older board members asked.

"She's going to be fine," Hudson said with a reassuring nod. "She just needs rest."

"Well, please extend our wishes for a full and speedy recovery," another added, and the others nodded in agreement.

Hudson acknowledged their words with a brief nod, then smoothly moved on to the next topic on the agenda.

Later that afternoon, he strode into the HR department, knocking once before entering Rosa Collins's office. Rosa, sharp-eyed and seasoned, looked up from her screen.

"Hudson," she said with a warm smile. "Everything okay?"

"I need to talk about my assistant," he said, getting straight to the point.

Rosa leaned back in her chair. "Is there a problem?"

He hesitated only for a moment. "I think she has a bit of a crush."

Rosa's brows rose. "Ava?"

Hudson nodded once. "I want to nip it in the bud. Don't need those sorts of problems—especially not now."

"Good move," Rosa said with a knowing look. "I'll organise a transfer for her."

"She's good at what she does," Hudson added. "Efficient. Smart. So, find a position that suits her. But I'll need a new personal assistant by the end of the week."

Rosa was already making notes. "Understood. I'll prioritise it."

"Thanks," he said, turning toward the door.

"Oh—and Hudson?"

He glanced back.

"I'm glad Renee's okay."

Something shifted in his expression—just for a second. "Yeah," he said softly. "So am I."

Then he was gone, already thinking about getting home early and rewarding the woman who turned his penthouse into a place worth returning to.

The city lights glittered through the floor-to-ceiling windows of the penthouse as Hudson stepped through the elevator doors, loosened his tie, and set his briefcase down on the console table. The apartment was quiet, the kind of soft, contented stillness that made his shoulders immediately relax.

"Renee?" he called, his voice low but expectant.

A soft voice answered from the direction of the bedroom. "In here!"

He walked down the hall, smiling to himself. The bedroom door was cracked open, and he pushed it gently to find her sitting up against a pile of pillows, dressed in one of his button-down shirts—clearly raided from his closet again. Her hair was loose around her shoulders, her bare legs stretched out over the duvet.

"You look entirely too pleased with yourself," he said, leaning against the doorframe.

She grinned lazily. "I followed doctor's orders. I rested."

"Oh? All day?"

"Mostly." She patted the bed beside her. "But I was promised a reward for being good."

Hudson chuckled and walked over, perching on the edge of the mattress. "And what kind of reward are we talking about?"

She gave him a coy look. "The kind that starts with a kiss and ends with me breaking another one of your rules."

He leaned in, brushing a slow, teasing kiss across her lips. "I'm beginning to think you enjoy testing my boundaries."

She kissed him back, then whispered, "Only when I know you'll cross them with me."

Hudson exhaled, his hand sliding through her hair as he deepened the kiss. But after a long moment, he pulled back just enough to rest his forehead against hers.

"I had a talk with HR today," he murmured.

"Oh?"

"I'm getting a new assistant," Hudson said as he settled beside Renee on the bed, loosening his tie.

She tilted her head, eyes dancing with curiosity. "Oh? Why?"

"She was getting a bit too familiar," he replied, voice dry with a hint of annoyance. "A little handsy. A little Hudson this, Hudson that." He gave a wry smile, then met Renee's eyes. "I don't want anything—or anyone—complicating this. Us."

Her teasing expression softened into something far more tender. "Neither do I."

Hudson leaned in and kissed her gently, his fingers sliding along her jaw to cradle her face. When he pulled back, he kept his forehead pressed to hers, their breath mingling.

"Now…" he murmured, voice low and warm, "how can I possibly reward you for being such a good patient?"

Renee smiled, a slow, knowing curve of her lips. She shifted, lifting herself to straddle his lap, her knees settling on either side of him. With deliberate care, she began to unbutton her shirt—one button at a time—until the fabric slipped open and revealed bare skin beneath.

His breath caught.

"Oh," she whispered, voice laced with mischief and heat, "I can think of a few ways, Mr. Waterford…"

Hudson's hands found her waist, reverent and eager. "God help me," he murmured, eyes locked on hers, "but I'm already yours."

Hudson's hands slid beneath the open edges of her shirt, his palms warm against her bare skin. He took his time, tracing the soft curve of her waist, the dip of her spine, as if reacquainting himself with every inch of her.

"You drive me crazy," he whispered, his voice rough now, thick with feeling.

Renee leaned in and brushed her lips over his. "That's the idea," she murmured.

Her fingers slipped to the buttons of his shirt, undoing them with practiced ease. When she pushed it off his shoulders, she pressed a kiss to the centre of his chest, right over his heart, which thundered beneath her lips.

Hudson caught her chin and tilted her face back to his, searching her eyes. "I still can't believe I get to love you like this."

"You always could," she said softly. "You just had to catch up."

With a groan that was half-laugh, half-need, he kissed her—deep and slow and full of reverence. Their bodies shifted instinctively, finding rhythm in familiarity and desire. Renee arched against him as he guided her back against the pillows, his mouth exploring the path down her throat, over her collarbone, along the slope of her breast.

Each movement was deliberate, intimate—no rush, no distance left between them.

When he entered her, it was with a gasp against her lips, like he needed to breathe her in to survive. Renee curled her fingers into his shoulders, her legs wrapping around him, drawing him closer.

They moved together, quietly at first—gentle moans, soft murmurs, hands tangling in hair and bedsheets alike. The world outside faded into silence, leaving only the rhythm of their love and the heat that built between them.

This wasn't just passion.

It was a reclaiming.

A promise remade in touch and breath.

By the time they stilled, tangled in each other's arms, skin damp and hearts racing, Hudson kissed her temple and whispered, "You're my home."

Renee's eyes fluttered open, and she smiled, her fingers brushing through his hair.

"And you're mine."

Later, the city lights still glowing beyond the glass walls, Hudson reached into the nightstand drawer and pulled out a small velvet box.

Renee, still curled against him, tangled in the sheets and the warmth of his arms, blinked up at the movement. Her breath caught when she saw the box in his hand.

He held it for a second longer than he meant to—his thumb brushing over the velvet, the weight of what he was about to say settling in his chest. For a fleeting moment, his confidence wavered. What if she wasn't ready? What if he wasn't enough?

Then he opened it.

A ring—elegant, timeless, unmistakably meant for her.

"I was going to wait," he said, his voice slightly rough. "Make some big speech... maybe even get down on one knee." He let out a quiet breath, almost a laugh, but there was a tremble in it. "But I almost lost you, and I don't want to waste a single second."

Renee stared at the ring, then at him, her eyes wide, shimmering, and full of something fragile and fierce all at once.

"Marry me again, Renee," Hudson said softly. "No contracts. No conditions. Just… us."

Her answer was a whisper, but it rang with certainty. "Yes."

His hands didn't shake, but they weren't steady either as he slipped the ring onto her finger. She looked down at it, then back at him—and in the next instant, she was in his arms, laughing through the tears spilling freely down her cheeks.

This time, there was no doubt.

No deal.

No hesitation.

Just love.

The next morning arrived gently, the city still stretching awake beneath a sky brushed in pale blue. Renee sat curled on the couch in one of Hudson's button-down shirts, legs tucked beneath her, a mug of chamomile tea warming her hands. Sunlight streamed through the tall windows, casting soft gold across the room and catching on the delicate ring now resting on her finger. She couldn't stop glancing at it—her left hand—where the diamond glittered quietly, confidently. Like a promise she never dared to imagine, now made real.

The penthouse doors opened with a ding and a voice called out, "I brought those magazines you wanted and one very overpriced green juice you're probably going to hate—"

Vivian walked in, stopped cold, and narrowed her eyes. "Okay, what's that smug little look on your face?"

Renee tried to play innocent, setting down her mug. "What look?"

"Like the cat that swallowed the entire damn canary look. Spit it out, Fitzgerald."

Renee didn't say a word. She simply lifted her hand and wiggled her fingers.

Vivian's jaw dropped. "No. Freaking. Way."

Renee bit her lip, eyes twinkling. "Way."

Vivian let out a dramatic gasp and launched herself onto the couch beside her, grabbing Renee's hand like it was made of solid gold. "Oh my god, it's gorgeous! When? How?

Wait—was this before or after you disobeyed doctor's orders and got a different kind of cardio?"

Renee burst into laughter. "After. Very much after."

Vivian clutched her chest. "My best friend is engaged. Again. But for real this time." Her voice softened as she looked back at the ring, then at Renee's face. "He loves you."

Renee nodded, her smile turning quiet and full. "Yeah. He really does."

"And you?" Vivian asked, though she already knew the answer.

"I never stopped."

Vivian pulled her into a tight hug. "Okay, okay, I'll allow it. But only if I get to plan the most epic wedding ever. No compromises. No courthouse nonsense. I want flowers, I want music, I want champagne towers—"

"And you're giving the toast," Renee said, laughing against her friend's shoulder.

Vivian leaned back, grinning. "Oh, baby, I was born for that moment."

They both laughed, and for the first time in a long while, Renee felt like everything was exactly where it was supposed to be.

Chapter Sixteen

Thursday morning, Hudson stood at the floor-to-ceiling window of his office, a cup of coffee cooling in his hand, untouched. The city stretched out before him, but his mind wasn't on the skyline, or the quarterly reports stacked on his desk, or the board meeting scheduled for later that day.

It was on Renee—still asleep when he left, curled on her side, her breathing soft, steady. The quiet resilience in her smile lingered in his memory, a fragile peace he clung to.

That peace cracked the moment Ava's voice buzzed through the intercom, smooth and clipped.

"Mr. Waterford, there are two detectives here to see you. They say it's about the fire."

His grip tightened on the cup. "Send them in."

Detectives Lang and Rivera entered moments later, all measured steps and unsmiling eyes. Lang, tall and weathered, offered a handshake. "Mr. Waterford. Appreciate you making time."

Hudson nodded, voice crisp. "Have a seat. What have you found?"

Rivera got straight to it. "The fire wasn't an accident. The sprinkler system was manually disabled just minutes before the flames started. The person responsible was one of your night security guards—David Knox."

Hudson stiffened. "Knox? I know him. Quiet, reliable. That explains why he didn't respond to Renee's call… But why the hell would he sabotage the system?"

Lang exchanged a glance with Rivera before answering. "We believe he was coerced—or bought. Knox is in debt up to his neck. Foreclosure on his mother's home, mounting credit cards. Classic leverage. We think someone exploited that."

Hudson's jaw clenched. "Do you have any idea who paid him off?"

Rivera shook her head. "Not yet. Knox claims he wasn't paid. Says he was just 'doing someone a favour'—no names, no details. He's lawyered up now and refusing to talk further."

Hudson leaned forward, his voice lower, darker. "Was Renee the target?"

Lang hesitated. "Knox insists he didn't know anyone would be hurt. He says he was given instructions—time, location, and what to disable. Said he assumed it was sabotage. Maybe a rival company trying to cause disruption."

Rivera added quietly, "But once he saw the news—realised Miss Fitzgerald had nearly died—he cracked. Told us he never would've done it if he'd known."

Hudson stood, the air around him charged. "So, someone used him. To hurt Renee."

Lang nodded grimly. "It's likely. He wasn't acting alone. Someone else started the fire near her office. We believe that person is still out there."

Hudson's voice dropped to a razor's edge. "Find them. Whoever did this—whoever gave the order—I want their name before the press does."

Lang met his gaze. "We'll keep you updated."

As the detectives left, the silence that settled wasn't peaceful—it pulsed.

Hudson turned back to the window, but the skyline blurred. All he could see was Renee—her soft laugh, her warm hand in his… the lifeless weight of her body in his arms as smoke filled the air.

Someone had tried to take her from him.

And Hudson Waterford didn't believe in second chances.

Not for people like that.

The door had barely clicked shut behind the detectives when Ava knocked lightly and stepped into the office, a tablet in one hand, her expression composed but tinged with just the right amount of concern.

"Sorry to interrupt," she said gently, closing the door behind her. "I thought you might need an update on your afternoon schedule… and maybe a refill?" She held up a fresh mug of coffee.

Hudson glanced over from the window, his expression unreadable. "Thanks," he said, accepting the cup. "Just leave it on the desk."

Ava obeyed but didn't leave. Instead, she lingered, tablet forgotten in her hand.

"I, um…" She hesitated, brushing a strand of hair behind her ear. "Was that about the fire?"

His gaze flicked to her. "Yes."

Her voice lowered. "Is there anything I should know? For statements, or… damage control?"

Hudson's eyes narrowed slightly—not suspicion, but fatigue. "It's under investigation. The detectives are handling it."

Ava nodded, her tone soft, casual. "Of course. I just—I heard the system was disabled. That's what people are whispering anyway." She looked at him, feigning reluctant curiosity. "Is that true?"

Hudson hesitated a beat too long. "Yes. They think it was deliberate."

Ava's brows knit together, her concern artfully performed. "That's awful. Who would do something like that?" A pause, then, "Do they know who's responsible?"

Hudson's jaw flexed, a flicker of something cold in his eyes. "They've got a name. One of the security guards. David Knox."

She blinked. "David?" Her voice caught just enough to sound surprised, not alarmed. "He's always seemed… harmless."

"So did a lot of people," Hudson said curtly, walking back to his desk. "But it looks like someone used him."

Ava tilted her head. "Used him how?"

Hudson sat, not looking at her. "That's all I can say for now."

There was a beat of silence. Ava stepped forward, laying the tablet down, her tone light but knowing. "Well, if there's anything you need me to handle—media inquiries, board fallout—just say the word."

He nodded once, already half lost in thought.

Ava lingered a second longer, then smiled faintly. "I'm just glad Renee's okay," she said, voice quiet.

Hudson looked up, his eyes sharpening. "So am I."

She dipped her head and turned toward the door. But as she stepped into the hallway, the practiced mask on her face slipped—just for an instant—and her smile faded into something far colder.

Then it was gone, replaced by calm efficiency, as she walked briskly back to her desk.

Friday morning brought a rare chill to the air, and an unmistakable storm into Hudson's office.

Ava Sinclair didn't knock. She burst through the door, her heels clicking sharply against the polished floor, blonde hair pulled back with surgical precision, eyes blazing.

"You're replacing me," she said flatly, accusation simmering beneath each word.

Hudson looked up from his desk, unfazed by her dramatic entrance. He set down his pen and leaned back in his chair, expression unreadable.

"Yes," he said, calm but firm. "Effective Monday."

Ava's breath hitched. "Why? After everything I've done for you—for this company?"

"It's not personal," he said, though even he heard how hollow that sounded. "It's just for the best."

Her lips curled, not into a smile, but something sharp. "Right. Of course. For the best."

She crossed her arms, took a step closer. "This is because of her, isn't it?"

Hudson's jaw ticked. "Ava—"

"She's jealous of me," Ava snapped, voice rising. "That's what this is. She sees the way you and I work together—she feels threatened. She's always hated that I know you better than she ever could."

Hudson stood slowly, his eyes darkening with warning. His voice was quiet, but it hit like steel.

"Enough. That's my fiancée you're talking about."

Ava blinked. For a heartbeat, she looked genuinely stunned.

"What?" she whispered, then louder—sharper— "You're engaged to her?"

But the shock quickly morphed into something colder, uglier. The polished mask she wore so flawlessly every day slipped, just enough to reveal what simmered beneath.

"I can't believe you're actually going back for round two," Ava snapped, her voice sharp with disbelief. "I thought you came to your senses when you divorced her."

She took a step closer, eyes blazing.

"I've been by your side for eight months," she hissed. "I've cleaned up your messes. Anticipated your every move. Protected you—and this company—from disasters you didn't even see coming. And now you're throwing me away for her?"

Hudson's jaw tightened. The air between them crackled, but he didn't move, didn't flinch.

"This has nothing to do with—"

"Yes, it does!" she snapped. "She's a spoiled heiress who's never worked for anything in her life. She fluttered her lashes, played the victim, and you handed her everything— including getting rid of me."

His voice dropped to a dangerous low. "You are out of line."

Ava's breath came in shallow, clipped bursts. But she didn't back down.

"You'll regret this," she said quietly, with a venomous calm that chilled the air between them. "She's not who you think she is."

Hudson didn't respond. He didn't need to. The way his gaze hardened was answer enough.

Ava stood still for a moment longer; eyes locked on his like a challenge.

Then she turned and walked out, heels clicking like gunshots on the marble floor, the door snapping shut behind her.

Hudson stared after her, jaw clenched.

That hadn't been about losing a job.

That had been personal.

And it made everything inside him go still.

Ava didn't return to the office after lunch.

Hudson noticed—but only in the way one might register a change in temperature. It didn't bother him. If anything, her absence was a relief. Her outburst that morning had left a bitter aftertaste, one that lingered long after she stormed out. He'd known Ava was ambitious, even protective of her position—but the venom in her voice when she'd spoken about Renee had unsettled him. It was personal. Too personal.

He was still staring out the window when the door opened without a knock.

"You look like someone just walked over your grave," Marcus said, striding in with two takeaway coffees in hand.

Hudson cracked a dry smile. "If you brought bad news, now's not the time."

"On the contrary," Marcus said, handing him a cup. "I'm here to drag your brooding ass out for a drink after work. Come on, one hour. You've earned it."

Hudson shook his head, setting the coffee aside. "Can't. I want to get home to Renee."

Marcus raised an eyebrow, a grin tugging at the corner of his mouth. "So, it's home now, huh? Look at you—domesticated and everything."

Hudson didn't answer, but the small smile that crept across his face said plenty.

"Well damn," Marcus muttered, smirking. "Fine but at least let me come by for dinner. I'll even bring dessert."

"Deal," Hudson said. Then, after a beat, Marcus caught the flicker of tension in his friend's eyes.

"What's wrong?" Marcus asked, easing into the chair opposite the desk.

Hudson hesitated. "Ava. She... lost it this morning. Accused Renee of manipulating me. Claimed I was making a mistake."

Marcus blinked. "She said that. Straight out?"

"Among other things," Hudson muttered. "I told her she was out of line. She stormed off and didn't come back."

Marcus leaned back, thoughtful. "She's always had... sharp elbows, but that doesn't sound like the Ava I know."

"I thought I knew her," Hudson said, rubbing his jaw. "But the way she talked about Renee—it was personal. Jealous. Almost angry."

There was a pause. Then Marcus said quietly, "You don't think she'd... I don't know. Do something."

Hudson looked up, and for the first time, let the thought he'd been suppressing rise to the surface. "The fire. She knew Renee was working late. She knew she'd be here alone. And she hired the night guard."

"David Knox," Marcus said slowly. "And Knox disabled the sprinklers."

Hudson stood abruptly, grabbing his phone. He called Renee. Straight to voicemail.

He frowned. Tried again. Same result.

"She always picks up," he muttered.

Marcus stood. "Let's go. Now."

Hudson didn't hesitate. He was already moving.

"Penthouse?" Marcus asked, grabbing his coat.

Hudson's expression was grim. "Yeah. I'm not waiting around to find out."

And they left together, dread hanging between them like smoke.

The kitchen was filled with the comforting scent of garlic and fresh herbs. Renee stood at the counter, barefoot in one of Hudson's old T-shirts, her hair swept into a messy bun. She'd been home for a week now, recovering and slowly reclaiming her rhythm. But restlessness had crept in, and she'd finally decided to channel it into something useful—dinner.

She was slicing vegetables with precise focus, the soft clink of the knife against the cutting board the only sound in the room. The quiet helped. It kept her from overthinking everything—Hudson's marriage proposal, the fire, the strange way the detectives had danced around their questions.

The intercom on the wall buzzed, interrupting the moment.

Renee wiped her hands on a dish towel and pressed the button. "Hello?"

The doorman's voice crackled through the speaker. "Miss Fitzgerald? Miss Sinclair is here. She says Mr. Waterford asked her to pick up some documents from his study."

Renee hesitated, the name giving her pause.

Ava?

It seemed odd. Hudson hadn't mentioned needing anything, let alone sending someone over. But she didn't want to be rude—or overly suspicious. Not without reason.

"Um… okay," she said, pressing the talk button again. "Send her up."

She turned back to the cutting board, shaking her head at herself. Maybe Hudson had called her while he was at the office. Maybe it was urgent. She reached for another bell pepper and started slicing.

A few moments later, she heard the soft ding of the penthouse doors opening.

"Hey, Ava," Renee called over her shoulder, keeping her tone polite, but cautious. "Hudson didn't mention you were stopping by, but I can show you where—"

She paused.

A faint, familiar scent drifted toward her—something sharp and floral, Ava's perfume. Then came the creak of a floorboard behind her. Too close.

The words died in her throat.

Something slammed into the back of her head—hard, fast, merciless.

Pain exploded behind her eyes, sharp and blinding, swallowing everything in white-hot static as the world tilted out of reach.

Her knees buckled, the knife slipping from her hand and clattering to the floor.

Everything went black.

Renee groaned softly, her head pounding as though a drumbeat echoed inside her skull. Everything was hazy—light fractured across her vision, and her limbs felt heavy, disconnected. The tiled kitchen floor was cold beneath her cheek.

She blinked, trying to remember what had happened. Her hand instinctively reached toward the back of her head—tender, wet. Pain flared. She winced.

Voices. No—just one voice. Hers.

Renee lifted her head slightly, vision swimming, and saw Ava standing at the kitchen island. Calm. Too calm.

She was methodically crushing something—small white tablets—into a fine powder and stirring it into a glass of water. Her movements were clinical, focused.

"Ava?" Renee's voice came out hoarse and fragile. "What happened?"

Ava didn't flinch. She looked down slowly, her expression no longer pleasant or polished. There was nothing professional or composed about her now—only a cold, burning hatred in her eyes.

"What happened?" Ava repeated with a bitter laugh. "You happened."

Renee tried to sit up, but the room spun wildly, her body sluggish and uncooperative. A low thrum pulsed in her ears—her heartbeat, heavy and frantic.

Ava stepped closer, the glass still in her hand, eyes alight with bitter triumph.

"I thought he was done with you," she hissed. "Divorced. Forgotten. And yet—here you are again. Back in my way."

Renee blinked, vision blurred, trying to hold on.

"I... I don't understand..."

Ava's expression twisted, fury flickering beneath the surface.

"No. You don't. You never did. You walked into his life like you were entitled to it. When he married you, I couldn't believe it. But then I saw it—he wasn't happy. You two were never together unless it was for show. Then he finally woke up. Left you."

She crouched beside Renee, lowering her voice to a dangerous whisper.

"You don't see him, not really. Not the way I do. You don't deserve him. You never did."

Her next words came like poison, sharp and deliberate.

"He was mine until you came crawling back. But don't worry…" She tilted the glass.

"You won't be a problem much longer."

Renee's breath caught, and instinct jolted her body, even if it was weak and slow. Her fingers scraped against the tile, searching for anything—anything at all.

Ava just smiled.

"Drink this," Ava said softly, her tone syrupy-sweet as she held the glass just inches from Renee's lips. "It'll help with the headache."

Renee turned her face away, but her limbs were leaden, her strength slipping fast.

"Please… stop," she whispered, her voice barely audible.

Ava's smile sharpened into something razor thin.

"Oh, I will. It's what you deserve, Renee." She leaned in, eyes gleaming with malice.

"One last favour… from me to you."

And in that moment, Renee understood true fear—not the distant, abstract kind—but real, suffocating terror that made her bones feel hollow.

Chapter Seventeen

Renee moaned, her limbs heavy and uncooperative as she struggled to sit up. Every movement sent a fresh wave of pain through her skull, blurring her vision and making her stomach churn. Her head lolled as Ava lifted her just enough to prop her against the cabinets.

"Easy now," Ava cooed, though there was no kindness in her voice—only a sickening edge. "Can't have you lying on the floor like a stray dog."

Renee's eyes fluttered open again, struggling to focus. "Ava… don't…" she murmured, the words barely audible.

Ava crouched in front of her, the glass of water in one hand, her other cradling the back of Renee's head with calculated tenderness.

"Come on, Renee," Ava crooned, syrupy sweet—like poison wrapped in lace. "This will make everything better."

Renee turned her head weakly, lips pressed together, trying to avoid the rim of the glass as Ava tilted it toward her mouth.

"No," she whispered.

But Ava's grip tightened. She forced the glass against Renee's lips, tilting it sharply. The water spilled down Renee's chin, soaking her shirt, but some of it slipped past her lips.

Renee coughed and sputtered, trying to twist away, feebly raising a trembling hand to push Ava back. "Stop…"

Ava's smile widened, eyes gleaming with rage and triumph.

"Too late for that, sweetheart."

Renee's arms shook violently as she tried again to push Ava away, but her limbs sank like lead, heavy and numb, as if gravity had doubled. The bitter, chalky taste coated her mouth, crawling down her throat with every forced swallow.

Panic flared in her chest.

Her heart pounded against her ribs, but her body refused to respond.

"No—please…" she gurgled, twisting her face away, but Ava's grip was merciless.

"Oh, I will," Ava hissed, tipping more of the liquid into Renee's mouth. "When you're gone for good."

Renee coughed, sputtered, trying to turn her face, to spit it out—but Ava only pressed harder, her knuckles white around the glass, her other hand gripping Renee's jaw.

"I waited," she spat, eyes blazing with hatred. "Eight months. I was there when he didn't look twice at you. Until your grandfather intervened. But you—you had to come back."

Renee whimpered as more of the liquid slid past her lips, choking her. She tried to twist her head away, but her body wouldn't respond. Her vision swam—edges blurring, the world narrowing to the cold tiles beneath her and the cruel voice in her ear.

Ava leaned in closer, her breath hot with fury. "He was mine," she spat. "And you ruined everything. But it's fine. I'll be there for him—helping him through the heartbreak of your suicide."

Her words dripped venom, each syllable slicing through the haze in Renee's mind like shards of glass.

Across the building, the elevator dinged softly.

Vivian stepped into the penthouse, keys still in hand, balancing a bag of takeout. She hadn't called—just decided to stop by and check on Renee, maybe cheer her up with Thai food and trash TV. The place was quiet, unusually so.

"Renee?" she called, her voice echoing faintly through the space. "I brought those dumplings you love. Where are you, girl?"

No answer.

A flicker of unease danced up Vivian's spine. She moved farther inside, frowning as she passed the empty living room and spotted the glow of kitchen lights.

"Renee?"

Then she saw her.

Renee was slumped on the floor, her limbs limp, eyes fluttering. Ava hovered over her, one hand gripping her hair, the other trying to force a glass back to her lips.

For one stunned heartbeat, the world froze. Then instinct snapped her into motion.

"Get the hell away from her!" she shouted, launching herself forward.

Ava whirled just in time for Vivian to slam into her. The glass clattered to the floor, shattering on impact. Ava staggered but didn't fall—she lunged, clawing at Vivian with shocking strength, fury contorting her face.

"You stupid bitch!" Ava shrieked, grappling with Vivian, trying to shove her back. "You don't understand! She doesn't deserve him!"

Vivian fought back, fists swinging, blocking Ava's wild attempts to reach Renee. But Ava was feral—driven by something twisted and unhinged.

With a savage shove, Ava hurled Vivian backward. She slammed into the kitchen counter with a gasp, pain exploding through her ribs. Dazed, she tried to scramble to her feet, but Ava was already lunging, eyes wild, teeth bared.

Then—

The elevator chimed.

A beat later, the penthouse doors slid open.

"Renee!" Hudson's voice rang out, raw, desperate.

He and Marcus burst into the room, eyes locking instantly on the chaos. Hudson froze—a breath, a heartbeat—then bolted across the room. Renee was collapsed on the floor, Ava looming over her, Vivian trying to get up.

He crossed the room in seconds, grabbing Ava and yanking her back with a force that sent her sprawling.

"Get away from her!" Hudson roared, placing himself between Ava and Renee, every line of his body poised to kill if he had to.

Ava scrambled to her feet, hair dishevelled, face flushed with rage—and for the first time, fear.

Marcus rushed to Vivian's side, helping her up. "You okay?" he asked, eyes flicking to Renee, then back to Ava.

Vivian nodded breathlessly. "She was trying to kill her. Poison—glass—she was choking…"

Hudson dropped to his knees beside Renee, his hands trembling as he cradled her face. "Renee? Renee, stay with me. I've got you. You're okay now."

Renee drifted in and out of consciousness, her eyelids fluttering as if each blink was a battle. Her lips parted, forming silent words she no longer had the strength to speak. One trembling hand twitched against the cold tile, reaching blindly for him—her last tether to safety.

Hudson looked up, eyes blazing.

"Call an ambulance," he ordered. "Now."

Marcus was already on the phone.

And Ava—silent now, wide-eyed, and breathless—backed slowly toward the wall as Hudson tried to wake Renee.

But Hudson didn't look at her again.

All he saw was Renee.

Marcus shoved Ava down onto the couch, pinning her arms with one hand as he fumbled for his phone with the other. "Don't move," he growled, his usual levity gone. "You so much as blink wrong, I swear—"

Ava hissed and struggled beneath him, but Marcus didn't budge. He had one knee braced against the edge of the cushion, his full weight keeping her in place as he called emergency services.

In the kitchen, Hudson knelt beside Renee, cradling her limp body against his chest. Her head lolled against his shoulder, her skin pale and clammy, her breath shallow.

"Renee," he whispered urgently, his voice breaking. "Baby, wake up. Come on, open your eyes."

Vivian hovered close, her hands trembling. "Hudson?"

He looked up, wild with desperation. "Do you know what she gave her? Did you see anything?"

Vivian spun around, scanning the kitchen. Her eyes landed on the shattered glass Ava had dropped during the struggle—liquid still pooled on the floor—on the bench, a small amber bottle, its cap laying next to it. She snatched it up, read the label, then froze.

"Oh my God," she breathed. "Sleeping tablets. The bottle's empty."

She turned the bottle toward him with a shaking hand. Hudson stared at it, his face draining of colour.

"God—Renee, hold on, please." His voice cracked as he pressed his lips to her temple. "Don't leave me. Not now. Not like this."

Renee didn't respond. Her body was frighteningly still in his arms.

From the hallway, Marcus called out, "Ambulance is on its way. Five minutes."

"Not fast enough," Hudson murmured, tightening his hold. "Come on, sweetheart. Stay with me. I just got you back..."

Vivian knelt beside them, one hand resting on Renee's knee, the other gripping Hudson's arm. "She's strong," she whispered fiercely. "She's going to make it. Just keep talking to her."

And Hudson did, his voice low and urgent, refusing to let go—even as the sirens began to wail in the distance.

The elevator doors burst open with a sharp ding, and two paramedics rushed out, flanked by the doorman who pointed frantically toward the kitchen.

"In here!" he called.

They surged into the apartment with practiced urgency, medical bags swinging at their sides. The moment they saw Renee on the floor, pale and unresponsive in Hudson's arms, they sprang into action.

"What's she taken?" one asked briskly as he knelt beside them, already snapping on gloves.

Vivian held out the empty bottle with a trembling hand. "Sleeping tablets. We think… we don't know how much."

The paramedic snatched the bottle, read the label, and nodded to his partner. "Get the injection ready—we might still have time."

"What are you giving her?" Hudson demanded, voice raw.

"It's flumazenil. It can counteract the effects of the sedatives," the other paramedic explained as he prepped a syringe. "But we have to act fast."

Vivian and Hudson moved back to give them space. The paramedic found a vein and administered the injection swiftly, then began checking her vitals while his partner assembled the stretcher.

"She's breathing, but shallow," one of them murmured. "Heart rate's low but holding. We're getting her out now."

They gently but efficiently transferred Renee onto the stretcher, securing her with straps and oxygen before wheeling her toward the door.

Hudson stood, his hands still shaking. His eyes followed every movement, refusing to let her out of his sight. Then he turned, jaw clenched, to Marcus and Vivian.

"Make sure the police take that bitch to jail," he growled, nodding toward Ava, who still sat restrained on the couch, her expression a twisted mix of rage and desperation.

Marcus's eyes darkened as he nodded. "Don't worry. She's not going anywhere."

Vivian stepped to Hudson's side, touching his arm gently. "Go with Renee. We've got this."

Without another word, Hudson followed the paramedics out, his gaze never leaving the fragile woman lying on the stretcher.

And back in the penthouse, as sirens wailed again in the distance—this time from a police cruiser—Ava Sinclair finally looked afraid.

The sterile white light of the hospital room buzzed faintly overhead. Machines beeped steadily beside the bed, the sound somehow both reassuring and terrifying. Hudson sat in the hard plastic chair, his elbows on his knees, head bowed, hands tangled in his hair.

Renee had been unconscious for hours.

She lay pale and still, her lips dry, her breath shallow but steady now thanks to the oxygen mask. An IV line ran to her hand, and a nurse had just adjusted the monitors before quietly stepping out to give them privacy.

Hudson reached for her hand again, cradling it between both of his, brushing his thumb over her knuckles as if sheer will could bring her back.

"Come on, Renee," he whispered. "You've survived worse. Not now. Not when we just found our way back…"

He stopped himself, eyes burning. Swallowed hard.

The door creaked open behind him. Vivian stepped in quietly, her face drawn with worry, but she offered a small nod when their eyes met.

"She's stable," she said gently. "The doctors said the injection worked. The dose was high, but… they think she'll wake up soon."

Hudson looked back to Renee, unable to speak.

And then—her fingers twitched.

Her lips moved faintly. "Huh…"

"Renee?" he breathed, sitting forward instantly.

Her lashes quivered like moth wings before her eyes slowly opened. Her gaze was hazy at first, eyes flickering across the room in confusion before settling on the face she knew best.

"Hudson…" Her voice was little more than a rasp, raw and fragile. "Ava…?"

"You're okay," he said quickly, his voice thick with relief, his hand tightening around hers. "You're safe. The paramedics got to you in time. You're in the hospital now."

She blinked, struggling to process his words. Her brow creased. "Ava… she…"

"I know," he said gently, leaning closer. "We know everything. She's in custody. She can't hurt you anymore, Renee. Marcus is making damn sure they throw the book at her."

Her lips quivered. Tears slipped silently from the corners of her eyes. Her whole body trembled with exhaustion and emotion.

"You saved me… again," she breathed, her voice a ghost. Her eyes fluttered shut, sleep claiming her.

"Of course I did," Hudson murmured, brushing a damp strand of hair from her forehead with trembling fingers. "I'm not letting anything happen to you. Not now. Not ever."

Vivian stood at the foot of the bed, eyes shimmering, but quietly stepped back to give them space.

Hudson brought Renee's hand to his lips and kissed it softly, his voice a broken whisper.

"I love you, Renee. I can't—" He exhaled shakily. "I can't live without you. I need you."

A faint smile touched her lips, even as her eyes remained closed.

"I love you too," she whispered, drifting into sleep with that smile still lingering.

Hudson bent low, pressing a gentle kiss to her forehead, then stayed there, forehead against hers, his breath mingling with the steady rhythm of hers.

Late afternoon sunlight slanted through the hospital window, casting a golden glow over the room. Renee had managed to sit up a little, propped by pillows, a blanket drawn over her lap. She was pale but alert, a quiet strength behind her tired eyes. Hudson sat beside her, his arm gently around her shoulders, protective and unwavering.

A knock at the door broke the silence.

Detective Joanna Lane stepped in, her partner, Detective Ryan Chen, close behind. Both wore serious expressions, though Lane softened slightly at the sight of Renee awake.

"Miss Fitzgerald, Mr. Waterford," Lane greeted, offering a respectful nod. "We're glad to see you on the mend."

"Thank you," Renee said softly, her voice still raspy.

Hudson gave a curt nod. "What did you find out?"

Chen stepped forward, flipping open a notepad. "We thought you'd want an update. Ava Sinclair is in custody, and she's not going anywhere. We talked to the night guard—David Knox again. He admitted to disabling the sprinklers and deactivated the fire alarm system the night of the fire for Miss Sinclair."

Renee stiffened. "So, it was deliberate."

"It was," Lane confirmed grimly. "Knox cracked first. Once we told him Ava was in custody, he started talking. Turns out, they were having an affair. That's how she manipulated him into helping her. Promised him money, a future. He claimed he thought it was just to 'scare' you. But once the charges started stacking, he stopped pretending."

Hudson's jaw clenched. "So, she seduced a guard to commit arson."

Chen nodded. "And she tried to stage Miss Fitzgerald's death to look like suicide. It's all premeditated—assault, attempted murder, arson, conspiracy. She's going away for a long time."

Renee was quiet for a moment, absorbing the weight of it all. "She really would've let me die."

Lane's expression softened. "She would have. But she didn't. You survived—and that changes everything."

Hudson tightened his grip around Renee. "What happens next?"

"We'll need formal statements from both of you," Chen said. "Once you're ready. No pressure today."

"And Marcus?" Renee asked. "Is he alright?"

"He's fine. Gave us a full statement. He was still demanding we throw her off the balcony when we left," Lane added with a faint smirk.

Hudson managed a dry chuckle. "Sounds about right."

Lane handed Renee a card. "Call when you're up to it. We'll take it from there."

As the detectives stepped out, Renee leaned into Hudson, her voice low.

"She nearly killed me."

"But she didn't," he said, kissing her hair. "You're still here. And now... we get on with our lives... together."

Chapter Eighteen

The elevator doors slid open with a soft chime, and Renee stepped out, Hudson at her side. The familiar hallway of Fitzgerald Enterprises greeted her like an old friend—gleaming marble floors, sleek glass walls, and the faint hum of productivity in the air.

It had only been a little over a week since Ava had tried to kill her, but it felt like a lifetime had passed.

Hudson walked her all the way to her office, his hand lightly resting at the small of her back. As they reached her door, he turned to face her.

"You okay?" he asked, his eyes scanning her face with quiet concern.

She nodded, smiling up at him. "More than okay."

He leaned in, kissed her gently, and whispered against her lips, "I'll see you later, Mrs. Almost-Waterford."

Renee chuckled softly, shaking her head as she stepped inside her office. "Don't start calling me that unless you're planning to make it official before lunch."

Hudson grinned. "Don't tempt me."

With a final wink, he left her to settle in.

Renee closed the door behind her and stood for a moment, breathing in the familiar scent of her office—vanilla, fresh paper, and the faintest trace of sandalwood from the candles she liked to burn during late nights. It was all exactly as she remembered yet somehow felt brand new.

The fire had done more damage than she'd initially realised—scorch marks across the walls, smoke-stained ceilings, melted electronics. But the repair crews had worked fast, and with meticulous care. Now, the space was fully restored. Fresh paint gleamed under the morning light, new fixtures blended perfectly with the old, and even the rug she loved had been replaced with a near-identical version. It looked like nothing had happened.

But she remembered.

She walked slowly to her desk and eased into her chair, letting her fingertips trail across the smooth surface—no longer charred or cracked, but whole again. Just like her.

This office had been a place of ambition, of pressure, of duty. Today, it felt like a place of survival. Of resilience. Of second chances.

Everything looked the same. Her framed photo of her grandfather, her favourite fountain pen, the stack of neatly arranged documents waiting for her attention.

But she wasn't the same.

Her gaze drifted to the window, where the skyline stretched wide and glittering. The past week played like flashes in her mind—Ava's rage, the shattered glass, Hudson's arms catching her before everything went dark. Then the hospital room. The beeping machines. Hudson's voice anchoring her to the world when everything else had blurred.

Ava had been officially charged and so had David Knox. Conspiracy to commit arson, attempted murder, assault. The detectives told her she wouldn't be seeing either of them again for a long, long time.

She wrapped her arms around herself for a moment, grounding herself in that truth.

And then—there was Hudson.

He hadn't left her side. Not at the hospital, not at home, not for a single breath. On Saturday morning, over coffee and half-eaten croissants, he'd looked at her with those steady, storm-grey eyes and asked, "When are you going to marry me again, Renee?"

She'd smiled through a tear and answered without hesitation, "As soon as it can be arranged."

Vivian had practically exploded with excitement the moment she heard. She'd instantly declared herself wedding planner-in-chief, already sketching dress ideas on napkins, and calling in favours from vendors before Renee could even say yes to a venue. Her boutique was thriving, and she promised she had the best team running things while she focused on "getting her best friend hitched again to the man who worshipped the ground she walked on."

Renee's heart swelled just thinking about it.

Vivian had pulled her aside just yesterday and said, "I never doubted he loved you, you know. Not for a second. You don't tear through fire and poison and fear like that unless you're in deep. Hudson Waterford is yours. Always was."

A soft knock broke her thoughts.

She turned to see her assistant poking her head in, a warm smile on her face. "Welcome back, Miss Fitzgerald."

Renee smiled, rising to her feet. "Thank you, Jess. It's good to be home."

And as the office stirred back to life around her, Renee felt it deep in her bones—she was back. Stronger. Wiser. Loved.

And this time, she wasn't alone.

The weeks blurred into a flurry of fabric swatches, cake tastings, vendor meetings, and late-night checklists. Between board meetings and bridal fittings, Renee barely had time to think. But every decision, every detail, brought her closer to the day she never thought she'd get to have—not like this. Not with love.

And now it had arrived.

Sunlight streamed through the tall windows of the bridal suite, casting golden halos on soft ivory silk and fresh white peonies. Vivian stood behind Renee, adjusting the delicate buttons on the back of her gown, her fingers surprisingly steady for someone who'd had two coffees and cried through the makeup artist's first attempt at waterproof mascara.

Vivian caught Renee's gaze in the mirror. "Your first wedding was a farce," she said quietly, her voice thick with emotion. "This one—I'm hoping this one is the best day of your life."

Renee turned slowly, reaching for her best friend's hands. "It will be," she said with a soft, sure smile. "I'm marrying the man I love… and he loves me."

Vivian let out a shaky laugh and wiped at her eyes. "Damn it, don't say stuff like that before the photos. I just got my eyeliner right."

Renee laughed, her heart full. "You've been with me through everything. I'm so glad you're here for this."

"I wouldn't be anywhere else." Vivian squeezed her hands. "Now go out there and marry the man who would walk through fire for you—because he already did."

And with that, Renee took one final breath, lifted her skirts, and stepped toward forever.

Meanwhile…

In a private room off the chapel, Hudson stood in front of a full-length mirror, straightening his cufflinks for the fourth time. Marcus leaned against the doorway, watching with a grin that danced dangerously close to smug.

"You keep fussing like that, she's gonna think you're the one walking down the aisle," Marcus said, tossing him a white pocket square.

Hudson caught it mid-air, then glanced at his reflection. "I just want everything to be perfect."

Marcus tilted his head. "Man, she doesn't care about your cufflinks. She loves you. That's the part that's perfect."

Hudson let out a quiet breath, nodding. "Yeah. I just… I can't believe we made it here. After everything."

"She's tough. So are you. And I'm pretty sure you'd burn the world down to keep her safe," Marcus said with a wink. "Which, for the record, is romantic—unless you're the world."

That earned a low laugh from Hudson, who shook his head and turned back to the mirror. But then his eyes drifted—unfocused, no longer seeing his reflection, only memories.

He could still see her—eyes blazing with hurt and pride during their annulment mediation, refusing to let him see her break. He saw her pale and unconscious in the hospital, her hand limp in his as fear gripped his chest like a vice. He saw her smiling shyly across the candlelit table, her guard slipping just enough for him to glimpse the woman who still loved him beneath all the pain.

And now… now she was about to walk down the aisle and promise forever.

Hudson swallowed hard, emotion rising in his throat.

This time, he wouldn't let her go.

Marcus clapped him on the back. "Come on, lover boy. Time to get married."

Minutes later, Hudson stood at the front of the chapel, his hands clasped loosely in front of him beneath an archway of cascading white orchids and soft linen draping. Golden sunlight filtered through stained-glass windows, casting soft colours over the polished marble floor. The hush of the guests behind him was broken only by the soft strains of the string quartet beginning to play.

This was it.

The moment he'd been waiting for his entire life—

Even if he hadn't known it until her.

The chapel doors opened with a quiet creak, and Vivian stepped into view first, radiant in a flowing royal blue gown, her face beaming with pride and emotion. She gave Hudson a wink as she passed, her bouquet clutched with the grace of someone who'd done this before—but never with stakes this high.

And then, time stopped.

Renee appeared at the threshold, framed by the open doors and the light pouring in behind her. The music swelled. Every breath in the room hitched.

Hudson couldn't move. He couldn't think. His world narrowed to the woman walking toward him, each step echoing like a heartbeat in his ears.

She was breathtaking.

The dress was a perfect blend of elegance and softness—lace detailing across the bodice, delicate cap sleeves, a flowing skirt that caught the air like mist. Her hair was swept into a loose up-do with soft tendrils curling around her face, and her eyes... they never left his.

But what struck him the most was her smile—glowing, serene, filled with so much love that it cracked something wide open inside him.

She looked like she belonged here. Like she'd always belonged to him.

As she came to stand before him, Hudson took her hands, grounding himself in the feel of her fingers curled around his. He could feel the slight tremble in her grip—and knew she could feel his.

The officiant began to speak, but Hudson barely heard the words. He only had eyes for Renee—her steady gaze, the way her lips curved in nervous excitement, the subtle quiver of her breath when she whispered, "I do."

When it came time for his vows, Hudson cleared his throat, voice thick with emotion.

"I thought I knew what love was. I thought it was strategy, duty, timing. But you... you taught me that love is brave. It's fierce. It's forgiving. And it's standing right here in front of me, looking at me like I'm worthy of all of it. Renee, I vow to spend every day proving that I am. To love you, protect you, honour you—for the rest of my life."

Tears shimmered in Renee's eyes as she whispered her vows in return, and moments later, the officiant smiled.

"With the power vested in me... I now pronounce you husband and wife."

Hudson didn't wait.

He drew Renee into his arms and kissed her—deeply, reverently, like a man who had almost lost everything and would never take it for granted again.

The chapel erupted in applause. But to Hudson, there was only her.

Forever had never looked so perfect.

Epilogue

Two Years Later…

Laughter floated through the candlelit garden like music, blending with the soft hum of string lights swaying overhead. Clusters of guests gathered around tall cocktail tables, sipping champagne and catching up under a sky dusted with stars. The air was warm, fragrant with blooming roses and jasmine, the perfect evening for a celebration.

Marcus looked dazed in the best way possible, his arm wrapped tightly around his fiancée, Jasmine, as friends raised glasses in their honour.

Hudson clapped him on the back. "You're finally joining the club."

Marcus grinned. "Yeah, yeah. Don't act like you didn't drag your feet getting there yourself."

Hudson chuckled, but his gaze drifted across the garden—drawn like a magnet to the woman who had changed everything. Renee stood a few feet away, laughing at something Vivian had said, her hand resting casually on her hip. Her hair, longer now, curled over one shoulder, and the soft green dress she wore caught the light every time she moved. She looked radiant.

Vivian—now Vivian Carter—was positively glowing herself, holding hands with her new husband, Greg. Their matching wedding bands gleamed as brightly as her smile.

"I still think she married Greg because he makes her laugh harder than anyone else," Marcus muttered.

Hudson smirked. "She married him because she finally found someone who wouldn't try to keep up with her. Just stand back and admire her."

Marcus raised his glass in a quiet salute. "Fair."

The music shifted, and as couples drifted onto the dance floor beneath the strings of fairy lights, Hudson made his way to Renee and extended a hand.

"May I have this dance, Mrs. Waterford?"

She smiled like it was still the first time he'd asked. "Always."

He pulled her close, his hand resting at the small of her back, and they began to sway. The world faded around them—just the hush of music, the warmth of their bodies pressed close, the rhythm of two people who had learned how to move through life together.

"You're quiet tonight," Hudson said, brushing a soft kiss against her temple. "Tired?"

"Hmm," she murmured, resting her head against his chest. "Maybe a little. Or maybe I'm just soaking all of this in."

He twirled her gently, then pulled her back into his arms. "I still can't believe we're here. Together. Happy."

"I can," she whispered, smiling up at him. "I knew the moment you ran into that burning office for me."

His lips curved. "I wasn't going to lose you."

"You didn't," she said softly. "And you're not going to."

She hesitated for a breath, her fingers brushing his chest, just over his heart. Then she looked up at him, her eyes shimmering with more than just the garden lights.

"Hudson?" she said, voice low.

He immediately stilled, searching her face. "What is it?"

She smiled gently. "You're going to be a daddy."

His eyes widened, every muscle in his body freezing for half a heartbeat. Then—

"What?"

"In about seven months," she added, her smile trembling now. "I found out this morning. I wanted to tell you when it was just us."

Hudson stared at her, blinking like he was trying to process the words. Then a slow, awed grin spread across his face, and he pulled her in so tightly she laughed.

"You're serious?" he asked into her hair.

She nodded; her cheek pressed against his chest. "You're going to be an amazing father."

He pulled back just enough to cup her face in his hands, his expression undone. "And you're going to be the most incredible mother."

Around them, music played, laughter carried, and the world kept spinning. But for Hudson and Renee, time had once again narrowed to just the two of them—dancing in the middle of everything they'd built, everything they'd survived.

And now… everything yet to come.

Forever had never looked so full.

The End

Thank you for reading Dark & Dangerous!

If you enjoyed this collection of irresistible alpha heroes, keep an eye out for more upcoming romance collections by Alison Reid, including:

Alpha Kings - *A Billionaire Alpha Male Romance Collection*

Cautious Hearts - *A Trust-After-Heartbreak Romance Collection*

Final Surrender - *Alpha Heroes Yielding to Love Collection*

Forbidden Hearts - *A Forbidden Love Romance Collection*

Forever Mine - *A Longing-for-Love Romance Collection*

Guarded Hearts - *A Surrender to Love Romance Collection*

Hearts & Secrets - *Small Town Romance Collection*

Hearts in Peril - *A Suspenseful Romance Collection*

Hidden Truths - *A Secret Identity Romance Collection*

Lies & Hearts - *A Lies, Secrets & Betrayal Romance Collection*

Love After Regret - *A Second-Chance Redemption Romance Collection*

Misjudged Hearts - *A Love After Judgement Romance Collection*

Torn Between Hearts - *A Love Triangle Romance Collection*

All of Alison Reid's books feature standalone stories, swoon-worthy heroes, and guaranteed happily-ever-afters.

Books by Alison Reid

A Billionaire for Christmas

A Heart in Florence

After The Storm

Always You

Before I Fell

Before the Thaw

Beneath the Lies

Billionaire Bodyguard

Billionaire Rancher

Blueprints of the Heart

Branlow

Collide

Echoes of Deception

Falling for the Billionaire

Forever Yours

Heart of the Outback

Hearts on the Line

Hidden Gem

Kept Promises

Mended Hearts

Mistaken Hearts

New Year's Eve Kiss

Quiet Danger

Reckless Hearts

Find all my books on Amazon:

https://www.amazon.com/author/alisonreid1970

About the Author

Alison Reid writes contemporary and small-town romance filled with heart, passion, and second-chance love stories. Her novels often feature strong heroines, irresistible heroes, and the happily-ever-afters readers adore. When she's not writing, Alison enjoys reading, spending time with her family, and imagining new love stories. She hopes her books give readers a few hours of escape, joy, and swoon-worthy romance they won't forget.